Donard

G000163159

Donard Anthology

Edited by Mike Graham

Donard Publishing

Donard Anthology

www.donardpublishing.com

Manufactured in Great Britain

This book is a result of the efforts of the many writers who have visited our site and it features winning competition entries as well as contributions from others. We appreciate all their efforts.

Title	Page

THE WIZARD By Gordon Phipps

It must be near sunset because the only thing visible from the two windows of my Broadway studio apartment - Broadway, George Street, Sydney, i.e. - which is the west-facing wall of the Matthew Talbot Hostel for Homeless Men, is now completely in the shade.

Also, I am hanging out for a beer, not having had one since breakfast, my bar fridge, which is my only fridge, beer-wise, looking like Mother Hubbard's cupboard.

But very soon, Merlin will be here.

Merlin is my best mate and he is on his way here this very minute for our weekly poker game, bearing in his beefy arms as always, a carton of life-preserving, cold cans of Victoria Bitter (VB).

But the first to arrive is, as usual, my cousin Benny whose arms are completely empty as he lets himself in without knocking, banging a chair and rocking the blanket-covered, folding, card/dining table as he does so.

With his beady eyes fixed on my bar fridge in the kitchen, he warmly greets me with "Merlin not here yet?", his x-ray vision already revealing the beerlessness of the fridge, and his pointed tongue licking his desiccated and disappointed lips.

Since, if Merlin is here, the only place where he will not be visible is my bathroom if its door is closed, and which is two square metres in area, and whose door is presently open, I take the question to be rhetorical. And also, since Benny always makes it a point to be the first to arrive for our weekly meeting, I decline to answer except to say: "How are you today, Benny?"

Benny answers: "Dry as a Salvo's bar fridge, me. Tried to pick up some beer on the way, but couldn't get any."

I am always surprised at how someone who likes to drink beer as much as does my cousin Benny, has never found out how one goes about buying some. So, purely out of curiosity I enquire of

Benny has every pub and liquor outlet between his place and mine run out of every brand of beer, or are they all closed? To which Benny replies in the affirmative.

Now this might normally cause me more than some disquiet and anxiety, except that were such a catastrophe to occur, Merlin is such a resourceful bloke as will find the only pub in Sydney that is open and with some beer on the shelves.

Installed in his usual chair at the card table, Benny again enquires "So Merlin's not here yet?"

So I then say to Benny: "Benny, if our good friend Merlin is here in this room, not only would we be able to see him, but as a result of his benevolence we would be holding, each of us, instead of this pointless and futile dialogue, a cold can of beer."

The reason why Benny is always first to arrive for our weekly card game is so that he can secure his favourite chair, which faces one of my two windows, and such has been his practice for longer than I can recall.

Now the only thing visible through this window is the same wall of the Matthew Talbot Hostel for Homeless Men that I have already mentioned, and therefore the odds are somewhat long against Benny's catching sight of a beautiful lady at her daily ablutions, or of a honeymooning couple resolutely working their way through Mr. Karma Sutra's extended repertoire. And since Benny seems to have more good fortune at the poker table than is justified by his grasp of the game, one day while contemplating going on the wagon - at least until Merlin arrives - I am doing some serious wondering about is there some connection between the aspect from Benny's chair, and his anomalous roll of luck?

So when sitting down in Benny's favourite position, what do I see, apart from my window, but my shaving mirror, which is at approximately the same height as would be the head of a seated poker player, and which hangs to the left of the window that I had assumed to be the feature that draws Benny like a magnet.

I feel constrained to explain that this mirror and the nail on which it hangs were inherited from the former tenant, whom I never saw but who, I must assume, was either a narcissistic child of either sex, or a clean-shaven male dwarf. And since my bathroom boasts no mirror, and I am equipped with neither a hammer, a nail, nor the experience required to drive one, I am condemned to forever shave my face in a stooping attitude.

With my suspicions of Benny's motives then aroused, I wondered could it be something that he sees in that mirror during a game of poker that renders him these consistently good results. So I go and get my bar stool from my kitchen/dining room, and I set it on the chair that is under the mirror, in such a way that the upturned legs terminate at about the position as would be the close-to-the-chest cards of the most cautious of poker players. And again I sit in Benny's chair and I look at the mirror.

Even to an intellect such as that of my cousin Benny, a ten, jack, queen, king and ace all of the same suit, in mirror image would still read exactly like an unbeatable poker hand.

Thereafter, during each session when Benny is winning hands in numbers inversely proportional to his knowledge of the odds of filling a full hand or a routine flush, I resolve to remove the mirror. But each time, when rehearsing this manoeuvre and sitting in Benny's chair and staring at the perfect rectangle of newly-revealed, clean and unblemished wall-paper, I decide that I will not be able to face Benny's look of hurt and recrimination.

Furthermore, it would mean confronting Benny with his improbity, which would be less than the courtesy expected of a perfect host and which would then cause Benny, being the sort of bloke he is, to give up attending a game where he has only an even chance of winning. And even furthermore, blood being thinner than water to the sort of person that is my cousin Benny, he might let the word get around that I have been hosting a poker game that is less than kosher.

In any case, the chair under the mirror is always occupied by Hardluck Harry, whose luck is not in the least very hard - except when playing poker with Benny - and who, it is widely known, can afford to lose quite a few hands of poker before he is lining up for the soup de jour at the Matthew Talbot.

It is the unwritten code of the serious card player to never make enquiries regarding the size of the purse that a fellow player has brought to the table, just as one would never speculate aloud as to his annual income. But due to Hardluck Harry's being sole heir to a chain of therapeutic all-night massage parlours, it is safe to assume that his take home pay is somewhat more than considerable. Also, it is universally appreciated that Hardluck Harry is as mean as catshit and is also the sort of bloke that if you happen to be on fire and he has a full bladder, he wants to know what is in it for him before he takes it out of his trousers and points it at you.

Another less-than-admirable practice of Hardluck Harry is that he will pick up anything that is lying around loose, and some things that are nailed down tight, and that once when Hardluck Harry is on business in Cairo, before they let him onto the aeroplane, they send out somebody to count the pyramids.

So, taking Hardluck Harry's many qualities into account and conceding that Benny will always be on the lookout for somebody to fleece, I figure that Hardluck Harry makes a better candidate than almost anybody that I know .

Right on schedule, Merlin arrives, and Benny holds the folding table steady as Merlin negotiates the promised carton of lager around the door and the adjacent chair. Benny, as his sole contribution, eagerly and neatly stacks the chilled-to-perfection cans in the bar fridge as I greet my mate Merlin.

Clutching one twenty-fourth of Merlin's bounty, Benny regains his chair just as the door again opens and the furniture is rearranged by Slim Stanley's precarious entrance into the crowding room. As you might have perspicaciously divined, Slim Stanley is slim like Hardluck Harry is generous with his cash, and is also not too bad at drinking other folks' beer, for which, as his corpulence attests, he has remarkable capacity.

Tonight, Stanley struggles in under the weight of two whole twist-top stubbies, which he ostentatiously bears to my bar fridge, his eyes then caressing the glittering iridescent green containers therein, before installing his contribution out of sight behind them. Affronted by this display of parsimony, Benny, whose VB can is already empty, darts to the fridge, extracts Stanley's two stubbies, untwists one, and with largesse normally foreign to his nature, offers the other to me.

As I unscrew its cap, I say to Stanley as follows: "Stanley, I do hope that you did not give yourself a hernia carrying all this beer up the stairs."

And Stanley, who has a hide to match his avoirdupois, rejoins thus: "You get your lift fixed and I'll bring in six cartons of the best boutique beer that can be bought." Which is a very safe offer, my landlord being as likely to have the elevator repaired as is Hardluck Harry to give away his entire fortune to the Salvation Army.

So the four of us; my best mate Merlin, my cousin Benny, Slim Stanley and myself, are sitting around the table, Benny, Stanley and myself on our chairs, and Merlin on a cushion mounted on a milk crate, as he is the most recently-joined member and I own only four chairs. Drinking each other's beer and discussing foreign affairs, the market and the state of the economy, we wait for Hardluck Harry and his stake to show up. But we are all getting older and we are beginning to think that maybe Hardluck Harry is not showing and perhaps we will start the game nonetheless.

This notion causes Benny considerable anxiety, depending as he does on Hardluck Harry for the greater part of his weekly groceries, to say nothing of the odd can or bottle of beer if only he could figure out how to buy some.

Each time that I declare that we are waiting for Hardluck Harry no longer, Benny urges us to reconsider as he thinks that at this moment he hears Hardluck Harry's well-shod footsteps on the stairs.

When he is outvoted three to one and I commence to shuffle the deck, Benny, now quite distraught, prepares himself for the terrifying challenge of playing poker equipped with nothing but luck and skill, and for slim pickings at that.

But then, to my horror and to Benny's delight, Merlin elects to restore his milk crate and cushion to my lounge suite and to occupy Hardluck Harry's now vacant chair.

My tactful remonstrations fall on deaf ears as Stanley claims more elbow room by moving his chair into Merlin's abandoned space, and the four of us are arranged at uniform intervals around the blanket-shrouded table; Stanley sitting opposite to myself, and Merlin to my left, with the shaving mirror behind him and Benny in front of him.

Since Merlin is the only one of us to be gainfully employed, Benny can hardly believe his partly-restored good fortune as we cut for the deal and the first hand is dealt by Stanley.

With one of everything in my hand, I do not even draw, and Stanley folds after drawing one card, leaving Benny and Merlin to fight it out, each raising the other as if they both hold five aces.

Because, via my shaving mirror, Benny knows already what cards Merlin is playing, and is raising with such vigour, I reckon that Merlin is about to take a bath, and I am hoping that he has such a poor hand that he will minimise the damage by either calling Benny, or better still, declaring himself out as soon as possible.

But Merlin's air of confidence indicates that has no intention of doing either and that he must therefore be holding some pretty fancy cardboard. Although obviously, not as fancy as Benny's.

As the host, and since I am already out, I feel entitled - with Merlin's consent of course - to peek at his cards, which I am then doing and wishing I am never born. Merlin is the proud owner of three aces, which normally can be considered a somewhat bankable hand in five card draw - except for when your opposition has already seen it and holds an even better hand - and subsequently, he is betting like a millionaire. And given Merlin's tenacity, it is a hand sufficient to make him go on raising Benny all night unless he suddenly drops dead.

But eventually, Benny's non-professional snorts of delight and my under-the-table shin kicking combined with Merlin's unshakable respect for my opinion, undermine Merlin's conviction. So he matches the last bet, takes a look at Benny's ten-high straight, and without rancour, which is always Merlin's style, he concedes defeat by scooping up all of the cards and thoroughly shuffling the deck, without having to disclose his three aces.

Now feeling responsible for Merlin's loss, I resolve to put a stop to the carnage. But to simply remove the shaving mirror will not only expose Benny's chicanery, but will be an admission of my complicity, and will inevitably generate speculation as to whether or not I am taking ten percent of Benny.

As Benny eagerly shuffles for another massacre, I announce to him "Deal me out Benny. I need a shave."

The following silence from Merlin and Stanley tells me that they are trying to think what it is that I have just said that sounds like I am about to shave my face, while Benny fumbles the shuffle and gasps such astonishment as I am never before seeing, signifying that he alone appreciates the underlying design of my intentions.

Stanley, justifiably in view of the extended delay in starting the game, wants to know why I cannot wait until morning to take a shave, and Benny, who now sees his newly found source of groceries slipping through his fingers, simply exhorts me to grow a beard in which he claims I will look quite distinguished.

Distinguished or not, I am resolute, and while I assemble hot water and shaving tackle, Benny is looking at me more than somewhat miffed, unable to complain any further in case it alerts Merlin and Stanley to the significance of the mirror in his poker-winning strategy. So, to achieve one more hand before his view of Merlin's cards is extinguished by my occupancy of the shaving mirror, Benny is now dealing those cards faster than I am ever seeing anybody deal a hand of poker.

In spite of Benny's urgent exhortations for Merlin to pick up his cards and look at them, they lie facedown on the blanket while Merlin stares in mystification at my preparations, and Benny sags resignedly in his chair as I adopt my shaving crouch.

As, with my imitation badger-bristle brush I apply the thick, creamy lather to my face, Merlin takes up his cards while in the mirror I watch Benny and I bob and weave to counter each of his neck stretches as he tries to catch one final glimpse of Merlin's poker hand.

Now normally, while going about my personal toilet, I am fastidiously tidy. But on this occasion, by the completion of my shave, the surface of the mirror is almost fully coated with accidental, albeit with some artful brush strokes, splashes

of shaving lather, whose effect is not lost on Benny as he studies his cards and grapples with the novel concept of winning a hand of poker by fair and square means.

Finally at ease with my conscience and very clean shaven, I sit down as an observer of the current hand, which will now be played according to the Marquis of Queensberry rules and also those of Hoyle.

Merlin, it is widely known, is never an ear-basher and communicates mostly by gestures and facial expressions. And also being an ingenuous bloke, incapable of any guile, and whose every gesture and facial expression reveal his innermost feelings, he is not perfectly designed for playing poker. So by his glum visage I can already tell, before I take a peek - maintaining my privileged observer status – that he has a handful of rubbish…except for a pair of threes.

Then I and the other punters watching Merlin draw three cards, can clearly read by his demeanour that he has not improved that much. So we are surprised when he opens the bidding with the kind of bet usually associated with a full house, and which immediately squeezes out the cautious Stanley. But Benny, who is taking Merlin's face at face-value and who is thinking that he can easily win this hand without outside help, raises Merlin, it being clear to all that know him, that Merlin is bluffing.

Now as you know, a bluffer cannot call, nor can he afford to be called. So Merlin has only two options, which are either to raise the last bet by an intimidating sum, or to throw in his hand and humiliate himself as a called and defeated bluffer. Merlin's usual humility is not evident today as, in a display of bravado, he doubles Benny's bet, which is exactly what Benny is praying for.

Even though Benny is thinking he has Merlin on the ropes, lacking his customary shaving mirror-inspired confidence, he plays it safe and merely matches Merlin's bet, which is exactly what Merlin was not praying for, and so, Merlin has to show his pitiful pair of threes - easily beaten by Benny's three jacks - and watch Benny's greedy hands encircle the very large pot and gather it to his side of the table.

I am so peeved at Merlin's recklessness that I want to clean the shaving cream from the mirror and throw him to the wolves. But watching Benny's gloating fingers caress his new pile of winnings tempers my chagrin, and I signal that I will sit in for the next hand, in which I will be dealer, and which is eagerly anticipated by Benny the poker maestro.

As Merlin takes up his cards one by one, Benny is more interested in Merlin's reactions than he is in his own hand, and we all of us watch in fascination as Merlin's face lengthens with each revealed card. Then Benny's delight is boundless as Merlin's hand movements indicate that he intends to hold one card and draw four. This surprises us more than somewhat, because Merlin is a seasoned player of draw poker, and as anybody who has ever played five-card-draw will soon tell you, only your aunty holds one card hoping to improve by drawing four, the odds against your achieving a respectable hand in this fashion being as long as from here to Mars.

But Merlin, who has not quite tabled his discards and is therefore not yet committed, seems to reconsider. And then, after much theatrical pondering and lip-biting, he decides to hold onto the four cards that he was about to discard, and draw one.

His transparent expressions aside, Merlin's reputation is as a cool and calculating player with a good head for assessing the odds of filling a winning hand. So this manoeuvre has us, and especially Benny, mystified. If Merlin was about to discard four cards, they must be rubbish, I can almost hear Benny laboriously calculate. But, since he then retained those same four rubbish cards, which could contain neither a pair nor anything else worth keeping, the only possibility is that they are four parts of an inside straight. And as any punter with even a rudimentary grasp of odds in draw poker will soon say to you, you are never ever filling an inside straight. Meaning, that if you are dealt four fifths of a straight with a gap in its middle, and also a pair of anything, go with the pair. And if you don't hold a pair of anything, save your money.

But Benny's knowledge of Merlin's skill notwithstanding, he must now be convinced that trying to fill an inside straight is exactly what Merlin is doing.

As for Merlin, as he takes his single drawn card to the light, he probably is thinking that he is wearing his best poker face and giving away nothing. But his imperceptible - except to the finely-tuned Benny - sag of disappointment is no doubt making Benny so cocky that he wonders why he is ever thinking that he needs my shaving mirror in the first place.

So now the world knows that Merlin has a handful of junk, and to add to his problems, his is the first bid. Which means that he has either to embark on a bluff to the death or to fold immediately. Much to the delight of Benny, Merlin does

the former, squeezing out Stanley who by now must be wondering whether there are any halfway decent cards in this deck and why is he here in the first place, except for the free beer.

With relish, Benny doubles Merlin's bet, which, since I would need at least a routine flush to stay in such a high-priced game, forces me right out of the race.

Now, the arch rivals, Benny and Merlin, face each other across the blanketed field, and Benny, reviewing Merlin' recent history as an unconvincing bluffer, is already counting the money. So when Merlin, his long face still reflecting his worse-than-poor hand, matches the last bid and raises by the same, Benny decides that there is a Santa Claus, and vigorously and also with some élan, he matches Merlin and raises again.

With again no option but to either tap the canvas or bluff on, Merlin recklessly pushes more perfectly good currency into the centre. Benny, convinced and certain that Merlin can be holding nothing more superior than one pair of anything, and still having a pile big enough to prove it, turns up the heat by raising yet again.

As he contemplates the considerable pile of cash in the centre of the table, half of which is Benny's, Merlin's heretofore glum face relaxes into an at-least-three-of-a-kind type faint smile, which has a signal affect on Benny, who must be thinking that the shaving mirror would now not be such a bad asset after all.

Not that it would do him much good because at this juncture Merlin's cards are face-down on the blanket, Merlin having indicated by standing and mentally plotting a path across the beer can-littered floor between his chair and my bathroom, that the pressure of the game - to say nothing of the several cans of VB - has been transferred to his bladder, and to allow comfortable consideration of his next gambit, he must take temporary leave, confident that in this gentlemen's game, the secret of his poker hand will remain face-down and intact during his absence from the table.

Benny is clinging to the hope that the few coins on view is the last of Merlin's cash, and since markers and cheques are not customarily exchanged in this cash-only venue, that Merlin will be unable to match the last bet and consequently will have to ignominiously throw in the towel.

But as the now relieved and consequently clear-headed Merlin regains his chair, his hand slides into his pocket and extracts a wad with which you could choke the fields of the two previous Melbourne Cups, and which evokes a gasp of grudging admiration from Benny as his beady eyes watch Merlin peel off paper sufficient to match and raise Benny's previous bid.

At this stage, I am hoping that to take it this far, in spite of his recent bluffing debacle, Merlin must be holding onto some pretty fancy paper after all, a possibility that has not escaped Benny, who is now probably considering folding as graciously and as cheaply as is possible. But he would also be thinking that if he does not call, he will never know exactly how fancy is Merlin's paper, and even though it will be the first time that he has had to pay for the privilege, he signals by counting out sufficient only to cover Merlin' last bid, that he will look at Merlin's hand.

So Benny pushes the last of his cash into the centre, and holds his breath as Merlin reaches for his face-down cards.

By now, the table is covered with cards, cans of beer, coins and notes. So to provide more space for Merlin's dramatic unveiling, I gather up the face-down discards and the remainder of the deck.

Merlin smiles enigmatically, pauses for effect, turns over his cards, and clean takes the wind out of Benny....with four beautiful bullets.

Now the deck of cards with which we are playing and with which we have had many a game, is my own. Yet I never know until this moment that it contains so many aces, having just noticed the ace of diamonds among Stanley's discards, causing me to hope that Stanley's short term memory is not too hot, and to suspect that were I to go through the rest of the deck, I might discover another three aces closely resembling the ones in Merlin's hand, which would be a big relief, because it would mean that there could be no aces in Benny's as-yet-undisclosed hand, because if there were even one, Benny might be wondering is he seeing double, or is there something on the nose.

Also, I am silently wishing that if Merlin is unsatisfied with my deck and bringing his own cards into the game, he would consider this possibility and not allow himself to be called until he knows the precise disposition of every bona fide ace in the game. Although, and on the other hand, I have observed that except for Stanley's current ace of diamonds, not one ace has been evident since Merlin had a whole three of them in the first hand of the evening, none of which was the diamond, which could indicate that the precise disposition of those three bona fide aces is already quite well-known to Merlin, at that.

Benny is still regarding with stark disbelief and some shock, those four aces, and I am fearful that if he regards too hard and for too long, he might regard some detail of one or of all of these aces that is not too consistent with the rest of the deck.

So smartly, I scoop up all of the cards and I shuffle them into the deck, keeping a tight grip as I do so, in case Merlin's four aces decide to jump out of the deck and land in his lap.

But since Merlin seems to be so relaxed about things, I concentrate on the next problem, which is how to covertly recover four - or perhaps seven - redundant cards that I am sure to find on the floor around Merlin's feet. But a casual glance in the direction of Merlin's size-elevens reveals nothing, which is a relief bigger than I can describe, but which does leave me puzzled more than somewhat.

Next day, when I encounter Benny in the soup-de-jour queue, my love of poetic justice is rewarded when he glumly informs me that having so recently been to the cleaners, he will be unable to attend the next game, it being not too likely that he could assemble an acceptable stake by such time.

And my love for my fellow man is reinforced when on the same day, Merlin presents me with two brand-new cellophane-wrapped decks of poker cards and a suggestion that I get rid of my old deck which must be getting quite worn-out by now.

I do not ask, and he does not volunteer, about the fate of the seven cards now depleting my old, quite worn-out deck. But the same day, after insufficient water is being issued by my toilet cistern, I discover floating face-up inside it, six bloated poker cards plus another lodged underneath the outlet valve, three of which are aces – none of which is a diamond – and the other four, never remotely resembling four parts of any straight - inside or otherwise.

I am still pondering the significance of this when Merlin arrives with yet another gift; a handsome and elegant shaving mirror, mounted on its own, head-high stand of solid mahogany, with which I can now do all of my shaving standing upright and in the privacy of my two square metres bathroom.

While I am admiring it and looking forward to my next session with the razor, he produces a claw hammer with which he expertly extracts the nail supporting my erstwhile mirror, and with a poker-faced expression that says it never will be missed, he drops the mirror and its nail into my kitchen pedal-bin.

Later that afternoon, I'm near a phone booth with the price of one phone call in my pocket, so I use it on Hardluck Harry, to find out why he didn't show up last night. But before I get a chance to put the question, Harry says to me: "Merlin told you why I wouldn't be able to get to the game last night?"

Of course, I'm not going to let Merlin down, so I say "Yes".

Harry continues: "Merlin didn't mind at all. He said there'd be less money in the game, but at least he'd be able to sit in my chair, instead of that milk crate."

Brighid by R D Williams

Brighid rode out of the trees and into the clearing, in which was settled a small Knobbin village, her golden armor shinning in the sunlight, her red hair spilling over her shoulders, her green eyes shinning with an inner light. Behind her came a group of about a dozen Elves on horseback, their hair the color of pale gold, and on their armor, and on the standard they bore, was the emblem of a tree on a green field. Several of the Knobbins came out of their small wooden houses to see what was going on. In the very center of the village she halted, casting her eyes about at the small fury faces that looked up at her.

"From this day forward I declare this village to be under my protection," she began in a loud voice. "In return for keeping your lands safe, a tithe of your harvest shall be given over to the feeding of the army under my command. I further ask that you shall abide by, and enforce, the following commands, so that peace and order shall be ensured."

An elder Knobbin cleared his throat loudly from where he stood upon the ground before her horse.

"You have a question?" she asked looking down at him.

"Who are you to issue commands to us?" he asked simply.

Her eyes widened slightly. "I am Brighid of the Tuathan," she said with an air of authority.

"I know that," responded the Knobbin. "And I am Dallath of the Knobbin people, yet who gave you authority over our village? What gives you the right to demand our crops, or to issue commands to us?"

"You are simple farm folk, so perhaps you do not fully understand," she began.

"We are simple, yes," he interrupted her. "Yet we are not stupid. There is a difference, and perhaps we must excuse you for now seeing that."

"Why you little rat!" an Elf that rode at Brighid's side said harshly. "How dare you," yet Brighid cut him off with a motion of her hand. "But milady," he started to protest.

"That is enough Eallath," she said quietly, and the Elf nodded his head to her. She turned her attention back to Dallath. "I ask only for what we need to protect your lands."

"Protect from what?" he asked.

"From the servants of Astoth should they attack again, and from others that would make you their slaves."

"I see," he said in a tone as if he were speaking to a young Knobbin. "From those that would command us and demand our crops."

"I have defended these lands," began Brighid, her voice rising slightly. "Therefore..."

Dallath cut her off, stomping his small wooden cane on the ground as he began to speak. "And we have defended these lands for generations beyond count, and we have aided the Elves against the Great Enemy since before the first rising of the sun. Spare me the further lecture on who you are, and what you have done to protect us."

"How dare you speak to me in such a manor!" her voice rising more. "Do you not realize," suddenly she stopped short. *"What am I doing? What am I saying?"* a voice deep inside asked her. *"Why should I be angry with this creature when all he wants is to be left alone?"* Through her mind ran several of her own actions as of late, and of more than a few she suddenly felt ashamed.

"We return to Siartalla," she said to Eallath. "Forgive me for the intrusion," she added to Dallath, and then turned her steed and rode back into the trees. The Elves glanced at one another for a moment, and then followed.

A day and a half later they arrived at Siartalla, and there she found that Ondin was gone. He had led a small force east and south, for Laron was again encroaching on their borders, and Ondin had wished to speak with him about it. Something deep inside warned her that there would be bloodshed from this. Commanding her escort to remain behind, she set out to follow him, for she could travel faster alone.

The next dawn found her far afield, and even as she came over the hills to see Ondin's banner in the distance, she saw that a fierce battle was already being fought. Forward she charged, and a cheer went up from the Elves gathered about the standard of the tree as she came into their view. As she came nearer she noticed something strange. Not far from Ondin's banner was that of Laron, and suddenly she realized that they were not fighting one another, but that they seemed to be drawn up together in defense against another force. Striving against them was a large force of men who wore the colors of Arlure. Unsure what was happening, she turned her course for the standard of the tree, and when she was perhaps one hundred yards distant, she saw for certain that these men were Arlurians. What treachery was this?

She urged Naeya, her steed, onward, and soon they were near to the lines of battle. War cries and challenges were called out, even as with a great leap, Naeya bore her over the front ranks of the men to land in the midst of those beyond, the horse's hooves cleaving the armor and flesh of those that stood in the way.

Brighid leaped from the horse, her sword Lonthar in hand, and a green fire shown in her eyes as the battle fury ran hot in her veins. Through armor and bone Lonthar cleaved and soon the grass all about was soaked with blood. She clove her way through the ranks of her opponents, red blood covering her golden armor, and red was stained the blade of her sword and her hands, for none could withstand her.

The sun had climbed high into the sky when she saw that the men were now in rout, fleeing before the elves as they drove forward, crying her name as a rallying call. She halted, and lowered her sword as she looked at the bodies about her. Suddenly she felt as if she had been kicked hard in the gut, and she gasped, her eyes locked upon the face of one of the bodies at her feet. Her sword fell from her grasp to land upon the ground, as she fell to her knees. There before her, cloven nearly in two by her own sword, lay one that she recognized, the body of Gallen, her own son that she had born to an old lover. Why was he here she wondered, and then the words of several conversations between her and him flooded into her memory, only half heeded when they had been spoken. *"Yet we fight against those that should be our friend and allies,"* he had said to her. *"This seems the work of the Dark One rather than of the Source,"* She looked around again, at the bodies of the men she had slain, counting their numbers. Had she really killed so many? And for what? There was no cause for this, no cause for such enmity between allies. In her mind she heard an echo of laughter, and she knew that somewhere Astoth would be joyous to hear of these things, his own enemies fighting one another.

Her body felt numb as she climbed slowly to her feet, and watched as the Elves continued to drive the Arlurians in rout further to the south of where she stood. With trembling hands she put her horn to her lips and sounded it, calling for retreat, hoping that they would leave what was left of the men in peace.

Without looking to see if the Elves had obeyed the horn signal, Brighid turned and made her way through the field of carnage towards the banner of the tree, where it still stood with only a few Elves about it. They were tending to a few of their wounded when she came near, and they began to stand and bow at her approach, yet she waved the gesture away.

"Where is Ondin?" she asked, her voice sounding strange and hollow in her own ears.

Two of the Elves looked at one another and then back at Brighid before one of them answered. "The Master is no more Mistress," he said slowly.

She just stared at him for a moment before her mind grasped the words he had spoken. "What happened here? What began this?" she asked slowly.

"We encountered Lord Laron along with a force of several score of men under his command," the Elf began. "Master Ondin greeted him, asking for a parley. They were both unarmed when they met with only a few guards each. As they were speaking to one another, Master Gallen rode up with a score of men, and he asked to speak with them both. What ever he had to say they must not have liked it, for I could hear Master Ondin's laughter, and two of Laron's men were apparently armed and upset by what he had said, for they suddenly struck out at Gallen. The men with him struck back, and before we could reach them I saw Ondin fall. I could hear Gallen yelling for them to stop, but it was too late, too many tempers had been flared too hotly by then. Soon there was an all out battle engaged, and more men came suddenly over the hills from the south, for they must have heard the sound of battle and suspected some treachery. They had just joined the growing battle when you arrived Mistress."

Brighid turned and saw the rest of the elves, and the remainder of Laron's men, come striding back across the field of battle. She could not help but feel that this was her fault. If she had only heeded Gallen's words in those conversations, yet she had heard them and had ignored them, thinking that she was above such concerns. As she stood there in thought, she began to see herself in another way, almost as if she stood outside of herself, watching her own actions of the past, hearing her own words more clearly. What she saw she did not like. Lording her abilities and powers over others, thinking that Men, Elves and others were inferior to her, for she was Tuathan. Commanding others because they let her do it, bullying when her commands were not followed as she wished, and intimidating others with her power. Men and Elves had considered the Tuathan to be Gods when they appeared among them, knowing that they had come from the High Plane, and she had grown so use to it that she had nearly thought herself to be one, a Goddess that should be respected, feared, obeyed, and worshiped. Yet now she saw what she had really become, no better than a tyrant, and she had stooped so low as to let herself become lost in the rage of battle, not caring who or what she killed, as if those about her were merely sheep to be slaughtered, for after all they were only Men. These were the people that they had been sent here to help and protect, to aid them and council them in their fight against Astoth, not to command them. Was this how Astoth had fallen to the dark path he was now on? Had he had good intentions in the beginning also?

"Mistress?" asked one of the elves nearby. "What are your orders?"

"None," she said quietly. "I have no authority to issue you orders."

"But milady," he began, confusion on his face. "Master Ondin is no more, you are our sole commander now."

"I am no commander," she said turning towards the elf. "Do as you see fit, though I suggest sending messengers to try and salvage what peace is possible with the men of Arlure. As for myself, I am going to see to those that are wounded upon the field." And with that she turned and strode out among the dead and dying that lay sprawled about, healing those that were not yet beyond her aid.

It was late that night before Brighid left the field, for all afternoon she had labored in healing, trying to make some small amends for her actions, though in her heart she knew that it could not be enough. She did not return to Siartalla that night, and she wandered aimlessly upon Naeya, her mind whirling with painful thoughts. At last she halted just as the sun was again beginning to rise into the sky, and dismounting she knelt upon the ground, looking towards the sun rise. She drew her sword and laid it upon the ground before her, the point away from her, laying her right hand upon the hilts. Then and there she swore a solemn oath, vowing that never again would she raise her hand against Men or Elves, save those that served Astoth, and then she cried out in a loud voice to the heavens above, begging for the Source to grant her forgiveness for her actions. Then, weariness taking her at last, she lay herself upon the ground unheeding, not caring what should become of her, hoping only to find some solace in the forgetfulness of sleep for a short while.

The Hitchhiker By Nichole R. Bennett

Do you remember ghost stories? The ones they tell 9 and 10-year-olds at scout camp or sleepovers? I never put much stock in those. I mean, they're just a collection of made-up stories to keep kids in line, like the Bogey Man and the Tooth Fairy.

Well, that's what I used to think, at any rate.

I remember the day I changed my mind. Actually, I remember it like it was yesterday, even though it was more than a decade ago. I've thought about it a lot since then.

I was 16 at the time, had a job at the local fabric store. I know, I know… That's not a cool job to have, but I was never really a cool kid, so it didn't bother me. Besides, it was either learn to make my clothes or find a better paying job so I could afford to shop for name brands. But, I digress.

It was a hot, muggy summer night; the kind of night that left you damp with sweat by just opening your front door. I was driving home with the windows down and a new "Guns N Roses" CD blaring on the radio. The air conditioner never did work in that car. It was late since I had to close the store and I really just wanted to get home. Ghosts and bogey men were the last things on my mind.

Since it was so late, I opted to take the less-traveled road that went near the cemetery. It was about a third of a mile longer, but the speed limit was higher and there were never any cops that way. In fact, no one really traveled it. It was pretty much out of the way to almost everywhere except Forrest Lawn Cemetery and that place didn't get many visitors this time of day. I usually managed to justify my lead foot with the lack of traffic and the need for keeping air moving in the shoe-box-sized car. Hey, I had to cool off somehow, right?

Anyway, I was driving up 71st Street, with the cemetery on my right, when I saw her. She was just standing there on the shoulder. She looked familiar, about my age, and just as hot as I felt. In fact,

I was sure I'd seen her just a few weeks before at Scott Davis' pool party. Although, I don't think I'll ever know what made me slow down for her. I'd never done that before.

"Hey, you need a ride somewhere?" She nodded and slid into the passenger's seat. Funny, I still don't remember her opening the car door. Hmm… "Your name's Amy, right? Haven't I seen you around somewhere?" I started to accelerate as she mumbled something. "Where do you need to go? Do you live around here? What are you doing out here so late? I'd be afraid to walk through here at 11 o'clock at night!"

Nothing but silence. Man, didn't this girl ever talk? Oh well, I could just drive and listen to my tunes. Amy didn't need to say much. Besides, maybe she was escaping something or someone I was better off not knowing about.

I drove toward home thinking that Amy must just need to escape while wondering were I was going to drop off my passenger. No big deal, right? I mean, really, what teen girl hasn't wanted to escape from a boyfriend or her parents? I was headed up the hill and decided I ought to slow down a bit. The hill is steep, but the drop into the ravine below is even worse! It must be at least 40 or 50 feet straight down to the rocks below. Rumor had it that many a car had gone over that edge to only be found during the annual city road clean-up day.

When I took my foot off the gas pedal, though, the car didn't respond. I was still speeding – and headed right for the guardrail! I know I screamed. I looked at Amy only to see her vanish right before my eyes. Talk about freaky!

Later, when I came to, I realized what had happened. You see, Amy was a ghost. She had been killed in a car crash along that same stretch of road and the only way to be at peace was to get another soul to haunt that area. Had something to do with ghosts and cemeteries, I guess. Of course, I had to practically pry that out of her. She never was much of a talker.

So, you see, that's why I had to do this. It's nothing personal.

Oh, and thanks for the ride. I've been waiting for quite a long time. I am really sorry about your car, though.

HER MOTHER'S CRY by Susan Tognela

Judith stood in the arrivals lounge, anxiously scanning the thronging, late night crowd. She stood apart from Ross and the children, aware of her fast heartbeat, her quick breaths.

'Are you sure Carol knows we're coming home tonight?' Ross asked.

Judith jumped, her nerves rattling like one of Isabelle's toys. 'Yes, Ross, she knows. She'll be here. I can see her now,' she added, watching her sister push her way through a giggling group of returning netballers.

'Darling,' Carol said, wrapping long, purple clad limbs around Judith, smothering her face with flowing red hair. 'Sorry we're late. Hullo, Ross. Hullo children.'

Judith, her greeting muffled in the purple, saw her father through a gap. He was older, thinner, his hair gray, his skin a blotchy red. He came forward hesitantly. Judith smiled, twisted her blonde bob behind her ears.

'Hullo Dad.'

'Judith.'

They hugged; she smelt the amber liquid on him. 'Mum didn't come?'

His eyes shifted. 'No. You know...'

Judith knew. 'Dad, meet your grandchildren,' she said.

Aidan smiled; Rebecca hid behind Ross, baby Isabelle slept on. Her father stood, saying nothing.

Carol grabbed Judith's canvas carryall, and said into the silence, 'Wait till you see your new house. I hope you like it.'

Judith gathered everyone together with a tight smile. They walked out of the airport into a warm night, her father walking behind, his head down. 'I might just be a minute, something to do,' he muttered, and veered off. The sisters looked at each other.

'Where's the car?' Judith asked.

'Shouldn't we wait for him?' Ross said.

'No,' Carol said. 'You know he'll be hours now. Let him get a taxi.'

Ross parked the second-hand Nissan in the driveway of their new home. As they got out of the car, Carol handed him the keys to the house she had purchased on their behalf, and left for her own home in her grubby yellow Volkswagen, saying she would see them tomorrow.

Ross jingled the keys in his hand, and glanced at Judith, his blue eyes crinkling at the sides.

'I'm going to carry you over the threshold,' he said. 'We can be newlyweds again.'

Judith laughed. 'Have a look in the backseat.'

'Come on.' Ross unlocked the door, then picked Judith up. 'Gawd,' he said, 'are you sure you're only fifty seven kilos?'

'Yep. Ross, I wish Mum had been at the airport tonight' Judith said.

'Jude...'

'It's been six years. You'd think...'

'Judith, stop.' Ross put her down onto the tiled floor of the entry. 'This is our first night in our new home. Let's not spoil it wondering about your mother.'

3.00am. Judith sat bolt upright in bed, her heart pounding. She'd had that same nightmare again. Someone was holding a pillow over her face, suffocating her. She wished she knew where it came from.

Judith stood with Ross and the children in the hot sunshine the next morning, her finger poised over her parents' doorbell. She pressed the button, then quickly stepped back beside Ross as the door opened.

Judith looked at the tall woman standing in the doorway; her once blonde hair now steel wool gray; her thin face etched with tiny lines on pale, sharp cheeks.

'Hullo, Mum.'

'Hullo Judith.' Her mother glanced at Ross, then looked quickly at the children.

'Mum, meet my children,' Judith said proudly. Her mother said nothing.

'Can we come in please? It's hot out here.' Ross forced a laugh, and stepped over the threshold into the unpleasant mustiness of a room whose windows are never opened. Judith's father shuffled in from the kitchen.

'Hullo again, Dad,' Judith said, then turned as Carol stepped through the doorway.

'Good morning everyone,' Carol said. 'Did you all sleep well in your new house? Mum, aren't they gorgeous kids?' Carol stared at her mother. 'Mum? Are you okay?'

Judith looked quickly at her mother. She was staring at Aidan, her face the colour of off-white cardboard. Then, with a small, anguished cry, she walked from the room.

Judith turned to her father, her head tilted in question. He shrugged, wouldn't meet her eyes.

Judith walked swiftly down the hall towards her mother's bedroom. 'Leave her, Jude,' Carol called.

'No. Not this time.'

Judith pushed open the bedroom door, found her mother staring out of the window.

'Mum! What is *wrong* with Aidan, for God's sake?' Judith asked.

Her mother didn't answer.

'Mum, I *asked* you...'

'Aidan. *Aidan.*' Judith's mother's eyes swivelled to the wall opposite her bed, where a large framed photograph of a little blond haired, blue-eyed boy was hung.

Judith's eyes followed. Aidan? No. He resembled Aidan, but it was a photograph of Neil. 'You're punishing me because Aidan looks like Neil?' Judith whispered. Tears filled her eyes. 'But I thought you'd be glad I had a son.'

'Leave me, please.' Her mother's voice was like iced water. Judith shivered, and left the room.

Later, in the park, the sisters were pushing the older children on the swings.

'God forbid, Carol, if I ever lost one of my kids, I wouldn't stop loving the others,' Judith said. 'Although, she's all right with

you. It's me she doesn't like. She didn't even come to Sydney when the kids were born.'

'You know what she's like.'

Judith twisted her head to look at Carol. 'No I don't. How could I? She sent me away when I was twelve.' Judith pushed Aidan hard, and he screamed. 'I know she wishes it was me who drowned, and not Neil. She hates me.'

'She doesn't hate you.'

'What else would you call it?'

Carol stopped pushing Rebecca's swing, and turned swiftly to Judith. 'You were the lucky one. Going away to school. You didn't have to put up with her, or their fights, or Dad's drinking. So don't blame me. It's not my fault you don't get on.' She walked off in an angry swish of red and orange skirts, and sat on a wooden slatted seat near the car.

Judith sighed. 'I know it's not your fault, Carol,' she called across the park. 'I never said it was.'

Judith's mother frowned when Judith arrived with the children the next morning. 'Why didn't you telephone Judith? I'm busy,' she said.

'I *did*. I spoke to Dad. He said he'd mind the kids.'

'He went to the hotel.'

'But...' Judith stopped. 'Could you mind them Mum? Please? I'll only be a couple of hours.'

Her mother sighed. 'Two hours, Judith, and that's all,' she said.

Judith tucked a packet of small white pills into her bag, and smiled brightly at her mother as she pushed Isabelle's pram into the house a couple of hours later. 'Thanks, Mum,' she said. 'I could use a cuppa?'

'Did I hear someone say cuppa?' Carol asked, appearing at the kitchen door.

'Carol. Is that you?' Judith heard the relief that her older daughter had arrived in her mother's voice.

Carol made a face at Judith. 'Yes Mum,' she said.

Judith grinned at her sister. 'Not working today?' she asked, as she filled the kettle with water.

'Nope. Day off. And do I need it.'

'You wouldn't need to work if you settled down and had a child,' her mother said.

'You've got three grandchildren, Mum,' Carol said. 'You want more?'

Judith saw her mother scowl. 'That's right, Mum,' Judith said. 'And those three need to know their grandmother. And *you* need to know them.'

'Don't you *dare* tell me what I need, Judith,' her mother said, pressing her thin lips together.

Judith stamped her foot. 'For God's *sake*, will you *stop* punishing me because your son is dead. *Okay?* It's time you got over it, and put the past behind you.'

Judith's mother's face twisted. She took a step towards Judith, her arm raised. Judith stepped back quickly against the cupboard in alarm.

'My son is dead because of you. You pushed him into the river.'

Judith stared at her mother, her mouth open. 'No.' She shook her head. 'I did not.'

'You did.'

'I don't believe you.'

'Jude...' Carol said.

Judith flapped her hands at her sister. 'I did not push Neil. *I couldn't have,*' she said.

Her mother stood before her, a mixture of triumph, loathing and relief on her face. 'You did.'

Judith swung around to Carol. 'Tell me I didn't,' she said. But she saw the answer on Carol's face.

'Oh, my God.' Judith slid slowly down the front of the cupboard. She sat on the floor, her head cradled in her arms. 'I had no idea,' she whispered. 'Mum, I'm so sorry.' Judith looked up, her blue eyes locking with her mother's.

'Get out of my sight,' her mother said.

Judith went home. She phoned Ross, and told him what she had learned. Then she took the packet of pills from her bag. She swallowed, and waited for oblivion.

Ross came home early to find Judith asleep on the couch.

'Judith, wake up,' he said, shaking her.

'Mmmm.' Judith's head lolled off the lounge.

'Have you taken those pills?' he asked.

'Mmmm.'

'How many?'

'Nuff.'

'What? What've you done?'

'Wanna sleep.'

'No. Wake up. Where are the kids?'

'Carol's. I pushed Neil.'

'Judith.' Ross pulled her into a sitting position. 'How many pills?'

'Two...'

'Two? Are you sure?'

'Yes.'

Ross blew air out between his lips in relief. 'I'll make some coffee. Get you something to eat.'

'I killed Neil.' Tears rolled down Judith's face.

'Jude, you were *five years old*. Okay? It'll be alright.'

Judith waited in the Nissan outside the hotel the following afternoon. Her father would come out sooner or later. Tanked? Talkative?

He finally rolled out of a brown room, the smoke haze still visible around him.

'Dad.'

'What're you doin' here, luv?'

'I need to know what happened.'

'Aw, luv...' He slumped into her car, and reached for a cigarette. Fumbled with the match. Looked forlornly back at the bar.

'Please Dad.'

'All right. I'll tell you.' He took a drag on the cigarette, blew the smoke out slowly. 'Neil was four that day,' he said, his voice just above a whisper. 'Got a fishin' rod for his birthday. He wanted to go fishin' on the pier. Your Mum said no, she had to go...somewhere else, but I said, I'm takin' him fishin'. You girls came too. Sean O'Leary was fishin' on the riverbank, an' I stopped to talk to him. You kids got impatient, so I let you go along to the pier.' He stopped, took a breath, his pale blue eyes watering. 'Next thing, Carol's runnin' towards me, screamin' that Neil was in the river. I said to her, get home, get the doctor, then I ran an' jumped in, but I couldn't find him. When I did, he was limp. Dead.' Tears rolled across the tiny red veins crisscrossing his cheeks. 'I never should've let him out of my sight. My beautiful boy.'

Judith sat stiffly in her seat. 'And I pushed him?'

He wiped his eyes, nodded slowly. 'You girls were cryin' and screamin'. First, Carol said he slipped, but later, she told us you'd pushed him.'

'Carol told you.' Judith looked at her father. 'But did you ask me?'

''Course. An' you admitted it.'

'And you believed me? A five year old child?'

Her father sagged into his seat, looked at her sorrowfully. 'Your Mum did. I wasn't so sure. Thought he might've slipped.'

'And now?'

He took a long drag on the smoke. 'I dunno, luv. If you did, you didn't mean to.' He bit his lip, swallowed hard. 'He wasn't even mine.' He said it so softly Judith wasn't sure she'd heard right.

'What?'

'The day before Neil died, your mother told me that he was some other bloke's kid. She was plannin' to leave, take him with her.'

'Oh, Dad. I had no idea.'

'No. But in the end, no one got him,' he said softly.

Judith met Carol at the front door later that day. 'I can't believe you never told me that I caused Neil's death,' she said.

'What was the point?' Carol asked, stepping inside.

'The *point?* For God's sake, I'm responsible for my brother's death. And no one ever told me.'

'I'm sorry, Jude. I thought you'd be better off not knowing,' Carol said, sitting down.

Judith glared at her. 'How could you *possibly* think that?'

'I was wrong,' Carol said softly. 'I need a scotch.'

Judith poured Carol a scotch and soda, and banged it onto the table beside her. Carol picked it up, and gulped it down.

Judith took a deep breath. 'Do you remember that day Carol? Did I really do it?'

Carol put the empty glass on the table, and clasped her hands together as if she were praying. She touched her fingers to her forehead. 'I remember Mum was hysterical. She kept saying, "what happened?" over and over. *You* wouldn't speak, but they made me. I had to tell them.'

'But do you remember me pushing him?'

Carol picked up her empty glass, and sucked at the dregs. 'Yes,' she said softly. 'Don't you remember anything?'

Judith shook her head. 'I've tried,' she said, 'but all I remember is Mum screaming. Mostly at me.'

'Yes. She screamed at everyone, but after you admitted it...well, Dad had to take you away from her, or she would've killed you. It was horrible.'

'My whole childhood was horrible,' Judith said.

'Mum needs to forgive you.'

'Like that'll ever happen. You saw her yesterday.'

Carol shifted in her seat. 'She was always going to leave after Neil died. But she never went. God knows why, because they fought all the time.'

'Did you know she was planning on leaving before he died, and taking Neil with her? Don't know if she was taking us,' Judith added.

Carol frowned. 'What?'

'Dad told me. Turns out, Neil wasn't even his.'

Judith lay in bed the next morning, watching Ross dress through half closed eyes.

'Are you getting up?' Ross asked.

'Nup.'

'What about the kids?'

'I'll see to them.'

Ross pulled up the knot of his tie. 'Have you taken more of those pills?'

'No.'

'Look, Jude, you've got to get over this. No one blames you for your brother's death. You were *five,* for God's sake.'

'My mother blames me. She hates me for it.'

Ross rolled his eyes. 'You know your mother's cracked. Sort it out with her, then put it behind you.' He picked up his briefcase and walked out of the room.

'Thanks for the sympathy, Ross,' Judith called after him. She heard the front door slam. She took the packet of white pills from her bedside drawer and popped one from its casing. She swallowed it, then turned over and sobbed into her pillow.

Judith sat on Carol's back patio in the cool of the afternoon, Isabelle asleep in her carrycot between them, the older children playing in the tiny garden. Carol sipped at a scotch and soda. Judith's drink was going warm on the table beside her.

'You know, I think Mum always wanted to tell me that I was responsible for Neil's drowning,' Judith said.

Carol swirled the ice in her glass. 'They used to fight about telling you. And then one night Dad got angry, and said you were never to be told. She never brought it up again. I think she was afraid of his temper. He had one back then.'

'I thought she'd like me a bit more once she saw the kids.'

'She needs help,' Carol said.

'I wonder if...I can build a bridge between us now?'

'Won't be easy.'

'No,' Judith said. 'But I have to try.'

A few days later, Judith answered her phone with Isabelle screaming in her ear.

'Judith?' said her mother. 'You're busy, obviously.'

'No, Mum, Isabelle's teething, that's all.'

'Oh. I...um, need a prescription filled at the pharmacy. Your father's...out, and Carol's working. But it doesn't matter, I'll call a taxi.'

'Mum. I'll be there in fifteen minutes.'

Judith strapped the children into the car with shaking hands. Did this mean her mother wanted to build a bridge too?

Judith's mother climbed into the passenger seat of the Nissan, and glanced at the children in the back seat.

'Hullo, Nanna,' Aidan said.

Judith smiled at him in the rear-view mirror, then looked expectantly at her mother. Her mother said nothing. Judith's smile faltered. 'You're not sick, are you, Mum?' she asked.

'Sick? No, of course not. Just some pills I've run out of.'

'Nanna, in twelve more sleeps I'll be five,' Aidan said.

Judith saw her mother close her eyes.

'Nanna? I said in...'

'Okay, Aidan,' Judith said. 'Nanna's not feeling well.'

'But she just said she wasn't sick!'

Judith smiled at her mother. 'He's so quick. Mum?'

'I heard you, Judith.'

'Well don't ignore me. Or him.'

Her mother pursed her lips. 'The pharmacy is on the corner. If you wouldn't mind waiting.'

Judith slumped in her seat as her mother got out of the car. Nothing had changed. The hoped for bridge had fallen back into the sea.

As Judith's mother climbed back into the car she dropped her bag onto the floor. The contents spilled out, and Judith saw a familiar packet amongst the clutter.

'Valium, Mum?'

Her mother snatched the packet of pills off the car floor. 'I need them.'

Judith looked at her. 'So do I,' she said.

A short time later, Judith pulled into her mother's driveway. She stopped the car, and turned to her. 'I really hoped things would be different between us when I came back home, Mum,' she said.

'I didn't ask you to come back.'

'Oh. So...you prefer me to be on the other side of the country?'

'Yes I do.'

Judith started to cry. Aidan reached around the seat and put his small arms around her neck. 'You're naughty, Nanna,' he said to his grandmother. 'You make Mummy cry.'

'Mum, can't you please forgive me?' Judith sobbed.

'No, I can't!' her mother said. Then she too burst into tears.

Judith had never seen her mother cry like this. 'I'm so sorry, Mum. I wish it was *me* who drowned,' she said.

A dam opened in her mother, tears running in little rivers down her face.

'Now Nanna's crying,' Aidan said, and put his arms around his grandmother. 'You're not naughty, Nanna,' he said. 'I love you, Nanna.' He offered her a tissue from the box in the back of the car.

Judith watched as her mother took the tissue from Aidan, then turn and pat his arm.

The following week, Judith was having coffee with two old friends. She switched on her mobile and it rang instantly.

'Judith,' Ross said.

Judith's heart slammed against her chest as she heard the fear in his voice. 'It's Isabelle. Her temperature's up, she's sick. Where are you?'

'On my way.'

Judith ran into her house, and stopped. Her mother was leaning into the screaming baby's cradle, her hand on Isabelle's forehead. 'I think she may have an ear infection Judith. Possibly from teething,' she said.

Judith picked up her baby. 'Yes...' She looked at Ross, who shrugged. 'Your phone was off, so...'

'Mum, thanks for coming.'

'I'll stay with the children while you take her to the hospital.'

Judith nodded. She touched her mother's shoulder as she passed, then drew back quickly, waiting for the rebuff that didn't come.

Two hours later they returned, Isabelle sleeping in Judith's arms. Aidan smiled at them. 'Nanna gave us a bath,' he said.

Her mother walked in from the kitchen, an apron tied around her thin waist. 'Is Isabelle alright?'

'Yes. You were right, an ear infection. Thanks, Mum.'

Her mother nodded, relief flashing across her face. 'I've fed the children. I'll phone for a taxi.'

'No, Mum, stay. Have a cup of tea. I'll drive you home.'

Her mother hesitated, took a step towards the phone, then stopped. Her eyes met Judith's. A brief smile passed between them. A beginning.

Months later, Judith drove alone down the narrow, wet road towards the river. She parked on the gravel verge, and climbed out of the Nissan into a gray, cold day. She stood on the riverbank, trying to remember what had happened there twenty-two years ago.

With a sigh, she stepped onto the pier, treading carefully over the old boards until she had walked along the length of it.

A gust of icy wind picked up her hair, and whipped it into her face. Judith pulled her parka around her and stood listening as a bird screeched in the trees above her, the noise echoing a memory from the past...

Neil screaming, '*No*,' and pushing her, his little hands flat against her chest, after she had demanded a turn of his new fishing rod...

'*I want a turn*,' she'd yelled, and pushed him back. Hard.

And then she watched in horror as he fell backwards into the river.

Carol had raced along the riverbank, screaming for their father. He had run onto the pier; yelling at Carol to run home, ring for the doctor.

Her father had jumped into the river. He'd found Neil quickly beneath the bubbles that were just below the surface. Neil had come up spluttering, coughing up the river water...

Judith cried out. Her body collapsed like a folding concertina onto the pier.

She remembered now.

The fierce red anger on her father's face.

How he'd turned his back to her.

How he'd pushed Neil below the surface of the river again.

How he'd held Neil beneath the water like he was holding a pillow over his face, until there were no more bubbles to be seen.

IF ONLY by Susan Tognela

Wednesday.

Scott hung himself this morning.

Mum found him, swinging from an exposed beam in the games room. He'd tied a hangman's noose around his neck, and jumped off the pool table. A printout from the Net on "How to make a Hangman's Noose" was on the floor.

Mum is in hospital, under sedation. Timmy is bawling in the kitchen. He doesn't know what Scott did, only that he's dead. Dad is in his bedroom. I can hear him banging on the furniture, screaming, 'Why? Why?'

I know why.

But I can't tell them. Not yet. Not until I know for sure how much trouble Scott is in. Would have been in.

The grandparents are coming. Both sets. Dad's are flying over from Melbourne; Mum's are driving up from their farm in Albany. I hope Mum is out of hospital before they get here.

Thursday morning.

Day one since Scott died. It's unbelievable he's dead. My hunky brother, just seventeen. This time last week we were looking forward to his birthday party. *He* was looking forward to his license. Mum and Dad gave him a car, a big surprise. Be careful, Mum said. He just grinned. Freedom!

Nana and Pop are here from Albany. Nana's in Scott's room now, crying. Pop's trying to be strong, but I saw him standing in the doorway of the games room, sobbing like a baby.

Mum is still in hospital. Dad will get her later, after he picks up Grandma and Grandpa from the airport.

The police are here! I nearly had a heart attack. What if they question me about...what do I say? I can't tell the police anything until I've talked to Mum and Dad. But it's okay. They weren't here about that. They were here because a suicide has been committed in our house.

A suicide.

In our house.

It feels weird, like it's all happening to someone else.

Thursday afternoon.

Dad picked up Grandma and Grandpa from the airport, and Mum is home. She's trying hard to keep it together, but she's losing it. I heard her tell Dad she wants to sell the house; she can never go into the games room again. She said she keeps seeing Scott swinging on the end of that noose. His face all blue. His eyes bulging; his tongue hanging out. I can't bear to think of Scott looking like that. I threw up in the loo afterwards.

Grandpa keeps asking Dad if Scott left a note. Dad says no. Grandpa says, 'He must have, David, you haven't looked properly.' Dad clenches his teeth and says, 'We've searched everywhere, and there is *no note*.' Dad's face looks like gray cardboard. He looks older than Grandpa.

The funeral people are here, sitting at our dining room table with Mum and Dad and the grandparents. Grandma wants them to keep Scott's death notice brief; she says it's not proper otherwise. Mum shut her up with one look.

I tried to write a poem to my brother, to put in my notice, but nothing sounded right. In the end, I just wrote, "I'm sorry Scott, I'll love you forever big bro. Jen."

Later Thursday afternoon.

Andrew Bennett just rang. I can't believe what he told me. I'm so *angry* with him. And with Scott. *If only* he'd waited.

Thursday night.

Nana and Grandma aren't speaking. They never did get on. Nana heard Grandpa make some dumb remark to Timmy about him being the only one who can carry on the family name now. Timmy is only seven; he didn't know what Grandpa meant, but Nana did. She hit the roof, told Grandpa he was a stupid old man. Grandma lost it, said how dared Nana call Grandpa stupid. Nana

told her to shut up. Then Pop tried to calm them all down,
at a time like this, families should pull together. Grandma to.
he was just a doddering old farmer, what would he know? Dau
started yelling, and then Mum screamed, *"I've lost my son."* She
sat on the lounge, crying, saying "My beautiful boy" over and over.
I had to go outside. I can't watch her being ripped apart.

Friday morning.
Day two.
Scott's funeral is tomorrow. I *have* to talk to Mum and Dad
alone before then. They have to know why Scott hung himself. But
I'm scared. How do I tell them this?

I want to see Kathy, but her Mum won't let her come over.

Heather came round about eleven. She's totally devastated.
Her eyes are red and swollen from crying. She really loved Scott;
she can't understand why he didn't confide in her. At least when
she knows the truth she might feel better about that.

We talked about Scott, about some of the dumb things he
did. Like when he jumped over the counter at McDonalds and
pushed Paul Bradley's face into the chips, because he thought Paul
was trying to crack onto Heather. Heather was working at Macca's
at the time, and was so mad at Scott she wouldn't speak to him for
a week. And Scott couldn't work out why!

Friday afternoon.
No one can look at Dad. I've never seen him this angry. Even
Grandpa's staying out of his way.

I needed a break from the house, so I went into town. I saw
a few kids from school on the bus, but they put their heads down,
and pretended they didn't see me. Did they really think I wouldn't
notice?

When I got to town, I saw Rachel and Kim standing outside
Woolworths. They saw me get off the bus, but they took off before
I could walk over to them. I couldn't help it; I just stood there on
the path bawling my eyes out. I got a few funny looks, so I put my
sunnies on, and waited for the next bus home. It's unbelievable. If
Scott had been killed in a car crash, everyone would be around
offering sympathy. But not for suicide. No one wants to talk about
what Scott did, it's embarrassing, a real stigma thing. Only Mum

nd Dad's closest friends have been to the house, and some of Scott's friends. I hope more people come to his funeral.

When I get home, I'm definitely talking to my parents.

Friday night.

I knocked, and went into Mum and Dad's room. Mum was in bed, with Timmy asleep beside her. Dad was standing by the window, staring out into our backyard. He said, 'Scott was going to help me finish the shed this weekend.' I looked at Mum. She patted the bed beside her. 'Come on, Jen,' she said, 'hop in.' Then Dad turned around and looked at me too. He said, 'You okay Jen?' I couldn't speak because I knew I would cry, so I just nodded. Then I said, 'I know why he did it.'

You could hear Mum's scream right through the house. Nana and Pop came running from their room. Grandma and Grandpa were right behind them, but they stood in the doorway, like they didn't know if they should come in or not.

Mum was screaming "Oh my God" over and over. Dad sat on the edge of the bed, groaning like he was in pain, his face covered by his hands. Timmy was awake and bawling. I couldn't stop crying; couldn't stop saying I was sorry.

Nana was beside herself. She kept saying to Mum, 'Gail, what's happened?' When Mum didn't answer, Grandpa said to Dad, 'David for God's sake, tell us.'

So he told them.

Grandma took a step into the room, and looked at me out of fierce eyes. She said, 'How do you know this, Jennifer?'

'Scott told me,' I said.

'When?'

'Late on Tuesday night.'

I was on the Net, trying to finish an assignment. Mum and Dad were out with friends, so I was also babysitting Timmy. Scott came in about eleven. His eyes were red, and he was shaking and sweating.

I said, '*Scott*, you've been drinking...Dad's gonna kill you.'

He didn't answer me, just sat in Dad's chair and leaned forward with his head in his hands. He was crying hard and I got scared. I said, 'Have you pranged the car?'

He shook his head, then threw up all over the floor. He just sat there, didn't even try to clean it up. I grabbed a glass off the bar, and poured in two capfuls of brandy. Dad reckons brandy cures everything. Scott drank it in one gulp. Then he said, '*Fuck*. I shouldn't have drunk that. Now they'll think I was pissed. *Fuck*.'

I handed him some paper towel from the bar as well, so he could clean up his mess, but he ignored it. So I spread it over his spew, and said, 'What have you *done*?'

He didn't answer for a minute, then in a low voice he said, 'I killed Tony Moore.'

'*What*? You did *what*?'

He shouted, '*I killed Tony Moore*. I knocked him off his fucking bike. *I didn't even see him*.' He got up from the chair, and started pacing the room, tears and snot running down his face, his voice rising higher and higher. 'All I felt was his bike under my front wheels. I didn't know what it was, and when I got out of the car to look, I saw Tony lying in the gutter. Blood everywhere. And he was dead. I must've run over him after I knocked him off his bike.'

I couldn't speak. My mouth opened and closed, but nothing came out.

I ran over to the phone. I said, 'I'm going to ring Mum and Dad.' Scott ran after me, and yanked the receiver out of my hand. He said, '*No*. I don't want them to know.'

'They *have* to know.'

'*I promised them I'd be careful. I'm not telling them*.' He said it with his teeth clenched.

A terrible thought hit me. 'You called the ambulance, right? You stayed with him?'

His face crumpled like a folding concertina, and he started sobbing. 'I got scared and I *took off*.'

'Oh, God. Scott!' I ran for the phone again. 'We've got to call an ambulance. He might be still alive. And the police.'

Scott yelled so loud I jumped. 'No! Don't you get it? If you call them now I'll go to jail. I *panicked*. I ran off and *left him*.'

'Someone's gonna find out it was *you*, Scott. The sooner you own up to it, the better.'

He was crying hard now. He said, 'I know. I will. I'll...go to the cops tonight. But I'm scared, Jen. What's gonna happen to me? Mum and Dad are gonna hate me.'

Those were the last words my brother ever spoke to me.

Saturday.

I'm standing beside my brother's grave. My father is beside me, his arm around me. His other arm is around my mother. My little brother, Timmy, is pressed close to him. Scott's girlfriend, Heather, and her family, are just behind us.

Beside us are my grandparents, both sets. And in front of us are Scott's friends, and my parents friends, and my friends, and even some of Timmy's friends. Most of them crying. Crying for a person they knew and loved. A seventeen-year-old boy with his whole life in front of him. Crying because they knew he shouldn't be in that grave. Such a waste.

The funeral is over, the crowd parts. I look up, and see Tony Moore standing on crutches, his head bandaged, his arm in a sling, injured when Andrew Bennett knocked him off his bike on Tuesday night, and left him lying in the gutter.

If only.

Eulogy by Luigi Marchini

Lewis sat in the middle, his brothers on either side. Rob, being the youngest, tended to get what he wanted, sat on his left looking out of the window of the Boeing 747. Joe, the intellectual, the educated one, sat on his right. Even in his slumber he managed to keep the air of aloofness that surrounded him in his waking hours. Lewis smiled as he noticed the Times crossword, barely started, hanging loosely in Joe's hands.

Lewis' thoughts concentrated on the purpose of their trip: their grandfather's funeral. A feeling of wistfulness tinged with bitterness came over him as he remembered his grandfather, Giovanni. He had been no saint, far from it in fact, but Lewis did have happy memories of him. However these were interspersed with darker, painful ones.

It was almost time to land so he adjusted his Rolex, one of the many presents his grandfather had bought him. He knew where the money had come from. At first he had been too young to understand; then as he grew older he chose to ignore his conscience. After all he was his grandfather and Giovanni had always told him 'Family comes first'.

Lewis himself had never followed that path, and neither had his brothers. True, the temptation had always been there: how could it not have been? He could experience the 'fruits' of this career choice almost every day of his life but, in reality, he had never had the stomach for it. Nonetheless he had respected his grandfather, or at least on the surface. For show. Inwardly he harboured other feelings mingled with the natural ones of family love.

Lewis looked at his brothers and pondered on how much they had all suffered and whether this suffering would now ease:

for it could never be completely extinguished. And, as he always did when his thoughts touched on unpleasant memories, he hummed a nursery rhyme.

****

The church sat at the top of a steep hill. There was only one road in the village and this led up to it. Cars were parked at the bottom of this hill and the mourners had to walk the 300 metres or so up to the top. It was a clear, cold day: the two seasons had made fleeting acquaintance with each other and the trees had acquired sparse white coats.

Lewis arrived at the summit some minutes before his brothers and looked up at the small white provincial church – *it's strange,* he thought, *it looked much bigger from the bottom.* As Lewis gazed upon it he remembered holidays here at Nella in his childhood. Sunday worship with his father, mother, and Giovanni. Then just his grandfather. And it was on those later 'holidays' that Lewis first formed the idea of retribution. Or revenge. It was a long time since the three siblings had been here though. Shortly Rob and Joe arrived and they stood, side by side, backs to the world, resembling, he imagined, three tall burnt-out tree stumps.

As they gazed upon the church, Lewis was certain that it seemed to increase in stature. It had a quaintness about it, sure enough, and from the outside it was not much to look at but to Lewis it had something else – an inherent sense of power, and death. He could almost taste it in the air. The seasonal smells were prevalent but there was another aroma, one of rotten decay. He turned to look at his brothers. Brothers to be admired. However he wondered if their mental scars would ever heal. And he also wondered if they suspected….

He looked about the hill and noticed that it was surrounded by woodland; and he wondered how many people had been led into the depths to receive their justice. As he contemplated this, a shaft of sunshine lit the woodland scene and he could discern a cluster of snowdrops. Lewis had never seen snowdrops (or snow piercers as his mother used to call them) in Italy before. He was then diverted by what sounded like a bird in song. He turned round again to face the church and he could see a pair of canaries, the brightest yellow, sitting on the roof, next to the tower. Canaries in Italy? At that time of year? Lewis was puzzled but his mood was lightened by their melody. He turned to his brothers to see if they were sharing this experience with him but they seemed oblivious – no matter, they were *his* birds! *His* flowers of song!

****

Lewis stood up on the altar and inspected the congregation. It was a funeral service and everyone was dressed accordingly. Black, or very dark clothes; women veiled; everyone with prayer-books or bibles; men with collars and ties, their hats by their sides; rosary beads in abundance.

At the back of the church, standing up, Lewis could make out two men who were obviously not mourners. True, they wore black, but not ties – they wore black sunglasses and matching polo-necks. Their complexion was darker than was normally found amongst Giovanni's 'family' and Lewis reckoned they were hit men brought in from somewhere in South America, probably, to find his grandfather's killer. *God this is just like a scene from a Coppola or a Scorcese film*, he thought. He suddenly felt uncomfortable – he wished he could see if their eyes were on him. He had been composed, cold even, ever since he had landed in Italy. Now he was starting to feel nervous; he loosened his tie and undid his top button.

He cleared his throat and began his eulogy:

'My grandfather, Giovanni, was a devoted father and loving grandfather; and I feel very humble even attempting to speak about him. I certainly feel honoured to have been related to him. He was so full of love, patience, great endurance and infinite kindness. Words really cannot do justice to him'.

At this point Lewis paused, sniffing slightly. The irony of what he had just spoken almost causing him to smile. He took out a handkerchief and blew his nose. Then he glimpsed the two men again and suddenly his stomach tightened, and he felt his hands and neck moisten. His heart thumped and his legs buckled slightly – he held on to the microphone and steadied himself. He looked at the congregation again and saw that no-one had come forward to help. '*Maybe they know*' he thought. With the clean side of his handkerchief, he dabbed his eyes and then dried his neck and hands. Now ready, he carried on:

'Everyone that knew him knows what he was like and anyone that did NOT know him, to my mind, has missed out on a life-enhancing experience'.

Again Lewis stopped, this time reflecting upon his latest words. He wondered how many lives had been spared by not knowing his grandfather. He looked at the congregation. On the front row the only people who weren't looking directly at him were Rob and Joe. Their heads were bowed. Everyone else was staring at him, some with tears in their eyes. Others expressionless, cold. He trembled, fear started to eat away at him. Composing himself he spoke. Or he tried to. Nothing came out. He swallowed and moistened his mouth. He tried again:

' For us who are left behind it has been an unhappy time, obviously but I feel he is still with us and that should give us hope because as G.K. Chesterton once said: "Hope is the power of being cheerful in circumstances that we know to be desperate". Giovanni, we love you more than words can say'. Finished, he glanced at his brothers who were now looking at him. Rob had tears in his eyes and Joe wore a pallid expression. *'For you'*, Lewis thought *'I did it for you'*.

****

I remember the first time you held me. To comfort me, you said. Why, I asked. You need me, you said. Why, I asked. Your father is in prison, you said. I remember the first time you came to my bed. To comfort me, you said. Why, I asked. You are family, you said. I remember the first time you hurt me. Why, I asked. It's love, you said. I remember the second and the third times you hurt me. You loved me more and more, you said. I remember you comforting Rob and Joe. Why them, I asked. They are family as well, you said. I was jealous, I said. You are special, you said. I remember the pain. The greatest love, you said.

****

There were many times over the years, until his grandfather had grown tired of him (them) when Lewis had felt sick; sick almost to the point of death with the pain and the agony. The ecstasy, Giovanni had called it. And on these occasions Lewis felt his senses were leaving him. These led to bouts of blankness (his so called vertigo).

In the middle of frequent endeavours to remember and earnest struggles to re-gather some token of the state of seeming nothingness into which his soul had lapsed, there had been moments when he dreamed of happiness.

Lewis now called to mind the blankness, the dampness and the pain; and madness, the madness of a memory that busies itself among forbidden things.

****

He shook the priest by the hand and stepped down from the altar, joining his brothers as they walked down the aisle towards the exit. He stepped into the fading daylight where he was soon flanked by the two men he had noticed inside. He turned round, saw his brothers and nodded. They returned his greeting simultaneously. They understood. Lewis permitted himself a wry smile as he remembered the snowdrops in the woods and, on an impulse, he looked up at the roof of the church but his canaries had gone.

As he was led down to a Mercedes, he recited a nursery rhyme he had sung to himself many times, 'If you go down to the woods today you are in for a big surprise'. And as he entered the vehicle Lewis wondered what the snowdrops would look like up close and what sweet rest there must be in the grave.

That Visionary Hollow by Luigi Marchini

He draws back the curtains. The sun is setting, a pale, whitish yellow football peeking out from behind its hiding place – a blue blanket sprinkled with white smoke rings. He looks down on the street below and notices the shops seem to be closing for the evening: advertising boards are being taken inside, as are goods that have been on display outside. He can hear the sounds of shutters being pulled down further up the street. He looks at his watch and this confirms the time: 5.30 or so. He is never sure if his watch is fast or slow or by how much. He had only wanted a little nap – at his time of life he tires easily but five hours is overdoing it a bit. He glances at the wall mirror – *no bad if I say so myself.* He really has to stop this obsession with mirrors. Ever since that time…His mind shuts the door at this point. He pulls a black overcoat over his striped pyjamas, steps into his black shoes, rushes as fast as he can to the door, almost stumbling over the empty bottles. The lift is opposite his flat: he pushes the down button. Within moments it arrives, empty. He steps inside and presses the button for the ground floor. He looks into the mirror hanging on the side. He takes a step back. In the reflection, he sees a face peering at him over his shoulder. A face he thinks he recognises. He turns round. The face is gone. He sits down. He had recognised her face - he had started to see it recently - but that thing on it-what was it? It had looked like a black hole, in the very place where her left eye should have been. He pats his pockets – empty of course, he remembers the bottles in his flat. Sighing, he gets back up, heart beating faster than it has in years. He had forgotten he had one. Glancing once more in the mirror, he notices that his own eyes seem bloodshot. He shakes his head as the lift reaches the ground floor. At the bottom he exits the lift, walks to the main door of the apartment block, opens it and steps out.

That is he tries to step out – a gust of wind forces him back against the door. He feels his head thump against the metal frame; the pain reminds him of how old he really is. As he falls, he sees her face again, the eye larger now, covering her right eye - a void. He wants to jump into it, and as he does so he hears her scream. Again.

The darkness outside was questioning itself, asking if it were time to take a break. That brief time where hesitancy reigns supreme is an appropriate time to analyse a situation and form a plan of action. Theoretically. It is also a time where long distant memories seem as fresh as after supper indigestion. Moments where rationality, in many cases, gives way to impulses that act on repressed emotions and desires.

And her name was Lauren.

He opens his eyes and looks at his watch – 5.40: he must have been out cold. Why does no - one help him? He puts his right hand against the door. The left hand stretches out and rests on the join between the floor and the wall opposite. He breathes in and pushes himself up slowly. When he is in a crouching position, his strength gives way and he slumps back down. Sitting now, he turns himself round so he is facing the street. People are walking past, on their way home from work, but no one stops to help him. He does up the buttons on the coat and pulls up the collar. He hunches his knees to his chin.

There are moments in life when we have to take responsibility for our actions. Not often, true, but our past has a habit of creeping up on us at some point. Sometimes when we are dead, sometimes very early in life - either way would be fortunate. We live, we die, and we disintegrate. Or we die in life and we disintegrate in life.

He sits there for maybe half an hour, staring at nothing. That is, nothing tangible though he thinks he can see her again, smiling at him. Only now there is hardly any face left, just a round nothingness. But he can't really see that much; his eyesight seems to have put on a grey coat. The traffic is becoming thinner almost by the second, yet the noise from it seems to have increased. His eardrums reverberate to that and the relentless march of his heart.

The moon shadows start to introduce themselves, and the shops seem all to be shut now. Suddenly he feels lighter, as if he had regressed to a little boy of four or five. His energy, his life force seems invigorated. He looks down at his feet, and back up at the world. To his relief she has gone. Something seems familiar – he feels his heart quicken even more. It doesn't seem cold now and he has a sensation of light-headedness. Just like that time.

Now he stands up effortlessly, remembering why he came out in the first place-whiskey, Jack Daniels. *I should have come out before my sleep.* He always was a procrastinator. The only shop that sells alcohol now open is the new 24 hour store around the corner. He steps onto the pavement and turns left. He walks past the jewellers, the newsagent, and the baker. He looks at his reflection in the shop windows as he scuttles past. Old habits die hard. He walks quickly, much faster than he has walked in years. Why? He looks at his legs; they are hidden by his pyjamas and coat, but parts of his feet are visible. They look like rotten bananas; punctuated with bean shoots. They feel different however, as if they are treading atoms.

He hadn't always drunk of course. In fact before that night he only drank with his meals, or a glass of wine in the office to toast a birthday. Things were different after.

That night - her eyes pleading, frightened, as his hands gripped her throat tighter, the contours and smoothness of her naked back and bum reflected in the ceiling mirror as she lay on top. He had tried to stop but the excitement had gotten to him, and the more she screamed the more he squeezed. There was no reasonable reason for his actions - they hadn't quarrelled and the lovemaking had been natural. Hidden deep in his smallest brain cells was the fact that he had enjoyed the killing more than the sex. He blamed the mirror.

He turns the corner and sees the lights of the shop at the end of the street. In two minutes he is outside. He hesitates. *Jack Daniels.* He almost forgets why he is here. He opens the door and steps inside. There are two female assistants behind the till to his right. They ignore him. He looks around the shop and sees there is another assistant picking up that morning's croissants in the bakery section to the left. He can see two other customers in the shop: one is helping himself to a cup of Kenco at 60p and the other is heating up a sausage roll in the microwave next to the coffee machine. He wrinkles his nose – why can't he smell anything? Not even the coffee.

He undoes his coat and checks the inside pocket to make sure he has money. He hasn't been in here for a long time – being closer, the newsagent has always been his first choice – so he looks around for the drinks section. He sees it behind the till at the checkout. Of course – isn't it always there? He walks up to the till and stoops at the counter. Neither girl raises her head. They seem to be sorting out some paperwork. He says:

"Excuse me, could I have a bottle of Jack Daniels please?"

Again, there seems no sign that he has been noticed. He repeats the question but louder. Nothing. Annoyed now, he shouts:

"Can't you hear me?"

One girl looks up, but not at him. She talks to the other assistant who continues doing whatever it is she is doing:

"Christ, it seems to have gone cold all of a sudden."

The other girl nods. He ponders his next action. Not for long though. He is upset, puzzled, and angry. But he has learned to control his emotions, freeze his feelings, and ensnare his nerve centre these past years. There are lapses from time to time, but very rarely. He has so little human contact anyway. Calmly he walks to the end of the counter, and pulls up the entry hatch. He looks at the girls. Again nothing seems to have disturbed them. So he steps inside the staff section of the checkout, reaches out for a half bottle of Jack Daniels and puts it quickly into his pockets. He turns and walks towards the exit. His walk is firm, calm and confident even though he expects to be apprehended at any moment. As he walks he listens for the voice, the one calling him thief. Instead all he hears is Lauren, screaming. As he exits, he sees her across the road. She is staring at him, the blackness reaching out, inviting him.

All of existence is embedded in the alien landscape of empty space, the vacuum, the void. For some people time spent here may only be a moment, for others it may well seem like eternity.

Back out on the pavement now, he stops. *What the hell is going on?* He really can't make head nor tail of it. What he does know is that he feels much younger and happier than he did half an hour ago. He heads back to his flat.

To experience enlightenment or to take a large step to atonement, we must first enter deep into the very heart of darkness.

Again as he walks he has the sensation of light-headedness, of floating, of freedom. He soon reaches the apartment block. He stops. There are people gathered in front of it. They seem to be surrounding something. He wonders what it could be and approaches. As he does so, he starts to make out the odd phrase – "has someone called an ambulance", "poor thing", "I wonder what happened". He is part of the crowd now. Through a gap he can make out something on the floor. Someone. An old man. A very old man. His hair as white as ivory, his face wrinkled like a walnut. He recognises this head. He also recognises the black overcoat and striped pyjamas. Most importantly though, he recognises the woman in the crowd, a demonic grin on her face, beckoning him. It is only now he realises how much like him she looks. He takes out the bottle and looks away from the woman. He steps through the crowd, glances back at the now invisible woman and places the bottle by the dead man's side.

BITTER SWEET by RAKIE KEIG

Her fingers turned the small glass round, watching the way the clear liquid coated the sides and left barely visible vapour trails on the smooth surface. The rim was marked with traces of her lipstick, and opaque fingerprints decorated the outside. The girl had been drinking from the same glass all night, ever since she had convinced the barman to sell her the entire bottle of vodka so that she didn't have to stand up and make her way back to the bar every five minutes.

She knew that the barman was watching her, and it made her smile. He was watching her pour neat vodka down her throat, and he was worried that at some point she would pass out and he would have to throw her out onto the street. Esme smiled because she knew that that wouldn't happen. She was working her way steadily through the bottle but she was still no more than halfway drunk, although she did plan on making it all the way there by the end of the night.

Someone else was watching her as well. She had been aware of his attention for several minutes now, but she hadn't bothered to look up and return his stare. Instead she concentrated on her glass, turning it between her fingers and watching how the smeared surface refracted the dim light of the bar. If she closed her eyes just a little and stared through her eyelashes she could imagine seeing all the stars in the universe within the clear liquid.

Finally she looked up, smiling as she saw that the man was coming towards her table. He was tall and well built, with black hair that was slightly longer than suited him, and he looked a little older than most of the regulars that came into the bar. He was also breaking the unofficial dress code by wearing anything other than black—in this case a white t-shirt and blue jeans. It was too warm to be wearing a jacket, but he looked the type who would forgo one anyway. Esme studied his open, friendly face as he approached and she found herself smiling. It had been a while, and she guessed that tonight of all nights she could use the company.

'All alone?' the man asked.

Esme made a show of looking around at the empty table. 'Sure am,' she smiled. 'Wanna join me? You'll have to leave the beer behind though—this is a vodka only table.'

The man laughed, setting his half-empty bottle of beer down on one of the other tables. Esme waved at the bartender until he brought over a second glass, which was noticeably cleaner than her own.

'What are we celebrating?' the man asked, dragging his chair a little closer.

Esme shook her head, pouring a liberal measure into his glass. 'Not celebrating. Commiserating. But don't ask until I'm a *lot* drunker.'

'Okay. I'm Bobby.' He held out his hand politely and Esme pinched it between two fingers to shake. She noticed him staring at her nails, which were long and curved and painted ebony black.

'Esme.' She took her hand back and cupped it again around the small glass. 'Drink,' she instructed.

Bobby did so, choking on the uncut liquor. 'So,' he asked, 'are you here for the convention?'

'Mostly.' Esme shrugged, her gaze wandering off across the room as if bored already. The bar was small and the windows were blacked out, making it look like a poorly lit tomb from the inside; the effect accented by the short, stubby candles that stood on each table. The air was thick with cigarette haze and waxy smoke. 'I was hoping to find a real psychic among all the charlatans, but I've not had any luck.'

'No? There's a lot of them here.'

'Well, maybe.' Esme made a face. 'But either the real ones are all avoiding me, or the whole thing is for the birds. I've not quite decided which yet.'

Bobby sipped at his drink. 'What're you looking for?' he asked.

'I want my fortune told.' Esme made her eyes wide, like the dozens of young girls she'd seen that day wandering around the stalls with expressions of vapid delight. 'Or more specifically, I want to know when I'm going to die.'

The man blinked, although he had heard crazier things that day. 'And no-one could tell you?'

'Not truthfully, no. They all told me that I would lead a long and happy life untinged by tragedy.'

'You don't believe that?'

Esme drained her glass; poured herself another. 'Nope. Not the happy bit and definitely not the long bit. None of them would be honest and tell me the truth.'

Bobby watched as she rotated the glass between her fingers. Just by looking at the girl, he had known that she would be strange and at least a little drunk, but he was surprised to find out exactly how strange and how drunk. 'So... when do *you* think you're going to die?'

'Soon.' The girl's eyes flicked up and held his briefly. 'Probably tonight.'

'Seriously?'

Esme nodded, and Bobby knew that she wasn't joking, not even a little. 'I had a premonition,' she told him, carefully enunciating each syllable of the long word. 'I've never been psychic or anything like that... although my grandma was, a little... anyway, I had this dream and when I woke up there was this date in my head. Twentieth of August, this year. And I knew that that was when I was going to die.' She raised her glass in a mocking toast. 'That was about ten years ago, so I've had a bit of time to get used to the idea.'

'Wow.' Bobby had heard a lot of stories during his life—especially at this time of year when the conference came to town—but it always surprised him to hear the different ways that people reacted to the knowledge they were given. 'So, this is what we're commiserating here, huh?'

'Yep. Guess I didn't have to be that much drunker before I told you.'

'And you came here to find out if your... premonition was true?'

'Well, partially. Also, when I had that premonition thing, I knew *where* I would die as well. It kinda made sense after all—I was born here, in this town, so it figures that I would die here.'

Bobby frowned. 'You think you're going to die here, to-night?' He laughed suddenly. 'Hell, if it were me I'd be on the other side of the planet right now, probably hiding in the safest place I could find.'

Esme's smile was serene. 'What's the point of that? When you've got that black cloud over your head, it's your time to go, whether you accept it or not.'

'Black cloud?'

'That's what my grandma used to call it.' She refilled his glass, motioning for him to drink up. 'When a person's about to die they get this aura around them, like a big cloud of mosquitoes or thick smoke or something. She sometimes saw it around people and when she did, that person would die within the next couple of days. She told me that her aunt could see it even more strongly, and it drove the poor woman mad. Wouldn't even leave the house in the end, because she couldn't deal with knowing that someone was going to die and not being able to do a damn thing about it.'

Bobby set down his glass and Esme immediately filled it again. 'And that's why you were looking for a psychic today? To tell you whether you've got a black cloud around your head?'

'Oh, I know it's there.' She waved an unsteady hand around her head, describing a wide halo. 'I don't need anyone to tell me. I just... wanted to make sure...' Esme laughed. 'I'd hate to think I'd spent the last week calling all my friends and family and telling them that I loved them for nothing. Also I'd have to pay back the money I borrowed. And I've spent it all.'

Bobby lifted the vodka bottle, tilting it to see how much was left. 'Are you planning to die of alcohol poisoning?' he joked.

Esme shrugged, leaning heavily on the table. 'I'll take whatever I can get at this point. I always figured I'd die through violence, but passing out in my own bed and never waking up... I guess I could deal with that.'

'You are seriously messed up.' Bobby shook his head, still laughing. 'Do you realise how weird it is to hear a young girl talking like this?'

'Never too young.' Esme spoke quietly, as if talking exclusively to the glass in her hand. 'Once you're ready, you're ready. But yes.' She raised her head and smiled, her green eyes sparkling. 'I guess I am a little messed up. Drink with me.'

Bobby held up his hands in surrender and drained his glass, refilling it himself from the rapidly emptying bottle. 'I'm here for the convention as well,' he said then.

'Really? Business or pleasure?'

'Business mostly. I'm a psychic.'

Esme sat back, eyeing him with sudden interest. Are you re-ally'' she cooed.

'Uh-huh. Not a great one, but good enough to be able to stumble my way through life and make a living out of it. And you know what else?'

'What else, Bobby?'

'I can see the black clouds too.' He raised his glass, returning her toast.

Esme sat watching him for a moment, then started to laugh. She tilted her head back, her dark hair tumbling down over her shoulders. 'And what do you see right now, Mister Psychic?' she asked, her half-closed eyes gazing up at the ceiling. 'What do you see when you look at me?'

'I see a long and happy life.'

Esme laughed even harder, rocking back precariously on her chair. 'Ah, it's so cute that you do that!' she managed to say. 'Maybe everyone I've spoken to today has just been too damn nice to tell me the truth.'

'Would you really want to hear someone tell you you're going to die?'

'Yes!' She rocked forward again and thumped her hand down on the table. 'I know that it's true and I'm sick of people telling me I'm a liar! If I say I'm going to die, then dammit, I want people to believe me.' She lifted her glass again. 'Bastards.'

Bobby watched her swallow the vodka as if it were water. 'I believe you,' he said at length.

Esme looked up at him through her long lashes. 'Really?' she asked. 'You see this?' She traced the air around her head again, questioningly.

Bobby nodded.

'Cool.'

'Not really.'

'So, am I right? Is it going to be tonight?'

Bobby's gaze followed the swirling darkness around her head. 'I think so,' he said truthfully.

There was a long silence between the two of them. Finally, Esme leaned back in her chair again and dug in the pocket of her jeans, pulling out a handful of money. 'That's the last of what I own,' she said, pushing it across the table. 'Go buy me more vodka. I'm going to try for the alcohol poisoning thing.'

Bobby took the money and stood up. 'Ever hear of a self-fulfilling prophecy?' he asked as he headed towards the bar.

Esme yawned loudly, then folded her arms on the slightly sticky tabletop and feigned sleep until he came back. Then she poured the last of the vodka from the first bottle into their two glasses and cheerfully opened the second.

'Here's to the future!' she laughed, topping up both glasses to the brim.

Bobby lifted his glass. 'Here's to blissful ignorance,' he suggested.

'That too.' They clinked their glasses together, spilling a fair amount of the contents.

They sat and drank in silence for several minutes, each lost in their own thoughts. Esme kept smiling to herself as if amused by some private joke. Eventually she leaned across the table towards her new companion.

'Bet you're glad you came to sit here with me,' she said, then laughed drunkenly.

'It's been an experience,' Bobby admitted. He emptied his glass for what felt like the hundredth time that night. 'Are you glad you're spending your last night on earth this way?'

'Yes. Hell yes.' Another laugh. 'So what's it like, being able to see the black clouds? Doesn't it drive you insane?'

The man shrugged. 'You try not to think about it. You pretend it's just a trick of the light. You don't mention it to anyone, not ever, and if you see it on someone then you turn and walk away as quickly as you can. Same way that everyone deals with death, I guess.'

'Not everyone,' Esme disagreed. 'But you see my point, right? That it could put you right out of your mind?'

Bobby raised his eyebrows quizzically but said nothing.

'I know it would for me.' She lifted her glass so that she was talking into her drink again. 'You'd start looking at the people you hate and wishing so hard that they were the ones with the black cloud over their heads, instead of all the innocent people out there. Then you'd wish for it to be there just so that you could walk up to them and smile and say nothing, and just *know*. Just know that they're doomed and there's nothing they can do about it.'

Bobby was shaking his head. 'I don't do that.'

'Hell, I wasn't saying you did. But some people would— you can see that, right? That sort of gift could push you over the edge, if you were a little disturbed already...' She made a vague gesture with her free hand. 'You know what I mean. You'd start laughing instead of crying when you saw the darkness. And then... then...'

'Then what?' Bobby wasn't smiling any more.

'You could play.' Her green eyes had gone distant. 'You'd see if you could change the world; if you could make the black cloud appear over someone. It wouldn't take much. You look at someone and think, *I'm going to be waiting for you when you get out of your car. I'll be there and you'll never see me, and I'll break your skull.* And then you could sit and watch the cloud form over that person's head; watch it condense and take shape and know that *you* had done that. *You* had changed the universe.' Abruptly, her eyes seemed to snap back into focus and she laughed, reaching for the vodka again. 'If you were truly out of it, of course.'

'Oh, of course.'

Esme didn't appear to notice the coldness in his voice. 'It'd be interesting, I guess. Something to play with... watching how a simple choice that you made inside your own head could mean the difference between life and death for someone else. Huh.' She shrugged, the idea seeming to slide away as quickly as it had come.

Bobby was sitting back in his own chair, his arms folded across his chest, and he had stopped drinking. 'Like the choice between whether I came to sit with you, or with some other girl?' he suggested coldly. 'Is that what you mean?'

'What?' Esme was concentrating hard on tilting the vodka bottle, the tip of her pink tongue protruding from the corner of her mouth.

The man leaned forward. 'Just how psychic are you, Esme?'

'Huh? Me?' She tipped the bottle too far and sloshed vodka across the table. 'Dammit! There, there we go...' She tried again and managed to fill her glass. 'I'm not psychic at all, I told you that. My grandma, she was the psychic one. And her aunt. I just had that one dream that one time, that's it. Never anything else happened like that.'

For a moment longer, Bobby stared at her, his eyes intense like he was trying to look right inside her skull. But then he relaxed and sat back. 'Drink your drink,' he said shortly.

'Certainly will.' Esme lifted her glass, then frowned. 'Did I say something wrong?'

'No.' Bobby shook his head and smiled. 'Nothing at all.'

'Good.' She took another sip of her drink, then glanced up at the clock. 'Oh my God, have you seen the time? It's half eleven… God, I've not got much time left.' She stood up hurriedly, stumbling a little as she retrieved her coat. 'I'd better go…'

Bobby helped her put the coat on. 'Do you want me to walk you home?'

'Oh… no, thank you. No, I'd rather be on my own now.' Esme smiled up at him. 'I think I'll walk down past the river… see it one last time. But thank you, for keeping me company tonight. And for telling me the truth.'

'You're welcome.' There was something dark and unreadable behind his eyes. 'I… I really hope I see you again.'

'You won't.' She laughed. 'Goodnight, Bobby.'

She stood on her toes and kissed him briefly. His mouth was flavoured with the sharp tang of vodka, and beneath that, a faint bitter sweetness that made Esme smile. She broke away and turned towards the door.

When she got there she supported herself on the doorframe and took one last look back at Bobby. He was just another weak, barely talented psychic, not strong enough even to break through her shields and see what she had really been thinking. But the drug she had slipped into his drink would silence his mind soon enough. If her timing had been right, it should start to take effect at about the same time that he got up from his seat to quietly follow her out of the bar. He would be dead in the streets by midnight.

There was always one, every year. She could always guarantee finding that one bad apple in the barrel, that one psychic misanthrope who pushed it too far and stumbled into the realms of the sociopath. It made her happy to think that there would soon be another one gone.

She paused in the doorway for a moment longer, watching the way that the black cloud curled and twined around Bobby's head; enjoying it doubly so as she knew her own was already fading. And then she turned and disappeared through the door into the night.

Urn of Life By Valerie Mahony

The sea was angry. Its violent waves fought against the hard rocks that barricaded them from the shore. They howled with rage, competing with the blistering wind which whipped furiously around the frothy water. The mournful cry of a seagull hovered over the dark water. The bird screeched in frustration before despairing of a catch and fading into the grey sky.

Rose sat still on a stony ledge and stared out at the ocean. Her cotton blouse flapped in the wind, stinging her arms which were growing numb with the cold. But she did not notice.

She did not see how the dark waves tumbled towards the rocks below, crashing against their jagged surface and spewing salty froth into the air. Nor did she hear the thunderous waves roaring loudly in her ears like the sound of a thousand winds rushing together.

All she heard was the familiar taunts of the demons that haunted her. The demons that could not be silenced.

"What have you done? You stupid cow!" The cold voice echoed over the water.

The spray lifting from a massive wave slapped against her cheek like an icy hand. She flinched and shut her eyes but it was more a trained response than a reaction to pain. She couldn't feel any pain. Dead souls feel nothing.

Her tongue wandered absentmindedly over her swollen lips. They tasted like salt. Salt and blood. It was the ring on his finger that had split her lip; the thick golden band that bound her to him for a lifetime. She played distractedly with the small gold chain on her own finger. Its smooth, polished surface slid beneath her frozen fingertips. The burden of the ring weighed heavily on her hand and she dropped it wearily into her lap.

The sharp smell of seaweed wafted up from the ocean but she could smell nothing but him. His sweaty chest pushed roughly against her back. Spicy aftershave as his prickly, unshaven chin brushed against her own. A breath saturated with stale, cold beer hissing at her, "You're nothing but garbage. Do you hear me?"

A small tear trickled from her eye and rolled slowly down her cheek, mixing with the blood, dust and salt that clung to her face like flies around a carcass. Tiredness filled her every pore. She felt as spent as the hollow shell of a used firecracker.

But it was over now. This was the end.

She couldn't remember the beginning. Was it on her thirtieth birthday when he had mocked her in front of her friends and she had said nothing? Or perhaps when he had gripped her wrist tightly, a stony glaze covering his dark eyes, before brushing her hand aside. It might have been when she felt his thick fingers clasp around her throat before releasing suddenly. Most likely, it was the moment she first saw him and knew that she would give her life to keep him.

But what did it matter now, when or where, why or how it had started? It was finishing, that was all that mattered. She was finishing.

She tucked her knees up under her chin and wrapped her arms around her legs. Her skin, covered with goose bumps, prickled with the cold – the cold sea air, her cold heart, an icy fear that she had known so long that she barely noticed its presence.

The same fear had been with her that morning as she sat trembling in the corner of her lounge. The faded purple couch had been pushed aside, its throw-cushions scattered all over the floor of the dark room. Thick curtains were pulled tightly across the windows, blocking out the morning light and smothering the room in their musty arms.

"What are you doing? Get up!" His voice was dry and just beginning to go hoarse.

Shakily she stood to her feet and shuffled backwards into the corner of the dim room until she could feel the coarse curtains shift behind her back. Her hands were shaking so she crossed her arms tightly over her chest and tucked the quivering limbs under her armpits.

"Don't even think about going anywhere," he spat at her before abruptly turning and leaving, like a hurricane suddenly changing its course.

The sound of breaking glass and the loud bang of the slamming hall door resounded like a gunshot as he stormed out of the room and disappeared into the kitchen.

She was alone.

Her three-year-old son was staying at her mother's house for the weekend, thank God. Rose wished she could leave him there forever. He would be safe under the protective wing of his grandmother in the cozy home with large glass windows that let in streams of light, away from the twisted dance of love and hatred that blurred together in the cries of angry voices and violent outbursts.

His little soul had already been bruised by his father's rage and his mother's weakness. The blue and purple swells on her cheeks had been reflected in his blue eyes. Her skin had healed but his eyes had not.

Every tear that poured down her face watered the weeds that were growing up around his small heart. Rose was glad that he was away and could not witness again how his mother had failed him.

Yes, it was good that she was alone.

Except that he was there. Somewhere in the back of the house. What was he doing? Fetching a tool? A weapon?

Rose stood motionless. She realised that she was not breathing and quietly let the air hiss out of her lungs, leaving her head spinning in its wake. She closed her eyes so that she did not have to look at her prison and waited for him to return.

She could hear the soft drone of cars passing in the street just behind the curtain, signalling the start of a lazy Saturday. Just beyond the hard walls that barricaded her in the lounge, people were laughing, walking, living.

He reappeared just as suddenly as he had left; a dark, menacing shadow filling the doorway. In his hand he held a beer bottle which dripped with cold condensation like it too could not contain the drops of fear that had now started to form on her brow.

Slowly he inched across the room, each footstep resounding like a gonging symbol as his heavy boots pounded the wooden floor. Rose stared blankly at the ground, fighting desperately to hold back the pool of unshed tears that balanced precariously behind her eyes. She only lifted her head when she could taste his stale, bitter breath in her mouth.

His eyes were cold, his hair sticky with sweat, his yellowing teeth jutted out from behind dry lips curled into a snarl.

Her knees buckled and she slid to the floor, the cold, hard wall pressed against her back.

She bit her trembling lip, trying to keep herself together but knowing that it was only moments before she would be shattered like a mirror splintering on a hard floor.

"I told you to get up, you bitch!" he screamed, ready for round two.

"Please," she whimpered as his tight fist clasped around her hair and yanked her to her feet.

With a sudden jolt of his arm, he flung her towards the couch where she collapsed and lay still with her head buried in the soft cushion.

He continued to attack her but she no longer felt the pain. Like a buoy being tossed about in the ocean, she resigned herself to her fate. She did not notice when his leather boot pounded into her stomach or when her cheekbone crashed against the small wooden table in the centre of the room. She never heard the sound of the wall clock tumbling to the floor nor the violent insults that spewed out of his mouth like bile.

All she heard was a soft, tender voice whispering her name. She knew it immediately - the way her name fell from her father's lips like water pouring down a gentle waterfall. She remembered the warm smile that spread across his face as she entered a room and the sound of his heart gently beating in her ear as she lay against his chest. She longed for the cloak of love that enveloped her when he took her in his arms.

That love had died with her father. The first piece of her soul had been buried in the ebony casket covered with white lilies. A sudden heart attack and he was gone. Rose's own death had been much slower and it was years before she realised that she was dead. It happened there, in the dimly lit room, the smell of cigarettes clinging to the air, the sound of shattering porcelain tumbling around her, the sight of her husband hammering the last nail into her coffin with his fist.

The final blow came with a crash. She turned and saw through blurry eyes the framed picture of her son smashing to the floor. His innocent face smiled up at her from behind shattered glass, the cracks marring his soft complexion like ugly scars.

Suddenly a surge of strength rushed through her limp body. She was lying next to the fireplace, oblivious to how she had gotten there, and covered in her own blood. Fresh blood poured out of a deep gash in her left arm as she pulled herself to her feet. She felt her hands grip the silver urn that held her father's ashes. Her crimson handprint was emblazoned across the polished silver. The sweet smell of blood filled her with strength like a wild animal picking up the scent of its prey.

She could hear him coming towards her, charging at her from behind, his heavy breathing marking out his every step. Quickly she swirled around swinging the urn in her hands like a baseball bat.

With a crunch the urn ploughed into his skull. She watched, as though in a dream, his body crumble to the floor like a puppet whose strings had been cut. A shower of dark grey ashes rained down on his limp body and flowed over the pool of red blood that gushed from his head.

***

Rose did not know how she had made it to the edge of the ocean or how long she had been staring out at its depths, wishing that it would swallow her up. The dying sun sank slowly into the water, filling the sky with streaks of orange and red like blood pouring into the sea.

"The ocean is the washbasin of the soul. It's deep enough to blot out any stain."

Her father's voice again, now much clearer, free from the chorus of ghosts that had inhabited her subconscious for so long.

Her tears flowed freely now. There was no fear to hold them back.

They washed away the stain of death that hung over her and fell like fresh rain onto the dark rocks.

With a renewed strength she stood on the rocky ledge and felt the strong wind rushing at her. She breathed it in deeply like parched ground soaking up the first spring rains. With a steady hand she removed the delicate gold ring from her finger and threw it over the ledge. It hovered for an instant before plunging into the ocean below and was engulfed it in its churning waters.

Slowly she turned to leave and then, through misty eyes, she suddenly saw it. A small, almost insignificant, yellow flower pushing its way up through a crack in the rocks. How it had survived on the dry boulders, battling against the sea breezes and harsh sunlight, Rose could only guess. What had given it the strength to grow in an environment that seemed determined to stifle it? What had it endured to earn the right to blossom?

Yet now in the shadowy light of dusk, it gleamed like a jewel hidden in the sand.

"My darling Rose."

How she loved his voice.

Magus and the Orb of Bethalas by D.M. Worthy

Act I
of the Great War

Chapter One
Flight

The night was dark—black as tar, and relenting to nothing. Heavy showers fell upon the eaves of the Lost Woods. A fox with a black-tipped tail ran apace, slipping around the dense collection of trees. Puffs of white breath issued from its mouth, cold rain beat on its fur. It was soaked. Ogres and wild-mastiffs had been chasing him nearly a quarter of an hour, and it was losing its oomph. Roars and yelps echoed in the distance, and with them came thuds all around, as the ogres hurled their stones.

The fox felt as if it would break at any moment, running at this breakneck speed. There was only one thing to do, to slow down, or pass out; the barks and cries drew a good distance closer.

The enemy was so close now the fox could discern the grinding of stones in the ogres' pouches, the pitter patter of paws in the mud. The fox dug deep inside itself, searching for strength, hoping—

The fox boosted up, putting more distance between him and the pursuers. The forestry of the Lost Woods fell away, and the ground dipped into the Corona Brook. The fox ran alongside, daring not to ford it, for the downpour had been relentless for hours, and the water level was much too high and rapid.

A quarter mile ahead, the two lampposts of the Mere Ferry glimmered at the delta of the Haw River and Corona Brook. Upon reaching the ferry he transformed. Into a man, tall, and clothed in a dark blue robe trimmed in gold. His eyes were dark, and his hair white-blond, tied with a black ribbon.

The man urgently untied the ferry, hopped on, and shoved off.

A stone arced through the air, and hit the water near the ferry, causing it to yaw hazardously. He paddled faster. Another stone was lobbed, and another, and another. He aimed his staff, and two green rays jetted forth, obliterating two of the stones; the third slammed into the ferry, and it pitched forward into the river, thrusting the shapeshifter headlong into the ferry as it buoyed.

The ogres and wild-mastiffs stood on the edge of the riverbank, watching their prey sail further and further away. The man struggled to his feet, and looked back at the river bank, where his enemies stood growling and shouting at him. He sat down and folded his legs, grateful to be out of the frying pan.

He thought of all the misadventures since his arrival to the Archipelago of Evermore. His boat floundered in a perilous storm, and stranded him on the island of Corinthia. That was two days ago, and from then on things haven't gone so well. First, there was a strange encounter with a mysterious person shrouded in black. The person said nothing, but he felt ill of it all the same. Then he stumbled upon the ogres' lair in the Woods; he slew many but due to disadvantaging numbers, he fled with all speed. In the chase he interrupted a pack of wild-mastiffs mauling a cadaver, and they followed his heels also, for the taste of new meat.

Night drew on, and the shapeshifter slept under the rain. At dawn he awoke to the caw of a crow hovering above. The rain had ceased. He was drenched and cold. There was a low *splat*, as crow dung landed but inches from his head. The bird let out a harsh call and flew away.

After a short length the man docked at the southern shore of the Lun Valley, thirty miles down river. He shapeshifted into the fox, shook off a bit of water, and trotted off. The grass was dark green and springy, moist from last night's rain, and glinting under the morning sun. He traveled northward all day across the valley. The sun slipped behind the horizon, all the western sky went red, and he happened upon the Downs of Nien. The fox was running apace now, streaming passed homesteads, casting long shadows in the pastures. Ere nightfall arrived he came to the town of Nien. That night the two moons were bright, an almost cheesy yellow, and larger than usual. He returned to human form and entered a small tavern.

The townsfolk eyed him funnily as he strolled through the streets. The people of Evermore had not seen wizard-kind since the world was young and the first king of Evermore reigned.

In a secluded corner of the tavern he ate his meal, heeding little those around him occasionally shooting him disapproving glances. Instinctively he looked up from his plate, and turned his head to the far right window. He spied a small silhouette perched on the win-dowsill; what it was he could not determine, some kind of bird, he reckoned. Since it appeared as no threat he returned to his food.

When he had downed his food and let it settle, he was on the move again, onward north. Light shone upon the soggy North-road on which the fox leisurely walked, his paws sinking in the mud. Two red bulbs of light glared afar. He transformed, and after a time he came before the Guard of Corinthia.

A pass ran through a stretch of mountains, whose slopes bore tight bushels of trees. At the entrance soared great iron doors, and two embattled towers were wrought into the slopes, their crests roaring with fire. Men paraded across a causeway connecting the towers, with wallse raised like a battlement; bowmen were posi-tioned here.

The shapeshifter came before the great iron doors. Trumpets rang out, and bowmen loomed from the causeway and tower win-dows, arrows set into the bowstrings. The bowmen said nothing, yet did not fire. The man waited patiently and unworried, for he'd been here before, long ago, when the Men of the Guard were mild-mannered.

Nowadays this is not so, the shapeshifter would come to dis-mayingly realize. In the early years, King Dorian ruled as Evermore's first king. Amidst the building of Bethalas, his castle, he found an orb while inspecting the progress. He kept the orb closed to him and called it the Orb of Bethalas, and he used its power to wrought a better creation of Castle Bethalas. With the orb he grew wise and powerful, aging older ever slowly, and his kingdom flourished greatly.

Years passed on, and the orb darkened with the growth of his power and pride, and ultimately turned black as impenetrable night. Dorian now went ahead of himself, his power fully wrought, and declared himself ruler over the southern world of Geneva. Thus, he confronted Lunasûne, High King of Geneva (emperors they were named in latter years when their kingdoms were wholly amassed). The high king accepted the challenge. In his grace and boldness, he sailed to Evermore and disembarked without escort, upon his pure white unicorn from Indaleen. An angelic aura was about him, and he was extremely fair to look upon, but something underneath was terrible about him. He had genially accepted the challenge, but the principle of the matter vexed him, and he was hot inside.

The High King wrestled Dorian and slew him justly; then took the Orb to L' Meran and there he set it in Rhavé Dûn, the mountain of fire. He declared no other king should have it save in dire need and consent from him, or his descendants. The untimely loss of King Dorian embittered the people of Evermore, and they became estranged with the other continents. Praxis, son of Dorian, was ill pleased with the High-king's arrangements, and declared the thirteen islands of Evermore sovereignty.

The great iron doors screeched open. Four guardsmen issued forth, in silver helmets, armed with long swords and round shields.

"Who are you?" one asked harshly. "You are not familiar and your raiment is queer."

"Queer maybe," said the shapeshifter. "But anyway, I am Magus."

"Magus what?" asked the guardsman rudely.

"Tidewater," said Magus pleasantly.

"Neither the name nor face is familiar," said the guardsman, scrutinizing him. "If you wish to pass, you shall need to speak with Tengrin."

With that the four men turned and walked away, and the doors creaked closed behind them. *I wish I had thought to bring the letter from the king with me*, he thought. *But who would have thought of that, especially if they didn't intend on the misshapen voyage?* Magus pondered the letter while he waited. The letter was rather strange, after all, and short. He had never met the King Taran, and his previous visit to Evermore was on other matters. Evermore felt small love for other continents, and knowing the current relations between the two kingdoms, Magus presumed the business urgent.

The doors opened again. Tengrin came forth, grim in face in a green cloak, fastened with a brooch like a golden badge; token of his Chief of the Guard status. Flanking him were a pair of guardsmen, and in tow, were three bowmen and the four guardsmen who originally answered the doors.

"Mr. Magus, stranger to Evermore," said Tengrin, a false pleasant smile on his face. Magus saw nothing but anger and agitation—hate maybe. Evermoree despised Setanians most of all in Geneva. And Magus was a Setanian. "By the laws of our lands, none should pass save they be familiar. Besides, your looks are ill to me. What is your business here?"

"A stranger perhaps, but not wholly," said Magus. "And as far as looks are concerned, to each is his own," he added smoothly. "Nevertheless, it just so happens I have business with the king."

"The likes of you would not hold in a king's presence," said Tengrin.

"I have counseled with the Emperor Tivoli, Tengrin, Chief of the Guard," said Magus irritably. "I am Magus the Sorcerer, fix your tongue! I know full well of Evermore's embittered feelings since the fall of Dorian by Lunasûne."

At that, swords were drawn and arrows readied.

"You should pay dearly for your insolence, wayward Magus," said Tengrin angrily. "What is preventing me from slaying you where you stand?"

"Me, I'm afraid," said Magus passively. "Lower your arms, for thy rashness may lead you to great hurt! Let me pass!"

The sorcerer was furious, his words commanding and powerful. There was a boom of thunder, and a streak of lightning. Tengrin and the guardsmen grew afraid—but just for a moment, and the bowmen fired. But a blinding light emitted from Magus' staff, an instant before they could do so, and the arrows flew astray. The sorcerer was enveloped in the radiance, his robe changed white, and the trimmings glowed bright gold. His robe and hair flowed in a sentient wind.

The guardsmen froze, blinded for a second, but their sight soon recovered. Onlookers stared aghast at the white figure shimmering like a star.

"It is your play, Tengrin," said Magus, his voice deep and carrying. "You have but to advance. Make your move!" The guardsmen did not respond nor step forward. Looking them over, and finding no contention, Magus said, "If you wish not to contend, let me pass!"

Weapons were lowered.

"You have been recognized as Magus the Sorcerer, and are free to proceed," said Tengrin. "By my leave," he added nonchalantly.

Magus chose to ignore the chief's latter comment, a feeble attempt to pretend to still have a control of the situation. His light died and dark returned. "Thank you, Tengrin, Chief of the Guard," he said bowing.

Tengrin nodded ever so slightly. Magus shifted into the fox, and the men started. He peered up to the moons, then to the guardsmen. He yelped and sprinted around them to the doors.

Several miles down the pass branched right, and ran across the clustered dwellings of Yurabar, at the base of a high precipice. Further on, the pass dipped sharply, and darkened, for the roof narrowed and little moonlight penetrated it. It ran this way for ten miles, then the land rose and the fox left the scene of mountains behind.

Chapter Two
Grabback

That night the fox journeyed along Blitz Run, curved northeastward of Blitz Falls. Blitz Falls consisted of seven waterfalls, four slender and spilling into a lake, and three wide, depositing into parallel furrows called the Triton. On the rim of the lake grew palm trees bearing fruit unfamiliar to Magus. The fox paused and admired the view, listening to the roar of the falls as mist sprayed him. The fox-Magus did not notice the crow hovering silently above.

By early morning he reached the rocky Shores of Gundar. White foam of the Selbring Ocean lapped the beach, rolling over the black stones, and dashing into rock formations. The fox stopped, surveyed the water for a moment, and continued on. He searched all morning for what he sought. Nearing mid-afternoon, the fox was tired and desired some rest. He awoke later to the smell of bird droppings on his nose.

The sky was purple; a faint orange dotted the western sky, as the sun neared the end of its daily descent. Finally Magus found what he looked for! It was a rocky black mound in the middle of the ocean. His first instinct was to bark, but he knew that would not do the trick, and transfigured into a human. Magus started whistling a song, resonating far out into the deep blue. During the melody, the black mound began moving slowly. Magus ended the song and waited.

Coming to shore, the water around the mound bubbled, revealing itself as the shell of a great turtle.

"Hello Magus," said the turtle, in a deep, dull, and slow voice. "What brings you to this side of the world?"

"Duties, Grabback, duties," said Magus. "It has been long since I have seen you. How is the ocean treating you?"

"Ok, I guess," said Grabback. "Floundered in a bad storm some days ago, but much of the same."

"I was in that same storm," Magus sympathized. "just ten miles from the coast of Corinthia. I hope I did not wake you from your slumber, but I need a favor."

"Not sleeping," said Grabback. "—just resting my eyes." The sorcerer knew that meant he was sleeping. "Tell me, Magus, how can I be of service?"

"I need you to take me to Avallone."

"Avallone?" asked Grabback, almost sounding amazed, if that were possible.

"Yes, my friend," said Magus. "I have to see the King Taran."

"Well, ok, if you wish. But you know the Evermore are not warm to Genevans…Setanians especially."

"Fully aware," said Magus. "That is why I did not choose to take my chances at the port. Dealing with the Guard of Corinthia was enough."

"Up you go then," said the turtle.

Magus climbed aboard the stony shelled beast. The sorcerer returned to fox form and curled up on Grabback's shell. Although bumpy and hard, he managed to get comfortable. Grabback slowly circled around and made for the water, which gurgled and fizzed as he descended into it. The ride was smooth, and he felt practically motionless. Magus the fox closed its eyes and relished the ocean breeze. However nothing could take his mind off the aching hunger of its stomach; the menial amount of bread he purchased at the tavern has been gone since yesterday morning. He cursed himself for not bringing more gold.

What was left of the sun's radiance disappeared in the horizon in a pink and purplish luster.

Grabback swam on.

The fox's ears perked up to the din of an explosion. He lifted his head and examined the night. In the far western distance he saw the silhouette of Mandalan Island, the second smallest island in Evermore. Magus the fox turned his attention to the eastern sky, alight, and flashing an ominous fiery red against a black nothingness. It was as if fire burned in the sky. He'd never seen such a sight. He gazed at this luminous marvel awhile, lay his head back down, and closed his eyes, trying to forget the terrible hunger.

Magus awoke just before sunrise. The eastern sky radiated a bright pink, with a hint of orange, and the surrounding scattered clouds were light purplish. Magus caught the view of palm trees on an island several miles off. Towards the far western shore was the quayside of Briscoe. Grabback drifted east.

The turtle came to rest on a sandy shore. The fox dismounted and transformed into a human. Magus peered around at the palm trees, and the brown round fruit they bared. The fruit was large and three times the size of an orange.

"If you head due north, you will meet North Mountain Road," said Grabback. "And that shall lead you to the Black Mountain."

"Very good thank you," said Magus, once again eyeing the strange fruit. "Grabback, what is that fruit?" he asked, tapping his staff against the tree. By the power vested in the staff, a fruit dropped from the tree. He caught it, and his hand fell under the weight.

"Oh those. They are coconuts."

"A what?" asked Magus, tossing it up and catching it.

"A co-co-nut," repeats Grabback. "Island fruit."

Magus lifted the coconut to his mouth.

"I wouldn't do that if I were you," Grabback laughed, a guttural sound. "You break it open."

Magus touched it lightly with his staff. It cracked open and milk spilled out onto his hand. He tipped the coconut and drank what remained.

"You can eat the white inside, as well," said the turtle. "If the flesh is yellow or yellowing. Don't eat it. Its rancid. Well, I'll be on my merry way. You know if you need me, just whistle."

"I shall," said Magus. "I shan't be more than two weeks, hopefully."

"Fine then," said Grabback slowly turning to the ocean. "Farewell."

"Farewell, my friend."

Grabback plunged into the water.

Magus slipped a lustrous dagger from his sleeve, with a golden grip encrusted with gems, rubies, and onyx; a dangerous weapon, a poisoned blade. Ivey was its name. He opened the fruit fully and scooped out some of the inside, ate it. It was good. After finishing the coconut he broke open another, drank the juice, shaved some of the flesh, and tucked the pieces in his pocket.

Chapter Three
North Mountain Road

The palm trees stretched for an acre before diminishing into the Azgabar Jungle. It was humid and damp, and the smell of rain lingered from the storm several days ago. Glittering sunlight peeked through the roof. Exotic birds were perched in the vine strangled trees, their calls foreign, beautiful. He passed a long, fat snake in a décor of black diamonds, coiled around a branch, hissing and staring fixedly at him as he crossed its path.

A flying insect buzzed annoyingly around his ear. He waved it away, but it kept coming back as if the little thing had some malicious intent to bite him. To Magus though, this winged pest was not so little, thrice the size of any mosquito he'd ever seen, perhaps larger. After a couple more violent swings of his arm the mosquito flew away, and he heard no more of it. Briefly after the encounter, the back of his neck began to itch. He went to scratch it, and groaned; a small bump had materialized there. The mosquito had bitten him after all.

Before long he was in fox form again, having grown tired of the vicious mosquito attacks, leaving him with at least ten bites. Now, he hated the jungle, but at least in fox form he'd have a better sense of direction if he were to get lost, though heading straight was a simple enough task. He wondered how far he was from the North Mountain Road. Grabback never said. The moment the thought crossed his mind his nose picked up the scent of food—mushrooms. The fox moved along, nose low to the ground trying to pinpoint the location. It strayed off course. The scent was close, so close he could almost taste the mushrooms. The fox squirmed through a thicket of bushes and found them. He could barely believe his eyes. The mushrooms were huge, the size of drums, sitting around the base of a very old tree. The fox surveyed the mushrooms with his nose. Their aroma made his nose tingle, and he sneezed. Deeming everything was fine, he dug in.

After eating half of one he was full and tired. The fox curled up and decided to take a nap. He would take more with him when he set off again.

When he opened his eyes sunlight was fading, casting the jungle under shadow. The fox yawned, licked his nose and stood up. His stomach was still full. Just then, an unwarranted nervousness set in. He frantically looked right and left, into the darkening bush.

He took a step forward, his stomach lurched. His knees buckled, and he collapsed with a whimper, instantaneously, and involuntarily transforming back to a human. Magus looked up from the ground. His head was spinning, everything was blurry. He got to his feet favoring his forehead.

"What's wrong with me?" he asked himself, squinting to a sudden throbbing pain in his head.

He peered down at the mushrooms and leapt back. They were different now. Dark green and mossy, their tops were mouths full of razor sharp teeth. Cruel swings of his staff sent pieces of mushroom flying everywhere. After taking another look, strangely, the mushrooms were back to normal. His mind was in a daze. Was he going crazy? A jolt of pain pierced his head. He favored his forehead again and leaned on his staff, staring at the chunks of mushroom scattered about. He was startled by ruffling bushes, and wheeled around, staff pointed, ready. Ferns shook and swayed. All around things moved. Sheer panic! He transformed into the fox and dashed off.

As he ran the jungle attacked him, vines tried to lasso him, or whip him. Conditions in his present form were no better. It was as if he ran through a pocket of hot air, thick, and slowing his movements to a crawl; it was like running in water, or running in a dreamscape. He felt nauseas, a moment away from regurgitating. The whole situation was unnerving, actually. He was fleeing from something he couldn't entirely flee from unless he escaped the jungle.

In the midst of his run, without any action of his own, he was human again. A vine snatched him up by his ankles, a second confiscated his staff. More vines wrapped around him, squeezing tight. He cried out. A vine coiled around his face silencing him. He struggled desperately to get free. Lastly, a vine caught him around the neck.

Next thing he knew, he was on the ground face down, wiggling crazily. He lifted his face from the dirt and scanned the area. Everything was peaceful. He rose to his feet and swayed like a tree in a breeze. He was hot, flushed, and sweaty, and his head was swimming. Nonetheless he had a job to do; he picked up his staff and labored on, queasy and uneasy.

Magus awoke the next morning to the sun glaring in his eyes, unable to remember falling asleep. From somewhere a crow cawed, but to him for some peculiar reason, it resembled a laugh. Magus found himself lying on his back—naked! He heard the fluttering of wings as the crow left wherever it was perched, flew passed his line of sight cawing laughter, and disappeared for just an instant as it passed in front of the sun.

Luckily enough he found his staff close at hand, his robe however, was nowhere to be seen. He did not know it, but his eyes were lightly bloodshot and dark patches were under them. After searching for ten minutes and coming up with nothing, he decided to transfigure to a fox and locate his clothing by scent. He felt lightheaded, but confident he could remain in fox form. At least long enough to find his robe anyway.

He found his belongings a quarter mile away. He didn't know when he'd taken his robe off. He dressed and started on his way again, realizing he was lost. He could tell by the position of the sun. By now, under the strain of his head condition, he lacked the will to change, and resolved to use his human sense to find a way out. He was off his present course. But how far off?

Throughout the morning he wandered the bush, beating off insects and once, averting a skunk's spray. The sky turned gray, the clouds flickered with the threat of rain. Magus passed through a cluster of ferns, and the earth sloped passively under his feet. From his position he spied the great height of the Black Mountain fifteen miles away.

Hours later he reached the foot of the mountain, meeting a road that wound up through a tunnel. He could see the light at the tunnel's end where the road continued on, and out of sight.

It was currently nightfall. Magus, continuing to suffer from the sickly conditions, stumbled upon one of the many small villages strewn about the slopes. From the start the villagers viewed him as a stray, a drunken man who appeared to lack many nights of sleep. His weary posture, and the way he labored forth on his staff didn't help matters. Ignoring their accusing eyes he trudged on.

Midnight came swiftly. He had passed another village, receiving the same reproachful glances. He was utterly famished. The mushrooms had long been walked off, but the side effects remained. He was tired but couldn't sleep. He found a cozy spot in a dark corner of a tunnel, and with the little strength he could mustered, he transformed into a fox and snuggled up. He closed his eyes but sleep would not come to him. Instead, he lay motionless listening to the serenity of the night.

The tranquility was broken, and his ears erected to the low rumble of thunder. The rumbles soon became booms and lightning flashed through the tunnel's entryways. There was the din of rainfall in the vicinity, growing steadily closer. A curtain of rain traveled down an 'S' curve, down the road, and over the tunnel, filling it with a steady drum.

Sleep was trying to take Magus when his nose picked up something; something human and something animal. His eyes popped open. Lightning flashed, and he descried two silhouettes at the opposite end of the tunnel. Barking resonated down the length of the shaft.

"What is it? Smell something boy?" a voice echoed.

Magus presumed the dog had caught his scent. Swift and slick, he slipped out from the tunnel's darkness and into the night. The rest had done him some good, although sleep would have been much better. He crept slyly from the corner, and raced down the road. Woofs echoed from behind him; he'd been seen.

Before long the dog was out of the tunnel and on the chase; it was a mastiff sporting a spiked collar. His master, who hadn't seen the fox, called futilely for his four-legged companion. There was a considerable distance between the fox and the dog, but the mastiff kept in hot pursuit.

The mastiff stayed on the fox's heels for a quarter of a mile; under better circumstances, he could've kept up the pace, but his body was reminded how sick it was, and he was exhausted and overheated now. A bend was up ahead, and he found hope in this; he mustered more energy and pushed harder. The bend seemed miles and miles away in his condition, and he swore he'd collapse before getting there. Thankfully he did not pass out; he rounded the curve and scurried up a slope, slipping and sliding in the mud. The fox located a section of a cliff to hide out if he stayed low.

Several moments afterwards, the fox heard the pitter-patter of paws splashing through puddles in the road. The mastiff rounded the corner. A voice was crying out, but he could not discern the words over the din of rain, and his racing heart.

The mastiff sniffed around, looked towards the cliff, and began snarling and yowling. The fox remained low, quiet. It was well hidden, but the mastiff had smelled him. The fox knew he could not escape this way, but he had a secure spot where he could plot and plan. The dog tried with much effort to scale the terrain but to no avail.

His trip to Evermore had been unpleasant, to say the least. But he thought of revealing himself to the man, but thought against it, reminiscing on the incident with the Guard of Corinthia. He was weary of the disgruntled island folk. He needed to think fast, to get out of yet another, sticky situation.

"Tryx! Tryx!" a voice cried. There was a loud piercing whistle. "Tryx! Where are you boy?"

Such a playful name for such a ferocious dog, Magus thought. Tryx growled and bared his teeth, then went into a fit of ecstatic baying.

The master came around the bend. He was in an ashen gray cloak, cowl cast over a helmet, with a brightly burnished round shield slung over his back.

"There you are, Tryx," he said. "What's doing?"

The fox leapt from his hiding place and pounced on the mastiff, plunging his face in the mud. The master cast aside his cloak, and reached for his sword; but before he could do so, the fox like lightning, pounced from the back of the mastiff, and slammed hard into the man's chest. He fell back into a puddle with a splash. The fox scampered off—but not far, and circled around. He had no strength for another chase, only to make a stand.

In the darkness of night, neither the dog nor master saw the fox revert to human form. He shifted to keep his balance, spread his legs a bit. The man stood to his feet. The air rang, and Magus saw a glint of steel rise in the night. A brilliant blue light followed thereafter. The man protected himself, and the sorcerer's spell was deflected; but the force of Magus's might threw him from his feet. Tryx very fond of his master rushed to his aid, concerned, letting the assailant get away.

Magus swore he recognized the man's face, he glimpsed in the light of the spell.

It was currently twilight. He was finally satisfied by the distance put between him, and his pursers. Right now, all Magus wanted to do was rest. But he dared not; he didn't want to get caught sleeping. His willingness to stay alert left him sleepless. However, fortune would smile upon him, and he happened upon a couple slices of coconut in his pocket; they were dry and warm, off white and covered in lint from being in there.

Light was breaking over the horizon. Magus lumbered sluggishly up a steep hill, but he had amazingly more stamina since the coconut slices. His eyes were droopy though, and he was still travel weary. Three miles off, the road veered sharply to the right and disappeared into a tunnel. Once out of the tunnel he met an intersection called The King's Crossing, where the East Mountain Road ran out from a tunnel, and traversed the North Mountain Road. A mile or two northward the castle Bethalas sat in a dell fifteen hundred feet below the mountain's peak, where a trio of flying things circled above. The winged creatures sighted his approach and homed in on him.

Magus was steadfast, having heard of these birds, these Dreschen they were called. The Dreschen were great exotic birds with long beaks and tail-feathers, and razor sharp talons. They landed and surrounded the sorcerer, peering at him inquisitively. The one in front of Magus spoke.

"What business do you have here?"

Magus straightened. "Business with the king. He is expecting me."

"I am sorry, Master Straggler. The King Taran is expecting but one visitor."

Neither Magus nor the Dreschen noticed a crow pass silently overhead.

"So if you please, stranger," it continued. "be on your way or be forced away, and more perhaps."

"Is this how everyone treats guests of the king?" Magus asked shortly. He was irritated all over again. Everyone knew wizards had short tempers. "I am tired and hungry and wish to speak to the king! If you would but inform King Taran that Magus Tidewater has arrived in response to his letter, I would greatly appreciate it."

The bird leaned down, stared into Magus' eyes, but it was looking far deeper. The Dreschen straightened, blinked.

"I see there is no lying in you. I shall return shortly."

It flew off. The remaining two stood still as statues, eyes fixed expressionlessly on him.

"The king will see you," said the Dreschen when it returned.

Chapter Four
Gilda the Witch

"First of all matters," said King Taran. "is the incident with the Guard of Corinthia."

"Your majesty," said Magus. "No one was injured, but they would not let me pass even though you requested me."

"I made no such request, and I sent you no letter," said the king surely. "Certainly I would remember such a thing."

"Taran, your highness," said Magus politely. "If you did not send the letter, than who did?"

Taran went silent.

"Do you have the letter you supposedly received from me?"

Magus heard the sarcasm in his voice and was greatly annoyed. But he'd hold his tongue, for he would never talk sharp to the monarch, unless unbelievably hard pressed. What bothered him though is the king's blatant lack of knowledge of the letter. Was he going crazy or something? He wasn't sure if he was directing that question to the king or himself. He *knows* he read that letter. *It was real, wasn't it?* "No," Magus replied heavily.

King Taran said nothing for a moment, deep in thought. "This is a strange mystery," said the king at last. "We do not correlate with those out of Evermore, but you do not tell a lie, for the Dreschen can see through deceit. Withal, I did not request..."

There was a hysteric knock on the throne room door. Soldiers stationed at the entrance answered it, and a soldier rushed in before the door was opened fully. "Sire! Sire! The prince!"

The king stiffened in his throne. "What is it?" the king asked worriedly. "What is wrong with my son?"

"Prince Farland, your majesty." The soldier could not get himself together for a moment, then said; "He has been turned to stone!"

"Stone?" Taran repeated appalled, rising to his feet. "How did this happen?"

"No one knows your highness. But there is worse... There is a stranger in the castle slaying guards and soldiers."

"Find this stranger!" demanded Taran, starting down the dais.

"There shall be no need for that," said a voice, and the room was consumed by darkness.

Three scarlet lights streaked through the darkness. Groans and grunts went up. A white light winked on and luminosity returned to the room. The guards and soldier lay on the floor, their dead gaze looking at nothing. Standing center stage was a tall figure dressed in a black shroud, identity concealed under a cowl. It was the figure Magus saw in the Lost Woods. But that was many days ago. And how could this person had followed him?

"Well, well, well," said the person in black, a woman's voice; sultry in a way, but dangerous and icy. She snapped her fingers, and fire returned to the torches. "The notorious Magus Tidewater. A pleasure to finally make your acquaintance."

"I wish I could say the same," said Magus mildly, extinguishing the light on his staff. "But I cannot see your face. If you are not a coward, show yourself!"

The woman snickered. "I believe I have already proven otherwise, but that is a reasonable request," she said, casting off her hood.

She was dark-haired and dark eyed, with a cold, sharp stare; her eyebrows were pointed, giving her a constant look of anger, although a wicked grin was on her face.

"Who are you?" asked Magus coolly. "I know you not."

"A better question is what do you want?" Taran interjected. "And what have you done to my son Farland?"

The woman did not respond, only looked at him. Even from ten feet away King Taran swooned, put his head down as if ashamed, returned to his throne, and said no more.

"I am Gilda," said the woman. "As far as your precious son, king, he has been stoned until I get what I want."

"What is that?" asked Magus.

Gilda laughed coldly. "What does Bethalas have to offer?"

"The orb."

"Very good," said Gilda, clapping her slender, long-nailed hands, mockingly. "That is why I chose you," she said, that grin on her lips. "Who else could have withstood the Dreschen's gaze though they were lying? In actuality though, you weren't, its just you were not completely accurate on your story. A minor oversight the Dreschen could not differ. The king did not send the letter, I did."

"Quite brilliant, I must confess," said Magus. He was mildly amused. "But surely you must know of a small little problem."

"And what would that be?" asked Gilda, folding her arms. "That the Orb of Bethalas was hidden away by the High-king Lunasûne, and it cannot be retrieved without consent? No Magus. I am fully aware of the circumstances. It is not good to get into a situation without completely assessing it first."

"Then you know the emperor would leave the prince stoned than adhere to such demands." Magus gave her a broad smile. "— Or kill the one who makes the request."

"It would be unwise to attempt that feat, Magus. You look peaked from those na-na jungle mushrooms."

Magus knew this to be true. But he wasn't listening. A green light issued from his staff. Gilda disappeared and materialized a pace in front of him, and her fingernails slashed his neck. Blood flowed down in four little streams. Magus flicked his wrist, and the white staff collided with her head. Since she was so close, the blow didn't inflict the damage he would've liked. But Gilda felt it all the same, and stammered back favoring her head. She extended her free arm, and a scarlet light shot from her palm—just as a shaft of green marked her. Magus' spell went wide, but hers struck him dead on, throwing him to the foot of the dais. A second scarlet beam jetted across the room. Magus transfigured to a fox, and dashed out the way at the nick of time.

The fox charged Gilda, dodging a barrage of spells; at the perfect moment, he pounced on the witch and felled her. Her hands went up just as his jaws targeted her neck. The fox snapped and growled at her. Then she did something Magus did not expect, and transformed into a crow. She took wing and flew in the king's direction. Magus reverted to human form, and shot a blast of searing red light. The spell nipped the crow's left wing, and she crash landed billowing smoke, wafting a brief smell of burnt feathers. Taran seized the opportunity, and jumped to his feet reaching for his sword. In an instant, the crow was human again, and vanished. Gilda appeared in front of the king, one hand clutching his throat, and the other pinning the hand grasping his sword, preventing him from drawing it any further.

"I'll rip out his throat!" she hissed, tightening her hold on his neck. "Get me the orb, Magus! Enough games! I want that orb! If not, the Prince Farland stays a statue forever."

"Do what she says," said Taran hoarsely.

"Your word or he dies," added Gilda, constricting the king's neck a tad more, and blood trickled.

"The orb is in L' Meran at Rhavé Dûn," said Magus plainly. He fought hard against the dizziness trying to overtake him now; the fight had left him spent. "You can go there and take it for yourself."

Gilda's eyes became thin slits. "You take me for a fool sorcerer. If it was that simple, just going to the fire-mountain and retrieving it, be sure of this Magus, I would've surely done it by now. But you and I know it is not at all that easy, don't we?" she asked the sorcerer with a sardonic smile. "Try again. Why would I take such a risk when I have a guinea? So what's it going to be, your word or his throat?"

Magus was loath to give his word, to give in. Anyone who is anyone knows wizards and witches keep to their word, even the wicked ones—to a certain extent. But he could not sacrifice a prince *and* king. However, the Emperor Tivoli would not bargain with an artifact as powerful and dangerous as the orb.

"You have my word."

"Good," said Gilda, pushing Taran down in his throne. "And no tricks, sorcerer, I'll be watching."

Gilda transformed to her shadowy guise, and glided through a nearby wall. Magus swayed and fainted.

Chapter Five
Journey to L' Meran

Magus awoke to the morning sun glinting through high slender arched windows, smothered under a thick down blanket on a warm, cozy bed. His staff! He sat erect, frantically peering around. He saw it propped against a chair, where his cleaned robe sat neatly folded, and settled down in relief. Last thing he remembered, he fainted after contending with the Witch. He reminded himself never to eat strange mushrooms again. One thing he could say was, he was well rested and anew. He had been given quarters in a luxurious guest room. There were two doors in the room, one to the left and another straight ahead. His stomach protested, and he favored it; he was hungrier than ever. He pushed away the blanket, and the silk sleeping clothes he'd been given to wear, swished when he slid off the bed.

He got dressed, and parked at a vanity table. As he removed his ribbon to comb his hair, someone rapped on the door, and through the mirror he saw the left door open, and a maiden come inside.

"Oh!" she said, surprised. "Master Magus, you're awake."

"I am," he said, combing his hair.

"Feeling better?" asked the maiden, closing the door behind her. "Only remedy for a case of na-na mushrooms is sleep and coconut juice."

"How long have I been sleeping?" he asked curiously, examining the scars on his neck

"Three and a half days."

"Goodness!" he said astounded, pulling his hair back, and fastening it with the ribbon.

"I've been waiting for you to wake. You must have eaten at least half a mushroom. Would you desire some breakfast?"

"Yes. Thank you."

Magus was fed well at breakfast, and urged to drink lots and lots of coconut juice. He drank so much that never again shall the liquid touch his lips. After breaking his fast a royal guard retrieved him, and brought him before the king. When he entered the throne room, much to his amazement, the mastiff, Tryx, and his gray-cloaked master were standing before Taran. The mastiff spotted him and bayed, sprinting for him.

"Tryx!" the master shouted commandingly, and the mastiff stopped in his tracks, throwing a look. "Come over here." Tryx glanced at Magus, his eyes saying, 'He's the one from the mountain-road.' Because he lacked the ability of common speech, he begrudgingly trotted back to his master. "Sorry 'bout that," he said to Magus.

"Not to worry about it, sir," said Magus dismissively, coming confidently, but warily forward. Tryx did not attack, but looked at him disdainfully.

He *did* recognize the man. And even more so now that his hood was removed, and his helmet tucked underneath his arm. He stood at least a foot shorter than Magus, but there was something appealingly regal about him.

"Magus the Sorcerer, your legend precedes you," said the man with a bow. Tryx growled and bared teeth. "Hush boy! Tryx, behave!"

"That is I," said Magus modestly, bowing back. "You are no stranger to me either, Cadence Dyar, winner of last year's Warriors of Fate Competition."

"Initially I called Cadence here to handle business with you," said Taran. "But the situation with the Guard shall be overlooked." Magus bowed in gratitude. "Now he will escort you on the quest. If you are in good health, Master Magus, I was hoping you two could set off tonight."

"Of course, Taran," said Magus with a nod. "But I'd like to see the prince, perhaps there is something I can do."

Magus, the king, and Cadence, with a dozen royal guards in tow went to Farland's chamber. Tryx pestered the sorcerer the entire way. Magus had a mind to tell the warrior that he was the assailant on the road, but now was not the time.

The prince's statue stood on his chamber balcony, overlooking villages and a seemingly endless scheme of jungle. The Dreschen could be heard circling and cawing above. Magus examined the statue. Farland's expression was one of shock and horror. Taran could not suffer to look upon it, and departed the balcony.

Magus tapped the statue with his staff three times and said, *"Presto Resendio!"*

Nothing happened. He placed a hand on the statue and closed his eyes. He began to murmur something that none of the others could discern. As Magus spoke his words became more audible, and the tip of his staff began to glow with a feverish blue light.

> ### naga imosa
> ### naga tumulta
> ### naga eshala itolsa

His voice lifted, booming, and chanted those words one last time. Magus removed his hand and frowned in dismay; he extinguished the light of his staff with a wave of a hand. Bewildered he re-examined the statue. He shook his head and returned inside.

"I am sorry, your highness," said Magus sincerely. "A stone curse is difficult to reverse as is, but this—I suggest we head for the L' Meran straight away."

Although puzzled by the sudden urgency, King Taran agreed.

Once preparations had been made, Magus, Cadence, and Tryx, and a company of soldiers trekked down the North Mountain Road, en route to Port Briscoe. The mastiff stayed worrisome to Magus, who grew to have grave worries about this dangerous and trig Witch, and paid the dog no mind. With the orb she'd become an even bigger threat. Thinking of her, he looked to the sky for any sign of a crow, but saw nothing. Tryx nipped at the sorcerer's robe.

"Tryx! Stop it boy!" said Cadence tersely. "What has gotten into you? Many apologies, Master Magus."

"Tis' nothing Master Cadence," said Magus waving it off. "It's just Tryx here smells something familiar."

"Whatever do you mean? Tryxie! Stop I say!"

"Tryx remembers me, is all," Magus replied. "Well, part of me, at least. The night of the storm…on the road…"

The soldiers and Cadence leapt back mystified when the sorcerer transfigured to a fox. Tryx snarled and showed his teeth. The fox stood unfazed.

The sun was bright, and a cool breeze blew in from the west. Briscoe was perched on an overhang with cobblestone streets and salt stone dwellings. It was alive with hustle and bustle, children playing and people purchasing food at the marketplace. Ships in the harbor bobbed on the dark water.

That night Magus heard thunderous rumble, and saw the red sky again

"Fire in the sky," said Cadence.

"Pardon?" said Magus.

"Fire in the sky," he repeated. "That is what the people of Evermore call the light from the volcano seen at night."

Magus looked at him thoughtfully. "You appear very different than the natives of Evermore."

"How so?" asked Cadence, but he never gave Magus a chance to reply. "Is it because I joined a competition not cultural of Evermore? Or perhaps because I do not carry my people's prejudice?"

"Both"

"I do not believe in prejudice, Magus. No man is better than another. That is my opinion."

"A good one it is. What made you contend in the competition?"

"To prove I was different, I suppose," Cadence replied with a shrug, and he looked down into the water. He sniggered. "But when I won that only fed flames to my people's discrimination."

Magus nodded. He was right. "I truly don't understand," he continued. "how folk of Evermore became estranged when it was our king who changed face? If anything, it should be those of Setan harsh against us for Dorian's arrogance."

"We harbor no hard feelings. That happened many a year ago."

"Do not get my people wrong," said Cadence turning to Magus. "We are good people. I feel that it is our shame that has turned our actions this way."

"Who can say?" said the sorcerer.

The silhouette of the mountain stood in the distance, a vivid river of red rolling down the slope. Magus suggested they not make the trip until morning.

At first early light the sorcerer, Cadence, and his four-legged companion disembarked from the ship. The shore was barren and gray. The air was harsh with fumes of sulfur and ash. Thirty miles northwards Rhavé Dûn endlessly spilled a river of lava into the steaming eastern shoreline. The ground shuddered briefly, and Cadence gave Magus a dark look.

"Rhavé Dûn is extremely volatile," said Cadence, as they started for their destination. "It erupts gently most times, but often it is known to be ferocious. If that happens…"

Magus clapped a hand on his shoulder, Tryx growled in disapproval. "We shall be up the creek without a paddle—and more besides."

Several times the volcano erupted but nothing explosive.

Nearing the mountain the ground became black, smooth, and billowy. Vegetation grew here and there. Smoke billowed from rents in the earth. During the latter part of the afternoon a series of tremors started. Evening approached, and the sky grew dark in the westering sun. There had not been a tremor in over an hour, and all seemed right. Tryx halted and barked intently at the volcano. Cadence rolled his shoulders. Magus shivered. Bay

"What was that?" Magus queried Cadence. "I caught a sudden chill."

Cadence didn't reply and fixed his eyes on the mountain. Tryx carried on with his fit of hysterical yapping. Ten minutes after they proceeded on, the land shuddered violently. The earth burst asunder near them. And just as abruptly as the earthquake began, it ended. Several moments later, the fire mountain spewed bombs and smoke. But still, everything seemed to be going fine.

They scaled the western slope, broad, and passive. Brimstone was potent in the air. Eighty feet up was a great fissure, formed during an enormous eruption four hundred years ago, that smothered the island in volcanic ash. Inside the heart of the volcano, at the end of a short ledge, the Orb of Bethalas sat comfortably on an obsidian pedestal. The orb was crystal clear, and the firelight of the magma gleamed through it, giving the impression of a ball of flame.

Within moments sweat masked their faces, their clothes clung to them. The sorcerer questioned the simplicity of the task. He wondered what the orb's protectoral device might be. He recalled all he knew about the orb's history. But no answer came to him. He reckoned before long they would find out.

Cadence offhandedly grabbed the orb. The fire mountain shuddered vehemently, the noise loud to their ears. Magma spurt in the air. Cadence lost his footing and toppled forward, landing hard on his stomach. The orb slipped from his grasp, and rolled crookedly along the ledge with an intense ringing sound, like a finger rubbed around the top of a wine glass. Cadence watched in horror as it veered off the edge. But it froze in midair! He looked up and saw Magus holding it afloat with a spell, barely, in his unsteady state. Cadence stretched, chest hanging over the ledge, and took hold of the orb. He heard Tryx howling but did not heed it. He blinked. The orb seemed to be weaving magic, for in it he saw the head of a red beast emerge. Looking closer he had a terrifying epiphany. It wasn't any power of the orb at all, but some beast rising from the lake of magma.

"Magus!" he cried, turning to the sorcerer.

Magus was stunned by the other eight looming heads of the creature. Cadence struggled to his feet, cupped the orb under his arm, and drew his sword.

The shuddering ceased.

The fire-Hydra swayed back and forth.

"Get out of here Tryx!" Cadanced yelled.

The mastiff needed only to be told but once, and bolted for the exit. A serpent made to attack him, and Magus shot a blast of ice. The serpent recoiled with a wail, the effected body cooled black. And Tryx was able to get away. The orb gleamed, and the blade of Cadence's sword shimmered blue. A head lurched at him, and he drove his weapon upward. Instead of melting instantly, like it should've done, the sword penetrated with a spray of cold snowy mist. The head billowed and began to cool, black spreading down its neck. It swayed backwards, but returned for another blow. The warrior's sword crashed against its head, the sound like metal striking stone. Frost spread everywhere, but did no damage to the already chilled quadrant of the body. It cried out and retreated.

"There is no defeating them," said Magus, releasing a stream of icy shards at an attacking head. "We may be able to cool there outside, but it is impossible to quench their inner fire." As he spoke a head gradually changed from black to reddish-orange.

Cadence held aloft the Orb of Bethalas, a stunning sea blue light burst from the orb, and the fire-Hydra quailed. Cadence and Magus loped. The serpent wriggled, recovered, and advanced. Just as they passed the opening, a head crashed into the ledge with a rancorous jolt. The sheer force threw Cadence and Magus out of the volcano, the orb once more slipping from Cadence's grasp. Watching it roll away down the slope, they scrambled to their feet, and gave chase.

A black winged creature descended from the sky. A horse mutilated by black magic, wild eyed and grotesque in appearance, but long-legged and solid in body; it had leathery wings, and a sheared tail.
Straddled it was a black hooded figure. The unknown rider stretched their arms, and the orb zipped into their hands.

Cadence and Magus skidded to a halt. The rider threw back their cowl. Gilda cackled insanely in her assertion of victory, and placed her hands around the orb. Pale light flared through her fingers, through her face, exposing her finger bones and skull; at that moment she looked like some sort of specter. A dazzling ray of light blazed forth, causing Cadence to squint his eyes. Gilda raised the Orb of Bethalas in defense ricocheting the sorcerer's spell, and sent it back to him. He was felled. He did not move. Cadence and Tryx charged down the slope. The orb jettisoned white flame, and Cadence put his shield in front of him. The spell struck the edge of his shield, spun him around, and he went tumbling down the mountain.

Gilda pulled on the reins, and she took to the sky cackling.

The Great Conspiracy by D.M. Worthy

Act II
of the Great War

Chapter One
On the Run

Wind whirled sand through the air. For as far as the eye could see was a monotonous view of sand, gray under the moonlights. Daralia, the second continent settled in Geneva, was mostly desert, hills, and mountains. The days were scorching hot, the nights chilly and breezy. Shade, the Master Thief, shivered and pulled his black cloak closer. He was clad in all black, and girt with a curved blade named Shitari, feather light and honed to perfection. It once belonged to the Prince Ameril of Jebil Sai—until he stole it.

Many amongst the criminal underworld daydreamed of pilfering it, but none made an effort; most never journeyed within thirty miles of the capital city.

But he wished to put those days of fell deeds behind him. He'd been a thief for thirty years, and now wanted a different life, a special holiday just for him. Find a nice plot of land and live fat the rest of his life. The Shitari was his source to liberation, so he devised his plan and made his move.

Six weeks ago he climbed Tor Brandír to Asul-Jer, the castle in the hill. He was a master of shadows, in an out of them in a blink of an eye. If you looked away just for an instant, you would miss him. And that's exactly what the Red Guards did. One time though, he thought he was a goner when he crossed a street, and a Red Guard looked his away. The guard stared hard into the shadow where Shade was concealed for several moments. He stepped forward to investigate, but just then a trio of guards came round a corner and hailed him. He greeted them in return and was distracted.

Shade at last located Ameril's balcony, and scaled the wall with a grapple. The prince was sound asleep, the beautifully crafted sword in his sights. He snuck in quietly, and unheeded—at first. For no reason at all, as if his very presence disturbed his sleep, Ameril sprang erect in his bed. "Guards! Guards!" he cried. But by then, Shade's hand had already found the dagger on his hip. Those were his last words, the prince's, before Shade hurled the dagger at him. Nefarious

At the end of it all, he barely came away with his life, and that made his retreat from this dubious life all the more alluring. A high bounty was on his head, and bounty hunters from far and wide were after him. He is on the run, with little place to go. All because of by some ill chance the prince woke up. What made it worse, he had to kill. Sure, he had slain many, but only those who sought him, never once during thievery. Killing while stealing, to him, was like slaying a victim after a successful pickpocket.

He walked up and down the dunes, wind rushing through his ears. He was westward bound, for the Outback, a mythical hideaway for all types of nefarious folk, on the outskirts of Bekistan. Its exact location he was unsure of. But he remembered what Low told him.

The thief stopped, hand under his cloak catching hold of Shitari. He fixed his eyes at the darkness of a high dune. Something was there, something moved! His profession made his eyes keen for the dark; he could see better than most, so he knew he saw something. He scurried down the side of a dune, laid flat on his stomach and watched. There was nothing. He began to wonder if his eyes had deceived him, when he saw a silhouette of a horse and rider approaching.

The rider was a dark-skinned man, with a grim face and prominent cheekbones; his ears and nose were pierced with gold loop earrings. His raiment was a tan shirt of flimsy material under a breastplate, with pants made of the same gauzy fabric, and black boots. Around his neck was a patterned black and white sash, and broad spear took up his left hand. Shade recognized him by the sash. The man was a Stygian Hunter, elitists of hunters and trackers among the Daralese, currently under contract from King Amire. If he reckoned right there were thirteen of them. *Curse them!* he thought. Things had gone from worse to worst. *How had I so carelessly come upon them? I have not seen the face of any in weeks. How did they find me?* But this was not what troubled him most, it was the direction from which he'd come, that really made him worried. *Did they presume where I was going? That there was no other place for me to go, except there.*

The Stygian Hunter checked his horse five paces from where Shade lay, and surveyed the area from the base of the dune. He appeared to sense something not quite right. Shade did not make a sound, tried not to even breathe too heavily. The horse swished its tail and neighed. The Hunter peered into the darkness at Shade, but didn't see the thief. He checked his horse and rode up the dune, passing by Shade so close that he felt a tug at his neck as the horse trampled his cloak.

§   §

Three hours of dark remained. The sand transformed into rocky terrain. Shade was hungry. He reached under his cloak, removed the leather purse from his shoulder, ruffled through it, and dug out a doughboy. He shouldered the purse and ate as he walked.

The Master Thief sighted the outline of the Kaziz Mountains, stretching the length of the horizon. They served as a dividing line of eastern and western Daralia called the Majestic Front. When Shade reached one of Kaziz's three passes, the Serpentine, the first light of dawn was touching the eastern horizon.

He slept tranquil on a cliff overlooking the pass. The sun glared too hotly upon his black hand, and he tucked it underneath his head; his other hand was under his cloak, gripping Shitari. He opened his eyes and sat up scanning the mountainside. His gaze turned up to the sun. It was mid-morning. The moment he lay back down and close his eyes, they promptly reopened to the faint whining of a horse. He peered over the edge of the cliff, and discerned a gray horse dallying lonely in the pass. Shitari leapt from its scabbard. Shade had the oddest feeling he was being watched, and wheeled around so fast the man creeping up behind him was startled. The thief was surprised as well, the man was so close. He was a Stygian Hunter (not the one from last night,) armed with two half moon shaped bladed gloves.

"So much for the element of surprise," said the Hunter, the corner of his mouth twitched.

He was amused Shade realized; he was looking forward to this. "Out in the wind," the thief agreed concurred, getting in his stance. Shitari shifted into direct sunlight, and shimmered like a stem of white fire.

"Shitari *is* a beautiful sword, isn't it?" said the Hunter.

"Want a closer view?" asked Shade, despite his racing heart. The Stygian Hunters were fierce warriors, and to meet them, more often than not, meant death.

"I mean to."

And with that the Stygian Hunter advanced.

They wrestled, kicking around dirt and dust; pebbles trickled off the cliff. The Stygian's blade ran across the top of Shade's left hand, and he cried out, retreating back a few steps. His foe, thinking he had him off guard, swung wildly for his head. The thief slipped deftly under the blow, stepping behind the Hunter; he threw his elbow backward, planting it square in the back of his head. Shade made a move to strike, and tripped over a jutting rock and fell. A singeing pain coursed his hand when it struck the ground. The Hunter attacked before he could get to his feet, and he was forced to fight on his back. The Stygian Hunter planted a boot underneath Shitari's handle, and it went flying over the ledge. Shade scurried back on his hands and heels.

"Nowhere to run except down," said the Stygian Hunter.

Shade's hand found a rock, thin and sharp, and whipped it; it whacked the Hunter's forehead, and he swayed in a daze, blood flowing between his eyes and down his nose. He took one wrong step backward, and toppled over the cliff with a cry. It was followed by a *thud*. Shade walked to the ridge favoring his hand, and looked down at the body motionless below. The Hunter was surely dead. Shade spat and made his way down.

He scooped up his sword a few feet from the dead body, shuffled back to the Hunter bleeding profusely into the dirt, and used the sword to cut off a piece of material for bandaging.

"Nowhere to run except down," he said mockingly to the slain bounty hunter, and spat.

§ §

Shade had taken the gray horse, and was riding hard down the Serpentine Pass. He began to think going to the Outback was an unwise choice. What if they tracked him there? But there weren't many options—and he knew it. He had no friends overseas; all his companions were either dead or in Vera Vera Island Prison. He had no access to a boat of any kind, nor could he chance entering a port no matter how elusive he was. Pictures of his face were everywhere, and he went out of his way to prevent any contact with the outside world. Some thirsty soul might try and collect on his head for a few gold zeni. The Outback was his only real option, lest he risk being caught.

By sundown he exited the pass and continued northwest through the realm of Mezu. Thereafter he rested briefly, nibbling on a doughboy. His hand stung every time he moved it. He told himself he'd better get used to it, for if battle were to come. Bekistan was two days from his current position, a day and a half if he covered enough ground, and there was no telling what sort of trouble he might run into. He bumped into two Stygian Hunters in as many days, only bigger problems could possibly lay in the horizon.

He hadn't ridden a horse since he was eighteen, and riding again brought those days back in a flood. He was sixteen again. He was Fawik Marzi, not yet Shade, the name that would make him one of the most infamous thieves in Daralese history. Living in Port Jero, and enjoying the peak week of the Commerce Days with his parents when the Black Cross Marauders blitzed the small city. The streets were crowded with merchants, market stands, and would be customers. On some of the corners illusionists, singers, and dancers performed. And the food! The air was ripe with suckling pig, stewed meat, freshly baked bread. Everything was fine until the bandits arrived.

Fawick's father was shot and killed with an arrow; his mother fell victim to two arrows in her back, but managed to get to a safe place with young Fawik before passing away. His eyes burned, and he wept heavy tears from a heavy heart. Both of his parents were gone.

After burying his parents in the back of their home, Shade snatched up their savings, some provisions, and fled into the night, never to return. It was unfortunate, for he had no friends being an introvert and all, and there were no relatives to rely on. Before long he was low on food, and soon on zeni. Once his coins were exhausted, he wandered for days without food, aching with hunger pangs. This being the case, he resolved to eat by whatever means possible.

He lumbered into a town, and aimlessly walked the streets searching for a solution to his dilemma. His spirits were downcast and his head was low, looking down at his feet. Although it was only late afternoon, he was having the distinct feeling there'd be another day without something to eat. A light jingle-jingle of a coin pouch from a group of men ahead, yanked him from his melancholy. He'd heard the sound countless times, but for some odd reason, it was like a beacon of light in his head. The jangle-jangle of jiggling money became a mating call to him, from that day forth.

The pouch was swinging at the hip of the man on the left. Fawik schemed, quickened his pace. One of them made a joke and they all laughed; Fawik pretended not to be paying attention when he bumped his victim, sneakily swiped his pouch and excused himself with a gentlemanly gesture. And said, "Oh gents, do you know whereabouts is the inn?" The men told him and the young man, now thief, ran there mouth watering. He ate to make up for the missed meals, and thought he was near to burst; also, he experienced a small shortness of breath. Content, he paid the innkeeper for a room and labored upstairs.

He didn't know long he'd been asleep, but it was rudely interrupted when his room door burst open. His roommate cried out, and one of the three shadows charging in hissed at him shut up. The room was dark, but he recognized the men when one of them said; "Steal my money will ya?" The next moment there was brutal fist to the eye, after which he remembered nothing. He awoke the next morning with a shiner of all shiners, a throbbing head, and no zeni. His hand darted to the chain he hoped to be still on his neck. It was. The silver chain his parents bought for him from during the commerce peak week, along with their wedding bands he adorned it with. These things he held sacred nowadays.

The incident in the inn that one fateful night would not deter him from his calling. He elevated his skills and schemes, staying at the inns and robbing unsuspecting roommates, and other occupants. One night he tried a man, the wrong man, one who always slept with one eye open. The man was alone in his room, easy pickings for Fawik...or so he thought. But the man drew a dagger on him, and asked sternly with a few clouts to Shade's head, what in the devil was he doing. The roles reversed, and the man stole *his* earnings, though light-hearted and amused as he was. He asked Fawik his name, and questioned as to why a smart looking fellow such as himself was stealing. The neophyte thief told the man his story.

Fawik and Low became close, teaching one another their trade. The seasoned criminal learned how to steal without killing, and the young man was learned in knife-fighting and horseback riding. Low named the young man Shade. "A fine name for such a sly one," Low told him.

For five years they committed dirty deeds and met others of their sort. But this all came to an untimely end when they were pursued one night by bounty hunters and Low was slain. Ever since, Shade chose to be alone; he kept losing the ones he loved. He had other constituents, yes, but he chose to be his own company. He would go on to be become a legendary thief in Daralia.

Chapter Two
Andrekka

The next morning Shade traveled Highland Road, with the Bluffs of Mezu rolling by in the east. All around buttes and mesas rose high above him. He closed his eyes and drew in a deep breath. He, like countless others, feared the sight of the place. The Forgotten Highway ran through there, forgotten and unused for centuries. The collection of crows and vultures there—superstitious signs of ill omens and death—weighed heavy on the hearts of those who entered. Furthermore, there resided the Den of Tauris, the Red Dragon; the ravenous chameleons were something to be considered as well. No one has traveled the highway since the Dark Age.

In the afternoon, he headed northwest and encountered a small dust storm. When it passed, he was able to descry the Djinn Sea, but the desert played tricks on the eyes, and it could be heat waves for all he knew. His hand bled through the dressing, and was ballooned and aching unbearably. The next time he took rest he could scarcely open it, and had to use his working hand to unfurl the fingers.

The sun was in a blaze of red and orange in its westerly descent. Shade had reached the boundaries of the Short Hills, casting evening shadows on each other. He pulled back on the reins, and the horse came to a skidding halt. He caught something out of the corner of his eye, heading east, about fifteen miles out. Six Stygian Hunters riding up a hill away from him.

"Seems like I just can't shake these bloodhounds," he said to himself. He flexed his puffy hand, wincing, and rode on.

After a short length he stopped again, and peered down at his pudgy hand, throbbing worse than ever. The bandage was soaked with blood. He began to worry about infection, and the possibility of losing his hand. He dismounted, sat on the lip of a hill, and gently unwrapped the dressing. Congealed blood was around the wound, in the lines of his palm, and imbedded in his fingernails. He tossed the useless dressing. He pulled out his water-horn, splashed a bit on the cut, and proceeded to wet his parched tongue. He turned his eyes to the west. The sun glared dim, barely visible behind the hills. He ripped off a piece of his shirt, and redressed the wound. He sure hoped he wouldn't lose his hand.

He reached the borders of Bekistan just as planned, a day later. Everything afterward would prove the most difficult. He was in search of Andrekka, the secret way leading to the Outback. *How did that rhyme go? Even on the brightest day, the sun can barely touch this place. Just beyond the Outback lay. If you search and do not find, there is no other way. Yes. That was it.* Little use it served him now, though. The sun didn't presently touch anything. It was nightfall.

His hand pained him so, but he'd primarily become accustomed to it. He sat and thought and ate while his horse piddled in front of him. He knew for certain the Outback wasn't a place you came and went at your leisure. An effort to keep the location undisclosed, Low told him. Spending the ending days of his life cooped in the Outback left him uneasy though. Now that he really pondered the notion, it was downright unthinkable. Perhaps, in six or seven years, possibly more, he could leave the Outback and sail away to another country. Two pouches full of gold should get him somewhere. He also had other things of value: a gold bangle, silver flask, and an aquamarine ring. Setan would be nice. But he fancied Yuri, on other side of the world as well, and it was far away from his troubles. When it came down to it, he didn't care where he went, as long it was away from Daralia.

Although none of their confidants believed in the fabled haven, Low wholeheartedly believed; growing up he'd listen to the old-timers gab about it, and later read old fantasy lore before going underground, and was intent on telling Shade everything. He swallowed every word, and before he shut his eyes to sleep, hoped it would pay off.

The pulsing pain in his hand prevented him from resting the way he desired. He tried to keep his mind off the injury; he wanted to sleep, not a lot, just enough to resurrect his vigor. When Shade was finally granted sleep, he did it with one eye open, with a hand under his cloak on his sword.

Once during his nap he startled awake at a noise he heard, or thought he heard, scanned the area, saw nothing then was snoozing again.

Hours before dawn he was on the move again, searching for Andrekka. He drifted into the Elekar Plain, but found nothing there. He went due west, and by nighttime he was in the Uplands. Here he called it a day and took rest. Summer had arrived, and the day was hot and had sapped his energy; he was exhausted.

Just after sunrise he set off. The air was already hot, and would be a preview for things to come. At the coming of mid-morning he slowed his speed to a trot, as not to spend the horse, for the sweltering heat was baking the hardpan. After a while, he stopped to tear another piece of his clothing, and redressed the wound. His hand wasn't any better, any worse either. Actually...it had grown numb. It felt strange and tingly at the palm as if he'd lain on it all night.

The blazing sun was a blinding shimmer in the sky. He was walking the gray horse. He took a swig, the last, from his water-horn. Frustrated, he tipped it all the way as if that would somehow produce more; he even took the time to shake it, and listen, for sounds of water. He put the empty container away, shaking his head. *It better be worth it you fool, you're now out of food and water.* He was beginning to regret this venture. He cursed himself for trusting the idea of a haven for crooks, undiscovered by the king's soldiers for nearly two hundred years. All of the other hideouts were now hot spots. During the winter of last year, the soldiers raided the last seven criminal refuges. There were no more places for the likes of him; nowadays you were either dead or imprisoned in Vera Vera. He cursed himself again. He would've rather taken chances at the port.

When evening dawned he relished it, thankful to be rid of that blasted sun. He took an hour rest and continued his journey. He took rest for the duration of the day, for tomorrow he planned to cover much ground. And regrettably, the sun was his guide.

When sunlight touched the earth he pressed on. After a full night's rest, Shade pushed the horse. The land grade climbed under them, leaving a scene of tall cactus behind. The ground soon lev-eled again. Then a sick feeling touched the thief's stomach. Squint-ing against the sun he gazed ahead.

All the while the gray horse sprinted for the life of it. His name was Sandwave, previously owned by the late Stygian Hunter Garik. He was a fantastic thoroughbred, and an utterly fast horse. Garik named him thus on their first day together, riding passed dunes that seemed to move in his speed. He'd paid quite a few zeni for him, and it was worth every bit. Well...not anymore.

Something didn't seem right, yet he did not slow. The horse be-tween his legs was forgotten, as Shade stared fixedly ahead. Some-thing was wrong. He couldn't tell what. He couldn't tell why. But he knew it. He blinked, and everything became so clear.

"Whoa! Whoa!" he cried, fiercely tugging on the reins. The gray horse's hoofs skidded, and for one dark moment, Shade thought the steed would not stop on time, and he (they) would go right over. But heaven would shine upon him this day, and they came to a grinding halt right at the drop; rocks and dirt clattered over the edge, and the horse whinnied.

Three hundred feet below, was a village of stone huts nestled in a gorge shrouded in shade. A flag fluttered lightly, a white one with a black cross. Shade understood full well what he'd stumbled upon, but there was no time to think of it. Not even time for anger, or hatred to curdle in his blood. Many of the Black Cross Marauders were already scrambling and mounting horses, and making their way out of the gorge via a mild slope on the opposite end.

Shade turned tail back down the hill.

§   §

Later that night he chucked about his dramatic experience. The Marauders had been a threat but posed no immediate danger. They'd pursued him, and it seemed that might actually catch him, for their steeds were quick, and they'd taken some sort of passage in the gorge. For five miles they took to his heels, but eventually gave up.

He made a mental note of the band's whereabouts

Seeing them made him drudge those past hurtful memories of the death of his parents; he was vexed and unable to sleep. His growling stomach didn't help matters either.

He opened his eyes, and looked around. He didn't know where he was. He didn't remember falling asleep, or where. Twilight was breaking, and the sun was sneaking up over the horizon. Shade examined his hand; all the fingers were swollen, and it clearly lacked feeling; he could scarcely open or close it now. He prodded the puffed flesh with a finger. Damn his hand. He clicked his teeth, spat, and got to his feet. He let out a hearty yawn, stretched, and his back cracked audibly. He groaned in ecstasy. He mounted his steed.

The town of Marush was discernable when he changed his course southwest. The sun shone bright as it approached its peak. Haze waved in the distance. All of the vigor he and his possessed the previous day was like a dream forgotten. It was so hot. He was severely thirsty, and was doubly sure the horse was too. By noon

Shade staggered near border of Djamar. Shade's lips were chapped, and licking them with his dry tongue only hurt. He was honestly going to die out there. No, no he wouldn't. Tomorrow he'd try his chances at a town; worried about being spotted was better than slowly dying in the desert. Yea, he completely regretted this quest now.

The afternoon grew late. And Shade couldn't take another step. His hand left the reins, but it remained poised as if he were still walking the horse. His legs gave out, and he collapsed. Sandwave grunted and nudged the thief, as if to say, 'Come on get up. You can't give up now.' Shade did not want to get it, but he must, the ground was hot. He slogged to his feet. Someone unknown force turned his head, and he was stunned. He didn't know how he didn't see it before. A sheer rock wall was about a tenth of a mile from him, severed by a dark, narrow crack. The thief screamed out in joy with a scratchy voice. He mounted the horse and galloped towards the wall. The sun gleamed against it, but only strings of light managed to penetrate into the cleft. He'd come to Andrekka, the Vulture Neck Passage. His heart told him it was the place but was leery. He stared unblinkingly at the blackness.

Chapter Three
The Outback

He led his horse into the passage. The walls hardly supplied enough room for the horse to turns its head. A few times it let out nervous neighs, resonating throughout the passage. Cracks of light glowed feebly here and there in the roof. He couldn't determine how far he had walked. Most of his tiredness was gone now, at the prospect of actually finding the Outback. He maneuvered his head around the horse, and saw the vertical line of light at the entrance shrinking at every step, until nothing but darkness was visible. He thought if he did want to go back what a business it'd be, he and his walking backwards. The passage was too small to do anything else. Now he realized how it got its name.

Further on beams of sun shot through substantial breaks spaced along the roof; enough to give Shade something to work with. It was good to see again. For a while he felt as if he'd been walking nowhere in some abyss. The glimmer was short lived, and the roof once again repudiated any light. But in the distance a pillar of light shone.

He exited the crevice, and his eyes were struck by an overabundance of sunlight. He put his hand inside the hood, massaging the inner corners of his eyes with his thumb and forefinger. During his momentary loss of sight he heard murmuring voices. He finally recovered his eyes and surveyed the land. The legendary Outback was a hollowed section in the rock, sparsely filled with tents wrought of makeshift material—and Daralia's worse of the worse. Some of the criminals gawked at the newcomer. People just didn't stray into the Outback everyday.

An olive-skinned man wearing a turban approached Shade, and the thief's hand immediately fell to his sword. He didn't know *how* he'd be greeted. It was always better to lean on the side of caution though.

"Welcome, fellow outlaw and stranger from over yonder," said the man in the turban; he extending his hand. "I am Sherk, Leader of the Outback." Shade extended his. Looking closer, he thought he recognized the man. But he could've been wrong.

Sherk did not shake Shade's hand, only looked down at it, up at him, and frowned. "Stranger you might be but we are one in the same. We share the same black blood. What am I to think of a man who wanders into our abode, though welcomed you are, without the respect of showing his face to his new family?"

"I beg your pardon," said Shade, casting off his hood. His skin was dark like smoke, his jaw was strong, and his nostrils wide; his eyes were a brown many shades lighter than his skin.

"Better," said Sherk, taking Shade's hand, and giving him a one armed embrace. "And what is your name so I may properly introduce you?"

"Shade".

"Ah, the Master Thief," Sherk added with a nod. "It is an honor."

"The honor is all mine, Sherk the Ruthless, Sherk the Terrible, Sherk the Red-Handed," said Shade with a graceful bow. "All in compliment, of course."

Sherk smiled. "What of your hand?"

"Stygian Hunter."

"Really?"

"Don't worry, he's expired."

Sherk's eyebrow perked. "You've killed one of the Hunters? Well done," he said clapping a hand on Shade's shoulder. "This calls for celebration!"

The Leader of the Outback called all the men around, and introduced the newcomer. Some of the hellions he knew of, like: Salin, whose game was plundering inns and slaughtering a few people for pleasure; Gale, along with a band of men attempted to steal gold out of the Sandarin Mine, before a tunnel collapsed. He was the only survivor; Rush robbed and slew a Master Merchant from overseas during the Commerce Days. And Shade knew of other men by their unsavory reputations. Sherk stated that four men were on errand, and would return some time tonight. He could stay in one of their tents until then, Sherk told him.

"Break out the rum boys! We've got celebrating to do!" the Leader of the Outback proclaimed. "Our new brother has slain one of the Stygian Hunters."

Whoops and cheers went up, and the men scattered to make preparations.

The Leader gave Shade a guided tour, showing him the well to get water, and a tent used to store provisions; it was practically empty. Shade was taken to his temporary quarters, toting rations and drink. Sherk said he'd return in a while to examine his hand.

The inside was just right for two people, but there was only one makeshift bedroll wrought of the same collection of fabrics as the tent themselves; there was a wash pan, a small frying pan, and a jug of water. The moment his head touched the bedroll he fell asleep. It had been decades since he was able to sleep unwarily. But it seemed that he'd just closed his eyes when Sherk roused him. In one hand he carried a bowl with a stirrer inside, in the other three pouches, and a cloth thrown over his forearm.

"Let's have a gander at that hand, shall we?" Sherk removed the dressing, examined the wound. He turned Shade's hand over. Black and blue spots were on the palm. "Does it hurt?" Sherk asked him, lifting his eyes from the palm, and fixing them on Shade's eyes.

"No, not at all. It's dead."

Sherk smiled and patted him on the shoulder. He opened one of the pouches, and poured some green powder into the bowl. The second pouch contained an orange-reddish powder, which he also dumped in the bowl. He grabbed the jug of water, and added just enough to make the concoction lumpy. Thereafter he stirred the concoction slightly. Swathe

"This may hurt a tad," he said, scooping some of the clumpy mix with his fingers.

Sherk began caking the wound with the mix. Shade felt nothing. *Why would I? It's dead as a stone.* When finished, Sherk opened the last pouch, and a mint aroma swathed the hut. He plucked out three leaves. A white-hot pain suddenly coursed Shade's hand, and he winced. Sherk placed the leaves on the remedial paste, and immediately the pain subsided. He removed the cloth from his forearm, and dressed the wound.

"Its not *water of healing* but it will do," said Sherk. "Now, my friend, return to your slumber. I am sure it's been long since you've had any descent. We shall postpone our tribute to tomorrow."

Shade wakened feeling well rested and vigorous. He stepped out into the night under a profusion of twinkling stars. The two moons shone full and pale. He espied Salin and Gale guarding the Vulture Neck Passage. He presumed that guard was only set at night. Better to lean on the side of caution, he always said. He lifted his arm and looked at his hand. The swelling had reduced slightly, although none of the feeling returned however.

Two refugees sat cross-legged on the ground facing each other, both silent, staring down at a chessboard. Each man seemed deep in thought. A hand touched on his shoulder, and he wheeled around, hand slipping in his cloak. In a flash Shitari leapt. Sherk jumped back drawing a curved knife. Their eyes fixed a moment then both men smiled weakly, and sheathed their weapons.

"Sorry friend," said Sherk, taking a step forward.

"No harm done."

"Good. That is a remarkable sword you have there."

"Its descent," said Shade modestly, scrutinizing Sherk.

Sherk laughed. "Do not worry, Master Thief. We do not steal from thy own."

That was good for Shade to hear, but still— "A strange condition for a pack of villains."

"Maybe, maybe not. We fled the outside world. We are all we have. There must be *some* honor amongst thieves, Shade."

"Surely."

"Surely is right. Believe it or no, Shade, but many of us have grown soft in our professions. We do not live to wreak havoc as we once did. Often the occupants of the Outback stay ten, twenty years before leaving. Sail to another country and start anew. Whether they revert to their old ways I cannot say."

"That is my intent, but I do not wish to stay so long."

"Only time will tell."

A gentle night-wind swept dust along. It was late, late night. Salin and Gale were still on guard duty when they heard footsteps and hooves. Both men faced the darkness weapons drawn.

"Why did the straw break the camel's back?" Gale cried.

"Because it was the last straw," a voice replied.

Four men emerged from the gap walking horses, laden with sacks.

"Hail fellows," said the one in front.

"Hail," said Salin and Gale.

"What's new in the outside world, Graf?" asked Salin.

"Bad business out there these days," said Graf, shaking his head.

"Why do you say?"

"Word is some thief stole Prince Ameril's sword, Shitari."

"Slew him in the process, too," added another man.

"Really?" said Gale.

"Yes," said Graf. "and that is not the half. This man, Shade, has—."

Salin and Gale's exchanged looks.

"Shade you say?" said Salin.

"That be his name if I heard right. All the bounty hunters are in search of him, the Stygian Hunters included. Certainly a bad business for him. The bounty on his head is half a million zeni."

"Makes me almost want to join the hunt," said the man fourth man. "Almost."

"This Shade must be a nasty piece of work, Ihraem," said Salin. "If he's stout for such a feat you might want to watch yourself. Besides, he's here."

"Who?" Graf asked incredulously.

"Shade."

"When did he get here? I'd love to shake his hand."

"Tomorrow, Graf, tomorrow. Most likely he's asleep. He was sun-beaten when he arrived. Take the paraphernalia to the storage tent."

Some hours later Shade lay awake in the hut, staring at the roof of the tent. Oddly, he was unable to go back to sleep. Aside him, an outlaw named Graf lay sleeping, snoring obnoxiously. But this was not the hindrance of his rest. Graf had come in and introduced himself, told of the information he'd came about, and shook his hand.

The next morning he made the acquaintance of the remaining members of the Outback; Ihraem, Verde, and Slader. To his relief these men were uninterested in the details of the tale. Their only desire was to view the sword. He showed the men and they marveled it; the shimmering Shitari in the morning sun attracted an audience. He thought one of the men among the congregation gave him a rather shifty stare. *The man ought to know better*, Shade thought. *But if not—*

Shortly after breakfast, Sherk relayed the news of Shade's defeat of a Stygian Hunter, and drinks were passed around. Slader lured Shade to his tent, where four other men…including Graf and the shady-faced man…were sitting in the sand. Graf held a two-foot long pipe, and a large brown pouch sat on his lap.

"Come, sit," said Graf, motioning to the ground. "Sit among our circle and smoke the mandrake with us."

Shade had heard of the leaf, but in Daralia this was an ordinarily rare commodity.

Shade huddled in the smoking circle and puffed the pipe.

The smoke, the rum, and long palaver ran well into late afternoon, and he was walking (stuttering) back to his hut when Sherk called him.

"There are things to discuss, my friend," the Leader said, placing an arm around his shoulder, and steering him in the opposite direction.

Sherk showed him to his tent with two roofs. It was twice the size of the other tents, housed the same belongings as his shared quarters. Save for the chest in the corner. A rolled up bundle was adjacent it. Sherk asked about his hand. Much better, Shade remarked. The swelling subsided to the point where his hand almost looked normal, but it was still numb.

"Now to business," said the Leader. "As you well know we are exiles of Daralia, withdrawn from our trade and possess no real means of profit. Folk do not traipse to the Outback eager to give handouts. So there is the business of taxes."

"Taxes. I see."

"Yes, taxes. For our food and drink run every three months or so, and life's little…" he trailed off daydreaming. "A taste of woman. We are men here, off course. There are needs." Shade agreed. He wasn't a stranger to harlots. "We toss a little coin or two for a harlot—or two. She is shared and…"

"You bring them here?" Shade asked astounded.

"How else do we get our piece? If your worry about the secrecy of our location, worry not. They are blindfolded here and back. Harlots do not question. Their profession is lying on their back."

"True this. About these taxes—."

"Just a trifle is given until funds are depleted, and taxes are collected again."

"Fair enough. What if our zeni is exhausted?"

"Not likely. Only trig villains here. Those who are heavy at the pouch, I might say. If not, there are ways to earn coin, if need be," he added, smiling.

"Of course."

Shade's hand disappeared under his cloak. He fumbled around for a moment then came up with a gold bangle. Sherk received it gratefully. He dug into the collar of his tunic, and brought out a key on a fine chain. He fit the key in the chest's lock and unlocked it with a *click*. Shade shifted to get a better look at the contents. It was about a quarter full, with copper, silver, and gold zeni and challots (Yurian currency), jewelry, an onyx, and a rather sizable emerald. Sherk dropped the bangle inside, closed the chest, locked it, and snatched up the bundle.

"Here," he said, tossing it to Shade. "I've made a bedroll for you."

"Thank you," Shade said gratefully with a nod.

The sky was a beautiful collage of blue, purple, and pink during sunset. With his mind swimming with mandrake, Shade felt up to a game of chess. He strolled about the Outback, searching for one of the two men he saw playing earlier. He located one, and was directed to Gale. Gale and Salin were having a round while passing a flask. He took a seat and watched.

After a long and grueling match, Salin claimed winner and Shade stepped into position to defeat Salin, with a few precise moves.

Sherk came over, and told Shade he was up for guard duty. Shade nodded and proceeded to Vulture Neck Passage. He and Ihraem posted there until relieved at nightfall.

Chapter Four
New Visitors

The mouthwatering smell of sizzling sausage roused Shade the following morning. Even though he's eaten well since he arrived to the Outback, he's been starving almost nonstop. The Master Thief stepped outside and whiffed the morning air, delighted. Graf was hunkered in front of the frying pan cooking eggs and sausage. Shade's nostrils flared.

"Mmm, smells good," said Shade.

Graf smiled. Over the meal the men talked and became familiar, and swapped stories about dastardly deeds, life, and women. Shade told him everything, except the death of his parents. No one needed to know, and he didn't feel like talking about it. It happened to be a small world, for Graf knew Low and thought highly of him. He had caught wind of the grievous news of Low's death not long after the incident. Graf was an Outback resident two years by then. For twenty-six years the Outback has been his home.

In the hour before twilight, black clouds in the dark sky shunned the moons. Stars peeked sporadically through notches in the puffy masses. A brisk wind howled. Rush and Slader stood guard at Andrekka, gusts ruffling their clothing. Rush leaned against the wall crossing his legs, hand falling to the dagger sheathed on his hip. Slader yawned, and began chatting needlessly to keep his partner alert. Rush interacted in the dialogue, but soon the conversation became one-sided. Slader speechless for the time being, heard Rush's light snores in the wind. He watched him a moment as his head nodded like a buoy, leaned over, and shouted:

"Hey!"

Rush awoke with a start, reaching for his dagger.

"Wake up, Rush, we're on duty."

"I know," replied Rush yawning, freeing the hand from the dagger, and covering his mouth. "Although I do not see the need to rouse me in such a manner. Why couldn't you have given me a polite nudge? Those kind of antics can get a man killed."

"Right. Just stay awake."

"I was," said Rush defensively. "Was relaxing that's all. A man can't—."

"Quiet," Slader hissed. He thought he heard something, but the wind obscured his audibility.

"What is it?"

"Silence, Rush. Damn you," Slader whispered acidly.

Rush said no more, and listened attentively.

Slader lifted his cutlass and turned to the passage. Rush followed suit. Although it was pitch black, and they could see nothing, they watched it and strained their ears for signs of movement. The wind calmed just enough for them to discern the soft clopping of hoofs; the hoofs picked up speed. A spear darted from the curtain of darkness, piercing Rush in the chest. Slader saw someone come forth, and he fled crying. "The Stygian Hunters have come!"

The Stygian Hunters emerged like trick riders, standing, knees bent on their saddles. The remaining twelve had come.

The rider at point drew a black scimitar. He was their captain, Djidi. Slader glanced over his shoulder and saw Djidi overtaking him. The captain made a sweep for Slader's head, but he dodged the blow. The Hunter did not make another pass. Instead he advanced on the other residents popping out of their tents.

A bola whirled through the air, and entangled Slader's legs, tripping him up. A Hunter armed with a bow, sent an arrow into his back. Another cruelly trampled his body.

§   §

Shade was in a serene slumber; he'd spent most of his time in the Outback, making up his lost sleep. "The Stygian Hunters have come!" was a low reverberation in the back of his mind. But he felt himself being rattled. Graf was shaking him.

"We are under attack by Stygian Hunters," he said darkly, and dashed from the tent.

Shade was no longer sleepy; he jumped to his feet, Shitari in hand.

A Hunter equipped with a nailed club prowled around bashing heads. The bowman picked off foes from afar. One Hunter, twirling a chain, grappled Gale around the neck and dragged him. Ihraem's head was dismissed from his shoulders by a metal boomerang with a serrated edge. Verde stabbed a Hunter in the back, and another bore an axe down on his skull. Salin intervened, and jabbed his hunting knife into the Hunter's ribcage, and threw him down.

Shade glanced around at the turmoil. Bodies of his new found family littered the ground. Sherk was battling with Djidi in the distance. He espied Salin contending with the Hunter with the spear, and hurried to his aid; with his help they slew the bounty hunter swiftly. There was a twang, and Salin fell without a cry, an arrow through the back of his neck. Shade wheeled around. The bowman charged, and let fly another arrow, pricking Shade in the upper left division of his chest. But the thief was not stayed, and his sword sliced his enemy from his steed.

The thief grunted, and snapped the arrow. He ticked off in his head two dead Stygian Hunters from twelve. Ten left. (Although in actuality, only eight Stygian Hunters remained.) He looked upon Salin, face down in blood, and sighed deeply. Guilt pulled at his heart. The Hunter wouldn't be here if it wasn't for his presence. Shade caught something mysterious in his peripheral vision. A Stygian Hunter not too far away, was flailing his arms wildly, then lowered his head and galloped off.

Shade mounted the dead bowman's steed, and charged the crazed Hunter. He treaded on the Hunter slain by Salin and counted eight. He gained on the fleeing Hunter until only forty feet separated them. The rider swatted the air as if fighting off flies, but looking closer Shade saw a black bird attacking him. The thief heard clanking chain behind him, and a searing pain engulfed his back. He cried out, and turned to see the source, and received a second lash to the nap of his neck.

Shade changed course, and tried to lose the Hunter, but thrice more the chain smote him. And if matters couldn't be worse, four additional Hunters closed in on him from the right. The noise of battle was dead, and Shade realized he was the sole survivor, and might soon be dead himself; he gigged Sandwave, and headed for the Vulture Neck Passage. A whistling sound approached, and out of nowhere something ripped through his side. Agony seized him, and he swayed. The boomerang curved right, disappearing behind him.

His will faltered as warm blood spilled down his body. He pressed forward, pushed the horse harder, harder. The Stygian Hunters were hot on his tail. The boomerang came whistling back round, marking his head; he dodged the projectile, but suffered a severe head blow from the chain. Spots appeared in front of his eyes. Dazed, he slid off the horse, landing sideways unpleasantly hard on his injured midriff, dislocating his shoulder. He released a cry, heightening, when Sandwave's hind hoof stomped his thigh; the Hunters barely missed stamping him.

The Hunters checked their steeds, and doubled back. He perceived death imminent, but was helpless to delay it; he could not move, was in too much pain to move. He seemed to hurt every-where.

"Seems that we have you now," said Djidi, speaking native Daralese tongue.

Chapter Five
Unlikely Savior

Shade didn't suffer himself to speak to these animals, and glow-ered at them defiantly. He thought they meant to toy with him.

"Your head is worth quite the fortune," said Djidi grinning. "Never in history has a bounty been set so high. You should be proud, Shade, Master Thief. You shall be legend. Savor this small comfort at least, before you perish. But," he said as an after-thought. "you may plead for your life if you wish."

Shade replied by spiting on the captain's boots. If they thought they'd get the satisfaction of seeing him grovel, they were sadly mistaken. He shall die on his feet, never on his knees. Djidi sig-naled. Chain clinked, and fresh pain coursed his back.

"Enough, enough," said a female's voice, partly entertained. The darkness near the Stygian Hunters shifted. "Business is done here Hunters. Move on with what is left of your pitiful band. Shade is my cull."

Djidi laughed. "I know not who you are wench," he said, squinting at the darkness. "but best keep out of Hunter affairs or join this thief. Mayhap we use you for our liking a bit before kill-ing you." He guffawed, and the others joined.

An icy laughed interjected, silencing the Hunters. "Release the thief for collateral for your lives."

"Guess again," said Djidi boldly. Underneath him his black stal-lion shifted nervously. "Show yourself or be gone with you! Last warning!"

Two rays of scarlet light streaked out of the darkness, and a pair of Hunters fell dead. Shade saw a shadow glide by him. Gilda dispelled her shadowy guise, holding a flail with three spiked balls. With an unearthly cackle she let fall her mace, bashing Djidi from his horse. A Hunter hurled his serrated boomerang, but she vanished into thin air.

The Hunters gazed around bewildered. And for a second, things were quiet save for the whistling boomerang making its return, until the Witch materialized aside the chain wielding Hunter. She ripped him from his horse, and crushed him with her flail. During this, the wielder of the boomerang was heedless of his weapon, and it slit his throat. The remnant Hunters attacked Gilda in full force. Shade, conscious drifting, observed his unknown savior contending the Hunters, beating them. Her dark hair flowed like silk, as did her graceful movements.

The onslaught was over in a few brief moments.

Shade blinked, amazed at Gilda's performance. Blackness blanketed his vision.

The Witch's eyes fixed on Djidi's horse, a black stallion. Gilda mused, and a smile touched her lips. She reached out, and the steed stepped back whining. Gilda advanced murmuring sweet words, lulling the horse.

"There, there," she said tenderly, massaging the stallion's flank. "You're a fine beast. I shall name you Rogue."

§   §

Shade regained consciousness. The sun flared in the horizon. The Witch paced back and forth at his feet. His shirt was torn, the arrow removed and the wound bandaged. His side was treated as well. Though pain throbbed along his back and leg, and his head radiated grave hurt.

"Come," said Gilda. "Time to go."

"Who are you?" Speaking sparked head pain. He winced. He'd be wise to keep his talking to a minimum.

"Later," said Gilda, seizing Rogue's reins. "Now we ride."

Shade tried to rise, and his body surged with pain, especially his leg. The world blurred. He hobbled forward, arm dangling limply, then collapsed.

"My leg." He winced. "My shoulder."

Gilda aided him, and reset his shoulder. He gave it a testing roll and everything seemed fine. Using her as a crutch, he struggled toward the horse laden with a pack. She assisted him on Rogue, and walked the horse through Andrekka.

None would ever know what became of Shade, and the Stygian Hunters.

Once they left the Vulture Neck Passage behind, she mounted Rogue behind Shade, and trotted southeast. During the journey his agonizing head made everything fuzzy. He rocked. Gilda secured him against her bosom. It felt almost maternal, as if his mother were holding him—well, perhaps not quite.

Now was the time for questions. He needed to know what was going on before things got out of hand. Shade turned and peered into her face. The sense of being a child was nostalgic; he felt so small and insignificant next to her. She looked upon him for a moment then returned her attention to the landscape. He opened his mouth to speak, and she muttered something unintelligible to him. Drowsiness abruptly set in, and sleep took over.

It was nigh dark when his eyelids flicked open. Thudding hoofs drummed in his ear. They'd been riding hard and relentless for some time. Shade's stomach begged for sustenance, and the grumble of his rescuer's stomach, said she craved the same.

"Rest well?" she asked.

"Yes, but I'm hungry," he said groggily.

They stopped to eat.

Shade eased off the saddle, and a jolting ache stroked him. Sleep served nothing for his incessantly pounding head. He limped to the camp and sat, which proved difficult; he felt despondent. The meal was eaten in uncomfortable silence. A thought came to him—his purse. He reached a hand under the cloak, and there it still remained, slung over his shoulder. He sighed with relief. He wished he remembered the valuables in Sherk's hut. Of what use would it be to him, or any of those men? For the second time the guilt was upchucked to his throat.

Shade could no longer endure the silence, and shook off the remorse. (Although deep down, he knew none of them would be dead if he hadn't come to the Outback.) There were many questions that needed answering. Why did she save him? How did she

gain knowledge of the Outback's whereabouts? And most importantly, where were they going? He meant to break the ice no matter
what.

"Where are we?" he asked, taking a swig from a water-horn.

"Northern rim of Bekistan."

That was a start. "Where are we going?"

Silence.

"Why did you save me?"

She didn't answer this, simply stared into the fire.

"What is your name?"

"Gilda Loveless."

"I'm…"

"I know who you are."

"Oh. You're no Daralese native. Where are you from? How did
you know about the Outback?"

The Witch gave no reply.

"Like to leave people in the dark, I see." He spit. "Either way, I
thank you for saving my life. I'm forever in your debt."

She turned to him, and her eyes seemed to say. *Yes, you are.*
They were unsettling, her dark eyes. Shade withdrew babbling
more questions and concentrated on eating.

There was no rest for the weary, because after the meal they set
off again, and managed to reach southern Baijan by night's end.
Rogue's long, strong legs helped them to cover a lot of ground.
Shade thought Gilda made a rather fine choice for their steed.

The morning brought sweltering heat, and dust was a brown
screen in front of the world. The hardpan was cracked at places,
split open like dry and broken skin. The heat only intensified later
into the day.

Rogue had been pushed to the limit, and was sweating badly.
Gilda gave him a break, and poured water over his head, neck, and
inner legs. Then she fanned him with a folded bedroll. The thief
and Witch rested a spell also; they were weary and hungry. When
they headed off again, Gilda allowed Shade to ride while she
walked. The horse could do without the extra weight for a while;
he was overtaxed in the heat as it is.

The day ended, and cast the traveler's shadows against the hardpan. Shade appreciated the abatement of hotness. His head felt better. His back was still sore, undoubtedly marred with welts, but

better than it was. The land changed, and weeds sprouted up here and there. Two coyotes were fighting for one reason or another. And a desert eagle shrieked overhead.

Before long Gilda mounted again, steering Rogue at a sprinting pace. It became substantially cooler in the coming hour. The moons were a Waning Gibbous in a starless sky. The journey entered into the heart of Baijan. This roused even more questions in Shade of their destination. North of Baijan was nothing save the Djinn Sea. He queried Gilda, but she answered not.

They discovered the Ubaine Road, and took it straight to the sea. They strayed off the road down a steep hill to the beach. A ship with a black sail bobbed on the dark water. Two figures standing at the edge of the water approached them; they were knights fully clad in black armor, girt with broadswords. Gilda stopped Rogue a few feet in front of the welcoming duo.

"Our friend here is injured," she said dismounting. "Help dim down, and show him to his quarters. And take the horse aboard."

"Yes, master," said the knights compliantly.

Chapter Six
Evermore

For seven days they sailed west. Further and further away from King Amire, and the Emperor Tivoli, and into the sovereignty of Evermore. Shade could begin his new life much, much sooner than he expected. And he stood at the bow, as the Witch's ship sailed over the beautiful aquamarine water. He'd never seen such water before. In the distance he could see an island practically covered in jungle, and at the far northern end, stood a dark mountain higher than any in Daralia. The scenery was jaw-dropping. Yea, he could get used to this.

On the night of the eighth day, they arrived at an island in the far east of Evermore. Two lampposts marked the quay. The knights assisted Shade off the ship; he could see the shadow of Gilda astraddle Rogue between the lampposts. A beaten path led from the quay up a passive hill, looming darkly above them. The knights helped him onto Rogue, Gilda gigged the horse, and they started down the path. *Where are we?*

"I shall answer one of your questions now," she said.

"Which one?" he queried, looking over his shoulder at her.

No reply.

Use your head, Shade. "Where are we?"

"We are in Azamaz, my private island. And before you open your mouth to question, I am taking you to Ravencroft, my mansion, where you shall do something for me."

Do something like what, be a servant? Not this one. I'll die before that. Shade put aside those feelings for right now, and wait to see what Gilda had in mind. He had never dealt with a wizard or witch before, so he didn't know what to expect.

Ravencroft was a dark place, before acres of even darker trees. *It's nighttime Shade, calm down.* Here, a man waited them. He wore a black robe, and a gray pointed hat, with the wide brim drawn low over his eyes. A long ponytail lay placidly over his shoulder. *So Gilda is the servant?* Shade thought. *He is the headman.*

"Things went well I see, Master," he said bowing.

Guess I was wrong.

"They did," she replied bowing back. "Take the horse to the backyard."

He bowed. "As you wish."

Shade wondered who the black wizard was. The man had not introduced himself, and Gilda didn't bother to. He figured he'd meet the man before long.

Gilda escorted Shade inside, and down the foyer alit with black chandeliers. They came upon a junction of halls, where an even larger chandelier hung from a high alcove in the ceiling. Gilda continued straight, Shade gimping alongside her. The hallway was decorated with large paintings created by a disturbed artist. Even more disturbed would be the one to hang them, Shade thought. One was of a dark forest under pale moons, and from the dark spaces between the trees gazed red eyes. In another, a goblin carrying a bludgeon was creeping out a door, a broad, wicked, grin on its face. It was the most vivid one, and the biggest, and Shade felt the goblin would attack him at any moment. He labored by it as quickly as possible, hand on his sword. Ravencroft was elaborate, even luxurious and elegant, in a morbid sort of way.

The Witch brought him to a door at the end of a hall on the second floor. She waved her hand over the knob, and the door creaked open. Shade followed her into a grand room, same black chandelier and high ceiling. Large windows took up one entire wall, flanked by dangling curtains that bore big tassels. The room was complimented with an enormous bed fit for four, a writing desk, a wing chair, and a vanity table with a green cushioned oak chair. A handful of those disturbing art pieces lined the walls, which Shade would remind himself to take down. Otherwise he'd never get any sleep. Lavish this room, in the similar gothic manner as the rest of Ravencroft.

"Here is where you'll stay," she said. "The door shall remain unlocked for your comfort. Feel free to tour the mansion, but mind you, many of the doors are locked. I'm sure the leg is badly wounded I'll tend to it once I return. In the meantime food will be brought. Any questions?"

"No."

"Good."

Gilda left, closing the door behind her.

Shade listened for the click of the lock, but it never came, and he labored over to the windows to see the view. From the side windows he descried the Selbring Ocean and the dock. The back windows revealed the shadowed woods and backyard, where Rogue milled around. The room had a spectacular view, better than any he's ever seen, and he grew up near the ocean. He flung off his cloak, removed the purse, kicked off his boots and got comfortable.

An hour the later the black wizard arrived, carrying a tray of steamed mushrooms, foot-long fish, and a tankard of red wine. Folded neatly underneath the tray was Shade's sleeping gown. *How thoughtful.*

"Many thanks," said Shade, grabbing the tray, the sleeping the gown.

"Welcome, sir. I shall need your garments so they can be de-spoiled. Shade placed the tray on the bed and began to undress.

"What is your name?" he asked the wizard.

"I am called by no name," replied the wizard, turning his back on Shade to give him privacy.

"A pure shame for that," said Shade, easing off his pants. A hoof print was gouged into his leg. The Nameless Wizard Shade mused.

"Not really."

Shade threw on the gown, and felt slightly awkward. He couldn't remember the last time he'd slept in anything other than his clothes. "Your may turn around." The wizard did so. "Everyone has a name, and everyone should be rightfully called by it," he said, handing over his dirty clothes.

"I'm sure your real name isn't Shade. Have a very good night, sir."

The wizard bowed and left.

§   §

Sleep devoured Shade, and he did so head hidden underneath the covers like when he was a child, and it wasn't until the fourth knock did he wake. He poked his head over the blanket and called. It was Gilda, bearing a decanter of water and petals, and a cloth. The decanter contained *water of healing*, or healing water its common name; a simple concoction of water and any sort of petal. But this potion is ineffective unless spelled, which could only be performed by anyone knowing the right incantation. Gilda dressed the wound, and doused the dressing with *water of healing*. Shade realized the water was more of an oily substance than actual water. Gilda checked his chest, side, and back, poured healing water over the wounds, and massaged them.

"What of your hand?" she asked.

Shade unraveled the dressing. The wound was caked with the paste, the healing process slow, but effectual. The feeling was yet to be restored though.

"Shaman powder," said Gilda. "Never was that a good remedy. Much to my dislike, I am forced to allow the paste to completely dissipate. No matter. I'll touch it up tomorrow."

§   §

Shade spent the next several days recuperating, occasionally hearing metallic footfalls as the knights patrolled the mansion. He had positioned the wing chair between the sets of windows so he could admire the view. Gilda hadn't revisited since the following day she treated his wounds. One morning he awoke to a racket outside. Investigating, he found Gilda and the Nameless Wizard hacking at a tree in the woods. Shade was surprised to see Gilda working hand in hand with him; he thought it was a master-servant relationship, but more like a master and apprentice rapport. Gilda called, "Timber!" and a tree came crashing down. They cut quarters, cut planks, and felled more trees. Between breaks the wizard brought him food. It was long after nightfall when the two abandoned the task for another day. In the morning Gilda came to see on him.

"When will I know what is it you ask of me?" Shade queried.

"You will know when I ask" she deflected. "Are you not appreciative that I've saved your skin?"

"I am."

"Well then, do not trouble yourself with it. I ask for very little in return. Perhaps you need entertainment. Would you desire a book from my study?"

"Fine."

She returned with a thick book named *Foosa*. Shortly after, ruckus commenced outside.

§   §

A week went by, and Gilda and her apprentice continued to work diligently on their project. Shade's left hand was wholly restored but often stiff, the arrow wound gone, the side laceration disappearing, his welts reducing, making him capable of sleeping on his back. The leg healed also, but he walked with a slight limp. The book Gilda gave him kept him deeply submerged in its stories.

After another week and a half of labor the construction was completed. It was a stable for Rogue. Shade had finished the book and was feeling in tip-top condition; his hand as good as new, and the limp hardly noticeable. When the Nameless Wizard brought his evening meal, he asked whereabouts was the study.

Three walls of the study were taken up by bookshelves twice his height. In the center of the room three more stood, two parallel, and the third horizontal so they formed a U. A pair of wing chairs faced a cold hearth. He wandered about searching for an empty slot to place the book, found it, and returned it, and found another. The books were meticulously organized, and after skimming the pages and deciding against it, he returned them to their proper place. He retrieved the rolling ladder and browsed the upper sections. A mammoth book called the *History of the World* caught his interest. Tired of being cooped in his room, he lugged it to a chair, sparked a fire, and opened it up.

A tragic bit of history occurred during the first age, in the northern world, at an island named Aklabeth. A devastating earthquake and volcanic eruption destroyed the island, sundering it into three sections. Three-fourths of the population died in the event.

He read on.

Another piece happened right there in Evermore, during the construction of Castle Bethalas, when the first king found an orb in a cavern, and grew obsessed with it, and gained power. The book told how he later challenged the sorcerer-king of Setan for control of Geneva. Shade thought how foolish such an act was. The high-kings' powers were daunting.

He read on and on, and the hours passed, the fire turned to embers, and his eyes burned. It was late and he resolved to go to bed.

With the history book tucked under his arm, he trudged the dim halls to his room. The corridor echoed with approaching footsteps, and from the staircase up ahead a knight descended, visor raised. In passing Shade lifted his hand to greet him, and opened his mouth to speak, but no words issued forth. He was left speechless, bewildered, and lightly fearful. For the between the space in the helmet there was no face, only blackness. Shade peered behind him warily, but the knight continued on his way—its way? *What the…? It was like living armor, and it could talk!* He hurried to his room.

Chapter Seven
Shade's Task

One afternoon while sitting in front of the windows reading his book, he espied Gilda and her apprentice hauling a large pewter cauldron to Rogue's stable. They came out and sauntered back to the mansion, disappearing under the windows. They emerged again, Gilda carrying an axe, the wizard two water pails. He entered the stable, and she headed for the forest. Shade watched all this in wonder. Rummy business was at work here. A whacking sound came from the woods. The wizard returned to the mansion, and appeared with more water, then left the stable towards the noise.

After a time the two emerged from the trees, the apprentice transporting an armful of faggots. They brought the sticks to the stable, came out several moments later, returned to the mansion, and didn't come out again.

Shade was nestled in his bed, *History of the World* beside him on the pillow. The songs of crickets drifted in from the open windows. An owl hooted in the woods. Rogue's sudden outburst startled the thief awake. From somewhere in the woods there was a fluttering of wings, as the owl took flight. Orange smoke billowed passed the windows.

The stallion was in a fit, whining and grunting. Shade leapt from the bed and scurried to the windows. As he observed the stable, the smoke changed from orange to green. Just when he made a move to warn someone, Rogue bolted from his stable in the direction of the forest. Gilda rushed out after him, and transformed into a crow. Shade was in awe. The crow flew in pursuit of Rogue, cawing into the night. Things were definitely becoming quite odd around Ravencroft, and it left Shade ill at ease.

In the coming nights Shade witnessed more colored smoke, sometimes red, sometimes purple, sometimes yellow, and endured the stallion's baleful cries. His purpose at Ravencroft was yet to be addressed. The sooner the better, he thought, because he desperately wanted to leave this place.

One day the Witch departed and was gone for a month. Gilda returned late one night, and left again straight away, with her altered stallion bequeathed with the ability of flight.

§   §

Three weeks went by.

Shade was enjoying *History of the World* in the study, while wind rattled the rain-covered windows. Ear piercing booms of thunder frightened him a few times. He wasn't accustomed to rain, for Daralia rarely got any. Nasty thunderstorms like this didn't occur in his homeland. Last time there was a terrible storm it was before he was born, and it rained for a week straight, and the great earthworms living under the desert surfaced.

He heard the door open and close.

"Who is it? Who's there?" he called.

"It is I," replied Gilda.

He'd seen a lot of her in the past two weeks, whereas the apprentice was nowhere to be seen. Actually, he hadn't heard the metallic footfalls passed his room in recent weeks either. That was relief. Ever since he realized they were specters of some sort, he tried to keep his distance. Gilda parked in the wing chair beside him. Shade closed his book, and eyed her patiently. Something obviously was on her mind. A couple of long moments passed, and she said nothing. She's attractive, he thought, in a special way. Not that she was hard on the eyes, but her cold presence often belied her features. He noticed she'd grown deafly pale, and black bags bulged underneath her eyes. Sleep seemed to have eluded her for many days. Something appeared different about her, but Shade couldn't say what. What Shade didn't know was she'd been in her quarters obsessively using the Orb of Bethalas.

"You like my collection, yes?"

"Yes."

"To the business at hand." Her eyes met his, and Shade's stomach tightened. "Shade you will handle an important matter for me."

"What can I handle that you alone are incapable?"

Gilda clasped the armrest and pulled herself to her feet. His eyes chased the Witch's pacing steps.

"I am incapable of performing all my plans alone. Your part in this is an intricate one. You are to make an assassination attempt on Emperor Asilva of Desmon, Aries."

"Pardon me, but you cannot be serious. An empress is not so easily assassinated."

"As I very well know. Remember, "attempt" is the keyword.""

"I remember once being told that you ask for little in return. I'm likely to die on such a task."

Gilda stopped pacing and scowled at him, and an icy chill ran down his spine. He held her gaze firmly, but not for long and turned away.

"If not for me you'd already be dead," she reminded him. Then her expression lightened. "A handsome payment is included, enough to acquire a private island such as this, if you wish. And you shall be equipped rightly," she said recommencing her pacing. "You are in my debt, Shade. Have you forgotten? A man of your caliber surely has principles, though a thief you may be. Will you hold to those principles or renege and be thrown to the fish?" She quit pacing and looked upon him, eyebrows raised questioningly.

"Since you put it that way…When do I go?"

"Not now. Not for a long time yet, perhaps."

The storm had decreased to a drizzle. Gilda stood at the dock, arms folded across her chest. A ship— her ship—was sailing towards Azamaz. A broad smile touched her face. She was anxious to get on with her new practice.

The ship docked, and the plank was let down. The knights disembarked with figures slung over both shoulders. Bodies! Gilda ordered them to be taken to the backyard. She looked quizzically at the Nameless Wizard as he descended the plank, pulling a creature by a chain. It had tan-pinkish skin, long pointed ears and a long pointed nose.

"A group of them attacked us in Telle," said the wizard. "It's a goblin, I think. May be of use."

"Absolutely," said Gilda. "Absolutely. You have done well, my apprentice. For this you shall taste a bit of the prize."

"Thank you," he said, trying not to sound too excited.

"What is your name, goblin?" Gilda asked.

The goblin growled in answer. Her dark eyes flashed, and she pointed a finger at it. The goblin retreated a few steps.

"Tell me now!"

"Grundge," it said compliantly.

"Good, Grundge. Be thankful, you shall be a captain in my legion. Come now, there is work to be done," she said then muttered something to it in a strange tone.

"Yes, master," said Grundge.

The knights made a total of six trips to the ship, carrying off twenty-four carcasses, and piled them in the backyard. The newcomer, Grundge, was designated to dig twenty-four shallow graves. And he performed his labor late into the night, when the rain picked up again, his chain waggling from his shackle.

Chapter Eight
Gilda's Dark Liege

Shade spent many days brooding on his task in disquiet. How could a thief be appointed to assassinate, and an empress at that? This empress would be especially difficult to slay. He'd rather be going after Tivoli. He wasn't learned in northern world life, but everyone knew of the Elcrest wizards who frequently visited the palace. If a wizard happened to be present at that time he was doomed. Doomed perhaps anyway, but that would increase the risk. Moreover, this Empress Asilva had a twin brother Ayn. All those wizards, and one man...This was bad business.

Sometimes he wandered the halls thinking about how nasty this piece of business was, and the day he bumped into Grundge he wished to heaven that he'd brought Shitari. Fortunately, the goblin paid him no mind—just like the phantom knights—and moseyed on, his chain clinking and swinging back and forth like a pendulum. It reminded him all too well about his lashings in the Outback. He wondered what he had gotten himself into, and knew the answer: A lot of trouble. The only other option was to grin and bear it. So one night before bed he swallowed his worries, and awaited the time for his assignment.

He was in the land of dreams. A familiar buzz tapped his subconscious. He tossed and turned, trying to shake it but couldn't. Then it was as if his mind woke up. Joy filled him. He rolled over and opened his eyes. Graf lie on his back, his folded hands rising and falling slowly on his stomach. That buzzing noise was his snoring. Shade noticed he was clad in his traveling clothes, not a sleeping gown given to him by the Witch's apprentice. He turned back over smiling at the thought; there were no Stygian Hunters; his villainous hideaway wasn't littered with corpses; no Witch; no dark mansion on a hill where queer things happened, spirits occupied armor, and a creature ambled about shackled by the neck. Everything was the way it ought to be. It was all a dream. He even still had the wounded hand. Yes, things were fine. Things were—

Graf was shaking him. In the background, Shade heard dreadful moaning. His tent mate rambled something about them being under attack and scampered from the tent. Shade followed, armed and ready. When he stepped out into the night, there was not a sole in sight. Only thing visible were tents. The night felt eerie, and when a soft breeze brushed him, it carried with it the scent of death, and putrid flesh. Faint, as if in the back of his mind, came more bone-chilling moans

"What's wrong, Shade?" a voice asked behind him.

The moment he turned around he jumped back. It was Salin. But not the Salin he once knew; the arrow that killed him protruded from his neck. His dead, decaying face started at him puzzled as if he knew not why Shade was shaky.

"Friend," someone said, clapping a hand on his shoulder.

It was Sherk; his face an unsightly mess, gray and peeling. He was a dead as a doorknob.

"Up for a game of chess?"

It was Graf, eyes bulged, face purple and cracked; his neck was marred by a nasty black and blue welt.

"Come with us." This time Djidi with his head mashed.

Shade's head turned this way and that. All of the Outback's slain were in attendance, heading towards him, encircling him. His heart beat hard, and he thought it would pound through his chest, gazing upon these ghastly beings. They were coming for him; coming to take him away from the world of the living. Graf reached for him. Shade didn't hesitate one bit, and slashed his neck. Bugs and worms spewed from the slash. Hands grabbed him—

He awoke with a start, in the dark mansion, Ravencroft on the hill. He was in his huge, comfortable bed. He never thought he'd be happy at the sight of this place. Moans were coming from outside. He got up and went to the window. Completely mortified, he took a step back. It was as if his nightmare came to life. There were undead beings in the yard. Not anyone he recognized but undead nonetheless. Gilda was out there too, holding a round object radiant with pale light. It was some kind of orb or crystal ball from what he could tell. She was saying something, but Shade couldn't discern the words; they sounded strange and foreign. The zombies moved lethargically, some bumping into one another stupidly. Gilda spoke louder, more commanding, but it still sounded like gibberish to the thief. She held the orb or crystal ball, aloft, and it pulsed and shined brighter. There were hollers from the grisly crowd, and they put their hands up to shield their eyes. One advanced on her, arms extended to grab her. Her magical object shimmered red, and the zombie burst into flames. Witnessing this seemed to settle the others down, and they dispersed quickly from the fire as if it were their bane. And it was.

The odds were not in Gilda's favor, and felt inclined to take action. Although, he had half a mind to leave her to it so endangering himself on the crazy mission she planned for him. But that wouldn't be right, especially since she saved his life and all. Without another thought he scooped up Shitari, and hastened from his room.

He was nimble, and quick, and his footfalls barely sounded on the hardwood floor. He reached a curved staircase and slid down the railing. He peered left, right, descried the back door, and sped down the hall. He stopped at the door, and peeped out the square windows. The zombies had encircled Gilda, just as they did him in his dream. He could see her towering over their ranks, holding her weapon aloft, pale light gleaming off their dead heads. Shade crouched low, twisted the knob, and slid out of the door through as minimal space as possible. The dead people wailed, as Gilda spoke to them in that unknown language. He took advantage of the situation, and silently used the darkness to come up behind the congregation of zombies. Shitari glinted as he emerged under the shine of the orb, and darted, decapitating an undead. They turned around in unison, crying in woe.

"Shade," said Gilda. In a delayed reaction, the beings advanced on him. She spoke a word, and they halted. She stepped forward, and they parted so that she may pass.

"I looked out the window and saw you battling," he said. "You roasted one like mutton, but I thought you needed a hand."

"I'm fine," she said softly. "These are my soldiers for my army."

Army? But Shade kept his mouth shut, knowing the Witch was not inclined to answer questions.

"I'm merely weaving a spell of command. What you witnessed was an isolated incident. The unruly one was put down. Not to worry. I must say," she said, eyes scrutinizing him barefoot in his sleeping gown. "I'm rather touched by your concern," she said teasingly, and cackled.

Shade plopped on the bed holding Shitari with both hands lazily between his sprawled legs. The epiphany of the Witch's true evilness sank in, causing him to want to perform the task, get paid and get gone. What other spooks would she bring to Ravencroft?

Gilda was no longer a witch, but a necromancer.

Winter came and Shade relaxed in front of the windows, entranced by the snowfall. He had never seen snow before, you see, and thought it a pretty course of nature. Eight inches of snowfall lay on the ground already, with drifts twice that. Only thing he disliked was the immense cold. He walked around in two layers of clothes these days. Another thing he disliked, rather despised, was the fact Gilda let her "soldiers" roam the halls. They were fully disciplined by this time, but Shade felt no better about it. The zombies trammeled him. He'd like once to be able to step out and not see one. None bothered him but still…

Besides the strolling undead, days, weeks, and months passed without incident. Though, in the last week of the season a fierce blizzard came, bringing four feet of snow. Luckily He, Gilda, and the Nameless Wizard Raven had chopped firewood for the season. The wizard commented the amount was excessive, but Gilda stated it would be a bad winter. She would be correct. When Spring arrived, she speculated how she'd foreseen it. The Orb of Bethalas had empowered her, and she grew much during wintry season.

Shade heard thunderclaps overhead, although he noticed the sky was clear as can be. He would've inquired to the Nameless Wizard, but he watched him and Grundge sail away a week ago. Gilda was somewhere around, but he didn't feel up to looking for her. He made a trip outside to see what's what. He saw a phenomenon unfeasible. A black cloud hovered over the mansion, lightning flashing and thunder crackling.

"Anytime you're ready to send me off," Shade said to himself.

§   §

When the ship came home the next week, Gilda stood atop the hill ready to welcome them. Her apprentice and Grundge led an entourage of fifty goblins in single file up the path. Gilda greeted the newly arrived with enchanting words, and they were immediately spellbound; days later there was commotion in the basement and outside. Zombies and goblins were everywhere, and Shade couldn't stand it. He stayed to his books, to himself, in his room as much as possible. Sleep didn't come easy nowadays with all the chopping, sawing, crashing timber, whooping, and cries. A gap had been made in the forest, and three additional quays and ships were a result of this relentless labor.

Thereafter things became peaceful again.

Shade resolved to reading in a clearing in the woods for relief of seeing Gilda's minions. He heard calls, and two albatross flickered in and out of his vision flying passed the clustered trees, journeying east towards the dimming sun. He marked his book and closed it, and ambled to the western edge of the forest, where the trees descended a steep slope, ending a hundred feet above the ocean. He sat down and admired the view of the ocean, its tidal flow, propped his book on his legs and began reading where he left off.

The sun, a dull arch of light half behind the ocean, colored the sky pink and orange. The moons were already visible in the sky. He neared the conclusion of the book, marked it, and started back to the house for a bite to eat. Heserved himself jam and bread for a snack. He grabbed a mug and browsed a long counter in the basement, where five barrels sat with spigots. Four he recognized. From left to right it was whiskey, *magic ale*, a powerfully potent specially brewed drink, red whiskey and beer. The fifth barrel bared three white X's. This wasn't there this morning.

Curious, he positioned his mug under the spout, and released enough of a dark red liquid for a swallow. He tipped the mug, and it went down smooth, his chest burning like fire.

"Woo!" he shouted, and exhaled a long breath. "That'll certainly put hair on your chest."

Naturally, he poured more of the beverage called firewater.

He trudged the eastern wing staircase with newel posts of howling wolves. The stairs were draped in violet carpet, trimmed black at the edges. The master bedroom, Gilda's bedroom, was in this wing.

He passed a zombie and wrinkled his nose in disgust. Turning left at an intersection, a pale light shooting from underneath Gila's bedroom door caught his peripherals. He glanced both ways, making sure the coast was clear, gently set down his food. He moseyed to the door, looked around again for extra precaution, and reached for the handle. Locked! It's just as well. He peered down at his feet dipped in light. The light was warm, inviting. The glow blinked out. Shade looked up at the door, back to his feet, then to the door again. No glare. No pale, warm, inviting light. Nothing. He retreated slowly, picked up his bread, jam, and mug of firewater, and proceeded down the hall. After a journey of six steps he stopped and threw a glance at the door. Pink light glinted across the floor. The lock relented with a faint *click*, and the door came ajar creaking.

He eyed the door suspiciously a moment, placed his food on the floor, and started towards it. He paused at the door, and peered through the crack. Only thing visible in his line of sight was the crystal sphere perched on a small round table, now pulsing dully with gray light. He didn't have the nerve to go inside, see the interior, and see what odd possessions and decorations the room held. But the blinking ball held his gaze. Shade was no longer aware he was in the hall, gazing in the master of Ravencroft's bedroom, a perpetually malicious woman who would curse him dead if she knew. Something could walk up on him any time. All this was irrelevant to Shade at the present, hypnotized, gawking unblinkingly at the flashing light. He desired to hold it, feel its warmth. The color changed, and a lustrous purple light flared from the sphere and spilled into the hall. He opened the door and....

Stepped into a place not resembling Gilda's room; there was no small round table where the sorcerous ball sat. He wasn't in a room at all—he wasn't in Ravencroft anymore. He was standing in a snowy plain, confronted and flanked by mountains. Snow fell, but he could not feel it. Wind blew, and he couldn't feel that, either. Sounds of labor and harsh cries turned him round. A vast black building was being constructed—a castle it appeared to him—by countless goblins. Standing before the works was someone shrouded in black, hands clasped together behind their back, black hair billowing in the wind. From a point somewhere between them, a star of purple light winked.

Everything changed.

He was in the deep blue sea. On a ship crowded with zombies. In the vicinity was an armada of ships, transporting goblins and skeletons. Before being overwhelmingly repulsed, purple flashed in the middle of the sea.

The scene turned.

He found himself in the hall outside Gilda's bedroom, looking through an opened door. He saw himself inside her room, transfixed on the orb. Shade motioned to warn the other Shade, and the orb blinked.

The surroundings flipped.

Shade was back on a ship. He viewed his other-self standing by Gilda, clad in green and white with a black cloak. His counterpart appeared rather pleased. "Get the trunk," the Necromancer said to the knights. They went below deck, and they returned lugging the trunk, and set it down. The other Shade looked at Gilda questioningly, she nodded, and he went over to the trunk and flipped the lid. Shade the invisible one, moved to get a better view. His jaw slacked. He blinked. The trunk was filled with zeni. *My reward*, he thought happily. He watched himself scoop coins in his hands, and let them spill through his fingers. Footsteps echoed behind him. He spun around, but only saw the night and dark water.

The thief was in Gilda's bedroom once more. His eyes blinked rapidly as if he'd awoken to a bright light glaring in his face. He shook his head and recovered, and as moments slipped away, so did any recollection of the visions. Hearing footsteps and harsh voices draw near, he bolted to the door, slipped out, and closed it softly behind him; he picked up his food and drink, and rounded the corner just as four goblins approached.

He put home a gulp of firewater when he reached his room. He didn't know what to make of the other visions, but seeing himself rewarded a trunk of money made loads of sense. He was going to be rich! Really, he wanted to wave off the notion. What did the crystal ball show exactly? Did it predict the future? Or does it only mirror one's deepest desire? It had him in a trance, and it could've been a number of things. But the thought of being wealthy put a smile on his face.

Chapter Nine
The Wheels of Fate turn

The Necromancer had been gone over two fortnights, and two other ships sailed away from Azamaz; one loaded with Grundge, phantom knights, and goblins; the other carrying the Nameless Wizard. Grundge returned twelve days later with more dead to be buried, and wooden caskets containing skeletal remains. And when Gilda returned she used her powers of necromancy to reanimate the dead.

In late October when the wizard returned to Azamaz, he brought an entire shipload of goblins. More trees were felled. Shanties and three large building were built in the backyard to house the goblins.

Over the next couple of years hundreds of goblins arrived. Grundge had taken a host of fellow goblins and sailed to the Lost Woods in Corinthia, and flushed out the wild-mastiffs and ogres, and brought them back to Azamaz. Two more quays were constructed, giving a total of five all together. Recently built ships packed with the Necromancer's minions sailed away never to return.

It was not until the present summer did Gilda share the orb with her apprentice, making a priceless discovery. The orb by this time was black save a section at the heart, but when the wizard succumbed to it, it became crystal clear again. Gilda learned, the darker the orb became the less power it fed. Now it could be passed back and forth between them and unlimited power consumed.

The Necromancer and her apprentice toggled extended absences, and during the upcoming year they rarely were home together.

On the fifth year of Shade's arrival to Ravencroft, he wondered if he'd ever perform his duty and get paid. He wanted to leave Azamaz and get on with his life. At first arrival he thought he could've endured the mansion, but the years dashed all his assumptions. But nowadays Azamaz was quiet, which was pleasant, but he still would rather be someplace else. Despite the fact that there were only a dozen goblins, and the knights roamed the mansion. The shanties and buildings stood dark and deserted.

One May afternoon as Shade napped to the boom of thunder, there was a knock on the door. He'd grown accustomed to the black cloud, but sometimes, like today, it made him tired and lazy, as the affects of rainy days often do. He called to the door, and Gilda shuffled in holding something tucked under her arm.

"Tonight's the night," she said, pleased.

"Good," he said, sitting up. He was topless, his chest muscular and abdomen tight. The scar on his ribs where the boomerang struck was seeable. "I mean to get it over with and done."

"I'm glad to see you're ready. Here are some clothes." She handed over a blue shirt embroidered with a sunburst, and a black cloak not his own.

"What's the shirt all about?" Shade recognized the symbol of Setan.

"Never you mind," the Necromancer said, brushing him off. "I have weaved a cloak of shadows for you. Use it well. When you attack Asilva, be sure the symbol on the shirt is noticeable. It is key, Shade. You sail at nightfall."

"I'd favor a dagger handy."

"I'll see what I can do."

At nightfall Gilda and her apprentice retrieved him, and briefed him.

"Nix that," Shade protested, when he was advised to sail twenty miles south of Desmond, and ride Rogue into the capital. "I'm not riding that beast."

"Believe me, thief," said Gilda. "I'm not tickled about the idea, but it is essential."

Gilda informed him how to get Rogue in the air, land, and stated necessary precautions and other particulars.

That night the knights were waiting at the dock for him, one gripping Rogue's reins, the other a grapple.

"You'll need the hook to scale the city wall," Gilda said.

"I don't need that," said Shade appalled.

"It's up to you, but take it anyway," said Gilda. "Oh, I nearly forgot. If in dire need speak, *ali ashan*, and Rogue shall come. And here," she said, removing a dagger from her sleeve pocket.

"Thanks"

Shade followed the knights aboard Gilda's personal ship, the black sail now bearing a red X.

"Be safe," the Nameless Wizard called to him.

Shade turned around and nodded. "As I can be."

The knights raised the plank and anchor, and Gilda, and the wizard watched until the ship was out of sight.

The Mirror By S.J.Thompson-Balk

<u>Aug.26<u>th</u> 1924</u>

My shaking hand prevents me from writing too fast in case I cannot make myself clear. What I am to be setting down is an account of the findings that I unwittingly uncovered whilst hunting for a few antiques in the West country, and the horror that I have found waiting for me here. At this present moment in time I feel that I am not in any danger but that the abhorrence shall soon be closing on me, and that there is nothing I can do to prevent its coming. That I am alone is plainly clear. Time is non-existent. The very air of this place is oppressing, heavy like the calm before a tremendous thunderstorm with the promise of events to come.

Days ago, it seems so long, I took some holiday from my employer so that I may have two or three weeks to pursue a favourite hobby of mine, antique hunting. I do not have an extensive knowledge of rare or ancient objects but I do know what I like. Perhaps some of that knowledge would have prepared – or at least warned – me of that which I am to face. Value of antiques is not of any real interest to me. Curiosity holds more value in my book; something with a little bit of strange history to talk about and amaze friends with. Amongst my small but modest collection are various scriptures, sketches by supposed mad princes, articles of clothing and jewellery holding some strange secret, a rather intriguing wood - carving and the mirror. That damn mirror…

The wooden carving was acquired in Scotland three weeks ago in a small shop situated near Loch Ness, on its own and rather out of the way. I had been staying with relatives at the time who could not place the shop I described to them.

It was not only a shop but also a 'tea house', or so said the small neatly painted sign above the front door. Feeling that I had taken in enough of the countryside for one day I decided to stop for some refreshment before returning to my kin. Entering the green wooden door, I thought that I had walked into what appeared to be someone's living room. A small bell above the door behind me tinkled gently as the door slowly closed itself. Countless odds and ends, books, miniatures and other knick-knacks were scattered in a haphazard fashion either on shelves or in piles on the floor or tables. Untouched and unused were words that sprang to mind. As I was glancing over the room a small, balding man, who was in his late eighties by the look of him, walked through a door opposite me. He beamed a smile at me, not surprised to see me standing there. That smile seemed quite genuine at the time but when I think back it feels that he knew me or knew something about me, or had possibly met me before. Maybe…

"Tea?" he asked.

"Yes, thank you" I replied, smiling back. The old man looked about the room.

"Feel free to have a look around. If anything takes your fancy just let me know when I bring your tea."

"You mean that everything in here is for sale?" I queried.

"Of course. I'm sure you will find something to your liking." He turned and walked back through the door by which he had entered. I stood for a few seconds before walking over to a large oaken bookshelf, lined with some old paperbacks, new paperbacks, pulp novels and musty old leather bound volumes, some of which having no titles on their covers or bindings. One in particular was rather worn, covered in a deep red leather. It was very heavy for its size and felt warm to the touch.

The front cover announced its title as:

Translated notes of the
Original Latin version
Of
The Necronomicon.

No author was mentioned anywhere on the book. Inside, as I

turned the crackling pages, I saw strange sketches drawn inside the margins and round the outer edges. Creatures, produced from an obviously fantastic imagination, swam, flew, ran, lumbered and fell upon other smaller beings, devouring them with a cannibalistic evil and seeming utter disregard. Those creatures were mainly octopoid in appearance, with thin tentacles or feelers twisting from their faces. Fat bloated bodies suspended by huge bat wings. And the eyes. Dark, evil, brooding eyes that stared out from the page. Deep yellow they were. Hypnotic, all seeing and appallingly devilish. Glancing closer at one of the tentacled heads I could swear that it was reaching out for me…

I was brought around from the trance or miasma when I heard the door open once more and close rather loudly. Spinning round in surprise, I had momentarily forgotten that I was in the shop.

"Intriguing, isn't it?" This was spoken as more of a statement than a question.

"Mmm, yes…yes it is," I replied, unsure now as to what I had seen on that first page.

The old man had set my cup of tea and a plate of assorted biscuits down on a table. I took up my cup whilst the old man spoke. Referring to the book, he said, "Two hundred years old that book is, and it's a translation of words far, far older. But I'm afraid that book is the only item here not for sale. But there are plenty of other curios I think you would be interested in; if you liked the book." Whether I had liked the book or not I could not say, only that it had held me in awe? Wonder? I could not remember.

The shopkeeper took from one of the shelves a small carved figurine, the like of which I had never seen before. Or had I? The detail of the piece was so intricate that it appeared as a sort of 'still life'. This had most certainly been a painstaking task to carve. Standing ten inches it had a fat bloated body perched like a bird atop a large rock with its clawed, webbed feet gripping the stone. Short taloned arms hung loosely at its sides, and behind it were folded a pair of great bat wings. The whole thing vaguely resembled a flying frog, or would have if it had not been for the beasts head, for this mirrored the head of the creature I had glimpsed in the Notes of the Necronomicon. After studying it closely for a few moments I fancied that the figure quivered and moved ever so slightly.

"Forty two pounds." The shopkeeper had obviously noted my apparent interest. "It is a fine piece, after all."

"I only have thirty with me." I think I feigned my financial standing at that time, and put on an air of hopelessness.

"Thirty it is then," he replied, "and I'll throw in the tea and biscuits." I gladly handed over the figurine and the money and finished my refreshment whilst the shopkeeper wrapped up my purchase. I noticed that my hands had become wet after holding the carving. Sweat? After several minutes he handed me the neatly bound parcel, and I bid him good day.

"Before you go, sir," he beckoned me back, "I do believe that there is some small amount of paperwork dealing with the history of your figurine. If I could take down your address I shall forward it to you as soon as I have found it." Pleasantly surprised at hearing this I wrote my address down for the old man. When I think back…was that a mistake?

It was a week after this that saw me in Portloe, Cornwall. When away for two or three weeks at a time, my Mother stays at my house in Hastings, giving her the chance to visit some old friends. I had asked her to forward any post for me to The Ship Inn, where I would be spending the better part of a fortnight.

Portloe is a quiet fishing village nestled amid hills, trees and coastal cliffs, tucked away from prying eyes. Traffic is rare and the people are friendly.

My room at The Ship was small, but extremely comfortable, with a double bed covered in the plumpest and softest of blankets and a bedside table tucked to one side with a small brass lamp. An old but equally cosy armchair sat in one corner, slightly lower to the floor than normal, but this added to its comfort. And opposite this a small chest of drawers. The bedroom window looked out over a narrow road that immediately fronted the Inn, and then across to a well kept garden, at the back of which ran a small stream which spilled out into the sea at the harbour. The noise of a stream bubbling and trickling is a splendid thing to wake up to in the morning.

The first couple of days were taken up by exploring the surrounding countryside and seemingly secret cliff walks, known only to those who spared the effort to look for them. Forgetting my camera was a shame, for the scenery around this part of the country is always a pleasure and makes me feel at home, and at ease.

On the third day I decided to visit Falmouth, with a mind to see Fowey, Mevagissey, Truro and a number of other towns and villages at a later date until I found something that took my fancy or until I ran out money. Enquiring of the landlord about transport he told me that a bus called in to the village at around a quarter to nine, and left at approximately nine a.m. This was the only bus to Falmouth so it was essential to catch it on time.

I was up and breakfasted early and waited a little way up from the Ship. The morning sun had not quite warmed up the early air but it certainly promised to be a good day.

My bus journey was a pleasant one, shared with several other passengers who were picked up or dropped off at various stops along the way. We passed along plenty of narrow lanes, all too common in the West country, suitable for one vehicle at a time only to pass. Here was some of the most wonderful countryside that would have graced an artists canvas.

The bus travelled North then Northwest towards Truro before rounding back to Southwest towards Devoran, Penryn then finally to Falmouth.

We eventually arrived, being dropped off in the centre of the town, and were told that the bus would be returning at four o'clock. Our journey to Falmouth had taken around two hours, so that left me plenty of time for browsing the impressive selection of shops. Turning off of the main road I followed a smaller but equally busy side street. Gentlemen's tailors of the highest standard were there, catering for the business and country gent alike; countless bakers and confectioners; women's salons; fresh fish sold straight from the trawlers; and two antique shops. The first of these dealt solely in furniture and looked like it was a fairly new shop. I entered for a perusal, not noticing the slight mustiness you often get in these places. Spotless inside, and all the furniture was polished to a shine. The owner, quite a young man, mentioned that he had indeed just set up shop here two months ago. After a last glance round I exited and continued past two paper stalls and a bakers until I saw the second of the antique shops.

I assumed that this shop was well established here for it's windows were dusty or misty and had certainly not seen a damp cloth for some time. Even the cobwebs looked like they had been resident for years as they seemed to have picked up their own layer of thick dust. So bad was it that it was not very clear what sort of items were proffered within. Giving the outside a brief glance up and down I reached for the door. That was all I could remember before I found myself inside with the door closed behind me and a small bell tinkling above it. The opening of and passing through the door was a haze, a dream. Turning and looking back out of the window onto the street proved to be of little use for it seemed that I could see less of the street from inside than I could of the shop from the outside. It was that bad that the passing of people was not at all obvious. Back inside the shop the very air felt heavy. Tiny dust motes gently whirled slowly through the air where my entrance had disturbed them, pinpointed by whatever light managed to penetrate the soupy glass. A stillness smothered everything within, halting it in time. Strong, deep smells of foreign woods and spices assailed my nostrils, overshadowing an underlying odour. This was perhaps what I associated more with antique shops but not in quite such an oppressive manner.

Turning my head slowly about the shop I was reminded of the one I had visited in Scotland, with the goods in an apparent lack of order and disarray. More piles of books, small boxes, curios, figurines, newspapers and items of jewellery were placed haphazardly. Shelves were few and far between. It actually looked more like a jumble sale or flea market. Everything had a thin coating of dust. I dragged my finger across a small side table and looked at it. The dust was tinged with a grease or oil. Smelling it made me catch my breath. Rotten. Something certainly smelt so. Cleaning my finger on my handkerchief I continued to look the shop over. In one corner was an old leather topped desk with a small lamp, shaded with green glass, and in the opposite corner was an old cash register. From a door behind these came a shuffling. Presumably the owner...

...looking back now I remember that all sounds from outside the shop had ceased, not even the lapping of the sea or the engines of the ships was conspicuous...

From the doorway at the rear of the premises stepped a man of slight build with greying hair and of perhaps about sixty years of age. His eyes seemed dark in the gloom of the shop and showed no surprise at seeing my standing there.

The sudden overpowering smell of dead fish wafted across the room but, as good manners dictate, I made no mention of it and tried to show that I not noticed it even though it became fouler by the second. I remember hoping that the shopkeeper had not noticed the look of distaste that must have surely crossed my face.

Walking over he shook my hand. "Good of you to come" he beamed, with a smile like a Cheshire cat. If it was at all possible, the stench grew stronger as he approached. Fighting back the bile, I introduced myself.

"Harding. James Harding. And you are...?" I prompted his name and his smile grew wider.

"Hobbs" he answered. "Did you say James Harding?" He then gave me a queer look. Did he suspect?

"Yes" I replied, a touch curious.

"Well, *Mr Harding*, do look around. I'll be just through that door there if you have need of my assistance." Mr Hobbs walked over to his leather topped desk and pulled out a small book and a pen. He wrote in it briefly, muttering my name. I began to feel slightly anxious. Hobbs saw the look on my face and spoke. "I merely like to keep a record of who...or rather how many people visit my shop." This did not make me feel any easier. Was he telepathic?

He closed his book and placed it back in the desk drawer before locking it, then exited the room through the door he had indicated. The fishy reek noticeably lessened as he left.

It was a few moments before I began looking the shop over. I was after a picture, something in an occult or macabre fashion to go with my figurine. Most of the framed pictures were of typical country scenes. There were various old newspapers and several card folders containing prints or sketches. And a few large books which turned out to be albums or portfolios of some artists work. One of these held several small pictures drawn in black ink, signed by one artist, dated between 1670 and 1700. They depicted the burning of what I assumed were witches, until I examined more closely the faces of the executioners. They were not quite right, most being hairless with large eyes and wide mouths, with disproportionately large heads. Not inhuman looking, just scary. Another picture showed the chasing and then killing of one of the odd looking folk by normal looking people. And another, with a priest standing over one more of these odd people who had been staked to the ground in an effort to restrain them. An exorcism? Maybe. There was no indication of where these scenes took place, if they were supposedly true. They were also strangely titled. There was one called "Du Dower Ros", which pictured a ritualistic ceremony on a small outcropping or island just off of the coast. And another titled "Dagonne O Bos Pol" had hundreds of prostrate worshippers atop a huge semicircular headland of the coast praying or chanting to whatever was beginning to creep up out of the dark sea over the cliff head.

Each of these sketches was incredibly detailed, which was reflected in the price. Eighty pounds per sketch was forty pounds more than I was readily willing to pay. For quite some time I just stood there, trying to make up my mind as to whether or not I could afford just one of them, until I decided to look around the shop again. Another twenty or so minutes passed and still nothing had come to light. It was when I'd felt ready to give up and take one last look at the album when I caught a glimpse of a small round mirror, twelve inches across and slightly convex. The actual mirror itself was unremarkable but the frame struck in me a chord of recognition…

A being, obviously not of this world but born of a frantic imagination, spanned at least half the circumference of the mirror from the top down. The creatures head was at the top of the mirror gazing outward, flaying out tentacle like, but very thin, appendages down each side of the frame as if embracing that which it owns. The face of the beast could not be described with ease except that it was most definitely aquatic, of octopoid origin. It's eyes, small and piggish, radiated an evil such as I had never found before in any piece of art or antiquity. Below this malevolent creature and filling the rest of the frame were bi-pedal beings, but still portraying their aquatic origins with gills and webbed hands or feet, diving in or emerging from the water. Thin lipped with short fat necks and bulging lidless eyes, I stared at them for quite some time. And then I fancied that the glass shimmered.

Jerking suddenly I broke my daydream. Feeling a little foolish I checked the mirror for a price tag. The creatures on the framework were too closely related to those I had seen in Scotland, and to that which I purchased there. Disheartened to find no price tag, the mirror was replaced. Anyway, it was a picture that I was after.

Returning to the photo album, I removed the picture that I required and walked over to the door where Mr Hobbs had said he would be should I need him. He was arranging a bookshelf when I entered, and turned when my toe scraped the floor.

"Ah, Mr *Harding*. Any luck?" I was becoming distinctly irritated by the way he kept on emphasizing my name whenever he spoke. Have they followed me?

"Yes," I answered, producing the picture.

"Was that all, James?" Or did anything else catch your eye?" Jesus, how fucking familiar did he want become? Was he trying to provoke me? I replied, almost cautiously.

"Well, Mr *Hobbs*, there was a mirror that rather struck me as being a peculiar piece, but it was not price marked, and it did look expensive. Besides, I was only really looking for a picture." Hobbs beckoned me back through the door onto the shop floor over to where I had placed the mirror.

"Would this be the item?" he questioned. I said it was so, and he proceeded to pick it up and walk over to the old desk. From a drawer he produced some old newspaper and began to wrap it. He continued. "I was not asking much for the mirror by any means, and seeing as you are spending eighty pounds on that picture then I will let you have it for nothing." On reflex I almost began to protest but instead kept quiet, giving Hobbs a perfunctory "thank you, that's most kind". The mirror was wrapped and neatly bound, and the picture was slipped into a cardboard sleeve whilst I counted out eighty pounds.

That was two days ago now; the 24th. I remember very little of the journey back to Portloe, only that I had felt so lucky as to have received a gift that must surely have some worth to someone. I have since, I think, found its worth. Certainly not monetary worth, for the recent occurrences point to it being vaguely alien. An eye for spying. Is Hobbs a spy?

Aug.27th.1924

-The morning is light and clear, and the sea is calm. How often I find my gaze wandering to the sea, staring out to the grey vastness in awe, which then turns quickly to a shuddering fear-

I think this shall be the last day of my writing, so I must be precise in my dialogue, despite the events of last night(26th), in case my fears prove themselves to pass.

The night of the 24th was comparatively uneventful, with dinner being a brief but hearty affair. I had retired to my room early, shortly after eating. My days purchases were placed on the dresser along with my figurine from Scotland. Frowning, I looked carefully at my two parcels. Coincidence though it obviously was, my two parcels were wrapped in exactly the same fashion. Same folding in the same places, as near as could be, and both sealed with brown packing tape. Another little story I could add to tell my friends. Leaving them wrapped, I opened the bedroom window slightly for a touch of fresh air. Being a low first storey window, iron bars ran vertically across to prevent the ingress of unwanted visitors. Undressing, I slid into bed.

That nights sleep was not altogether restful, rather it was more fitful and uneasy. It was not long, it seemed, that I had been asleep when I started dreaming-

-everything was dark at first, until my eyes adjusted to the light. When they had become accustomed I found that I was drifting through deep waters. The sea. No sound reverberated through the misty liquid, and it seemed that I moved in slow motion.

Forces other than my own were guiding me towards some unknown goal, as I swam without any impetus. Slowly into view came a few blocks of green stone, jade, obviously shaped by hand for their angles were too defined with no sign of erosion, although their geometric shape was unimaginably hard to make clear. Drifting closer I could discern the faint outlines of a building in the distance. Small at first, I expected to be within reach of its walls soon, but it was taking an age for them to come any closer. This underwater structure was infinitely bigger than I had first suspected. Eventually I came to within around one hundred feet of the walls, staring in total disbelief. No human could have built this for its geometry was all wrong, and surely could not have stood as it was unsupported. But on a block to my left were the engraved words, 'Built by Randall Smith'.

The walls rose to over four hundred feet before my eyes lost sight of the topmost portions. The architect here (Randall Smith?) must have been a genius or a stark raving madman, for the angles of this structure totally defied every law of physics, geometry and gravity ever applied in science. In this asymmetrical world symmetry was being openly mocked. Order did not belong here. Everything screamed of madness and I found myself starting to feel claustrophobic. Ahead of me yawned a massive stone archway with a pitch black void beyond which light could not penetrate. The portal stood fully one hundred feet high and sixty feet wide. Its topmost portion was carved. Floating closer, a chord of recognition was struck within me, turning quickly to a chord of fear knotting in my stomach. The carving was an exact likeness of that on the mirror, and upon this realisation a wave of panic and nausea swept through me. A feeling of trespass and terror took me, and I felt that I had desecrated some forbidden temple. My breathing was becoming rapid and my claustrophobia growing. An immense feeling of dread began to overwhelm me and I turned to escape only to find that the maddening walls now surrounded me. I glanced in all directions in apprehension of what was to come. From the darkness of the archway I sensed a deep evil emanating, although nothing seemed to stir within. Except bubbles. Small at first, growing slowly larger and rolling round the top of the archway's lintel before spiralling towards the all too distant surface. Staring at the blackness of the doorway was all I could do; I was frozen to the spot in fear. A deep heaviness or oppressiveness swept out of the dark and washed over me, caressing. Movement was impossible, even to turn my head. Heavier and heavier became the pressure of the water until a shape started to emerge into the faint light. A dim shadow at first, which quickly moved forward to float within the archway. Tentacles writhed around the edge of the giant doorway, feeling their way, gripping the stone, getting ready to pull...something through. Stark terror now gripped me and I tried to force a scream but only screamed in silence as from beyond the dark heaved a huge bloated head. Fish, toad? I knew not. Slimy, monstrous, evilly glinting yellow eyes above rows of venomous black teeth and an enormous beak, like that of an octopus. Circling this beak were several more tentacles, tipped with black barbs, roiling towards me to where I floated. Two of these gripped me round the waist and chest, at which I tried to struggle. In vain. It was then that I started to shout and scream like a maniac, but the instant I opened my mouth I felt and then saw tiny little feelers emerge from my throat. Eyes wide in terror and panic like I had never known, I lost all sense of realism, if indeed there were any. Looking back at my nemesis I saw one single tentacle head for me and wrap itself around my neck and to slowly squeeze. The pressure in my head was immense, and as I was drawn up to the foul creatures eyes I could feel my skull begin to crack, when a booming alien voice exploded in my mind, "RANDALL"-

At the instant that voice called, I sat bolt upright in my bed gasping for breath and glaring round the room with wild eyes staring like marbles. A sweat chilled my body, and I remember feeling disorientated, taking a few moments to fully realise where I was. Leaning over and striking a match, I glanced at my watch, seeing that it was only three o'clock in the morning. I was about to blow out the match when I noticed a glistening on the surface of my dresser. Lighting the bedside lamp showed that the whole of the dresser was covered with what I presumed to be condensation, until a cold draught blew across my face. The window was wide open. It had obviously been raining and blew in with the wind. Swinging my legs out of bed to close the window my feet were instantly chilled as they touched the floor. The carpet was also damp, and very cold. It had rained harder than I expected. A quick glance round the room showed that even the walls were dripping wet. I was feeling far too tired to do anything about it at the time and so lay back in bed. But the sheer reality of the dream kept me awake for at least another two hours.

Rising on the morning of the 25th, I found that everything had dried out sufficiently. I felt reasonably good, despite my waking in the early hours, and so decided to spend the day lazing around the countryside. Whilst eating my breakfast that morning, I pondered over the dream from the last night, and at how I was actually holding my breath when I woke up. The realism of my dreaming had seemed fantastic, but then a lot of people feel that way upon waking, some even disappointed that they woke at all. I was not one of those. The slimy green cyclopean walls hinted at some memory I was not able to place, leaving me with a nagging familiarity. But the creature was easy to place. It was from the frame of my mirror and the figurine from Scotland. Images such as these are bound to play tricks on the minds of the weak or the over imaginative. Breakfast finished, I started to make my way to my room to freshen up before wandering outside. It was only when I had reached the foot of the stairs that I noticed how quiet and still everything had gone. Collecting a few items before I set out, I hung the mirror on the coat hook on the back of the door.

One of the precipitous cliff walks took me along the coast towards the West. It was not a strenuous walk by any means but had a steep path here and there when the land rose to the top of a cliff head, yawning away to my left onto the rocks below. Seemingly I had been walking for almost two hours, with various stops along the way, and the time should have been close to midday. My pocket watch told the time as being a quarter to twelve, but the sun was still fairly low and the day had not yet warmed up. My watch must have been running fast, I thought, so I set about adjusting it to an approximate time until I got back. Upon resetting my watch I had the feeling that everything around me was moving at a slow pace, even the waves seeming to break over the rocks and then hang briefly in the air before crashing back down. Apart from the sea there were no other sounds at all. No birds, insects, farm machinery or wind. Nothing. I did not know why this should seem so strange for I was quite isolated, alone on the coast. (Alone? Would that I were.) I decided to turn round and start a slow walk back. This proved stranger.

I had not realised, until my journey back, that the temperature was not rising but instead getting gradually colder. This I could not explain for there was still no wind with a perfectly clear August sky. Still no sound or movement. An uneasiness stole over me and I decided to quicken my pace. Eventually I neared the village and thought that I heard talking from below the cliffs, laughing as well I think, but very soft, and very eerie. My first impressions were that it had been the wind but there still was not the slightest breeze. Then came the feeling of a presence behind me. A stone clattered down the path making me spin round, heart racing. No-one. Then that soft voice again. Malevolent. Not laughing this time but calling out. To me? I could have sworn that it called my name. As I stared up the path another stone came rolling from out of nowhere. It didn't take anymore as panic set in and I turned running downhill towards the village in a blind sprint.

Upon reaching the road I raced up it towards the inn. Still no sound, no movement, no people. Barring the sound of the waves and the voice which still followed behind. Hauling open the front door of the inn I searched for the landlord or whoever else might be within. Empty. The bar, kitchen and dining room were all empty. Yanking out my room key I pounded up the stairs three at a time. Again I could not find a single person. My door was swiftly unlocked and I bowled inside.

(Present-My room is so cold now, and although by my watch a whole day passes, night still has not come. The sun is high above me now, but not moving. That soft but hideous voice still calls from below my window but I dare not look. Those deep wet footsteps are thudding through the earth again. God...I shall need sleep soon.)

The chill inside my room was remarkable. As cold as ice. Crossing to the window, I sought to see if there were any signs of my pursuer. The window would not open and no amount of pulling could move it. But I heard a frantic clicking or scraping on the road below, and a laugh more like a hiss. Quickly turning to the door I was going to risk a glance into the hallway before locking myself inside. But the door, too, was held fast. Frantically looking the room over I noticed that there was a thin sheen of moisture all over the walls, floor and furniture. Then, a musty smell filled the room. Fish? I could not be sure, but it was definitely the smell of the sea tainting the air. The dampness could not be accounted for as my window was shut. Wiping my finger along one wall I tasted the moisture. Saltwater. Seawater. Seawater with the foul stench and taste of dead marine life. Gagging, I spat out the disgusting dew just as a noise from behind made me freeze. It was more of a 'slop', like a wet sponge falling to the floor. Turning slowly with my breath quickening and heart hammering with fear, I saw a piece of thick brown seaweed laying on the floor at the foot of the door. Kelp. And it was wriggling.

Just as I felt confident enough to move towards it and examine it, another piece landed on the first. Staggering backwards and sitting on the bed, I couldn't believe that I had seen it fall from *out of the mirror*.

The surface of the mirror was now shimmering. It became slightly blurred, the sound of the sea grew louder, then the mirror creaked and grew to twice it's size. I needed to scream but my mouth had dried up, and I found myself gibbering. My stomach knotted and tightened when I heard the voice.

"Do not deny us, RANDALL, join Him in his dreams in C'marrah."

I think I must have passed out then, as the horrid laughter echoed through my brain.

It was after this episode that I awoke to my present horror, to which I am now resigned. Certainly there is someone coming for me...I hear Him in my dreams, suggesting things to me, threatening me with aeons of pain as His pale, sickly, wriggling larvae feed upon me for what would be an eternity. Several times I have woken from these nightmares crying.

(My feelings at the time of my waking cannot simply be put

down on paper, except to say that I must have come to terms with the inevitable. If I had not then surely I would be screaming.)

Glancing up from the floor where I had passed out my jaw fell slack, and I remember half shouting or choking something in my fright. The walls of the room were (and are now) layered completely from floor to ceiling in moist brown seaweed, seeming to emanate from the mirror, and disappear within the glass. Standing up, I reeled from dizziness instilled by the foul reek of fish and dead sea life, almost making me sick. I steadied myself on one knee and looked at my watch. It said one-thirty. Also the date had changed to the 26th. Obviously it was still running fast, for it should have been around three-thirty in the afternoon. Unless I had slept for ten hours. If that was so, then the real time was not much past midnight. But still the sun shone.

Another thing that I have noticed about the seaweed on the walls-it gently heaves up and down like it was breathing. What scared me though was when I realised that it matched my own pattern of breathing.

My preoccupation had been so intense that I had not at first noticed that my room had grown colder. I shivered and, rubbing my arms briskly, looked for my overcoat. It lay on the armchair, so I stepped over and quickly donned the thick garment. The chill within my room was now starting to frost the window. My breath fogged as I blew into my hands. Still the room got colder, with the temperature dropping noticeably by the second, making my teeth begin to chatter. I sat on the bed and wrapped blankets around my shoulders to retain any heat I could. The speed of the frosting was ridiculous. My nose, cheeks and fingers started to numb and my respiration was short and painful; my eyes began to close, feeling an unending desire to drop to sleep.

Then warmth. A wave of room temperature washed over me. A blessed release. The numbness left my fingers, replaced by an itching as they warmed. Outside was a typical summers day.

My attention was brought abruptly back round to the mirror when I heard a watery, bubbling noise. Staring at it, slightly confused, I moved slowly towards it until I could see the surface shimmering again. The bubbling ceased and was followed by a deep, regular echoing that I could only describe as giant footsteps, emanating from the very ground below me. Slow and heavy, they vibrated up from the foundations of the village itself. They became louder and closer, until I thought that they would burst through the door of my confined room. Until the noise lessened and moved farther away. Towards the sea? Pipes. Can I hear pipes?

The seaweed still matches my breathing.

I now hear soft voices, sighing in despair, becoming clearer, the moans and cries of tortured souls. Piercing screams and a bubbling, gibbering madness of laughter of those that had lost their minds. In the midst of all this noise, a face was growing in the mirror. It seemed that it was travelling from up inside the depths of the glass, small at first but growing steadily bigger. An old mans face. Familiar yet alien. Standing mesmerised, the face burst from the mirror, hanging out of the frame, staring with jet black eyes, themselves like inky mirrors. No pupils. No life. No soul. Apart from the ones stolen. It spoke a single word to me.

"COME", before folding in on itself and disappearing backwards within the glass, which became immediately still.

Evening?

There is no circulation of air in my room. It is musty and stifling. The seaweed heaves gently as if asleep.

As far as I can tell, it has been about five hours since the face last appeared. Nothing has changed. Outside is quiet and still.

The room is now becoming more odious and offensive. I can hear the sea, but it is coming from the mirror. Whatever happens will be very soon. Would that I had my father's old service revolver. I could have put a bullet through my head long ago. When I come to think of it…There is movement from the mirror…

Cornish newspaper clipping reads as follows

<u>27th August 1924</u>

At seven o'clock yesterday morning, local fishermen from out of Portloe found a body floating face down in the sea near the cliffs a mere three hundred yards from their small harbour. The deceased was said to have drowned, but no specific details concerning the bodies apparent "bizarre state" can as yet be ascertained. The body was of a young man, about early to mid-twenties, and was believed to have been staying nearby.

No more information can be gleaned from the Police at this time…

Notes from P.C. Dants report-Falmouth Police Station

<u>29th August 1924</u>

…the deceased, named as Randall Smith, architect by trade, was not a local man. He lived in the South East of England, and was staying at the Ship Inn at Portloe whilst taking some leave from his employer. Previous to this Mr Smith had been holidaying in Scotland…

…Mr Smiths family have been informed of his death and the circumstances surrounding it. They are due to arrive in Falmouth later on tonight or first thing tomorrow morning (30th). We also contacted Mr Smiths Scottish relatives, who were asked the whereabouts of a 'tea shop' close to Loch Ness. Apparently there are no shops of that kind in the area. We have chased up the lead on the antique shops in Falmouth. The first mentioned in Smiths account is genuine, dealing in furniture and the like, with the proprietor being a well respected dealer on that corner of the market. The other shop does not exist. All that we found was an empty building with windows boarded over. That is how it has stood for the past six years…

31st August 1924

...Mr Smith was not known to have had any enemies, outstanding debts or ever a crossed word with anyone. We are regarding this case as suspicious but are not as yet ruling out suicide or misadventure. The Coroner will determine the cause of death...

...the diary Mr Smith had been writing dated from the 24th to the 27th August, leaving a large question mark. He was last seen by the landlord of the Ship Inn on the morning of the 25th. Smith was found dead on the 26th, yet an entry in his diary clearly states the 27th. Perhaps a lapse of memory? It is still very puzzling, especially considering the bizarre condition of his body...

...the Coroner knows an excellent psychoanalyst who he hopes can give an insight on Smiths state of mind from the information we have. Still a fairly recent science, psychoanalysis...

Excerpts from the Coroners report.

31st Aug. 1924.

...upon initial examination the cause of death can only be that of drowning. No bruises, lesions, cuts, burns or any other sign of a forced struggle or possible accident are apparent, barring the red circular marks around his legs and lower torso. These marks are raised slightly above the flesh, and look for all the world like giant squid rings. Hmmm, too many stories of the sea as a boy put that in my head. Smith was brought to me with his left hand clutching a mirror, which proved quite a task to release. The mirror has no particular fascination...

2nd Sep. 1924

...and when Davies saw the marks he confirmed what I had took to be only flight of fancy. The rings were indeed made by a giant squid or octopus. But I did point out that the rings were six to seven inches in diameter. Davies merely shrugged...

...according to Smiths G.P. he had never suffered from any skin complaint/disorder in his life. Yet once his body had dried out sufficiently I could see that it was covered with small dry scales, not unlike those of a fish. He was diagnosed as having suffered from an acute form of Icthyosis. The degree of this condition would have been impossible to keep out of the public eye, yet his family insist that he had never suffered from anything like this, and wasn't one for staying indoors...

3rd Sep. 1924

...it has been found that Smith was told to take leave from his employer as he was having 'difficulty at work'. He had apparently claimed to hear voices on occasion, and hallucinated several times. Smith had confided to his G.P. that the voices sometimes said 'objectionable' things and that he was feeling increasingly persecuted. By whom he did not say. Much of his unstable condition is borne out in his diary...

...no drug use was known or found. He was not an alcoholic and was in good physical health, aside from the inexplicable case of Icthyosis...

...as far as we can tell Smith could have been suffering from a psychological condition known as Dementia Praecox or Schizophrenic Psychoses which may have driven him to suicide...

...with my side of the case now closed-or taken as far as is humanly possible?-Smiths effects will be handed over to his family. All except for the mirror, for I have been told that it has been misplaced...

END

My Brother Jim By S.J.Thompson-Balk

Most towns and cities in the surrounding 200,000 square miles had been laid waste, devastated following a series of tragedies. Totally unrelated incidents, but having knock on effects, happening within short periods of each other wiping out many of the inhabitants, or deforming them into bands of freaks, weirdo's, and cannibals due to lack of, or contamination of, food.

Some of the cannibals had been referred to as 'wasters', but that was only due to the state of their bodies and minds, slowly being eaten away by the unknown disease running rampant across the countryside. They were voracious. Vicious. Thought of nothing but food. Using anything alive as food. No chefs here. These folks liked their food raw, and still screaming.

Most people had been affected by the outbreak of the disease, nicknamed 'the wasting'. A lot of these died in the giant meteor shower that ravaged the county like a huge hail storm, destroying buildings and setting fire to almost everything. Even more died when a nuclear power station was hit by a meteor, taking out a third of the building in one hit and the rest in the explosion that followed. Radiation clouds floated like the caps of hanging judges, slowly brushing the land and leaving it's taint.

Those that had survived the wasting had been immune, carriers only. Out of these, the ones that survived the meteor shower and radiation, and there were very few, now faced a battle to stay alive.

The prison truck was the only serviceable vehicle that Alex could find. Everything else had been burnt, blown up, crashed or torn to bits for spare parts. He was able to siphon two hundred or so gallons of fuel into jerry cans, so there was at least enough for three or four weeks searching. Three or four weeks of crawling at 15-20mph, looking for someone for his brother, Jim. Jim was laid up in the secured rear of the truck with a broken leg and a rifle wound in the shoulder. For the most part he was quiet, until the truck hit a pothole or debris and then he would moan or grunt.

"You okay, bro?" Another moan from the back. "Don't worry, we'll get you someone real soon."

Sandy had been running from the waster for five days now. Wherever she hid he eventually sniffed her out, gibbering and drooling as he came. She had first seen him after he had killed a young woman, the only other survivor Sandy knew of. Her name was Nicky, a pretty brunette of about twenty five. They had talked to each other across the street from separate buildings for three days, and Nicky had decided to make the run across to Sandy. She never made it. One of the bodies laying in the street was not dead as they had thought. It wasn't entirely stupid either. It lay there, waiting, thinking, wanting, getting hard at the thought. Until it heard the careful footsteps turn into a run. Then it looked up and lunged, ran twenty feet and side-swiped Nicky from her feet, sending her down on her back, unconscious. It tore viciously at her track bottoms, exposing the bare flesh from her stomach down. The waster sat there between her legs staring, giggling to itself like a child, whilst tugging furiously at it's huge cock. A moment later and it had come over it's own hand. He licked it off and started to prod Nicky, trying to wake her. She came around and immediately started to scream, panic and desperation shaking her entire body. In a voice that bubbled like phlegm, the waster just said "Dinner", and smiled as he tore open her stomach with a shard of glass. He ate while Nicky gasped.

That had done it for Sandy and she screamed. She went cold and a metallic taste of fear crept into her mouth. Her first reaction had been to hide when the waster saw her at the window. She should have moved out, changed buildings, but she had panicked.

Now she was waiting for that filthy piece of shit to rumble her hideout again. She was weak from hunger and could not keep running like this. There had to be a better way to go than being raped, torn apart and eaten.

A distant rumbling, quiet, echoed down the street. She was hiding on the ground floor of a pharmacy, behind a cabinet laying on it's side. There had not been any sound of the waster for at least two hours and everything else was quiet. Closer now the rumbling came. It was plainly a vehicle, a truck or van by the sound of it, not travelling too fast, maybe looking for survivors. Now or never, she thought. Get up, move and run. Fear froze her and she squeezed her eyes to shut it out. A tin can rattled ten feet behind her. That did it. Heart hammering she scrambled over the cabinet and headed for the door.

Alex sang along to the song on the tape he played on his portable radio – Another One Bites The Dust by Queen. He heard a distant scream. Up ahead a figure ran out from a derelict store front straight towards his truck. Behind this figure lumbered a waster, dressed only in a tattered once-white t-shirt. Alex pulled up to a halt, reached across to the passenger seat for his rifle and climbed out.

Sandy ran for all she was worth towards the truck. Glancing quickly back she could she the waster coming, grinning it's idiot grin and licking it's cracked bloodied lips. She turned back to the truck and saw it stop. Then a man got out holding a gun. She started to get edgy again. What if this man was no better than the wasters? But what if he was better? There was no choice but to head towards him.

Sandy watched him lift the rifle. "Don't move", he shouted. She had barely stopped when the weapon cracked out it's shot and the air buzzed beside her ear. Behind her came the sound of a cane striking a piece of leather. Her head whipped round in time to see the waster spin and drop to the floor, the back of it's head a gaping chasm.

"Get over here, quick", Alex shouted. Sandy needed no further encouragement and she sprinted the fifty yards to the truck and jumped in the passenger side. She sat sobbing as Alex climbed back in and then looked at him with red rimmed eyes.

"Thank you, I can't believe I've found anyone else alive." Alex started the truck forward again.

"Well, you're safe now. I have a little food and water that I've picked up, and I think that the three of us should move out somewhere quieter."

"Three of us?" Sandy questioned.

"Yeah, my brother Jim is in the back. One broken leg and a

hole in his shoulder. Bullet. He needs some attention." There was a moan from the rear as Jim heard his name.

"Well," Sandy said, "I know basic first aid, so that may help."

They came to sparse hillside outside of the town. Having no cover or hiding places it was the ideal spot for a brief rest, giving a wide view of the surrounding area. Alex and Sandy got out of the truck and moved to the back.

"Best we see how he is doing." Alex started unlocking the doors while Sandy grabbed a first aid kit from the front. She ran round the back and only saw the butt of the rifle before pain and blackness exploded from her forehead.

Everything was blurred, hazy. One voice was muttering somewhere near her. Another was moaning close by. Sandy opened her eyes. It had got dark out and the only light was shining from an old tilley lamp which she looked at upside down. She was inside the rear of the truck on her back, naked and held down at her wrists and ankles with her head towards the doors. The outline of Alex stood holding the lamp. Lifting her head and looking towards the interior she saw furtive movements in the shadow.

"What are doing?" she sobbed, struggling with her bonds.

"I'm watching", said Alex, his voice low and monotone. He reached into his pocket and pulled out a small white sachet, tearing the corner off. Leaning over Sandy's outstretched body he sprinkled the contents over her pussy and thighs. "Sugar. He's got a sweet tooth, y'know." Then looking up to the back of the truck he said, "Come and get it." There was a shuffling that made Sandy jerk her head back up. The face that came into the light stopped her breath. It was pale, lifeless, skin hanging off of one cheek, saliva dripping down it's chin past lips that were smacking in anticipation. In one hand it held a knife.

"Dinner," the figure gurgled.

"W…Waster," Sandy screamed

"My brother Jim," said Alex proudly.

Small Indiscretions by Christian Ayling

It was a cold autumn day. Jane jogged through the park, her daily routine in which she nutted out the problems of the world, at least her world.

This particular day was colder than usual. Her problems so much more wearing than ever before. She had to clear her head. Greg, her loving but distant husband, was trying to save his struggling company. He was always so serious. The responsibility of providing for his family was a heavy burden; she could see it in his eyes. She felt so lonely. It wasn't always like this. What happened to the days when they used to race each other to the phone when it rang, both too hysterical to even make sense to the poor person on the other end, or when they'd spend all day in bed just talking and being playful with one another. Now they barely spoke, he was too busy trying to avoid financial ruin. He didn't enjoy life anymore and he didn't enjoy her either. Still, he was doing all the things that were required of a good husband. He helped around the house, put food on the table and was faithful.

Jane felt out of breath. She didn't often stop during her jog, but her drive that day was low to say the least.

Whilst walking to the water fountain, she noticed a young couple in their twenties rolling around on the lawn laughing and carrying on. She felt envious of them. That was her, ten years ago. It seemed more like a lifetime ago. The water cooled her thoughts at least for a moment. That's all she ever had, moments. Nothing much, just a touch of happiness here or there, most of which came from the kids. "Are you right?" said a well modulated voice from behind. "There are others in line here you know."

Jane released her hand from the tap immediately and turned around ready to abuse the rude man for his impatience. To her surprise, there wasn't a line of people like the man inferred. There was just one man with a smiley, goofy look on his face. Her mood softened, he was just having a lend of her. He looked vaguely familiar. Brown eyes, average height, muscles that would be the envy of all men and last but not least, something Jane always found endearing, a dimple on each cheek, accentuating his smile. "Please, don't let me stop you, your royal highness," she taunted. He laughed and took a sip of water from the fountain. His mouth touching the spout where hers had been. Jane didn't know why she was still standing there. Their moment had finished. The joke was over. He turned around and smiled once again. It drove her crazy. His teeth were so white, like he was off a tooth paste commercial. This man could sell her anything. "Are you going for seconds?" he asked in a jovial tone. Jane felt like a silly little schoolgirl who had a wild crush on her teacher. Forbidden lust, probably all one sided, making it all the more exciting. "My name's Damon, " he said, holding his hand out.

They exchanged meaningless chatter as they walked along the path towards the swimming center. All the normal, light hearted conversation that took little investment or energy. 'Great weather isn't it?' 'Do you come here often?' 'Have we met?' "Do you want to go for a swim?" "What was that?" she politely asked, not sure if she'd heard him right. Damon set upon her with his weapon of mass destruction, a dimply smile. "I was just heading to the pool to do some laps, want to join me? I'll understand if you don't, I mean, not many people can out lap me so if you're….." Jane stopped him in his tracks. "You think you're so smug don't you? I could whip your butt buddy," she said rising to the challenge. Jane's competitive streak set in. Even beating her husband to the phone was a competition she just couldn't resist. "Sure, why not," she said, "I don't have anywhere else to be."

As they neared the pool, Jane had second thoughts about swimming with this man, as much as she wanted to. "I don't have any bathers," she said, thinking that would be the end of that, but Damon had an answer for everything.

After letting him buy her some bathers from the swim shop, she promised to pay him back.

They parted as they went into separate change rooms. Jane sat on the bench seat, thinking about whether to get changed or not. She could just duck out and he'd be none the wiser. But what if she bumped into him when jogging? She'd have to change her route. Why did she feel like she was cheating? It was just a swim. This is silly, she thought as she started to change into her bathers. He'd brought her a skimpy two piece. "He wishes," she laughed.

After putting her t-shirt over the bathers, she met Damon at the pool ladder. Wow, he was hot. He wore black, shiny speedos that told a story of their own. He didn't even give her a second glance as he dove into the pool. As hurtful as that was, it was for the best. He was a bit of a show off, splashing around like a performing dolphin. Jane could tell it was for her benefit. "Come on, let's go," he challenged. Jane swam over to the edge of the pool ready to race, the mood less flirtatious than before.

"Go!" shouted Damon as he pushed off from the edge. Jane had no hope; he was in his prime, at least 10 years her junior. She eventually caught up with him; her heart wasn't in it. Jane didn't even know why she was swimming with this man whom she had only just met. What was I thinking?

As she turned to climb out of the pool, Damon pulled her over to him like she was his possession. "You did well," he said in what Jane perceived to be a patronising tone. "Thank you," she responded politely. "You're very beautiful," said Damon like a bolt out of the blue. "I'm sure you say that to all the ladies," she quipped as she pulled away. "You're different," he said, without denying the womanising inference.

He placed his hand on her face and they kissed. Jane pulled away, Damon pushed in harder. He was so forceful. His arms wrapped around her, they locked together in a passionate embrace like the two young lovers Jane had seen earlier in the park. She felt loved, beautiful and wanted. Jane's inhibitions flew out the window. She could live with the fact she'd kissed another man, but they were heading beyond the point of no return. There were only two other people in the pool, playing and splashing down the other end, oblivious to the fact that a mother of two was committing adultery in a public pool in which her family often swam together.

Jane couldn't believe she'd allowed him to go further. Her body experiencing overwhelming bliss, her mind in torment. She'd never been with any other man but her husband and certainly never in a public place. Greg was conservative and predictable, same place, same time, same channel; just like clockwork. Damon appeared to be the complete opposite, although she didn't know him, his actions spoke clearly. He knew what he wanted and he wanted it now, he couldn't wait another minute to ravish her. Jane's breathing was shallow but evident, her guilt the same. Damon's head now rested on her shoulder.

As the warm feeling started to fade, her guilt now began to strengthen. Damon lifted his head to regain composure. "Thank you," he said as if she'd done him a favour. "Meet you at the gate," he added swimming towards the ladder. As he grabbed his towel, he walked toward the change room. Jane's mind started to go numb. Her mind too numb to process what had just happened.

She reached the change room and took a warm shower.

Oh my god, oh my god, what have I done? A shower wasn't going to make her feel any cleaner. Panic set in. She immediately grabbed her belongings. I don't want to see him, she thought heading toward the exit. Damon was nowhere to be seen. He was probably enjoying a shower, thinking about his encounter. Jane started to wonder if he was married. If he was, it wouldn't matter. He'd just go home, kiss the wife and never give it another thought. Men are all the same, except for Greg. Greg! She had to tell him. It may be hard for a while, but they could work through it. It happens all the time.

No one gave Jane a second glance as she ran through the streets in her bathers. She reached her home, grabbing the keys from her pocket. She felt colder than ever. Maybe she could just accept it as one of those things, not tell Greg, and just swear to herself that she'd never do it again. What would telling him do? He was the type of man who'd rather not know and just keep living his boring, predictable life. Like the time she dinted their new car whilst Greg was away on business. She could've just got it fixed without telling him and he'd be none the wiser, but she had to own up and confess. He turned around and said, 'I would've rather not know, why didn't you just fix it?'

This was one of those times. That's what Jane had to do; she had to 'just fix it,' change her jogging path and she'd never see him again. Anyway, Greg sort of pushed her towards this by neglecting her needs. Maybe if she works on Greg a bit more, it may improve their relationship and this whole thing would've actually helped their marriage. Jane could put it down as a learning experience. This could be a good thing. The first day of their new life. Jane took a deep breath, exhaled and smiled. Yes, she was going to turn this negative into a positive.

If only it were that easy. Everyday was a battle. Being intimate with Greg, sleeping at night, focusing on simple tasks, nothing seemed to ease her guilt. But living with guilt somehow seemed easier than facing life without Greg.

Jane looked at herself in the mirror. Even though it'd only been two weeks since her indiscretion, it was like she'd aged incredibly. It was beginning to wear her down.

"Are you ready honey?" asked Greg, eager to get to his business dinner. Jane didn't want to go but she always accompanied Greg to those sorts of things.

On arrival to the restaurant, they were greeted by Edmond Clarke, Greg's business partner. "I'm sorry Mrs. Clarke couldn't make it tonight, she has a migraine." She always had a migraine, being rich must have been one big headache, or maybe it was just being married to a snob like Mr. Clarke. Jane reluctantly pecked him on the cheek. Edmond felt her dislike for him. He was scrupulous in business, and probably the cause of their financial mess.

They sat and made small talk for a while, Jane looking decidedly bored. As her eyes flicked passed the door, she noticed a familiar face, Damon's. She looked away hoping he wouldn't notice her sitting at the table with her husband and his associate. She gave a quick glance back. Damon was walking toward her. Surely he knew she was married, although they never got that far in conversation. She looked up; there he was, standing right at her table. She swallowed, her heart pounding fast, blood rushing to her head. He looked good, dressed in a black suit, she felt bad for having lustful thoughts. If she introduced Damon to her husband, he was sure to get the hint and make an excuse for a quick exit. Greg looked at Damon and smiled. "Mr. Hardwood, thank you for coming," Greg said as he stood up to shake Damon's hand. Greg knows him? Jane hadn't asked Damon for his last name. Greg had spoken of this Mr. Hardwood before. He was the young gun who'd offered to buy Greg out. "Please, call me Damon," he said, staring at Jane. "Oh sorry," said Greg, "this is Jane, my wife." Damon stood up, leaned in and kissed her hand. "Cut it out," joked Greg. "She has a jealous husband," he added like he was some kind of stand up comic. The men laughed and continued to talk business. Jane tried not to look at Damon, but found it very hard. She was trying to read his thoughts. How could he act so calmly? He totally ignored her as if she was just the wife of a business associate. Jane didn't eat much of her entrée or main course. She wanted to leave as soon as possible. Maybe she could fake a migraine; it worked for Mrs. Clarke.

The discussion between the men was starting to get quite heated. "I'm not selling my half of the business, I know we can get it back on track," said Greg appealing to Edmond. But Edmond had a different agenda. He wanted Greg to sell his share to Damon so he would have the young gun as his business partner. "Damon can bring this company out of the red, he'll do whatever it takes. Look, it's not like this isn't a fair offer." Damon pushed a cheque across the table, 1.2 million dollars. It looked good on paper, but Greg had worked too hard to sell out now and besides, they owed the bank much more than that.

"I have to go to the gentleman's room," snapped Greg as he got up from the table. "I'll be back in a minute honey," he added. Jane felt very uncomfortable. At least Edmond was staying; the last thing she wanted was to be left alone with Damon.

Damon grabbed his briefcase off the floor and placed it carefully on the table. Instead of the two men talking business amongst themselves; their attention turned to Jane. "We have to talk quickly," said Edmond, as Damon grabbed a yellow envelope out of his case. "Jane," Edmond said sternly, "you need to convince Greg to sell; it's in your best interest, if you know what I mean. I'm assuming he doesn't know about your small indiscretion?" Jane couldn't believe it; they were asking her to sell Greg out. "It's up to Greg, I believe in him. If he thinks he can get the company out of debt, then he can," said Jane in her husbands defence. She felt like a hypocrite playing the good wife when Damon knew different. Damon slid the yellow envelope over to Jane. "I'm not signing a contract," snapped Jane as she looked away. "It's not a contract," said Damon, "it's photo's. I don't think I need to tell you what they're of." Jane was flabbergasted. They were blackmailing her into siding with them. "You set me up?" cried Jane, trying to fight the tears, "I was just a business transaction to you?" Edmond jumped in to prevent a large scene from occurring. "Look, no one has to know. Just convince Greg to sell his share to Damon." Jane was too angry. Not at the two businessmen, but at herself. She'd cheated on her husband once and now she'd have to do it again. "The choice is yours," said Damon.

A waitress stood at the table, waiting for a pause in conversation. "Excuse me," she said, "would you like to order hot drinks?" "No thank you," answered Jane sharply as her anger built, "this is my mistake and I'll fix it."

Greg walked over to the table, observing a very upset Jane. He assumed it was over the insulting offer and had had words with the two men over it. "What's the envelope for?" asked Greg. "Nothing," Jane said as she passed it back to Damon. "We're going," announced Greg as he grabbed his jacket. Damon stood and kissed Jane's cheek. "You still owe me fifteen bucks for the bathers," he whispered with a sly smile. Jane felt sick to her stomach. She'd been taken for a ride and didn't even see it coming.

On the way home, silence filled the car as they both thought about their next move. Jane was fooling herself into thinking that her mistake could just be swept under the carpet. Her husband had put his heart and soul into that company, even to the detriment of their marriage. This was the perfect opportunity to be rid of the very thing distracting him from being the husband Jane yearned for. As much as she wanted to, she couldn't. "What do you think I should do?" asked Greg, looking for his wife's reassurance. Jane looked at Greg and saw a vulnerability she'd never seen before. He loved her so much and would probably take her word as gospel. Right then, at that moment, she felt her words were un-deserving of being heard. "I think you should follow your dream," she said as she looked out the window.

As the weeks passed, Jane kept waiting for her husband to come home with the yellow envelope in his hand screaming, "Why? How could you do this to me?"

She couldn't bare it anymore; Jane had to confess her infidelity. She arranged for the kids to go to her mothers.

That night, over dinner, Jane and Greg had a chance to talk like a normal couple, without distractions. "We should do this more often," smiled Greg, gazing into his wife's eyes. Rolling her finger around the wine glass, Jane had an epiphany. All this time, she had thought her husband was the problem, but it was her. She didn't appreciate who he was, only focusing on what he wasn't. "Greg, I have something to tell you," Jane said, not believing herself at what she was about to do. She knew that saying those words out loud would shame her. "You know that night with Edmond and Damon at the restaurant? They gave me a yellow envelope with something in it. Something that I'm not proud of," she confessed as tears streamed down her face. Greg held Jane's hands and smiled. "They gave me the envelope the next day after I refused the offer," he admitted. "But I put it in my drawer without opening it. Do you want me to see what's in that envelope?" Jane shook her head, not able to speak. Greg squeezed her hands. "My love and my trust for you outweighs whatever could be in the envelope," Greg said so affectionately. "I have to tell you," she said pushing Greg's hands away. Greg interrupted, "just answer me this. Do you regret what you did?" he asked as he stood up. Jane nodded and looked away to hide her tears. "Then it's over, I don't want to know."

Greg held Jane tightly, like he never had before. Jane felt released from her guilt. She loved her husband and everything was going to be okay. "Do you want to hear something funny?" laughed Greg. "The company went bust today, it's gone. It's over!" Jane looked surprised by her husband's odd reaction. He smiled and then continued, "the funny part being that Damon bought me out yesterday. He was so anxious to seal the deal, that he paid 1.6 million into our account this morning. It's enough to cover what we owed the bank, plus these," he said, as he revealed two plane tickets to Bermuda. Jane smiled, thinking about the uncertainty of life. With the twist and turns of late, she knew just one thing, Greg may not be the most impulsive man in the world, but his love for Jane was real, and nothing was more certain than that.

Christmas by Pawel Podolak

For my son Irwin

„What to do?" – he has wondered for more than six hours. He always wanted to have a son, but at so high cost? His advisers say that this is the only way to do it. But could he convict his only child for such a terrible death in the name of his paternal ambitious? On the other hand, hasn't He, Almighty, the right to real moments connected with parenthood; happiness of first grimaces, steps and words? He created a human being using Himself as a pattern, so it's obvious that He has the same desires. To have a child. His own child. Blood from His blood, flesh from His flesh, soul from soul. Is it too much? "What to do?". Nobody forced Him to make the decision quickly, but He felt that the time has just came. They even chose the son's parents on Earth. He is to be a carpenter's child. This is – as they say - the best solution for everyone. No manor houses or palaces. Just an ordinary cot. Giving a birth is to be in a stable. The only thing He forced a warm climate. Especially in December. A schedule of his life is also already prepared. And of his death. The only thing to do is to make the decision. But what will He tell him after all of that? Would he understand, that He had to act this way? That there were no other solutions? Wouldn't His son accuse Him for trading him on? That all those things were just to give the proof? Would he believe in a real father's intentions? On the other hand would He be able to reward for all the pain to His child afterwards? Questions, questions, questions...

He slowly rose His eyes onto the advisors. Took a deep breath, as if He tried to make Himself more confident (does He???). "I agree. – He said finally – Send an angel."

Twenty first century catharsis by Pawel Podolak

Once upon a time, being a novice writer, I wrote a story. A man saw a manikin with a very vulgar make up standing behind the exposure glass of the female clothes shop. The stream of thoughts and feelings was taking him to the "red light" district but the whole story was just a pretext for the deliberation about the condition of a human being. During a meeting with my readers, one of them (critics were not interested in my art at all at that time) asked me a question: "How possible was it to live through all those things I wrote about, being so young ?" - I really saw disbelief in his eyes. I answered, of course, I did not experience any of these things, and the situation was just created in my mind as a pretext to say a few words about things that I recognised as the most important. As proof I asked a question "Must a writer of a detective story have killed somebody to write about murder?" The answer seemed to be obvious.

I didn't know whether he believed in what I said. But what could I tell him, if that was the truth?

However, when I came back home I started to think about the reader's question (I did not have in the end so many readers and questions). Rejecting the most literal meaning of living through the written facts, there was a great deal of thoughts connected with the considered facts. There was a possibility that if you thought about them, you would do it the same way you thought about it if they would take place in real life. If so, perhaps at the "mind" level there is no difference between created and real life? Going deeper, feeling are caused by thoughts – aren't we crying (although less and less frequently) with heroes of books we read? So if the reader's affection resulted in tears or anger, why not to go further and suspect that the author writes about the real affections? If so, what is the difference between things the writer lived through in real life and the ones created in his mind?

And suddenly I got the point! This is Great Thing that was on the Great People's minds, who were paying citizens for taking part in a theatrical performance two and a half thousands years ago. Eureka!

The Summer Adventure by Pawel Podolak

One summer evening we were coming back home with our son, who was two-years-old at that time. It was just after finishing one of the garden parties organised by one of my many cousins. This is the advantage of being part of a big family – there's always someone's birthday or some anniversary to celebrate. So we were going home, travelling mostly on country roads, some of which were difficult to call even a track. It was about 9 o'clock in the evening and Our Little Boy started to send signals that he was hungry and tired. Unfortunately to get home it was another 30 km, so – as usual – we decided not to understand the louder and louder signs of tiredness given by Our Son and just listen to another attack of the groans. The sun was setting in a picture postcard way, showing to us all kinds of yellows and reds (I heard that these colours in the sky meant that the next day would be sunny and warm). So we were just driving through bend in the road, when suddenly … nothing happened. Nobody appeared on the road asking for help. There were no animals unexpectedly crossing our way forcing me to prove how good driver I was after travelling behind the wheel for one million kilometres. No single drop of rain fell on the window of the car, dirty with dead flies and mosquitoes which didn't spread their flesh on the glass, decreasing the visibility. Nothing. Absolutely nothing. However there was something in that moment that caused till this day, many years after this summer as well as the age of Our Son, I have remembered this trip. Perhaps it was a fact, that during that single moment the sense that my life has been completely fulfilled. I needed nothing more. There was She, Our Little Boy and me, with the sun beautifully setting over our heads. And the big group of my cousins, with their children behind us and our house with a garden ahead.

I think it was the reason why this single moment, when absolutely nothing happened, won the competition for the most beautiful moment in my life.

Gargoyle Grin by Ruth Glover

Libby scowled. She didn't like this house with its creaky floorboards; she didn't like the jungle of weeds in the garden and she didn't like the quiet village. She wanted to go back to the city where she had lived for the full seven years of her life.

She wandered miserably over to the old, dry well and perched on the wall. If only she hadn't got sick, she thought glumly. If she hadn't got sick then they wouldn't have moved to the middle of nowhere.

She picked up a stone and dropped it into the well, listening for a splash or a thud as it struck the bottom. Instead, she heard a sharp yelp.

"Ow! That hurt!"

Libby looked round, thinking that someone must be playing a trick on her. "Who's there?" she called angrily.

"It's me, and that hurt!" the voice replied.

Libby looked round again, but she still couldn't see anybody. "Where are you?" she demanded. "Stop hiding, it isn't funny!"

"I'm not hiding!" the voice shouted back indignantly. "I'm in the well!"

Libby gasped and jumped off the wall. Peering down, she tried to see the bottom, but the well was too deep and the shadows were too dark.

"Are you all right?" she called anxiously. "Are you hurt?"

"Well," the voice sounded slightly mollified. "No. But it's so dark and lonely down here."

Libby heard a slight sniff, and she immediately felt terrible. "Wait!" she shouted. "I'll get you out! I'll get help! I promise!"

She hurried up the garden path, but she'd only gone a very short distance when her legs gave way and she sagged to the ground, trembling with exhaustion. She was so weak!

Libby tried to crawl towards the house, and her father found her on the path, sobbing and gasping on her hands and knees.

"Libby!" he cried worriedly. "What happened?"

He rushed to her side and scooped her up as if she weighed no more than a doll, and as soon as she could talk, Libby explained about the voice in the well, and how she was trying to get help.

"I couldn't go on, Daddy!" she wailed miserably. "I tried so hard, but I couldn't do it, and the Voice is trapped in the well! Please help him, Daddy!"

"Shh," soothed Daddy, carrying her to her bedroom. "Shh, it's okay, Libby. I'll go down to the well and sort it out. Now you just wait here; you've been very sick and you need to rest."

"But you'll help him…" Libby repeated urgently. "You'll get him out of the well?"

"Yes, Libby," Daddy smiled reassuringly. "If there's anyone down there I'll get them out."

Libby sagged back against the pillows and closed her eyes. Daddy would sort it out, she told herself drowsily. It would be okay.

An hour later, Daddy stood in the doorway, looking in at his sleeping daughter. He was troubled and after a few minutes he quietly went downstairs.

"How is she?" asked Jenny, the cheerful woman who helped him clean the house.

Daddy sighed. "I don't know," he said wearily. "I'm afraid she might be getting worse. She heard voices in the well and I found her crawling up the garden to get help, but I've just been down to the well and there's nobody there."

"Don't worry, Sir " Jenny said comfortingly. "She's been very sick; it'll take a while before she's right again. Just give her time."

Behind the door, Libby bit her lip. She had overheard the conversation and the idea that the voice wasn't real bothered her. It meant that she wasn't getting better at all, and she was tired of being sick.

Silently, Libby decided that she would be well again by Christmas. It was the first week of September so she had nearly four months to get strong and healthy again.

"I will do it!" Libby promised herself. "And I'll go back to the well and see if there really was a voice or not!"

She began to think about how she could help herself get well. She needed to eat properly, she thought; lots of fruit and vegetables, and food with iron in.

She'd heard the doctor talk about food with iron in, and she had been afraid that she would have to eat bits of metal, but Daddy had explained that the iron in food was a vitamin and not lumps of metal at all.

But, she mused, sitting down on the bottom step and thinking hard; food wouldn't be enough. She had to make her arms and legs strong again, and that meant exercise.

Before the illness, she used to run around with her friends, but she didn't know anybody here, so she would have to exercise on her own.

Maybe, she thought, she could find a skipping rope. A skipping rope would help her to get fit.

Libby worked diligently at her plan. The next day, it took her an hour to get to the well, and when she reached it, she leaned over the side and called down.

"Is anybody down there?"

"Still here," came the gloomy voice. "In the dark. Oh, how lonely I am."

"Don't worry," Libby called down. "I'll talk to you, then you won't be so lonely. And I'm building up my strength! Soon I'll be strong enough to come down and help you."

"Thank you!" cried the voice tearfully. "It's so good to have a friend again!"

So everyday, Libby went down the garden, managing a little further without a rest each day. Jenny bought her skipping rope to play with, and everyday she gave Libby an apple, a banana and a fruity cereal bar to take down the garden with her.

Daddy was delighted. Libby had only picked at her food since she'd fallen ill. It was very encouraging to see her asking for fruit and eating all her dinner. Her cheeks had lost their pale, hollow look and her tired eyes looked brighter. For the first time Daddy could believe that his little girl would actually get better.

Summer turned into autumn and the garden became an exotic jungle of red and gold leaves and late blooming flowers. Libby thought it was beautiful, and described it in great detail to her friend down the well, who wished fervently that he could see it too.

"Soon," Libby promised, twirling her skipping rope. "Very soon."

Then, one morning when Libby skipped down the winding path, she noticed there was frost on the ground. She would have to rescue the voice soon, she realised. Otherwise he would freeze when the snow fell.

Next week, she resolved silently. She would be strong enough then, and she could climb into the well and help the voice out.

She worked harder than ever over the next few days. She ate well, even having a second helping of pudding on a couple of days, and she ran and skipped round the garden whenever the weather was fine enough. When it was raining she did push ups and sit-ups in her bedroom to strengthen her arms, back and stomach.

By the Wednesday of the following week she knew she was ready. She found an old sheet and cut it into strips, which she knotted together to make a rope. She tested each knot carefully, and hid it under her coat. She also picked up a torch she'd had for her birthday.

Finally ready, Libby ran down the garden. The wind tugged at her hair and her cheeks glowed from the cold. Her eyes sparkled as she breathed in the cool fresh air and for a moment she felt so healthy and happy that she thought she could almost fly.

She arrived at the well and tied the sheet rope firmly around a sturdy tree. She tied the other end around her waist and climbed into the well. There were some metal rungs fixed on the inside, and Libby used those as well as the rope to lower herself into the darkness.

"I'm coming!" she called down to her friend. "I'm coming to rescue you!"

For the first time since she'd dropped the pebble on his head, the voice didn't answer. Libby climbed down faster, until at last her feet stood on the damp, squishy ground.

She turned the torch on and looked round. It was dark and dank and gloomy.

"Where are you?" she called softly. "I'm here! Where are you?"

She listened and heard her voice echoing off the glistening bricks. Then, as the last echo died, she thought she heard a hoarse whisper by her feet.

She crouched down curiously, and saw a small, stone creature half buried in the mud. As she examined it with her torch, it lifted its head slightly with a noise like two stones scraping together. There was a very faint light in its eyes and she knew at once that this was the Voice.

"It's you!" she said softly. She reached out and gently tried to wipe some of the mud away. "You're my friend in the well."

"You came," whispered the stony creature faintly. "You came for me!"

A gravelly tear formed in its eye, and its paw reached out to touch her hand. "Thank you," it whispered.

Libby frowned. "What's wrong?" she asked anxiously. "Are you sick? You're so quiet!"

The creature smiled faintly. "You're nearly well," it told her. "You don't need me anymore, so the magic is fading. I will be stone again very soon."

Libby stared at him in horror. The magic only lasted while she was sick? All the time she had been trying to get well so she could save him, she had been killing him!

"What can I do?" she asked, starting to cry. "I don't want you to die!"

"Not dead, Libby," whispered the creature. "Just stone."

There was a moment of silence, then he spoke again and his voice was fainter than ever. "I wish I could see the sun again," he murmured.

Libby wiped her face and stuck the torch in her pocket. Then she untied the rope from her waist and dug her stony friend out of the mud with her hands. Once he was clear, she tied the sheet rope around him firmly.

"I'll get you out," she whispered tearfully. "You'll sit in the sun forever and ever!"

She climbed out of the well, using the metal rungs to pull herself up. Then, when she reached the top, she hauled the rope up. It was hard work, but she persevered until he was out of the well. Kneeling down beside him, she untied the sheet rope and wiped as much of the mud away as possible.

"There you are," she whispered through her tears. "Can you feel the sun?"

"Thank you Libby," the voice was just the faintest murmur now and, with a painful creak, he tilted his face to the winter sun and smiled. Then the light in his eyes went out and he was just a stone gargoyle.

For a long time, Libby just sat beside him and wept. Then she got to work scraping away the rest of the mud. As the dirt came away, she noticed some words carved into the bottom of his stone back. They read 'Gargoyle Grim' but the second arch of the m had worn away so it now said Gargoyle Grin.

Libby smiled. Grin was a much better name for the friend who had encouraged her back to health. Without him, she would still be weak and sickly and miserable. She looked around for a sunny spot in the garden and spotted the old stone sundial. It looked just like a stone mushroom with a flat top, and it caught the sun for most of the day.

She picked him up and carried him carefully over to his new home, placing him right in the middle of the stone disc, where the rays of the sun would fall on him everyday.

Then she gently kissed his stone head. "Thank you, Gargoyle Grin," she whispered, and walked slowly up the garden path towards the house.

Eep's Quest by Ruth Glover

The sun was rising, creeping across the pale, grey sky like spilt syrup, and every time the warm golden rays touched a wild flower, a playing fairy paused and vanished from sight.

The fairies knew that daylight meant danger, but they liked to play in the meadow until the very last shadow had departed.

Grubert Goblin was watching the playful fairies from the bushes. In his stubby, dirty hand he held a small mesh cloth, about the size of a handkerchief, and on his shoulder sat a small, grey bird called Pidge. It looked dirty and scraggly, just like the goblin, and its eyes were sharp and shrewd.

As more fairies popped out of sight, Grubert the Goblin pointed at two fairies called Eep and Jey. Immediately, Pidge took the cloth in its clawed feet and took to the air. Before Eep or Jey knew what was happening, he dropped the little cloth over them.

Jey and Eep squealed in surprise and fear and the rest of the fairies immediately popped away to their dark, safe little nests. Trapped by the mesh, Eep and Jey exchanged fearful glances.

"What are we going to do?" whispered Eep fearfully.

"We have to escape," replied Jey firmly. She tried to move, but the net was too heavy and the weight of it pinned her to the ground.

Eep was wriggling forward on his belly. He found that if he kept his wings folded very flat against his back, he was able to move a little bit. And then, suddenly, he disappeared.

"Eep!" cried Jey in horror. "Eep! Where are you?"

"Down here," came Eep's muffled voice. "I've fallen down a wormhole! Quickly, Jey, we can hide until it's safe."

Jey began to wriggle towards the spot where Eep had disappeared, but she was too late. A great black shadow fell over her, and she just had time to scream once before the thick, grimy fingers of Grubert Goblin plucked her off the ground.

Hidden in the hole, Eep heard Jey's cry and he scrambled out quickly, just in time to see the goblin stumping off across the meadow with his prize clutched in his dirty hand.

He was too late.

Eep climbed onto a toadstool and wept because Jey was his best friend and the thought of never seeing her again was horrible. Then a strange idea came to him.

What if he went after the goblin, and rescued Jey?

The thought took root in his head and he jumped to his feet excitedly. That's what he'd do! He would go after the goblin and save Jey!

He would need a weapon, he thought to himself, and rushed over to the brambly hedgerow, where he selected a long, strong, sharp thorn to use as a sword.

All he needed now was a steed!

Eep thought hard about this, and as he was thinking, a small wren landed on the ground beside him, pecking at the ground without much interest.

This wren would be an ideal steed, Eep thought. I wonder if she will help me.

As if she'd heard his thoughts, the wren fixed one of her bright, inquisitive eyes on the little fairy. "A fairy!" she exclaimed. "I thought you all turned to dust in the sunlight!"

Eep was outraged. "Of course we don't!" he shouted indignantly. "We just like to play in the moonlight! Like..." he thought for a moment, trying to think of other animals that only came out at night. "Like owls, or badgers!" he finished.

"Oh," said the wren, losing interest. She spread her wings, as if she was about to fly away.

"Wait!" Eep cried. "Please help me, Lady Wren. The evil goblin has kidnapped my friend and I have to save her!"

The wren cocked her head to one side, then to the other side. "How terrible," she agreed. "Of course I'll help you!"

Eep jumped up, waving his makeshift sword. "Let's go!" he cried enthusiastically.

He vaulted onto the wren's back and they took to the air, flying after the disappearing goblin as fast as they could.

Grubert lived in a tumbledown little shack in the woods beyond the meadow. It was made from tree branches and moss, and woven grasses and mud, all packed together to make an odd misshapen little house. There was a crooked chimney in the lopsided roof and tiny wisps of smoke puffed out every two or three seconds.

They arrived just in time to see Grubert slam the little door shut.

"Bother!" exclaimed Eep as the door closed. "Now how will we get in?"

"Let's fly around the house," Wren suggested. "Maybe there's an open window we can get through."

Eep agreed that it was a good idea, but unfortunately, all the windows were locked up tight.

Eep began to despair. How could he rescue Jey if he couldn't get to her?

Wren landed on a windowsill and they peered through the grimy glass, trying to see into the gloomy little room. It was difficult to see anything, but Eep thought he could make out a fireplace with a small, orange fire glowing in the grate, a low table crowded with bits and pieces of things and a padded chair that was leaking stuffing.

He could also see Grubert and Pidge moving around the room. Using his sleeve, Eep scrubbed a little of the filth off the window so he could see better.

Jey was standing on the small table. Her hands were planted on her hips in the position she usually used when she was arguing. Eep was impressed. Not many fairies would be brave enough to challenge a goblin! He felt a surge of pride for his friend.

Suddenly, he saw something else in the room, and panicked.

It was a wolf cub!

Normally wolves didn't bother with fairies; they were too small to make a snack, let alone a good meal, and fairy dust made them sneeze. Sometimes though, when the moon was full, the wolves would go crazy and hunted the fairies.

Eep did a quick calculation and paled as he realised that it would be a full moon tonight. Jey was in terrible danger!

"We have to get inside, Wren!" he cried urgently. "The goblin has got a wolf cub in there and when the moon rises tonight, it will go crazy and eat Jey! We have to save her!"

Wren nodded and thought hard. "Maybe we could go down the chimney," she suggested.

Eep peered through the window and shook his head. "There's a fire," he said regretfully.

"Look," Wren cried suddenly, "There's a small hole in the wall by the door! We can squeeze in there!"

Eep looked, and sure enough, there was a hole just big enough for a small fairy. He hurried over to it and crawled through, but Wren was too big.

"I'm sorry Eep," Wren told him. "You'll have to go without me. I'll wait out here for you both."

Eep nodded and turned to face the room. The wolf cub spotted him immediately and snapped and snarled at the end of its silver chain, but Grubert, Pidge and Jey didn't see him. They were busy arguing.

"But I've told you," Jey said crossly. "I can't grant wishes! I'm a fairy, not a genie!"

"Well, I heard that fairies *can* grant wishes, and if you don't grant my wish, I will feed you to the wolf!" growled Grubert stubbornly.

Jey shook her head in despair. "But I can't do it!" she wailed. "I would if I could, but I can't!"

Grubert stomped over to the table. He snatched Jey up in his fist and shook her furiously. "Well you were warned!" he roared.

"Wait!" yelled Eep. "Wait! Mr Goblin, what was your wish?"

Grubert paused and looked round, searching for the owner of the small but determined voice that had shouted.

Eep hid inside a smelly, overturned boot and tried not to breathe.

"Who's there?" demanded Grubert. "Where are you?"

He looked round wildly, and Pidge began circling the room on silent grey wings, his sharp eyes searching for movement.

Eep held his breath and stayed very still, then when Pidge had moved on, he answered the goblin.

"It doesn't matter who I am!" he shouted. "Tell me your wish, Goblin. What do you want that makes you threaten the life of this fairy?"

Grubert was peering into dark corners, searching for the voice, but as Eep spoke again he stopped and plopped onto one of the chairs. He still held Jey in his fist and he peered at her distractedly as if he'd never seen her before.

"Do you see that wolf cub there," Grubert asked despondently. "Well, it's not really a wolf cub, it's my son Gaal. He's been cursed and," a tear crept down Grubert's dirty face. "And I want my boy back," he hiccupped sadly.

Eep was both shocked and confused. "So Gaal is a werewolf?" he asked doubtfully, peeking out of the boot at the snarling wolf cub and thinking about the bright sunshine outside.

Grubert looked surprised, then thoughtful, then shook his head. "No, it must be a curse," he declared. "Werewolves turn back during the day and the sun is shining bright outside."

"You great ninny!" shrieked Jey incredulously from the goblin's fist. "You great, stupid goblin!"

"Jey! Be quiet!" yelled Eep, erupting from the boot in alarm and flying up to the table. "He'll squish you if you make him angry!!"

"Another fairy?" exclaimed Grubert. "Where did you come from?" he demanded, reaching out and grabbing Eep in his other hand.

"I came to rescue Jey!" Eep replied bravely. "Let her go, Mr Goblin. We can't grant wishes and we don't need to!"

"Silly, stupid, idiot goblin!" fumed Jey, thumping her tiny fists down on the goblin's hand for emphasis.

"Don't you know that werewolves are allergic to silver?" she went on in a voice that was loud with outrage and disbelief. "If you put silver on a werewolf, you stop him from changing! Poor Gaal can't change back because you've wrapped in him in silver chains!"

"You mean..." Grubert stared at her, hope and disbelief mingling in his ugly face.

"Yes!" Eep cried hastily. "If you take the silver chains off the wolf cub and take him outside into the sunshine, he'll change back! I promise!"

Grubert jumped to his feet. "Pidge!" he yelled, tossing both fairies into the air, where they were caught gently in the talons of the swooping Pidge.

Grubert scooped the little wolf into his arms and hurried outside, where Wren was waiting anxiously. She watched curiously as Grubert knelt down and carefully undid the silver collar around the squirming puppy's neck.

The moment the collar was lifted away from the cub's skin, something began to happen.

The cub began to wriggle and squirm as if it was being tickled to death with a ticklestick, and then, all of a sudden, it seemed to pop and a very young goblin was sitting on the ground in its place.

"Goodness!" exclaimed Jey, dangling from Pidge's claw. "Look, it's a little Goblet!"

"See!" Eep called to Grubert. "Now please let us go, Mr Goblin. You've got your boy back. And as long as he wears silver when he's a goblin, he won't change back into a wolf!"

"Let them go, Pidge," Grubert cried happily. "And thank you, little fairies! Thank you so much! If ever *you* need any help, you can always come to me. Thank you!"

And he flung his arms around his son and hugged him tightly.

Pidge dived low and deposited the fairies on the ground, then soared over to the Goblins and circled above their heads, making little caws of glee.

Eep and Jey looked at each other and then Wren landed beside them. "Time to go home?" she asked.

"Time to go home," the two fairies agreed, and climbed onto her back.

Spontaneous by Antony Davies

So there I was, eating a curry and watching Saturday night telly, and my big iron-framed mirror just fell off the wall. Just like that, falls, the string holding it up all snapped and waving free. It hit the floor and the glass only cracked at first and I'm wondering if this counts as seven years bad luck or not, but the question soon died as the near-perfect triangles fell onto my carpet in a shower of silvery noise.

I heaved myself off the couch and stood looking at the little shards, hands on hips, and I was strangely impressed the way my reflection multiplied identically in each piece.

The first thing I notice here is my right leg. My boxer shorts are snagged up the top of my thigh and the inside of the thigh is bunched out and pasty white. Quickly, I pull it down but then I notice how much my gut hangs over when I bend even slightly.

Big deal, so I'm past my fighting best—a lot of guys my age are.

Not that I've ever had a fight, mind.

I'm thirty in two months.

Middle-aged spread a decade early.

But I exercise. I play *football*. What else?

Instead of clearing the mess, I decided to write a list of my regular activities. I got as far as football and stopped. The room felt awfully big without my over-sized mirror lording over it.

The idea that I did absolutely nothing with my life was just too ridiculous and the prospect made me jittery, like I had to do something, anything, just to get these thoughts out of my head. I checked off the positive things in my life, those things that everyone really needs:

A car ~ *check.*

Job ~ *check.*

Decent flat ~ *check.*

Girlfriend ~ sort-of *check*.

And there I am, wondering what the hell I have to be so anxious about. But that jittery feeling, that ants-in-your-pants sensation you can't explain, it just wouldn't go away. I was missing something.

Yet, at the same time, I was missing *nothing*.

There, in black and white, was everything I need to live a happy, fulfilling life. Except kids, but don't get me started on them. I want them, yeah, but my sort-of girlfriend is still only twenty-four so—

Girlfriend more than five years younger than you ~ *check*.

So I sit there, thinking. I've never skydived. Never been down rapids. Have I ever done anything exciting in my entire life?

Hang gliding ~ *no-check*.

Diving with sharks ~ no-check.

Hot air balloon ~ no-check.

I *have* been abroad, six or seven times: Ibiza, Faliraki, Benidorm.

Package holidays with parents ~ *check*.

Beer and birds holiday with mates ~ *check*.

And so I sit and I sit and I think. The curry's cold before I realise that it's coming up to midnight. I give myself until then to come up with either something that gives my life meaning … something, *anything whatsoever* that raises me above the mundane. And if I can't come up with anything, if my pen hovers, and refuses to touch down and write the one thing that sets me apart from every other curry-eating, beer-swilling lad that went past his prime without even noticing, I will, without a shadow of a doubt, throw myself from the window.

Either that, or I come up with a plan.

11:56.

Abseiling ~ *no-check*.

Snorkel the Great Barrier Reef ~ *no-check*.

Walk the Great Wall of China ~ *no-check*.

11.59.

It's taken me this long to realise it, taken me twenty-nine years and ten months, plus a few days that I can't be bothered adding up, it's taken me so long to get this far, to nowhere, and now I have one minute to decide what to do with the rest of my life. Time's running out.

I'm reflected a million times, from the big, obvious pieces to the tiny invisible flakes. I'm scattered on the floor, lying in pieces, my plans as a twenty year-old destroyed. My ambition, finished.

12.00.

The only answer is not to make any more plans. You'll only be disappointed in the long run. Don't plan anything, ever. If you do you'll fail. And you'll wind up in a nice apartment with designer boxer shorts, eating chicken madras on a Saturday night, not giving one single shit where your girlfriend is.

So that's my big plan: no more plans. I mean, after all, that's what screws you up. People making you think you need things. Wear Nike, you'll run faster. Buy Persil, you'll be whiter than white can be. Watch Ally McBeal or Sex in the City, you'll realise how utterly shit your own job is and go out and get into debt, trying to live a lifestyle you can't possibly achieve.

And that's how I decided to become spontaneous.

I'd just wait until a decision was required and I'd make it. Whimsical, old, *slightly* overweight, Alan. He'll be a crazy guy, your buddy, your pal. "You're thirty, Alan? I'd never have guessed. Had you closer to twenty-four."

Like my girlfriend.

Okay, so by now it's one in the morning and I don't know where she is. I call her mobile and it sounds like she's at a club. She says, "Hey, what's up?"

And the combination of hearing her speak and the afterglow of my life-affirming decision, these two things make me horny. Usually, I'd say something romantic like, 'I wanted to hear your voice,' but here, now, with my new spontaneity beside me, I say, "I need some sex. You coming round?"

"I can't hear you!" she shouts.

I shout back, "I want to shag you, right now."

She yells in my ear, "I'll call you back."

The phone went dead right then and I stood there considering whether or not to go down the club and break up with her. Too long. I considered it too long, so I had to come up with something else.

A run!

Yes, I'm going for a late-night-slash-early-morning run, work off a little of this excess skin, but on the way out, I grab my keys—spontaneously—and instead of running around the block I'm getting in my car, deciding where to go. Nowhere, that's where.

I'm driving nowhere but forwards in my designer boxer shorts and that black vest I got from Next. I pass a speed camera at under the limit and I think back to my list.

Received a speeding ticket in the post ~ *no-check*.

So I pull to a halt and turn the car and head back up the street, go a sufficient distance, then turn back and floor it. The limit here's thirty, so forty-five should be sufficient. I don't watch the road, just look for the telltale flash of the camera. Yup, there it went.

Cool.

What next? What could I do now?

Going by the park, the local square of grass where we play football on a Sunday before heading for a pint, I have a great idea.

I pulled off the road, bumped up the path, and sluiced onto the wet pitch. Mud erupted behind me, but I was going too fast to get stuck. I pulled a donut in the centre circle, not whooping and hollering as I'd pictured myself doing a split-second before leaving the road, but all calm, staring ahead, concentrating on the manoeuvre. Then I got bored and went for goal. I've seen this in a Jackie Chan film, but he parks between two cars, not sliding into the goal at sixty. I revved hard, floored it, and careered toward the white sticks, yanking on my handbrake and turning the wheel a bit. The car went sideways and slid right between them. I wanted to shout "Goooooooaaaaaaaallll" like the commentators do in Spain and Italy, but I was stony-faced, serious.

On a mission.

Back on the road, I'm wondering how I can be even more spontaneous, when I pass a police car. I check the rear view mirror and it hasn't followed. I'm a little disappointed. So I do a three-pointer and retrace my tracks, faster. The police car's still there. I slam on the brake, skidding to a halt. Still nothing. So I get out and march over to the car and tap on the glass.

The coppers are eating a pizza and one of them winds down his window. "Can I help you, sir?"

He's younger than me by a good couple of years, which makes me even angrier.

He says, "Sir? Are you okay?"

And I reach out and grab a handful of pizza, just like that, without thinking about it, and not a slice either, a big steaming glob of cheese and tomato and dough and meat. It burns like hell, but I stuff it in my mouth. By now, the officer, he's out of his car and has his hand on his belt.

"On the floor," he says, but I'm chewing.

He says again, "On the floor, sir."

The young bastard. The kid. Child. Telling me what to do.

I say, "Want some pizza?" and jam the gooey mess into his face.

The boy pulls back, yanks something from his belt, and aims it at me. My eyes explode, and I fall to the ground, sobbing.

Been strafed with pepper spray ~ check.

* * * * *

The copper and his partner took around fifteen minutes to establish I wasn't drunk or under warrant or absconded from anywhere medical, and by then I'd decided I was bored with the situation and just wanted to go home. I lied about a bet I'd had and eventually they let me go, advising me to keep washing my eyes out with fresh water.

At home, there's an answerphone message from Kerry, my sort-of girlfriend. It says she hopes I'm okay and not too pissed off with her.

I try to think what the least-expected thing I could possibly do might be.

Here's where I closed my eyes. Here's where I thought about what to do next. I wandered the flat and vowed to use the first thing of interest that I came across. I found my mobile, but rejected it for being a mundane necessity of modern life.

Mobile phones a necessity?

No they bloody are not.

I turned it on and dialled my voicemail, selected the option to change my greeting: "Hello, this is Alan. You can no longer reach me via this method as I have decided it is simply a tool of phone corporations, tricking you into buying their unnecessary crap. I am spontaneously disposing of this, and if you happen to be my sort-of girlfriend Kerry, then I don't care. You slag."

Girlfriend ~ no-check.

And that was that. I dropped the phone in the toilet and flushed. It didn't go all the way down, just stuck out from the bend.

Aching, festering anxiety that I may be out of touch for more than ten minutes at a time ~ check.

The next thing I find is my passport. I take this as a sign: my passport to a new life. A whole new life. YES! That is the one thing I need. A new life. Not lots of little things in this life, but a completely new one.

What I do next is my one, solitary concession to a planned, ordered lifestyle: my Visa card. The lesser of two evils. You can't be spontaneous without funds, after all. You are restricted, your freedom dead, everything bound and gagged. Without money, that is. Even if, in my case, it's someone else's.

From my front door to the terminal at Dover, it took four hours and ten minutes. The ferry got me to France by ten in the morning. I drew a few strange looks as I wandered the decks. Perhaps they were just too stunned by this pale, flabby man in his late twenties, whose greatest achievements in life are churning up a footie pitch and getting hit with pepper spray.

In Paris, a six-hour drive from Calais, I buy a strong little coffee and sit outside a tabac in the afternoon sunshine, baking, wondering if I dare take off my vest.

Four Americans go to the counter and start pointing at the board. One of the men says, "Do you have cof-fee? You know, proper cof-fee?"

The barista, he just shrugged casually.

Another said, "American cof-fee? Proper cof-fee?"

I finished my obviously fake coffee and volunteered my services as a fluent French speaker. I said to the barista, "Le chat dans le jardin," and he looked at me funny. I said, "Je voudrais un biscuit avec le chevaux," and the barista laughed. I said, "Les Americans a la mer," and tapped my head, and the barista laughed more and hit me with a torrent of good-natured French I couldn't hope to understand.

I turned to my American friends and said, "They're out of proper coffee," and they all left, shaking their heads at the lack of choice outside of the hub of the free world.

Make fun of dumb Americans without them realising ~ check.

Up the Eiffel Tower, after persuading the guards that my dress sense is all the rage in London, I decide against spitting off the top, as this is simply common. Instead, I just look. The city spans across the landscape as if it has always been there. Cathedrals, museums, hotels; landmarks, I have read about but never seen until today, all of them out there for me to visit, absorb, climb should I choose. I could watch the world from here forever. If it wasn't so cold. Even in the sun, the wind brings goose-bumps. I continue to look down upon every Parisian and tourist, every work of architectural art, I do this until I can't feel my naked feet, and when this happens, I head reluctantly for the elevator and descend.

The warmth builds as the ground nears and wave upon wave of depression wash though me. I want that view back, and I know I cannot have it, simply because I'm thinking about it all the way in that lift, going down, going down. I just want to do something, or at least see something that no one else in the world has.

That's all.

From here, I drove south through the French countryside, remembering memories I cannot possibly have, of fighting, of trenches, of mud, blood and human remains, congealing on a futile battlefield. Poppies grow. Corn grows. A splendid white blur shoots down a railway track, and I think how lucky the French are to have had their infrastructure blown to pieces fifty years ago while we Brits make do with 19th century shite.

More poppies.

Feel sorry for yourself whilst growing jealous of thousands of dead people ~ check.

Realise the true meaning of war in Europe ~ un-check.

It's soon dark and I stop for a proper meal of meat and garlic, a few vegetables that I poke at and try to eat but give up on in favour of a rich, chocolate pudding.

More driving, a sugar buzz helping me on. I speed, but no one stops me. When I'm doing around ninety, I see a police car in my rearview and relish the chance to try out my expert French tongue on the authorities, picturing myself saying, "Ou es la chat?" and the policeman's reply, "Le chat dans le jardin." But it never happens. The car speeds past me, probably a hundred, maybe one-ten, and the occupants are eating croissants, dipping the pieces in something red and gooey. They see me, and seem a little surprised, probably at my appearance, then instead of pulling me over, they nod, the driver casually salutes, and pulls away.

I feel cheated somehow.

At three-fifteen Monday morning, I see the sea. It's black and glittering in the moonlight. This is Marseille. Its hilly structure reminds me of how San Francisco looks on films. The harbour, oh the harbour.

Then it was a winding road that guided me down the coastline, the narrow beach where I thought maybe I saw two bodies writhing, locked together.

When I find a place to park, I do so. I turn off the engine and the silence is strange and sudden, like a switch has turned the quietness on rather than something else off. Like it is louder than the noise of the car. But the silence is not silent.

Waves seem to hiss on the shore and I open the window to listen. The waves breaking and, yes, they're more a hiss than a crash. I hear sand moving, coarse against pebbles and shells, and the scent of salt and water and a tinge of fish enters the car. I look upon the Mediterranean, eight hundred miles from my front door. The moon is full, up ahead, off to the right, casting its glow on each and every ripple, even as each ripple heads for shore, rolls up on itself, breaks, hisses, leaving a fine white foam.

Here's where I got out of my car. There was no wind. The air was warm, coating my skin with an invisible film. I came down from the road, ignoring the gravel biting the soft soles of my feet. Then onto the beach. Still hard with pebbles, I absorbed the pain, trivial though it was, and drove myself onwards, desperate to feel those moon-tipped waves, some pathological urge, uncontrollable, something making me experience waves, so far from my home, breaking on my bare, naked feet.

The sand grew finer the closer I got to the foamy edge. But when I put my right foot in the water, the cold gripped like a fanged beast. It's as if the moon had cooled the ocean but not the air around it. Like the polar opposite of the sun. Like a chunk of ice, not fire. Like it cannot defeat the sun any other way but from ground level up.

A morsel of advice for anyone who happens to be in Marseille at three in the morning: Warm air does not equal warm sea.

Freezing to death in a body of water famed for heat ~ check.

I didn't retract my foot. I left it there, finding solid ground, finding pebbles, my brief respite of sand now gone. My other foot joined it and I began to shiver. The cold spread up my legs, past my knees. I didn't feel it go through my groin, it just crept into my arms and neck.

Down below, I could still feel. I felt the water rise. A little of it broke on my knees and freezing drops splashed up the inside of my thighs. I stepped out a little further and more water splashed, this time reaching my designer boxer shorts, my scrotum retracting, trying to return inside my body where it was still warm. I remembered my first time at a swimming pool, at Scott Hall Sports Centre, when my father grew impatient and pushed me in. It's good for you, son. So here, now, in Marseille, I prepared to dunk my whole body, intending to float and feel the rise and fall of the Mediterranean beneath me.

Then I see something.

Moonlit water splashing upwards. The movement is maybe a hundred metres away. Someone is swimming. Swimming towards me. A man, I'm sure. He gets closer and yes, it's a man. A black man. His wet skin reflecting light. His arms pumping slowly, legs kicking.

Me, shivering, up to my knees in cold, cold Mediterranean.

The man finds his feet, five metres from me, and he stands up. He is really more of a boy than a man. Water beads in his fuzzy hair. He wipes his face with both hands and grins very white teeth at me. He holds his hands to the sky, as if trying to hug the moon itself.

He says something very quickly and happily in what I take to be French.

I say, "Le chat dans la jardin?"

His grin, somehow, it widens. He says, "English?"

I say, "Oui."

He says, "Ah. I too will be in England soon."

He wades from the sea, wearing only a tight pair of underpants, passing me without a strange look, without pity, without acknowledging that fat English men in vests don't normally stand in the sea at three A.M. He treads over the pebbles without looking back, without seeming to notice the hurt the ground brings, without one single thought.

Or that's how it seemed to me.

I decide, impulsively of course, that I will not dunk myself under the water. Instead, I return to my car, watching the black man, the boy from the sea, I watch him as he jogs along the coastal road. On his way, according to him, to England. I take a blanket from the boot, another symbol of my preparedness, my just-in-case life, and I wrap it around me. I sit on the bonnet and allow the engine's warmth to give me back my nerve endings.

Soon, I poked my big toe with a fingernail and, sure enough, I could feel again.

Soon, a couple came by, arm-in-arm, giggling at first, but silent as they passed.

Soon, I began to regret dumping my girlfriend by answerphone.

But soon, mercifully, the sun peaked over the horizon.

It started as a faint glow to my left. Then a dot of brilliant yellow. Then it was too bright to look at, but I felt it rise, the warmth on my skin, my shadow growing longer to my right.

Watch the sun rise eight hundred miles from home ~ check.

I should be in work now. It'll be eight o'clock-ish back in England. They'll be ringing my mobile, discovering that I've discovered the meaning of my life. Or rather its lack of meaning.

The car I'm sat on, I realise suddenly, it's a company car. I'll have to return it when they sack me.

Good job ~ un-check.

Car ~ un-check.

The ability to pay for my plush apartment ~ un-check.

A couple of backpackers wander by, both girls, Canadian flags sewn to their packs. They speak to me in broken French. Nothing about cats or gardens, so I can't help them. They leave.

The sun is up now and people are arriving on the beach. A tanned, muscular man is attaching some sort of kite to a surfboard, looking happily upwards as little clouds start to zip across the sky. The Canadian girls come back without their packs, and I must have been sitting here for longer than I thought. The girls strip to bikinis and hit the water. I take off my vest and follow their lead.

It's still cold, but tolerable. I float there, on my back, belly up, bobbing with the rhythm of the ocean. Inside me, something warm grows. I feel things drifting away from me.

Choice.

I've taken all the choices I ever had, and got rid of them. I cannot now choose whether to go to work or not. Can no longer say sweet lies to my girlfriend and have sex. Cannot drive anywhere I like.

My job, my girlfriend who never really loved me, my flat that meant I had to work like that young black kid is going to have to if he ever reaches England, all of it now gone.

I float.

I smile.

I choose to do nothing.

Dying a crappy, unfilfilling life, kidding myself I wanted it all along ~ un-check.

Stress ~ un-check.

Two Canadian girls splashing toward me, about to make conversation ~ check.

My new life, unpredictable, but probably more sensible than the last forty-eight hours…

…Check.

Conscience! by Charlie McGee

Tom Eastwood liked nothing better than fishing and so he cheerily trotted this fine morning towards the banks of the local river, right behind the old boat house. It was his favourite spot, not because of an abundance for him to catch, in fact it was often very poor fishing ground, but because of that fact, he was normally on his own, which is the way he wanted it. The serenity and beauty of the landscape added to the shelter nearby was the consummate climate for him to lose himself in his thoughts when he needed to and he felt the location was his own secret hideaway.

As usual he nestled ideally beneath an old elm tree, overlooking the calm waters of an undisturbed stream and set about organising himself to a comfortable position. The moist dew, glistening off the grassy carpet around him added a sparkle to the crisp atmosphere which engulfed the scene for a time, and since it was indeed his favourite hour of the day, he thought the setting was the perfect environment to relax. Happy and content with his lot, he whistled a jovial tune as he worked, which was carried through the air by a fresh breeze, until at last he could cast his line.

"Right," he uttered out loud, "let's see if they're biting today."

Suddenly he was startled as he heard another voice answering him.

"I wouldn't worry about that Tom; the river's well stocked this morning."

Glancing to the embankment on his right, he was surprised to see an elderly lady sitting casually with her arms folded and her hand under her chin taking in the view he had come accustomed to. She then turned towards Tom with a pleasant smile before apologising.

"Pardon me, it is Tom isn't it?"

Tom nodded before she continued.

"I didn't mean to startle you. I was just enjoying the peaceful-ness and it really is such a lovely spot. So different from the reality we are faced with every day. What, with all these wars and fam-ines, you must come here fishing regularly to get away from it all?"

The initial shock had left Tom, but he was still amazed he hadn't noticed her before, also since he had a good view of the area after coming around the old riverside building when he arrived. His first impressions were that she was a harmless old woman and be-sides, he was sure he knew her. How else would she know his name anyway? Thinking about it, he didn't mind answering her, and especially as it was, since he hadn't conversed with anyone in weeks. Not since his only sibling tragically lost their life in a tragic boating accident.

Tom couldn't come to terms with the loss and had been griev-ing his only remaining family member for at least a month, but this morning, there was an extra spring in Tom's step, so much so that everyone in the village who seen him strolling his way to the river-bank that early hour, came to the conclusion that Tom was finally accepting the demise of his sadly missed brother.

"I do," he answered gladly, "I love to get away from the trials of everyday life for a while on a regular basis, and the tranquillity out here is perfect."

As he spoke he perceived the rugged wear and tear of her skin to go with the tiredness which appeared on her face when she let her smile escape her features. Viewing her appearance, he immedi-ately pitied her sorry state, but attempted to disguise his concern by offering her one of his sandwiches as he allowed himself a quick snack. The generous gesture helped revitalise her pleasant expres-sion, however only to refuse whilst acknowledging the offer with gratitude.

Tom leaned back against the tree while the conversation main-tained its pattern.

"I know what you mean about all this bloodshed and starva-tion; there seems to be a new catastrophe commencing every single week. Only this morning they were talking about some regional conflict in the Far East that could easily spiral out of control, while some unknown disease is threatening livestock in South America that could have a devastating effect on local economies."

The old lady agreed.

"It's true; it's so sad, and on top of the atrocities which are ever present and worsening all around the world, as well as the on-going wars in the Middle-East, Africa, and Asia. You'd wonder where it's all going to end. There's also the mindless violence in most communities now."

She paused for a instant to reflect on what she had said and stared into the river waters which were now being disturbed by the first drops of a passing shower, before shaking her head slowly and lamenting.

"Life has become so cheap. It just saddens me how evil some people can get. Everything seems to be out of control and I just can't see anyway back for us."

Tom listened solemnly to her every word and humbly he observed how sorrowful she was by the sight of her red eyes slowly beginning to fill, nevertheless his interest was swiftly disrupted with the impending rain shower. He quickly grabbed what he could and followed by the grey woman, he hurried to the shelter of the boathouse.

The old woman was right to be worried, for at that very moment across the globe, events were being contrived to push civilisation further into an abyss. An alliance of evil and mayhem was falling into place between radicals who were brainwashed into believing it was their honour to kill and die for their religion in an unholy union with drug lords who had taken control of their destitute countries. Their only common goal was the destruction and elimination of the western world, be it for different reasons, and when and if they succeed in that, it was possible they had planned to turn their numerous deadly weapons, as well as their crazed hatred and greed, on each other.

The meeting place was organised at a small island off the East African coast, which was well protected both naturally and artificially, and was owned by Sydney Nanyukai. He was well-educated in one of England's finest private schools and he used his education to good use, becoming one of the Dark Continent's most influential leaders. He was also well documented in his views against the white-man's ownership of any part of Africa and he used his people's support of his opinions to stir unrest and anarchy in neighbouring territories. This fitted nicely in his designs for conquest and it was going to help even more-so if the preordained meeting, which he was going to use to impress his allies, went ahead without a hitch.

Having being informed of the news, he allowed himself a smug smile as he inspected the bodies of two NATO agents, which were slaughtered the previous night trying to infiltrate the decoy base he had set up deep in the chain of mountain ranges in the far west of his vast country.

God was disappointed with the way everything was deteriorating on Eden and it was decreed that a decision on the future of mankind had to be made, and so the Supreme Being gathered the separate entities together to pass judgement.

They were nearly all in agreement initially of the failure of mankind to co-exist, all except Memory, who reminded the assembly of the great achievements of man, of pacifists like Gandhi who stood strong in the face of adversary, of the artists who created so much beauty like Da Vinci and Michelangelo, or the geniuses amongst them whom over a short space of time have propelled mankind from creating crude utensils to exploring the realms of space, while their legend is littered with an array of martyrs who would rather die for the good they believed in, than bow on bended knee to tyrants.

However History quickly intervened, reminding all, of the consequences of the actions of these people; of the brutal murder of Gandhi and the resulting bloody war, of the greed of rich collectors who spend millions on the great works of art, so they can hide what they can get their hands on behind enclosed stone walls for their own enjoyment, while space rockets which send man out into the heavens, were also being used to carry devices of mass destruction. History argues that it can't speak for the future. It can only speak for what has passed and that the majority of the time it has been a catalogue of doom.

Reason however disagrees, and puts forward the notion that war is unavoidable and for man to progress he must challenge himself, adding that the favoured species had also done well of late, noting that most societies weren't turning to war unless it was a last resort. The discussion was fast becoming confusing, and with reason's statement, more questions were been asked, until it was finally and hastily decided to turn to Conscience to try and resolve the issue and decide man's fate.

The aged woman sat comfortably just inside the large opening of the open shed, on an ancient wheel which was slanted against a lifeless, decrepit red brick wall. She at first gazed wearily out at the accumulating raindrops in an ever-increasing puddle, but suddenly she spun towards Tom with a query.

"Tom! Tell me what you think?"

She quickly gained his attention before proceeding.

"Do you ever suppose all the hatred in the world will ever disappear?"

Tom studied the question cautiously for a moment until he was settled in himself to let the old lady know what he thought.

"There always has being hatred," he opened with, "just as there is always love."

Happy with his start, he stood up in the doorway.

"I mean its true what the adage says, there can't be right without wrong, or good without evil. They compliment each other. Sure, there are wars at the moment, there always has been, but as usual we'll find some way to find peace in every conflict. If you look at the other side of the coin, there's also a lot of good in the world. I'll give you an example."

Tom paused to take a deep breath and to lean towards the door jam with his elbow as he readied himself to reveal a personal tragedy.

"A couple of months ago, my brother, who I was close to, was out in his boat, fishing with two comrades, but they were having no joy. It was late in the evening and since it was getting dark and the wind was picking up, they decided eventually to turn for home. But then disaster struck; rushing back to shore, they collided with a boulder high up in the water, and it wasn't long before the small craft began to sink. Now, it was mentioned by the survivors, that they were still a nice bit out in the lake and they couldn't be certain if anyone spotted their predicament, so my brother, who handed his friends their lifejackets, advised them to try and get to a buoy which was a hundred metres or so away, while he promised to follow. Thinking my brother was coming along behind, his friends done what they were instructed, but..., well..., the bottom line is that my brother drowned."

Pausing to clear a lump from his throat, Tom then exhaled a deep sigh before resuming.

"Anyway, thank the lord God, the rest of the fishermen were saved by the quick actions of an eagle-eyed old mariner who spotted the incident from the shore while safely tying up his own boat from the ensuing storm."

Tom had a calm look about him and his gentle aspect bewildered the old woman, so on offering condolences, she also queried his feeling about his sibling having being taken so suddenly from him.

Tom looked deep into her well travelled eyes whilst he reminisced.

"I took it real bad. I wouldn't talk to anyone and I kept blaming my brother for being so stupid. But that's all changed now."

Immediately Tom Eastwood smiled, but he confused the old lady even more as she questioned his statement.

"What do you mean it's all changed?"

Staring directly at her now, he continued.

"There was an investigation into the tragedy and I received the verdict yesterday evening. You see, when my brother's body was recovered, he wasn't wearing a life-preserver and it has now being acknowledged that since it was down to my brother to organise the boat before they left, he and he alone could have known there were only two lifejackets when they began to sink. The authorities are convinced that was why he quickly took over and passed them to his friends, while pretending he had one. It's believed he knew that whatever chance his friends had, they would have little or no chance if they were concentrating in keeping him afloat, so he directed the other two towards the buoy while at the same time; he bravely went down with his boat."

Instantly he glimpsed at the old woman to notice her reaction, but was delighted to see an improvement in her appearance. Gone were the weary look and tired eyes to be replaced by a healthier, pleasant feature. She received the story with remorse, nevertheless the noble and courageous gesture of Tom's brother inspired her and Tom was pleased to see the sunshine return to her face. Leaving her to wallow in her emotion, he watched the last few drops falling, while he concluded.

"But now I know that my brother will be remembered for performing a heroic deed by giving his own life so his friends might live."

Tom gave a last heavy sigh before picking up his bits n' pieces to go back to his elm tree, stopping only to invite the grey woman to join him, however, he was startled for the second time that morning. This time she had disappeared, as fleetly as she had appeared. Tom swiftly scrutinised the landscape, but to no avail, so he shrugged his shoulders and carefree, decided to retake his original position.

The debate was silent and without decision until eventually Conscience put forward its own opinion.

"The question here is has man turned its back on everything God has provided him? And the initial answer would have to be 'Yes'; But not in all cases.

There are times in man's past, present and their possible future when men and women, the world over, when the time is right and the situation demands it, has stood tall to give their life so others might live. The selfish sacrifice of these people will never be forgotten by those nearest to them.

Then there are others who stand up for the small person, and fights for their rights and tries to feed, clothe and educate them. These people are numerous, but they seek no reward for their good deeds.

Tom Eastwood is right. There is a lot of good in the world and it's unfair that these people are punished for the mayhem that others cause. No! I won't have it on myself to condemn man when most are striving hard to be as it was intended. My final answer has to be; Let man live."

While the rest of the gathering acknowledged and agreed with what Conscience had said, later, as God viewed over the wonderful Eden, the feeling of joy overcame Tom and somehow, he instantly knew something good was after happening.

Unknown to Tom, on another part of the rock we call Earth, a freak hurricane has stranded a motley group of individuals on a small island off the East African coast. They are left without any contact to the mainland, but listening to their host, they go inside a very large cavern, which has being turned into a fortress. After securing themselves in, they now feel safe from the ravages of what has been hastily named 'Hurricane Michael', so it isn't long before they continue their plans, when in an instant their meeting is disturbed.

Without warning, a loud deafening bang echoes around the cave; then a louder one; followed by another and another. The place begins to shake and immediately loose fittings start to fall, as the ceiling strains under pressure. An odour of sulphur and brimstone poisons the air, and panicking, the host along with his guests', race towards the large entrance, only to be beaten back by the flames which spring up from the ever widening cracks in the ground. They're trapped and scared as they fall further back into their tomb, until they come to a river of molten rock edging closer from all sides. All hope is lost, and facing their fate, their cries of woe are immediately replaced by ones of anger, as they vent their wicked hatred on each other.

Elsewhere around the world, news reports are beginning to mention a dormant volcano erupting on a small, isolated, uninhabited island, while a freak hurricane pulverises the area for a time. With no life apparently in any danger, and the extremes ending as soon as they begin, there doesn't seem to be any reason for the media to carry the report for long so it's sensibly discarded. Especially considering a more interesting story has emerged about the bizarre disappearance of Sydney Nanyukai.

The Cursed Text! by Charlie McGee

A stunning, silver light, reflecting majestically from a shinning, full moon, allows dew crystals to glisten along the path of a dull grey roof top, and fall upon the murky waters of the Thames, before disappearing from view under one of the many stone, Georgian bridges which unites both banks of the London estuary. It's laughing trail flows without effort in her tide of passage, and conjures up images, caught in the stillness of time, to be touched on momentarily, and then let go. In the calm of night, the experience can be a lonely vigil, whilst perhaps, resting on a concrete barrier overlooking the scene, and without distractions, somebody with the tiresome burden of Atlas, could comfortably be hypnotised by such a sight, to be lost with a hint of salvation from their worldly worries. Somebody like Jason, an honest man, with good integrity; a man who always tries to do things right, but of course is prone to mistakes, temptations, vices, wrong decisions, and any other type of misdemeanours which betrays the souls of all of us, as weak-minded individuals at some point. His recent past aggrieves him so much, with the reason behind his misfortune a continuing mystery of perplexity casting it's harrowing shadow in each step he dared tread, every word which escaped his lips, and at any gesture he made to understand, ever since and all because, of a simple note, a token message, a soldier's mark of hope to a loved one, penned and sent as a text, during the lonely hours in the count-down to battle. As the chill air of a sleeping London encourages Jason Peterson to push his clenched fists further down into his overcoat pockets, he becomes lost in his haunting memories once more, flooding back yet again to remind him and march him step by step through the puzzling circumstances that had led him to the unfortunate position he now found himself in, and he can only wonder 'Why?'

Enter Sandman!

Sixteen hundred hours on a Friday evening, and all recreational activities are cancelled, or whatever it is you might be lucky to organise, to relieve the boredom in the middle of this God forsaken place. Operation Sandman has got the green light for tomorrow night, and finally, you're about to see some action, at last you get the opportunity to advance forward, proudly, from your camouflage tents and sand-bag castles to face unknown desert foes, a chance to show your true metal to your comrades; however, now it isn't a game anymore. Gradually, as you begin to think about it, and the reality of war starts to play its disturbing tune at the back of your mind, a deep down feeling of anxiety grows stronger in the pit of your stomach, whilst a bad taste sours your throat, as the realisation of how serious the situation is, slowly sets in. Some sit and think, in a hopeless state, about what can, could and might go wrong. More tell jokes or play cards, nervously; anything to change the subject, just for a small while, a return to normality, yesterday maybe, although all around, you notice the tension building up in the sandy air. Others, like you, remain silent to the outside world and sprinkled in every corner of the makeshift barracks are somebody's lover, sweethearts and romantics where private thoughts are kept secretly for loved ones, and that was the start of it!

Your captured thoughts sent in a moment of affection on your mobile to sweet Elaine and before long, your whole life has changed. Even though it seemed curious to you at first that Elaine never replied, you promptly conceded that the poor receiving network on your fiancé's cell phone was to blame again, and so you made a promise to her wallet-sized picture to renew the contraption for her as soon as your tour was ended. And then you slept, soundly, with visions of Elaine filling your head, to rise well-rested at the sound of reveille, after which you then went about your normal duties, before assembling with your comrades in preparation for the mission at hand. Or so you thought!

"Private Peterson to report to Captain Aldridge immediately"

It happened so quick, your feet never touched the ground, well, it appeared that way.

Kicked out of the army, stripped of all privileges, pensions, and thrown back into Civvies Street without even a court-martial for you to defend yourself with.

"Are you Private Jason Peterson?"

"Yes Sir."

"Do you know an Elaine Madsen from Osborne Road, Acton?"

"Am, yes sir. Why Sir"

"Just answer the question private? Did you send her a text message last night?"

"Yes Sir, several of us sent text messages sir. Our quartermaster said we were allowed to send one, and since all our phones are connected up to the army's telecom service, all our calls and messages are monitored for anything out of order and can be traced back."

"I am well aware of that private, how else do you think I got a hold of this! Now, can you confirm for me that you sent this text message last night to the same Elaine Madsen?"

After cautiously scanning its content, you recognised it and meekly agreed, and that was the spark. You can barely remember the captain bellowing at the top of his voice for you to get out of his army immediately, that there is no place for people like you in the armed forces and that you are the most despicable person he'd ever had the misfortune to be in the same room with.

The military police roughly grabbed you forthwith, and with a hastily collected package of your personnel belongings, you were bundled onto the first plane to England; but you didn't make it home as straightforward as that, did you?

Continental Europe

Flying over the clear blue Mediterranean Sea in a Royal Air Force Hercules cargo plane, you tried and tried again to contact Elaine, but there was no signal. No line and no answer from your sweetheart with your emotions now getting the better of you, on top of your bewilderment to the way you were treated. You couldn't understand what you had done wrong, and no matter how many times you went over the cursed message, your crime remained a puzzle, so you tried to involve a co-pilot in your attempt to discover your fault.

He seemed a mild enough gentleman with a pleasant smile which made you feel at ease, and on more than one occasion he questioned if you were all right, so you didn't think any harm would come to your query.

He sat across from you and listened with intrigue, as you relayed your confusing tale without uttering a word until you were finished, when he opened his mouth first, to emit a disbelieving snigger.

"Ah come on, are you telling me you were kicked out of the army over a bloody text message? You have to be having me on, or more like someone is having you on. Look, show me the text and let me put your mind at rest."

You handed it to him all right, where he read it in a shocked stance; and a growing appearance of repulse on his face. He instantly dropped your phone, took one disgusted look at your stunned reaction, walked straight to the cockpit, and directed the plane to be diverted to the nearest NATO airfield, somewhere in the south of Italy.

"Sir, only for I'm a practising Christian I would have thrown you out of the plane over the Mediterranean; …without a parachute. I'm putting the word out on you. People like you should be locked up."

Those were the last words he said to you before having you marched off military property, but what the hell had you done wrong? All you did was to compose a few words for your beloved.

Again you went over the piece on your mobile phone and yet again your wrongdoing eluded you, there was no sense or meaning to those confounded accusations, nothing that seemed out of order in any way. In a frustrated rage, you then strived in your fury to contact Elaine, however, recall after recall was left with no reply, until the depression of your situation suffocated you to such an extent that you tearfully decided to hide the offending device in the middle of your holdall. Out of sight, out of mind you thought; and it was at that point you contemplated discarding it altogether for good; but now, your rebellious heart persuaded you not to. You had done nothing wrong and you were going to prove it as well, by providing the text in its original form as it was wrote, for your solicitor, when you were then going to take the armed forces to court for unfair dismissal and abusive behaviour by dumping you just like that, in a foreign country and evicting you in a threatening manner from a military base. Ha-ha, you'll get them alright.

A train station in a nearby town afforded you the chance to purchase a ticket to France where you could then decide how to take the small hop across the channel, and so determined, you entered a spacious coach and found yourself a satisfying cushioned seat to relax and rest your head for a few hours on your already eventful journey home.

Merci France

You slept like a log, still and cumbersome, waking to find a middle-aged clergyman doing his best to be comfortable at the end of the seat you had taken up in the well packed carriage, but you quickly gathered yourself and offered an embarrassed apology. The padre acknowledged it and passed off your previous pose as a small inconvenience, while swiftly settling back into a more appropriate position as soon as you moved your feet.

"You're English?"

"Am; yes padre."

"I thought so from your apology. You had a good sleep?"

"Yeah, like a baby, but listen, I'm really sorry about that; you should have woke me. Honest, there was no-one else in the carriage when I nodded off."

"No, don't worry about that. Most of us got on in Lyon. Anyway, I could tell by your eyelids doing ninety that you were lost in your dreams.

You turned a lot as well. I hope you weren't having a nightmare."

"Not exactly Father, I've a lot on my mind.

Here, you've very good English! You wouldn't happen to be Irish by any chance?"

"Well spotted son. Trained in Maynooth and sent to the four corners of the globe like all the servants of the Lord that have gone before me. I got Rome, thank God."

The light-hearted banter lifted your spirits somewhat, but then you went too far. You couldn't keep your trap shut. What business was it of the priest anyway?

It's good to talk. It helps to lighten the burden of the soul; and who better to ask for guidance from, except a man of the cloth. Bullshit!

Father O'Malley listened carefully to your every word.

How you sent the message to Elaine.

How you were ordered before your superiors and discharged in disgrace from the army.

How you befriended a pilot on the flight home and explained to him what had happened you; and then how his reaction was to have you dumped in the middle of nowhere.

What was so terrible about the text?

You showed it to Father O'Malley and he scrutinised it, before swiftly blessing himself and all hell broke lose.

Conductors were called for. A sign of the cross was prayed for. Security was hailed for. And you were placed under arrest, in the baggage car, to remain, in cold exclusion, alone again for the rest of the journey to Paris, while Fr. O'Malley led who'd care to join in, in an extended version of the ten mysteries of the Rosary.

The French police were waiting for you with menace in Paris when you arrived and wasted no time in tossing you into the back of a Black Maria, while exclaiming in their native Gallic tongue, and very little English, expressions of profanity at your unwanted presence. You guessed as much, and were proved right, as you were handed over to the British authorities on a cruise ship at the port of Calais; when it was declared that you were never to set foot on French soil again. Your suspicion that the cursed text was to blame was confirmed when you were ushered into a holding berth after it was then shown to the captain of the vessel with words which seemed to suggest that you should be ashamed of yourself and if he had his way; he'd dump you in the middle of the English Channel.

And then it was back to dear old England; you, your holdall, and that blasted phone.

No sound left your lips during the short voyage and although you could feel the intense stares as you hurried down the gangplank at journeys end, you did your best to ignore your recently acquired infamy, and rushed to board the first bus to London, and the sanctuary of a safer environment.

Back in Blighty

You were still dumbfounded as you sat a solitary figure in Charing Cross, at the inexplicable allegations that had been directed your way, however, it helped to drift in and out of a haze, a wholehearted attempt to soothe your concern and focus on your next move. You used the phone kiosk beside the bench and were relieved to eventually make contact with Elaine, but her brother was waiting, with a list of foul-mouthed grammar which translated for you to stay away from my family, that Elaine is finished with you, and I'll do you if you ever come near any one of us again.

You were scared and sank into a fragile circle of one, as you wrestled with your thoughts, to open your mobile and view its contents for the umpteenth time, but terrified in case anybody eavesdropping might cause you more grief, so you trudged silently through the crowded streets of the metropolis, until hours later you found a quiet haven, and came to a stop, here on a concrete arm of a stony bridge overlooking the river Thames, but what are you going to do now?

In the distant, a crimson shade illuminates the skyline, drawing this suburban district to the majesty of the English capital as the early hours of a new day tick slowly by, leaving Jason Peterson in a forlorn disposition, isolated by everyone he knows and has met since fate fed by the need to be close to Elaine, urged him to send a text message on the eve of battle. A cry for comfort two nights ago opened a Pandora box of sorts, haunting his every movement, shattering his shaking confidence, dragging him closer to a point with no return; its job nearly complete now. He closes his eyes and mourns his lot, with a sense of despair enveloping his will to reason, and ever more the moonlit water seem so inviting, an escape from reality and the trials presented undeservedly in a carefree display of chance. Jason leans forward and imagines the weightlessness of the fall into the blackness below. The cold, noiseless splash and the strength of the tide; the struggle for one last breath; one last gasp before his living nightmare finally ends to float away in peace, his desperate soul now free; a decision so easy to take.

Suddenly his concentration is disturbed.

"I hope you're not thinking of jumping in there lad."

Panicking, Jason turns around and is confronted by a silhouette with a familiar helmet and a luminous yellow jacket studying his suspicious condition, a sight which encourages the decommissioned soldier to blurt out a reply.

"No constable, no; just thinking; that's all."

"You know, it's not worth it. It never is. We all have our problems, which sometimes make us want to do stupid things, but we get on with it. Remember lad, tomorrow is always a new day.

Here, why don't you tell me all about it and we'll see if we can resolve whatever it is that's bothering you together."

"It's not as easy at that constable; you think now that you'll be able to help me and I'll tell you all that's after happening to me; the way everybody has turned against me, ostracized me, banished me; from the army, from an aeroplane, a continental train; priests attacking me and my girlfriend disowning me; and all because of this bloody text message. And nobody; nobody has stopped for one minute to explain, to say to me what I've done wrong. Yeah you'll help me alright; until I show you the message, and then, you'll just be like the rest, so why don't you just do me one little favour and help me over the side. You'll be doing everyone a favour in the long run."

As Jason stressed his point towards the policeman, he stretched his arm holding his mobile in the direction of Officer Thomas Barnes, who, with a well-practised movement grappled the ex-serviceman from the wall and affixed the handcuffs he'd concealed in the palm of experience on the hapless figure.

"Now laddie, what message?"

Officer Barnes picked up the detainee's phone which had fallen during the arresting manoeuvre and with a controlled grin proceeded to scroll down through its private notes; however, the policeman's unprofessional attitude enraged the disorientated young man, who had been left sitting on the rough ground.

"That's none of your business!" Jason roared, jumping up at the same time to knock the constable, who fell back with a surprise, hard against the concrete wall, resulting in the

small device with its offending message, dropping from Tom Barnes grip, to descend effortlessly into the welcoming Thames.

…And just like that, as time stood still, it was gone.

Fin?

The Poet by Charlie McGee

It was November 1941 and a worried old man was feeling defeated. He was sick of hiding in dark n' dirty attics, behind tight, claustrophobic false walls, in damp rat-infested cellars, or anywhere else his few remaining trustworthy friends could find for him. Jakob was also feeling very tired. Not only was he on the wrong side of fifty, which wasn't an age to be on the run like a wanted fugitive, but with the Gestapo nearly catching up with him recently, he had put his hosts, a kind, young, sympathetic, Dutch family, in great danger.

When he first arrived there seven years previously to escape the Nazi purges throughout Germany, he'd quickly grown fond of Amsterdam, nevertheless as much then as now, he still longed for the picturesque scenery of the Bavarian mountains, with their snow-capped peaks and the endless idyllic walks, lost in the open countryside, by the inviting crystal tide of her countless lakes. Back then, he thought it'd only be a matter of time before the people at home came to their senses and got rid of that madman and his collection of uneducated thugs with their anti-Semite slogans and opinions, however it was now over two years into their brutal war and there appeared to be no-one able to stop their evil. Most of Europe was already under the jack-boot with England standing alone, along with Stalin's Russia, now that its farcical truce with their fascist enemies has been ripped up, by the S.S. as they goose-stepped resolutely to the beat of Operation Barbarossa in a betrayal the Communists should have known would come. Thrown together as comrades out of desperation, these last two bastions of old empires on opposite ends of an ancient continent were it seemed, the only obstacles left against the Third Reich's relentless march. Of course there was always the hope that the Americans would join in the fray and save the day like in 1917, and although there'd been rumours, that wasn't going to happen today or tomorrow.

He peered discontentedly between the gap in the makeshift curtain that was placed over the sky-light and stared solemnly into the welcoming, bright, moon-lit sky, and even though numerous red flashes in the distance accompanied with an eerie sound reverberating through the roof-tops fore-warned him of an impending air raid, their presence suddenly allowed Jakob to breath a temporary sigh of relief.

"Well at least I'll be safe from the Nazis while that's going on," he wondered quietly, although he then sighed with the conclusion that knowing his luck, a bomb would probably fall directly upon his hide-out and blow himself to kingdom come.

He'd a long time admitted what a fool he was for not travelling further onto England and maybe to America when he had a chance. It wasn't that he was penniless or anything back then, in fact to the contrary he'd accumulated a healthy bank balance as a consequence of his imaginative and creative writing during the bleak, hardship days of the Twenties, but Herr Himmler now had his greedy paws on the most of that, as-well as the wealth of the rest of Europe's Jewish population. His fortunes resembled a pit of despair, and of late he sometimes felt certain that the Armageddon of the Christian Bible, The New Testament, was now coming to pass for the Hebrew faith.

During the long, dark, drawn-out nights in hiding, he liked to reminisce about happier times and Jakob often remembered fondly the joy and surprise he felt when he was told for the first time that his writings were going to be published for the general public to enjoy by a reputable printing firm based in Munich. He was then encouraged to continue his work in the same manner about the same subjects that shone through his talent, the all too familiar wonders of nature and simple life in general. He loved it so much and his ramblings took him to such elegant and wonderful settings of breathtaking splendour that would be fixed in his mind forever.

<blockquote>
To see a splendid beauty,
Across an enchanted land;
Of a mystic lush green paradise,
Created by God's own hands;
</blockquote>

Jakob allowed himself a simple smile as he recalled some words of his which were written in his more youthful days, but nonetheless summed up perfectly his love for his Bavarian homeland. Since he was left with no copies of his writings anymore, only his memories remained, however some of these were pleasant indeed. At one stage his poetry was admired far and wide because it brought the reader to a different place, a sweeter place where the sun always shined, the birds always sang and a majestic brook with gentle waters always flowed through grass covered meadows at the foot of dizzy rolling hills or along by simple farms laboured effortlessly by their owners with Teutonic efficiency and sitting perfectly into the landscape like a masterpiece created by the famed German artist, Holbien himself. Alas, once the S.S. found out the author was Jewish, it didn't take long for his work to be ridiculed and his much coveted publishing contract tore up. They then set about to persecute Jakob the Poet, and it was really only by the skin of his teeth that he escaped to Holland, however it was now looking likely that they were going to catch up with him, sooner rather than later.

The droning noise of the aircraft were drawing closer and the cargo of lethal fire and blast bombs the British Lancaster's were carrying began to descend on the blacked-out and battered old city. Out on the street, policemen, German troops and civilians alike scurried quickly to the nearest underground shelter for protection from the deadly bombardment and as Jakob thought about it, he knew that given the chance, he'd be amongst them. He stared across to the river nearby and the sight that greeted his weary eyes of the Prussian fleet moored along the quayside now lit up by several burning buildings decorated by the panic of stricken sailors running to and fro to escape the deadly explosions and flying debris. In an instant it was obvious to his intelligence to quickly conclude that the target was the supply ships stranded along the wharf, as well as anything else of the German navy that was caught in the RAF's way, but to view the terrible destruction unfolding in front of him, brought a strange feeling of satisfaction upon Jakob's person, although the sensation didn't last long.

The brave couple that had been hiding the fugitive, had long left for the air-raid shelter along with their siblings, and Jakob was all alone in the house, however it was gradually dawning on him the real danger he was in as he watched another stray device miss its target and instead fall upon some unfortunates property. He thought about it for a moment, but it didn't take Jakob long to make up his mind since he was sick to death of running and putting other people's lives at risk and it was time he decided,

"To face my fears;"

Not only that, he assumed that if a bomb was to fall on the young families home, he and he alone would be killed, which would be bad enough, but what if his badly mangled body was found in amongst the rubble by the Nazis. There might be an investigation to identify the remains, where upon they could find out he was a Jew and then there'd be lots of questions, followed by arrests and God knows what would happen to his hosts and their children.

Jakob grabbed the one or two possessions he'd left in the world, namely his wired-framed glasses, and his worn jotter with its well used pencil. He left no farewell note or anything else to thank his protectors and soon after taking one quick last look around the gloomy attic room; he pulled on his torn, dishevelled overcoat and departed quietly through a side entrance. He thought it best that way so as not to leave any in-criminating evidence lying about for any eagle-eyed Nazi, or collaborator, and instead, dragged his hat down over his face, turned up his collar, and proceeded speedily in the direction of the docks to where the attack was concentrated, before quickly boarding one of the many small fishing boats left deserted. Jakob was content with the vessel he chose as there was an oil-skin cover stretched out over its opening and somewhat in a sense of pessimistic foreboding, Jakob hastily lay hidden under its fragile shell, after untying the craft from the quay. Lying silently in a foetal position in a vain attempt to shield himself from the onslaught, he then took a deep breath and waited for the insignificant boat to drift unceremoniously to its own doom.

With the wreckage from the exploding merchant ships and trapped naval destroyers landing in every direction, Jakob's found his fearless courage slowly beginning to recede. He felt that at any moment now, a red-hot piece of metal or any other manner of shrapnel was going to rip through the canvas awning and kill him, so in preparation for his demise, he shut his eyes tightly, clasped his hands over his ears and began chanting an old Hebrew prayer over and over again. It was a verse he loved so well since it was

taught to a young boy by his very affectionate mother and his belief was that by repeating it, the strength of his mother's spirit
would help him leave this world quickly and without too much
pain.

The attack continued noisily all around Jakob, even though his
self induced mantra began to drown out the horrendous din, while
at the same time it aided the terrified gentleman in losing consciousness. The nightmare claps of thunder shaking his trembling
frame along with the blinding red white flashes of burning carnage
dissipated, as a vision appeared, and he found himself in an enchanting place, sitting on a neatly built stone wall that continued on
into the distance. Inside the low construction, a shallow breeze was
brushing along the top of a large pasture of golden wheat, helping
the stalks to sway in unison, without any real effort. He was
pleased to hear several children playing happily in the flaxen field,
their laughter resounding through the air, noticed even above the
cry of the nearby woodland creatures, or the chorus of the many
summer birds which flew freely through the clear blue sky. On one
side of the wall was a dusty track of a mountain path sliding its
way purposely around a remote, overgrown, emerald forest, whilst
a natural grassy verge lay roughly, on either side of the road-way.
It had a constant sprinkle of a copper shade evident upon its pine-
green coat, but it added to the authenticity of the dry, sunny setting.
And then the water! Always a river of some type! Jakob was forever finding himself drawn to the flow, peacefulness and beauty of
water ripples swimming nonchalantly into one another, over rocky
out-crops or in a free-flow race as they draw nearer to its ever widening mouth to join a larger, more raging force on its journey towards the sea.

The layout was perfect for Jakob, a kind of Heaven with the
poet drifting in and out of a picture of nirvana, regularly in his
dreams. He couldn't imagine Paradise to be much better and in
truth he hoped he wouldn't have to wake up from his own private
Eden to face the ever present horrors of real life. Sitting comfortably on the stony surface, he turned with a smile to the children
playing in the distant, to watch them jump with a skip through the
tall stems, only to disappear momentarily as they landed. He em-
braced the display, taking delight to join their warm laugh, until a
small while later, his attention was captured by a lone, wild rabbit

which came into view, itself skipping boldly along the hill path, stopping frequently on its way, as it got closer, to rub its nose and survey its surroundings. Its proud leaps high into the air brought with them, small clouds of dust that were being disturbed from the dry surface and Jakob patiently watched the light brown mists settle softly upon the rough ground. He anticipated the curiosity of the timid animal as it approached him, wondering how close it would dare come, however suddenly, the calmness was instantly disturbed, when without warning, the atmosphere dramatically began to change.

From further up the trail, Jakob observed a much larger, denser veil, or was it a fog forming. It's threatening, wilder, more hurried appearance seemed to push it swiftly pass the woodlands and down the mountain, enveloping the immediate surroundings it encroached with its daunting advance. The poet also noticed how darker the sky was becoming as the spectacle closed at an alarming rate whilst the ever stronger gusts that accompanied it grew wilder by the second, bringing with them black smoke and clouds, which suffocated the summer scene. As panic set in, Jakob glanced helplessly towards the children to try and warn them to find cover from the ensuing storm, but was then aghast to see a mass of steel-helmeted foot soldiers with menacing faces, racing through the lea under the banner of a crooked cross. In a horrifying show of brutality, their destructive rampage cut down the innocents in an instant, and continued on with chilling hatred to Jakob in a frenzied, bloodthirsty zeal. He wanted to run and hide and even scream, but he knew it was no use as the deafening roar of countless, frightening war machines gained momentum with a crescendo of battle cries repeating through his head. Down-hearted, he collapsed onto the dirty track and it was now evident to the poet that there was no escape, no release from the persistent terror. A broken man, he crouched behind the stone wall in a pitiful pose, his tearful eyes lost in the hands which were once renowned to write such beautiful prose, while meekly accepting his fateful end. He almost immediately could hear the powerful, military voices getting louder and heavier, nearer and more fearful as the sickening smell of their bad breath filled Jakob's nostrils, until suddenly, just when their verbal overtones began to become clearer, he could feel a wet hand on his shaking shoulder.

"Alright mate? Are you okay? What are you doin' out 'ere all on your own anyway?"

Jakob was astonished at first when he heard the cockney slang, and to make certain, he quickly opened his eyes and sat up in his bobbling craft, while the sailor continued.

"Thought you were nothin' but a corpse there for a sec."

Immediately Jakob hastily interrupted with the little bit of English he had, especially after spotting the St. George's ensign flying proudly aloft the vessel that had pulled alongside.

"Where am I? Who are you?" he asked excitedly in quick succession, however, without a word from his saviour, his questions were emotionally answered when he recognised the welcoming white cliffs of Dover across the distant horizon. It was a sight which allowed him tears of joy for the first time in years and he shed them freely for at last he was truly free.

A short while later as he was recuperating in an English hospital he became a poet again by putting pen to paper in tribute to his much beloved Bavaria, when he wrote an ode which he often recited when gazing out across the English Channel towards Northern Europe.

> I saved a dream from far-away,
> A forgotten place I left someday;
> Where vivid hues danced across the land,
> Was such a life so full, so grand;
>
> I know I'll see my friends no-more,
> A broken heart I can never cure;
> My tranquil life is lost forever,
> But forget my land; I cannot; Never.

FIN

CARRIGEEN COTTAGE by Declan P.Gowran

ON that first night I lay quietly on the bed in the darkened room, drawing mental pictures over the dim walls. Jimmy, my big brother, was stretched out beside me, breathing softly in the first layers of sleep, and already half covered. A soft light diffused through the door from the stairwell that led up to the loft from the kitchen below. I listened aimlessly to the shuffling of feet, odd whispers of strange voices, those aware that we were probably asleep already. Aware that we might be homesick already.

I was really too fixated by the day's events to drift naturally into sleep. It seemed ages ago that our parents had hugged us goodbye, abandoning us to this weird new world. They may have been as upset as we had been in their own way, but they didn't show it. We weren't really upset as they left us, still excited about the benign unknown fate of spending holidays alone with new people. Our parents had been reluctant to leave perhaps out of a sense of guilt as this was the first time that we as a family had been parted. From early that morning Jimmy and me had put up a game struggle to avoid being dragged off on this sort of adventure. He had hidden under our bed, and I had taken to the Glory-Hole under the stairs to avoid detection. We had been trying every excuse to deter them since their idea of a country holiday had been first mooted:

"Yous are going to Baltinglass, and that's final!"

Daddy had spoken in his sea captain's voice. We had learned not to argue with the captain when his cheeks blew up like balloons, when his eyebrows curled up like Count Dracula's.

Mammy tried to reassure us:

"It'll be great for you! Just think: a holiday down the country with chickens and cows..."

"And pigs and muck!" Daddy added quickly, winking.

"Now how many other poor children would get such a treat?"

Mammy had hit the soft spot below our belts. But we kept on bawling anyway just in case.

"You should be so lucky!" Daddy scoffed: "Here! Look what I've got for yous!"

Like magic he produced two pairs of wellies out of thin air: the sort that farmers would wear. Jimmy looked at me. I looked back. Backwards and forwards. Next came the suitcase. Inside it newly laid out were two sets of fresh duds: tartan shirts and socks and canvas short pants. This was the business. Maybe things wouldn't be so bad after all. And there was a bag of bon-bons each, thrown in too! We'd be sure to see loads of tractors and machinery as well as all those animals. These were things us city kids only got to see in magazines, seldom in the flesh, except when the rag-and-bone man came tinkling up the avenue with his worn out nag and dray. Or when a wild herd of steers was hounded on the hoof, down the canal to the back of Bowyer's slaughterhouse.

It was a pleasant summer's evening. We could almost feel the hum of the countryside, alive with the buzzing of insects, and the music of birds, and the swaying of the trees as we arrived at our destination. The journey itself, begun with trepidation, but slowly becoming interesting, for me turned out to be brilliant. Who doesn't love a drive especially in the country. We had waved to the gang from the back of Daddy's battered green Bedford van as we headed out of the avenue, Baltinglass bound, trying to look grim to leave them with a good impression of our tearful departure. Daddy used the Bedford to haul for the grocery shop. It was only a two seater with a button starter beside the handbrake so we had to sit on the rickety orange boxes in the capacious back of the body. We spent the time reading or tossing tennis balls, all the time rocking, and sometimes hunkering down between our parents to see where we were going on the thin, winding road. Every now and then there was a junction like a triangle and another road would veer off into the distance, but to where exactly I could only guess. The further we got the more we had to climb and that's when I really got excited when the big, big mountains started to appear:

"Wow! Look at the size of that one. It's huge!"

"That's *Lug-na-Coille!* " Daddy said matter of factly. " Biggest mountain in these parts. Managed   to climb it once, doing the artillery training with the *Slua Mhuire* down in the Glen of Imaal. Do you know we're supposed to be getting a new fleet of ships with fast-firing guns. Those guns on the Corvettes take an eternity to lay . It must have been just then that I fell in love with mountains. How mountains endow the Earth with sheer power and majesty. Slopes, shapes, curves, drops, highs, lows, tops, saddles, clouds and mist. Mysterious, overwhelming. Heavens uplifting. Mountains simply couldn't be ignored.

Carrigeen Cottage was a Council Cottage. A quaint little house with a hall-door porch flanked by two windows. It also had two little gable end windows, providing a coy light for the bedrooms in the loft. It had a slate grey roof topped in the centre by a sturdy single chimney stack. Despite it being a sultry evening a wisp of blue smoke curled lazily through the still air from the chimney. Even as we arrived at the wicket gate I sensed a heady aroma in the air: the smell of the countryside. A musky scent seemed to waft from the shrubby hedge that formed the boundary of the front garden and the road. (The shrub, I was to learn later, was called Ornamental Currant or *Ribes*). It smelt to me then like the Scent of Paradise, and some feeling deep inside me told me that I would grow to love this place and its people.

Daddy tooted the horn as we arrived, playing taps, and waking the countryside from its slumber.

Mammy waved frantically through the open window as the occupants of the cottage emerged from the shadow of the doorway, which had already been open, closely followed by a pair of shaggy mongrel dogs who were bounding and barking joyously at the prospect of company.

Cathleen Carroll was the woman of the house. A countrywoman. She sidled up to the Bedford, circled it with her greetings before coming around to the back doors. She peered through the back window, and pressed her thin pointed nose up to the glass, examining us inside with a beady eye.

"Ah ha!" She cackled: "Well what sees I, says I!"

She spoke a mighty queer language right enough, and she had a mischievous sparkle in her pale blue eyes. She started to chortle and giggle and hum, and teasing us by contorting her bony face.

"Ah now, me boyos ye're not afraid o' me are ye. Are ye not comin' ou' to see oul Carroll an' she with a glass o' orange squash all ready fer ye, t' wash aw'y the dust o' th' road."

She stood at the back of the Bedford, tapping her foot on the ground and daring us to get out. The dogs were going mad by this stage. Carroll's husband, Ned was standing by the garden gate, sucking on his pipe and trying to calm them as they lolled about, licking our parents' hands.

"What's keeping yous," Daddy shouted: "Come and meet the Howlers!"

Often children have no control over their destiny, but we jumped out enthusiastically to mix it with the rest. We got a big bear hug in turn from Carroll. While Ned manfully shook us both with a mighty squeeze of his big paw. Ned had a crusty red face with a grey stubblely beard which he would rub intermittently. Every time he puffed on his pipe he would grumble and when he spoke he whistled like an old steam engine. He grabbed Daddy then to engage him in conversation.

"Now!" Said Carroll after we polished off our orange squash: "Ye pair may as well get yer bearings before breakfast-why don't ye go for a gallop round the garden while yer mother and' me get ye yer tae!"

Carroll had a funny way with words right enough as well as being a bit of an imp. But we felt that she had bidden us welcome in her own peculiar way, meaning for us to stay with her, as free as needs be. The woman of a thousand smiles had found the quickest way to our hearts.

Carrigeen Cottage stood facing the sun at the short end of an isosceles triangle. A flower garden, ornamental in style, stood to the front of the cottage. It was set with colourful flower borders enclosed by a series of glossy privet hedging that was clipped to a miniature size. To the right, as you looked from the door, beyond the garden stood the vegetable patch. This was sown mainly with potatoes, although carrots and beet and pungent onions also abounded. To the left of the door a large metal farm-gate provided access from the roadway for the likes of a motorcar or tractor though the Carrolls possessed neither. Their small holding hardly amounted to an acre which with the house was rented for a schilling a week. There was a working area to the left –hand eastern gable end of the cottage used mainly for the cutting of firewood as evidenced by a scattering of saplings and sallies, tree-trunks and logs, the imprint of cartwheels, and a saddle for the cross-cut saw.

To the rear of the cottage stood a one storey out-house made of granite. Above in the upper chamber the domesticated fowl roosted when they weren't out clucking and scratching around the yard or laying eggs in makeshift concealed nests. It was equipped with a small door which could be secured against foxes, and was reached by slabs of granite that jutted out from the walls like stepping stones of stairs. In the lower chamber the pigs resided. A pretty pair of porkers with curly tails that Carroll raised for Christmas. The pigs' quarters also had an outdoor extension sty. We noticed that the pigs' feeding trough was also gouged out of granite. The sort of crockery that you'd find very hard to crack!

To the back of the out-house stood the dung-heap. The soiled bedding from the sty and the chicken coop was collected here; as well as the contents of the Walpamur cans from the bedrooms after the slopping out from the night before! Ned said that it was this rich smelly compost that provided the food for his lawn-grass and flowers and vegetables so was not to be sneered at.

This was Nature's Bounty, Ned explained. You don't turn your nose up to Mother Nature. At that moment though, contemplating the dung-heap, it was just as well that we didn't realise that it too would provide us with our ' out-door convenience'! It was hard to reconcile the smell we made doing our 'No. 2' with the perfume of the rose. But such are the mysterious lessons of Nature. What goes out

must come back! But we were soon to learn how to dig a hole and do our business before applying the camouflage. It didn't really bother us as it often happened at home if the gang was out on a campaign. It was just that the clumps of grass were a bit hard to rub around the hind-quarters if you had forgotten to bring paper- the newspaper variety that is -like the *Leinster Leader*! Now there was a paper with plenty of coverage!

The western boundary of Carrolls' field was formed by a section of the main road from Baltinglass which lay about two miles to the north. The eastern boundary was formed by the hedgerows of Tom Doyle's field, the farmer who cultivated it. Although Carrolls' field sloped gently down to its apex, Jimmy figured it would still make a great football pitch. I figured it was too full of clover and buttercup; but maybe Carroll would let us build goalposts if we asked her nicely. And maybe Ned might build the goal, seeing that he had such fine lengths of wood in the saw-yard.

We were so debating when all of a sudden Jimmy spotted it. There at the end of the field stood a brown pony, browsing contentedly. Automatically we both started running to it, only holding up as we approached the pony for fear of frightening it. This was rapid. Heaven sent. It was a beautiful animal and big enough to ride. Although the top of my head barely reached the pony's shoulder, I reckoned Jimmy could have vaulted straight on to her back if he gave it a go.

I dared him, but Jimmy never was 'The bravest of the braves'. We were both good climbers being well able to scamper up the chestnut trees in the middle of our avenue. But being confronted with a real live animal was another matter. On the spur of the moment Jimmy said that he might as well just risk it. The cowboy in him almost broke through.

"Better not, not now anyways." He checked cautiously.

"You're probably right." I agreed. "Like I don't sees any reins or stirrups ....no saddle... an' you have to be an Indian to ride a horse bareback."

"I still bet ya I could do it all the same!" Jimmy boasted. "There's nuttin' to it!"

But I knew he wasn't being honest. He was scrunching up his face like he would if the master asked him an awkward sums question in school.

"I wonder what her name is?" I said with a sigh.

"Now you're presumin'!" Jimmy scoffed. "You see, I can tell!"

Jimmy knelt down on the grass and peered underneath the horse's hind legs.

"As I thought!" He scoffed again: "It's a *she* alright!"

Jimmy always annoyed me when he got haughty and inquisitive like that. He would often examine me and pinch me when we were in the bath together. His excuse being that when he grew up he was going to be a doctor so he had to find out all about live bodies- on boys anyway - he had to rely on his imagination to decipher a girl's anatomy though he claimed to have a fair idea on that score. I was mighty glad that he had never expressed a desire to become a dentist- I just couldn't bare to have him scratching my teeth with a rusty fork, looking out for cavities.

"I see you've met Lady!"

It was Ned's voice. He was strutting down the field with great strides, coming towards us. 'Lady' we called out simultaneously. Lady was no name for a horse!

"Why don't you call her Apache!" I blurted out.

"Or Comanche!" Jimmy hollered. " Comanche was General Custer's horse, an' the only livin' thing to survive the Battle of the Little Big Horn, I know 'cause I sawr it in the pictures!"

Ned pulled out his pipe. He lit a match and after a few sucking puffs he took a silver cap from his waistcoat pocket and placed it over the bowl. He puffed pensively for a moment, the balmy breeze stirring the straggly hairs on his head, the base of his pipe resting on the matchbox which he held in the palm of his hand. The match which he had used up had burnt right down to his brown finger tips, but he didn't seem to feel its effect as it flickered and died. He then crushed the petrified wood between his fingers, rubbing it out like a powder as it sprinkled on to the grass. Ned spoke in his unique chewy sort of way:-

" Comanche? Hmm. Well if I was goin' on the warpath, that would be a mighty fine name for
war-horse. But this horse is every inch a Lady. Have you ever seen such a shiny colour. Felt the lushness of her coat, the softness of her hide. Come over yourselves. Stroke her. She won't bite!"

We approached the pony timidly at first. Lady responded. She whinnied and nudged us with her nose to encourage us. I stroked the white blaze on her forehead. Her hair here was firm like a cloths brush. She also had white ankle socks to match. Her long tail swished about like a pendulum, now and then describing a flailing circle, swatting away a sleepy fly from her back. Ned began to talk to her, a language it seemed only know to him and Lady. He produced a sugar-lump from his waistcoat to reward her. I could sense instinctively the bond between the man and his horse.

"Time for tay, now!" Ned chuckled:- "You'll see Lady here ag'in tomorrow. We'll go fetch kindlin' wood after I finishes work. Promise!"

We galloped joyously up the field, whooping like Red Indians. I felt suddenly hungry. No, it was more like an empty hole in the pit of my belly.

"What's for tea! What's for tea!" We cried out in time honoured fashion, barely ducking to dip our hands in the basin of water by the fire as Mammy instructed. We attacked the table greedily, demolishing all the lovely fare laid out before us. The Howlers started howling then to get in on the act until Ned had to whoosh the pair of them unceremoniously out the door to restore a bit of order.

"Tis the country air.." Carroll mused. "Works wonders on all sorts o' life. Aye they'll sleep t'night alright, ye may count on it without worry."

Mammy jolted her head back almost in mock agreement:

" Country air did you say! Now amn't I the right baby to be dozing off like that!"

"Better get you home to your bed, so. " Daddy laughed.

And then we all laughed. Hearty rings of laughter rang around Carrigeen Cottage as the dusk gathered in the daylight. I laughed especially while a dollop of Carroll's homemade jam dribbled down my chin like blood from a vampire's lips. I felt so contented then.

Although Carrigeen Cottage was small the accommodation was economically arranged. Behind the front door there was a compact entrance hall. To the right as you entered you found the living room cum dining room cum kitchen area all rolled up into one. This ran the entire width of the eastern gable of the house. As you walked into the kitchen the expansive fireplace and hearth stood to the left, forming the centrepiece, the heart of the cottage. Behind the hallway partition an ingle nook was formed, furnishing a cosy seat out of the draught. The hearth was coloured a tarry black and was festooned with an array of crane-like hooks of various shapes and lengths that were used to swing the pots and pans back and forth over the heat of the flames. When we arrived a large tar encrusted iron kettle hung there as it whistled to the boil. An equally tar encrusted skillen pot heaped with steaming jacketed potatoes stood to the side of the range. The built-in sections of the hearth either side of the fire-grate formed seats large enough for us boys to sit upon. These seats were to become our favourite perches once you faced away from the fire with both feet forward.

Carroll used a wide four-footed table for eating off. It also served as her worktop. The table was covered with oilcloth with a floral pattern. For this first visit she had taken out the porcelain service

for the tea. This china was only used for auspicious occasions, ordinarily we used mugs with blue and white hoops (rather like the Synge Street football jersey) , and matching plates for the everyday meals. There was a sideboard and cupboards lining the kitchen gable wall and at the end corner at the bottom of the stairs, a bag of white flour was propped on the concrete floor. To the back of the kitchen, there was a tiny back bedroom, and adjacent to a closet, the stairs ascended to the two bedrooms in the loft. We were ensconced in the bedroom to the right at the top of the stairs. This would have been Granny Nowlan's room normally. (Nowlan was Carroll's maiden name). Granny Nowlan was away at present ' doin' the rounds o' th' family'. She liked to circulate amongst her family during the summer months,' t' keep a weather eye on them', but she always came home for the winter to stay with Carroll. Nowlan liked to sit at the back of the kitchen, like *Whistler's Mother*, rocking in her chair, and holding court for any local worthy who cared to call. She loved embroidery and would bleach the old flour sacks to make pillows and napkins and hankies and sheets. In that way she was like my own Grandfather:- nothing was allowed go to waste, partly I suppose because there wasn't much going around in the first place, and partly because necessity has always been the mother of innovation. Nowlan was a handywoman and taught her daughter most of what she knew. She had a wizened face and her hands were black and blue from ' from all that turkey pluckin' as she used to say. But she had a serene look about her, of being totally at peace with the world after years of hard struggle.

And she was always good for a penny for to go down to Hughes green corrugated shop for a bar of Cleeves Toffee.

Although there were few shops in the district, the travelling peddlers regularly brought their passing trade. There was one traveller in particular, an urbane gent who dressed like a dandy with a cravat and colourful tweed coat sporting a buttonhole, and with spats for shoes, who called about once a month to Carrigeen Cottage. He rode a bicycle that was painted a garish green and kept his wares in a box over the front wheel and in an old crocodile suitcase on the back carrier. He would knock politely on the door of the cottage, even though it was always open, and introduce himself, though Carroll knew him well. He would deliver his sales pitch then like a man from a Medicine Show, laying out his suitcase on the table, and throwing open the lid as if revealing the secret to a magician's master trick. Inside the case lay scattered the riches of the industrial world from safety pins to spools of thread, sewing needles, ribbons, scissors, pen knifes, pins, brooches, bangles, rings, badges and bracelets, trinkets and trifles. He would sometimes stay for tea which would give him the chance to extract some bottles from his box to tempt Carroll if she wasn't biting. These crystalline containers of *art deco* designs contained various potions, tinctures and perfumes. With the sale completed he would mount his bicycle and give a wave with his brown derby hat as he rattled off down the road to his next port of call.

The itinerant tinkers too, often called in their gaily painted horse drawn caravans. These might have blankets to sell, and rugs, and carpets, and doormats, and linoleum, and oilcloth. Some carried out their traditional trade of mending pots and pans, and working tin into plates and mugs, and rough toys and ornaments.

The room to the left of the entrance hall of the cottage was Carroll's very own pride and joy. The master bedroom with the master bed complimented by a varnished wardrobe and a mahogany commode complete with basin, jug, and a swivelling mirror. Usually on weekdays our ablutions would consist of a quick rub around the kisser with a wet cloth. But on Saturday nights we got the full works down to bare buttocks with the bar of Red Lifebuoy, standing on a towel on the linoleum in front of that glorious commode. On it Ned had all his grooming accoutrements laid out like his razor and brush and bowl and his hairbrush and hair-cream on one side and Carroll also had hers laid out on the other side together with more womanly items like a powder puff.

When we really got dirty and the muck and sweat of our frolics got stuck between our toes, the zinc bath was brought out into the kitchen and placed in front of the fire. That's when we got the real going over, finishing off with a hair shampoo. Over the mantle-piece of the fireplace stood a melancholy figurine of the Sacred Heart: a simple shrine to the Faith of the family. A deep red glow shone from the shrine as constant as the family's belief. To one side a picture of Our Lady held out her hands to the world while treading on a snake. There were other pictures too, hanging about the cottage. Rustic and Alpine scenes which Carroll liked to change around every now and then like a floating gallery. She liked to change the scenery as she put it, and once she professed to an unholy love for the famous 'Bubbles' illustration used to advertise Pears Soap when she was a little girl.

As night closed in on that first night Ned began to trim the wicks of the oil lamps. For the table there was a large brass based lamp with a bulbous golden glass cover, and a smaller version for the mantle-piece. There were others too, adapted for carrying, but we were forbidden to handle these for fear of burning ourselves or causing a fire. We understood. But Ned allowed us to manipulate them under supervision. It was a novelty for us to control the height and intensity of the flickering flame by turning the wick-wheel on the side of the lamp. The effect of moving about in the lamplight threw spectral shadows on to the ceiling and walls. The smell of the paraffin reminded me of medicine, and it tended to make me sleepy. Bedtime was suggested by a couple of jaw-breaking yawns. Mammy and Carroll got us ready and tucked us into our bed, together as always just like at home. That night we got two goodnight kisses each before we turned over to try and sleep.

I don't know exactly how long I had been slumbering when I perceived another voice coming up the stairs. This voice was different. It sounded girlish, young and gay and carefree, full of the *joie de vivre*. Now I was curious about this interloper, but kept my

head down anyway, leaving enough room to peek over the covers.
First an indistinct head peeped in around the door, followed by the
shape of a figure that was obviously female in form. I discerned the
swish of her skirt as she went to retire:

"Hello." I mumbled sleepily, sounding a little silly.

"Hello, Little Wan." The girl whispered: " I'm Eileen and
you must be....Jimmy...."

" Not on yer nanny!" I croaked indignantly: " He's that ugly
one beside me!"

I nodded in his direction, prodding, but Jimmy just snorted.

Eileen began to titter uncontrollably. I could hear Carroll
scold her then from down the stairs.

" Better get to bed." Eileen said gently: " See you in the
morning, please God. Goodnight Little
Wan, and sweet dreams."

" I suppose you were out with your boyfriend." I said
nosily, speaking off the cuff.

" Well aren't you the saucy one!"

That was enough for Carroll: " Get to bed! Go to sleep!"
She cried, fearing a revolution.

" If you must know," Eileen continued: " I was out dancin'
in Castledermot...and no I haven't got a Beau .....unless now, you
yourself might be interested...."

Perish the thought! I curled up with embarrassment.

" Goodnight again." She said: " Sure we'll have a chat
tomorrow."

She turned to leave, but paused and peeped in again:

" You can knock on my door if you need anything, I'm just
across from you. Don't be afraid now. And don't be shy now, sure
you won't?"

" Thanks Eileen." I said sincerely: " Goodnight!"

This time she left and entered her own room across the
small landing, closing her bedroom door softly behind her. The
lights from downstairs finally dimmed and I settled into the bed,
snuggling up beside Jimmy. He snorted again and kicked a little so
I covered him to keep him warm. A rich glow infused my veins
like the light from the Sacred Heart lamp. It was a feeling of
belonging, of family.

Our mother, being an orphan of sorts, (which is another story) had been brought up my the McDonald Family in Parkview in Dublin as one of their own. The Carrolls were second cousins to the clan and often called to the house when they came up to town. In time, gregarious as she was, Carroll added our own house to her list of visits on her downtown excursions. She would visit as needs be during the year, but the All-Ireland trip every September was always *de rigeur*. Although the All-Ireland Football final was a must go it never proved to be a must see as she never set foot inside Croke Park unless her beloved Lilywhites happened to be playing. Unfortunately the last time that that had happened was way back in 1928 which was always a sore point with her sporting sensibilities. Yes there had been a Leinster title in '56; but what was that compared to a coveted All-Ireland amount of bragging. Carroll wore her colours on her sleeve. She was the 'Sporting Man' about the house.

"Bad cess to them Jackeens!" She would curse as Michael O'Hehir recorded another Dublin score over the crackling of the wireless. We generally listened to the Gaelic matches on sultry Sunday afternoons, sitting out in the garden. Carrolls had an old wooden wireless with big knobs that was powered by an ancient wet battery, but the reception came in strong and relatively clear. We would forever tease her about the amount of All-Irelands that Dublin had won- even at Hurling -but this rarely fazed her:

"An' we was the first, the very first, to lift the sacred Sam Maguire! Beat that if ye can, an' sure ye never will in a month of Football Sundays!"

After the match was over I used to love to fiddle with the knobs on the wireless. searching for far away stations. The wireless used to make zany extra-terrestrial screeches as you tuned it in between the bands that had strange foreign names like Hilversum and Luxembourg. The AFN waveband was really hip while the BBC World Service seemed the most exotic. Carroll preferred down home programmes like Dinjo's Take the Floor or the Ceili House and she especia.lly enjoyed Hospitals' Requests.

For me everything would stop when Carroll came to town. I used to get hi-jacked as a sort of chaperone for her progress for a generous retainer of course. That was an incentive for her heart too was generous. She loved to visit friends she knew in Cork Street and Clanbrassil Street, and go shopping to the likes of Pims Store in Georges Street. It was her chance to get away from the drudgery of rural life, her chance to promenade across the town in her finery. Carroll favoured figured-in dressy suits of neutral colours like cobalt-blue for it favoured her straight cut short grey hair. She always donned an elegant hat stuffed sometimes with waxy fruit or maybe a long silver pin stuck in the side and sometimes a feather! She wore matching cloggy shoes often clasped with silver buckles. Indeed she would have done herself justice with her epochal style at the likes of Ladies Day at the Horse Show. I think her secret was she always dressed to suit her age. She had no pretensions. Nothing but natural airs and graces. No denims indeed for such a Grand Dame.

Carrigeen Cottage itself was barely inside the boundary of County Kildare. In fact the Three-County-Corner was just about a mile down the road to the Big Stone school. On an unmarked, indeterminate, and invisible spot in the middle of a certain field it was to be found:- the exact spot that County Wicklow, County Carlow and County Kildare fused together so that you could have a foot in two of them and a hand in the other. The real question was: Where would your heart lie? Which county would your heart follow?

If mountains were your first love then you had to lean to Wicklow, The Garden of Ireland. If it was rivers then it had to be Carlow, shaped like a cornucopia, the Horn of Ireland. But if you liked horses then it had to be Kildare with its famous Curragh, the Plain of Ireland.

So it was with Ned too, Kildare was his favourite. Unfortunately when you like the horses, you also tend to like a flutter. Being a working-man Ned would hardly be in town in between Sundays, and of course the Bookies wouldn't open on Sundays. Of course there was no moral or religious law forbidding a learned perusal through the pages of The Field or The Sporting Life even on Sundays. A man could take a fancy to a horse, trace its bloodline, follow its form guide or that of its jockey. Follow them like stars in the night sky. We too would read the racing press, and Ned explained about the science of betting with cross-doubles and accumulators and yankees and monkeys.

Ned wasn't really a gambler, he just loved the horse. He was really hooked on cards though and I'm sure he would have been the King of the Strip if he had ever got to Las Vegas. He attended religiously the Saturday Night card game over in Irongrange. 25's was the preferred hand. It seems it required more tactical skill than the likes of draw poker. Every Saturday night without fail Ned would wash and shave and dress up: 't' give the Sunday suit a bit o' an airin' before Mass'.

He would hop up on his big framed Rudge bicycle, trouser clips in place, his soft Fedora hat pulled down over his eyes and head to the wind. On darker evenings we could hear the whirr of his dynamo rubbing against the tyre, and watch the beam of his lamp stabbing the roadway as he took off, gathering speed, as the beam became stronger. We always shouted after him: " Good Luck now!" for when Ned won at the cards it meant a Sunday morning treat after Mass like an ice-cream or chocolate bar in celebration.

Of course we often wished that we could go and watch Ned play the cards; but he always insisted that it went on much too late for children. He said that even the women were barred. I felt that he didn't really want to encourage us. Some things like cards, it would seem, were totally sacrosanct in the world of grown-up men. But Ned made it up to us by showing us some of his card tricks and teaching us innocuous games like 'House'. My favourite game was 'House' and I used to love yelling 'House!' when my last card was called. Jimmy loved playing 'Beggin' me neighbour'. It was just like his brain-waves- there was no end to them or that game. Ned told us all about a game called 'Find the Lady', but warned us off it by saying: ' That's only a game for eegits!" It was great fun trying to build a pyramid with the cards. I don't think I ever managed to construct a full pyramid. I suspect that as soon as I turned my back, Jimmy would blow it down and blame it on the draught from the chimney as I went for him in a temper. At times like that I thought Jimmy was a little sly. But it didn't bother me that much. I had my own foibles. I always pinched more of the blankets when I snuggled down to sleep under the bed covers, mesmerised by that hawk-like eye on the Jack of Spades.

Every weekday morning, at cock-crow, Ned would leave on his bicycle to go to work on the Corcoran's farm near Hacketstown. He was a labourer there and general handyman. He would often bring home produce from the farm, and sometimes exotic items like marrows or cherries from the orchard plus the customary quart of milk in his can. Any time he had to take a special tool or implement he would sling these under the cross-bar of the bicycle while his bag of personal effects was fastened to the back carrier.

Carroll was like Ned and used a three-speed Ladies bicycle for her commuting. She cycled into Baltinglass regularly to do her business or perhaps visit Mrs Kearney up the town or drop into O'Donoughue's house where her brother John had lodgings. She also had another brother, Michael who was married in the town at that time. She would do her shopping in the likes of Timmons shop or Quinns or Gillespies. Clarkes beside the bridge over the Slaney was her fashion haunt. She seemed to have a privileged arrangement with some of these traders. Gillespies for instance always delivered her bag of flour out to the cottage while the driver of Quinns' truck often dropped in fresh eggs and butter to our house on its trips up to Dublin. Carroll must have been a well favoured customer though she didn't smoke and never crossed the door of a public house unless it was for medicinal or baking purposes. She was never a prude and never judgemental. Not for her the narrow mindedness of the parish gossip. She walked though with a superior, urbane air, assured of her standing, affording all and sundry the time of day and any sympathy deemed necessary for the sustaining of life.

Whatever else Carroll never forgot her pets. I reckon that The Howlers were better fed than the rest of the household with the prime cuts of beef that she used to toss to them. She would slice it and then toss it to them so that The Howlers would jump up in turn and catch the titbit in mid-air. It was rather like a Circus act, I fancied. Carroll also reserved a slice of choice liver for the feral cat who lived outdoors like a phantom in the field. We had spotted this cat- a furry creature -hiding in the undergrowth. It always kept a respectful distance from us much as we wished to go and pet it for we were very familiar with cats from our own home. This cat's tail seemed a trifle short to us perhaps the result of a chance encounter with an angry dog.

In later years Carroll acquired a nanny-goat to provide a rich supply of fresh milk. The goat roamed free, and did trojan service for the County Council, trimming the ditches around the cottage with all her nibbling. In the evenings Carroll would coax her into the kitchen with a fistful of oatmeal for to milk her. As Carroll milked Jinny into the bucket, every now and then she would aim a teat at a crater in the floor of the kitchen, and squirt a jet of milk to form a little pool in this depression. Now chickens may have a reputation for being dumb animals, but milking time was the cue for the flock to congregate in the kitchen. They would dip their beaks into the milk and sip away merrily the way that birds do. It seemed the stereotypical *'Stage Oirish'* scene of ' The pigs in the parlour'. I think in Carrolls' case it was an affirmation of the bond she had developed with her 'pets'; and an illustration that from ages past as Mankind and Animalkind began to live side by side they became as one. The goat, the chickens, the pigs, the cat were as much Carrolls' pets as her dogs.

Carrolls' domestic arrangements were in all probability a throwback to a more folksy existence. And it would have to be asked for instance if the Nativity scene with the cow and the donkey was purely accidental. All of Carrigeen Cottage's animals were part of Carrolls' extended family, and all were accorded equal consideration. She was to grieve inconsolable when one of The Howlers was knocked down on the road.

The sun was already high in the sky when we arose on the following morning. We had been left to our own hour to acclimatise. It was only on Sundays that a strict timetable was adhered to in order to attend Mass in Baltinglass.

" G' Mornin' lads," Eileen chirped as we came hobbling down the wooden stairs, *clackety-clack!* " I ken see ye slept well....Yer breakfast is on the table....So help yerselves..."

I yawned again.

" D' you know what, I never slept better....like a log!"

Jimmy sneezed:

" So if you slept like a log, then how come you were kicking me all night!"

He showed Eileen the backs of his legs;

" Just look at those bruises, will you!"

Eileen bent down to nurse him by rubbing his calves:

" There now Jimmy, ye're bound to survive."

Jimmy grinned mischievously:

" Oooh! That was nice." He cooed. " Would you mind doin' that again.....Please!"

" Why ye cheeky coot!"

Eileen let the dishcloth fly at him as he made a mad dash for the door. Then she was after him like a flapping swan, chasing him around the garden and around the piggery and around the field. He was laughing, Eileen was laughing and I was laughing too.

" Tax! Tax! Tax!" Jimmy cried hysterically, crossing his fingers. He was running out of space now and out of breath .

" Tax!" Eileen cried: " I'll tax ye good and proper when I ketches ye!"

" No! No! " I tried to explain: " He's lookin' for a pow-wow, a truce!"

Eileen pulled up, gasping for air by this stage: " I'm bet for sure!" She wheezed.

Jimmy stopped too and collapsed on the grass, panting:

" Can I have me breakfast now? I promise to be good."

" Ye can have your breakfast on one condition...."

" What's that?"

" That ye keep *both* yer fingers crossed....with *both* hands, mind !"

Jimmy hadn't much choice but to 'lap up' his breakfast. But he was delighted. He always enjoyed his food and this showed because he was much tubbier than me. Why lately he had begun to start bursting out of his older more worn out pants. Eileen herself was fairly fit and very lithesome then even though she was in her mid-twenties. She was a tall girl with short straight jet black hair that curled into the nape of her long neck. She had a vivid rosy complexion and a pair of fiery eyes that bulged with curious passion. When she dared you she would stand with her hands on her hips, legs apart and with her head leaning to one side; and when she would scold you she would stand in exactly the same way and wag her long finger in your face. Luckily we didn't annoy her too often. We would tease her, hoping that she might chase us round the garden.

Like her parents, Eileen too cycled everywhere, to the town, to her friends, to the neighbours, to the cinema, to the dance, and over the next hill just for the heck of it. When we first went to Mass Ned would give Jimmy a crossbar on his big 'Upstairs Model' bike while I got a carrier on the back of Eileen's machine. There was a certain knack to sitting on the carrier: you had to keep your legs well outstretched away from the chain and the wheel spokes. Balance was essential to ensure that you did not upset the equilibrium of the rider otherwise you'd wobble and crash to the ground. You could help steady yourself by holding the lip of the saddle or the rider's mid-rift with both hands. All Carroll had to do was to carry the prayer-books in her front basket and pedal graciously, sitting back like a peahen on her saddle, trailing the tail of her rain-mac in the slipstream.

Eileen often brought me off on trips on the back of her bicycle. I think she preferred company, not seeming to mind the extra effort required to haul me all over the countryside. I got to see many places in this way from Moone to Ballitore.

About the farthest place we visited was Carlow. Eileen would want to do some shopping in Shaws Department Store. We would have an ice-cream before setting off for home, resting here and there, discussing items of interest or various dwellings along the way.

" Someday I'll me married," She would say: " And I'll have a good husband, and m'ybe a little wan like yeself to dress up and bring out, and we'll all be livin' together in that lovely house..."

She would point to a certain house.

" No! M'ybe that wan over there might be better....or that wan...."

She would point to another and another:

" Which wan would ye prefer?"

" What about that one," I would venture, pointing in an entirely different direction. At a caravan pulled by a jaded horse, crunching along the road: " It's the travelling life for me!" I would assert, imagining that such a lifestyle was made of pure romance.

" Gow a that!" Eileen would say: " Ye'r like meself: too fond of yer comfort!"

Of course she was right. But we had great if simple comforts at Carrigeen Cottage. It was the cosiest place on Earth on damp summer nights; and cool as a closet on a scorching day.

Monday means one universal truth: Monday is washday all over the world. Every morning the fire was resuscitated in the grate by removing the excess ash and throwing on some firewood or turf. The cooled ash was cast beneath the fruit trees and tomato plants to plumpen up their fruits. Eileen prepared the fattest pot to boil the heavier clothes for the washing.

" Now me lads!" Carroll called to us as we finished our soda bread: " Which of ye will fetch me some water?"

" I will! I will!" We both shouted simultaneously.

She retrieved a large zinc bucket from under the table and rattled the handle:

" I think ye both best go...to carry it back from The Pike..."

" The Pike?" We both squirmed. " What's The Pike?" We imagined The Pike to be a lake of sorts named after the eponymous fish where the locals went to fetch their water. The Pike in fact was a water pump that stood at Carrigeen Crossroads a short distance from the cottage. The Pike wasn't so much the pump itself, but the general surroundings of the pump thus identified. This pump itself was a tall solid green instrument with a long curved handle on one side and an ornate spout with a bucket handle grip on the other. It was topped with a fancy scored finial and was set in a bed of concrete protected by a two-sided wall which looked into the Murray's front field. You hanged your bucket from the lug on the spout, primed the handle with a few strokes , and then you could literally hear the water being sucked up from underground, coursing up through the body of the pump which stood about five feet tall before the flow cascaded like a waterfall into your bucket. As soon as you stopped pumping the water stopped flowing and gurgled back to earth. Like any location where water was available for drinking, just like a desert oasis, The Pike was a special place of meeting, attracting the locals to discuss the general affairs and the prevailing conditions of the day be these political, personal, local or national. Even here in a country renowned for wet weather, drinking water was still a precious commodity. Kavanagh, for instance used to drive up to The Pike every day and load up his old Volkswagen Beetle with churns of fresh water for his household. Even the overflow from The Pike went to slake the thirst of passing animals.

Jimmy was busy pumping and I was busy leaning on the wall, gazing whimsically through the distance at the beautiful contours of a mountain range that stood off to the south-east. The tops of the mountains seemed to flow along the line of the horizon like gigantic dark blue waves.

" I wonder what those mountains are called," I said to Jimmy, pointing off above the retaining wall.

" How the hell would I know!" He gasped: " Can't you see I'm too busy to be idlin', admirin' a knuckle load of hillocks!"

" Them's the Blackstairs mountains."

The voice seemed to come from nowhere:

" And the tallest one there is called Mount Leinster. Ye can see her clear today so it should be a good day for cuttin' the Spring barley."

I turned in surprise at the voice of the interloper, and Jimmy stopped pumping.

Beside me stood a smallish man with watery eyes and a whiskery face. He was dressed in a dark shiny suit with a matching shiny waistcoat. His shirt had no collar and no tie. He was wearing a well worn peaked cap and his grey hair stuck out like clutches of straw from under the rim. In his hand he held a walking stick, a cane really, black like ebony, with a carved canine hand grip. His face was rough and unshaven and his lips were large and rubbery. He wiped some moisture from his eyes with a well used handkerchief. He dribbled ever so slightly when he spoke:

" Tom Byrne's the name," He said: " I live down yonder towards Graney. Ye lads must be here on yer holidays, I'll warrant, I haven't see ye around these parts afore, has I?"

" We're staying at Carrolls." I told him brusquely.

" At Carrolls is it," He continued: " An' isn't it the only place to stay."

He began to root through a host of pockets.

" I'm headin' up to Carroll this very minute for me dinner. She's the best cook in God's creation. An' she looks after me well, does that woman, mighty well. It's forever sorry I is that I didn't get me spoke in there afore ould Ned....But sure isn't that Life....A man's must strike awhile the iron's hot else he'll grow cold in his oulder age. O! I had me pick then o' all the girls; alas never got attached. Too busy at all, workin' night, noon and mornin', Life soon leaves ye in the lurch if ye let it, an' now in the Autumn o' me time, no memories to share man to woman...."

" Never say die!" Jimmy said cheerfully.

" Are you a farmer then," I asked inquisitively: " Or wha'?"

" Sure is I am an' I amn't." Tom replied cryptically. He held out his calloused hands: " An' what would ye make o' them."

His were leathery hands.. The sinews and blue veins stood out wormlike, fat and prominent like tubes under his skin.

" Feel them. Them hands has built houses and haybarns."

He spoke proudly, looking proudly as if he was conferring his hands with some distinguished personal honour, as if they weren't really a part of him, rather inanimate objects.

" If twas to be done, Tom Byrne was the hands to do it. If not fer himself then fer his neighbours, an' isn't that how the good Lord intended it t' be...Share our talents...Share our fortune...An' seein's that I'm possessed o' good fortune in me time...I'd take it kindly if you shared some o' it wi'h me."

Tom went over to the retaining wall, leaned over and plucked a few heads of the ripening beards of barley that was growing in the field. He rubbed the arrowlike heads between his sandpaper palms, blew away the chaff, and then tossed the grains straight into his mouth. He masticated thoughtfully for a moment. In doing so he slipped his other hand nonchalantly into his pocket and pulled out a pair of jingling coins after a quick shuffle. He gave us a coin apiece: two florins for two fellows. We were grovelling in our thanks. Tom just waved us away. It wasn't as if we had earned it. We hadn't done him a turn. And yet this must have been his way of welcome as far as we were concerned being very special guests of Carroll as he later put it.

" Don't worry Tom, we won't eat your dinner!" Is all I thought to say. He chortled in response.

We chatted at The Pike for an age. Jimmy became fascinated with Tom's pocket watch when he went to check the time. You could see its workings- cogs and wheels and jewels -

through the glass backing plate. Tom too smoked a pipe just like Ned, but unlike Ned's wooden pipe Tom's was made of white clay. A chalk pipe. Tom cut his tobacco off the block with a nifty penknife. I pestered him to have a try; but Tom restrained me by saying that he was afraid I might cut my finger off and smoke it instead! How silly, I thought, but Tom promised to give me my very own pipe as a sort of souvenir of

   our first meeting.

   " Dudeens are a dime a dozen in the tobacconists." He claimed.

   " Could you tell me the name of those mountains?" I said to Tom, pointing northwards.

   " Well now, for a start there's Baltinglass Hill....It has the Cross on top...."

   " So then Bray must be on the other side!" I butted in. I knew for definite that there was a Cross on top of Bray Head. But I was to be disappointed.

   " Heavens above, no!" Tom spat across the wall. " Ther's a rake o' mountains 'tween here and Bray. No, every other hill in Ireland has a Cross set on top o' it!"

   " But why so, Tom?" Now even Jimmy was getting interested.

   " Ye see, them Crosses be markers on the way to Heaven." Tom explained: " The Cross has t' be high t' be nearer to God, but not so high that ye can't get t' them handy like. I think the highest wan in the country is down on Mount Brandon in the Kingdom, but the chapel on Croagh Patrick might run it a close second. I climbed The Reek once ye know, in me bare feet, an' I still has the bunions t' prove it.."

   Tom tapped the ground once then twice: " T' restore the circulation." He explained how sinners climbed holy mountains to do penance for their peccadilloes.

   " What in tarnation's a pick-a-dillos?" Jimmy asked, scrunching up his face the way he always did when out of his depth.

   " Well," said Tom: " a peccadillo is like a small sin, well like eatin' a fry on a Friday like....Yer only doin' damage t' yerself, like...."

" Where's me bucket o' water, that I sent yis for an hour ago!"

It was Carroll, calling to us from the cottage gate.

" Gosh, we'd better git!" Jimmy blurted.

" We'll see ya later, Tom!"

Tom nodded: " I'll follow present."

We both grasped the handle of the bucket to cart the water back to the cottage, sploshing dollops of it as we waddled along the road, spare arms outstretched for balance, tongues sticking out like directional feelers, and listening to the splashes sizzle as they hit the hot tarmacadam of high summer.

Tom Doyle's field was next to the cottage. It was full of haycocks so we decided we might have a bit of fun trying to climb one. We had never seen haycocks close up, but we instinctively knew that they would make great playcentres. We climbed over the farmgate rather than opening it. The grass in the field was all cropped and coloured an anaemic yellow. We tried to scale one of the cocks, but every time we tried to grip the hay we pulled it away, and we ended up sliding back down to the bottom. We gave up easily, sitting down instead on the sunny side of the *rick*, chewing strands of hay. The atmosphere was heady from the strong scent of the hay. Some of the *ricks* had caps on them: an opened out jute sack like a tonsure, weighed down on each corner with a stone. We imagined that this was to prevent the *rick* being carried off with the wind, in reality it served to run off the rainwater to stop the hay from rotting as well.

In those days a special horse drawn haywain was used to lift and transport the haycocks. This type of wagon had a flatbed made of timber with sheet metal reinforcement at its trailing edge. The wagon was backed up to the haycock then tilted downwards with the trailing edge just under the haycock. A large wide circular leather tong was then placed in position around the body of the haycock with either loose end attached to a hand-winch on the wagon trailer. The haycock was then slowly winched onto the wagon with a cranking handle. When the centre of gravity was achieved the wagon trailer acting as the fulcrum, tilted the haycock upright to the level, and it was then simply carried off to the haybarn on the farm.

We used to love riding on the back of the haywain, listening to the hollow crunch of the iron wheels crushing soft grass and tarmacadam, on through Carrigeen Cross and up the back road to Baltinglass to Tom Doyle's farm. Tom Doyle had the finest orchards in the district and he would let us gorge ourselves on its fruit. Though we never forgot to bring back a few cookers for Carroll to make into appletarts.

In later years the more functional buckrake shifted the haycocks. John Doyle would drop the forks onto the cropped grass and reverse violently, lifting the haycock, and tilting it forward to keep it securely in place. He would then gun the tractor into life and trundle out of the field, doing wheelies on the big-foot rear treads to show-off as he sped up the road to his father's farm. It may have looked dangerous as the prongs of the buckrake raised sparks from the hard surface of the road: one could imagine a haycock going up in flames. If nothing else it was pure entertainment. And I wonder was that the reason why John Doyle always carried a bucket of sand on the front frame of the buckrake when he went shifting the haycocks.

Carroll must have baked the best homemade bread ever. It was like the Manna from Heaven. And tasted like it too. The secret must have been in her kneading, her knack in the baking, the proportion of her ingredients, her secret flavouring. She had the standard equipment:- an enamel basin, milled flour, baking soda, cool spring water from The Pike, and fresh milk as she needed. She would mix the raw ingredients on the table, talking away as she did so, purely mechanical, and turning the dough over and over again. She seemed to play with the dough:- bashing it, and beating it, moulding it, and fashioning it, and punching it before flattening it. The lump of dough was then placed in the flat-pan with the lid and placed over the fire for to bake it.

On top of the lid Carroll would place live-coals (a quantity of coal was kept by the household for this reason) lifted from the embers with her long tongs. In effect the pan had now taken on the aspect of an oven, the heat being applied from above and below.

Most amazing of all Carroll never used any fancy gadgets like weighing scales when measuring out her bread ingredients. She knew instinctively how much of each to add for best results.

Only a sieve was employed to sift the flour to make the bread mix smoother. Yet the consistency was always exactly right whether she was baking wholemeal or soda bread or fruit-cake. She knew when to lift the bread and she always tapped it on the bottom to test her baking. It was gorgeous bread especially when eaten hot in thick slices with melting creamery butter dripping off the edges and maybe homemade jam.

Carroll's gravy too was Chef's Special. After roasting or maybe frying rashers she would use the juices as the gravy base. This is a common kitchen ploy, but it was whatever way she blended the cornflour and the condiments, her gravy tasted somehow so different to any of those packaged powders. Perhaps it was the farm fresh food that really made the difference.

Jimmy in fact developed a fondness for cabbage pickled with pepper from Carroll's table. Funny how our taste buds are tickled. Very few children have a natural appetite for vegetables particularly if boringly cooked, cold or bland. Half the battle may be in the appearance, but Carroll's cabbage was always cooked in bacon or corned beef water, then finished off in the frying pan. Jimmy watched as Ned sprinkled pepper on his cabbage, tried it and liked it. It was the same with the salt and the scallions. We both loved to dip the white head of the scallion into the bowl of salt that always stood on the table. It seemed to bring out the hot flavour of the scallions even more. Carroll had a large china bowl like a delph basin into which she piled the pot of floury potatoes, dug up fresh from the garden. We'd fork a spud, peel it with the knife then mash it into the gravy or coat a slice with a wedge of butter before scoffing it. Sometimes if we were really starving we'd grab them, juggle them and eat them whole. The dessert on Sundays was always a special treat: fresh strawberries or raspberries and rhubarb. We might only get an ice-cream after Mass in Baltinglass.

Ned was a self-sufficient man in many ways. He had to be. He would do all his own shoe repairs for instance. For this he had a 'Manx Leg' as he called it: a three footed iron stand with three differently shaped impressionist soles for feet. He'd place the shoe for surgery on the correctly shaped sole, cut a sole or heel to size with his craft-knife, and then nail them with brads if the shoe was made of leather or use glue if the shoes were rubber. He would also attach metal strips to the toe or heel to prolong the life of the shoe. He had a special hammer for shoe-mending: it had a long handle with a small head, flattened on one side and wedgelike on the other. He would use his claw wrench for extracting rusty brads.

About once a month Ned would give us a haircut. He would sit us up on the back of a chair with a towel around our neck. He would begin clipping away with the scissors, following the shape of our head. For the 'short back and sides' he would use a small handheld set of clippers with serrated blades. This instrument used to tickle us on the backs of our necks and behind our ears. He would then rub Brylcreem through our hair, comb it and part it to the side, leaving the ' cow's lick' or the 'kiss-curl' across our foreheads. With such a hair-do we were every inch the 'Nancy Boys' from the neck up!

" Now ye looks like the bees-knees," Ned would whistle: " Just like Dan Duryea!" Whoever he was. Some Cowboy Film Star he told us like Audie Murphy who we liked best as 'The Chap'.

Ned for his part shaved with an open razor which he sharpened and cleaned on a long leather strap rather like the 'biffers' that the Christian Brothers used to leather the boys with if they misbehaved or reported late for school. Ned would never use the leather strap on us. He was much too gentle by nature. We were more afraid indeed of a scolding from Carroll's tongue or Eileen's wagging finger.

Granny Nowlan was a great knitter: cardigans, *baneens,* sweaters, no bother! Embroidery was her main forte. She initialled all the linen handkerchiefs so they wouldn't go astray. Regularly after tea a queue of old bachelors would form at the cottage, coming not to court her, but to have a few buttons sewn onto shirts, a few socks darned, a trouser rip repaired or a Christmas order for a patchwork quilt. Pillows were her speciality: his n' hers for the newly weds, costing a mite extra with matching sheets or towels. She would pluck the goose feathers for stuffing after accepting the goose for payment.

It was Carroll or Eileen who used to do the ironing. The irons were individual pieces of metal that were heated on the fire. When hot enough the iron was retrieved, placed into its shoe and clipped into place. An old sheet used as a dampener served to protect the clothes from the harsher irons. The irons came in different shapes: squares, rectangles, triangular and pointed and were heavy duty or light. It all depended on what sort of apparel you were ironing as to what iron you might use. Ned wore 'Grandad' shirts with detachable collars. The collars were fastened with studs. These studs could be fashion items in their own right, being made of precious stone or metal to match cuff-links or tie-pins; but the more utilitarian would be made of mother-of-pearl. As well as taking his main meal at Carrolls, Tom Byrne also contracted her to do his laundering, from shirts to long-johns underwear! You could always tell whose clothes were which on the clothesline. Eileen favoured plaid or tartan skirts with puffed sleeved blouses. One time she picked up a beret, tied a string of smelly onions around her neck and can-canned around the kitchen like a French Ma'am 'selle!

Eileen loved dancing. In fact she was the first to teach me the rudiments of Irish Dancing in the kitchen to the sound of ceili music on Radio Eireann. First she demonstrated the steps of a plain reel and I made sure to watch her carefully because I so wanted to be her partner. She started:

" *Right foot forward, toe to the floor, left heel backward, heel to the floor, now both angled out and ye're ready, a stor! Dee daah, dee daah, dee daah dee....Seven steps to the right, with hands to the hips, reverse to the left, toe to the floor, heel behind, and ye're ready for more...One, two, three, four, five, six, seven.....All good children go to heaven.....!.*

It must have been then that I feel in love with dancing, having Eileen as my teacher, sweeping round the floor. But dancing was one of the great pastimes of country folk, whether impromptu in the kitchen or at the Ballroom of Romance in the town or in the barn! Ned took the long slasher and the bow-saw to cut and chop the windfall wood down on Tom Byrne's farm. Ned did chores for Tom like cutting hay and mending fences as Tom was retired. In return Ned was allowed to use some of the outhouse facilities for stabling Lady in winter, and his two-wheeled farm cart. Ned fetched Lady from the field and fixed the halter and reins to lead her.

" Who wants to be first?" He asked.

Jimmy and me looked at each other unsure of what he meant, pondering a right response.

" Who wants to be first to ride her?"

" I do! I do!" We both cried out, jumping up and down, holding up our hands like at school when we were asked an easy question with a prize attached. Ned tossed a coin to decide it, and I won.   13   I was chuffed. Jimmy disconsolate.

" Shure ye can ride her home, isn't that the fairest." Ned said, patting Jimmy's head. He soon brightened up again back to his old self.

Ned lifted me bodily onto Lady's broad back.

" Hold the reins firmly but loosely," He told me: " Grip her by the flanks with your legs, sit erect and follow her movements as if ye're a part o' her."

I did as Ned instructed, feeling naturally a little nervous, but thrilled at the same time. I was amazed at myself, riding bareback like an Indian. Lady's back was wide, hard and firm. I could feel the life within her.

" Giddy-up!" I called to encourage her, and just as quick I felt myself slipping to one side, off-balance. Ned righted me and held me in position as I settled back. Lady's body was so round that I almost had to do the splits to sit astride her. I somehow managed to stay aboard till we reached Tom Byrne's farm, bouncing up and down like part of a piston!

Ned chopped the wood and we gathered it into the cart which he had hitched up to Lady with practised precision. As we completed our task, and prepared to haul it home, Tom Byrne came hobbling up the lane, tapping his walking stick at an odd clump of dockweed.

" God bless the work!" He declared in greeting: " Will ye not come in for a pick-me-up...."

This was a sort of indirect command and Ned nodded in response so we nodded too. We followed Tom into his ramshackle house. Tom's farmhouse had a thatched roof and whitewashed walls. The windows were tiny and very pokey. Although dingy, dark and damp, rough and ready it seemed comfortable enough for him, being a confirmed bachelor. The house contained a virtual treasure-trove of bric-a-brac, and we were fascinated at what we saw scattered around his living room. There were boxes everywhere of every description and every size and shape, tins and bottles just so, canisters and jars, ewers and jugs.

" Tis a bit o' a squirrel, I am!" Tom confessed to us: " Ev'ry'ing I lays me hands on I covet, if in it takes me fancy..." He picked up an inconspicuous earthenware jug and contemplated it lovingly by holding it aloft:

" Now this piece is pure delight!" He intoned enthusiastically like an auctioneer: " I'll have ye know, this jug once held the purest spirit in the country!"

" You mean a Genie!" Jimmy gasped with excitement: " A Genie in a jug! Tell us! Tell us!"

" Not at all! Not at all!" Tom shook his head vigorously. " Twas *poteen,* aye the smoothest *poteen* in the country. The excise man's dream. Elixir everlastin'. The heavenly dew..."

Tom was babbling on now.

" He means raw whiskey, " Ned explained: " The pure kind made on the mountain side, with a taste as sharp as a wild mountain stream, crystal clear like the snows of winter, what bites ye in the mouth when ye sip it with yer lips, the sort that starts the fire in yer belly that never quenches..."

Now the pair of them were rambling on.

" But now this will do ye nicely!" Tom exclaimed, rousing from his reverie. He fetched two fat brown bottles from a cupboard, and flipped the caps off them by knocking the tops on the edge of his oaken table: " Have some Ginger Ale, lads....Ye've earned it!"   1

An gabhar, the blacksmith worked in Hell! This Hell was a dark cavernous workshop surrounded by gigantic trees. Just inside the doors to this Hades the great cauldron of live coals glowed like black vermilion, like lava blisters. Slung to the side of the fire the handles of the bellows dangled. This lever the sweaty broad shouldered man worked purposefully in rhythmical strokes to breath venom into the flames and create heat. *An gabhar* dressed lightly in a sweatshirt and he wore a great leather apron bearing the brandings: the seared hieroglyphics of his work etched into it. His skin appeared to be pink like par-boiled bacon, and there were wet ringlets around his eyes, nose and mouth. At the entrance stood the great monolith of his trade: the anvil. On the backs of the doors there were hanging a selection of horseshoes, and around the doors laid out there was a collection of iron implements like plough shares, hoops of wheel rims, fireside companion pieces, spades, forks, shovels, and the odd artistic metal sculpture shaped undoubtedly in a moment of relaxed inspiration.

Ned brought Lady to be shoed. *An gabhar* patted the pony and circled her, passing comments on her fine physique, the lustre of her coat, the brawn of her back. In turn he took each leg between his knees, examining and cleaning, and measuring the hooves. Expertly and effortlessly he dislodged the worn shoes and cast them into a bucket, all the time soothing the pony with his melodious voice. He selected a set of shoes and in turn shoved them into the fire with his long tongs while working the bellows with his free hand. When satisfied he extracted the red hot metal, placed it on the horn of the anvil, took the hammer which had been resting on the flatter part of it, and with practised strokes of his bulging muscular arm, he worked the shoe into the desired shape and finish.

Clang! Clang! Clang!   Clunk! Clunk! Clunk!   Cling! Cling! Cling!

With an awl he punched holes into the soft metal to make slots for the nails as necessary.

So he worked, until satisfied, he thrust the hot shoe into the barrel of water where it cooled with a loud sizzle and a conjuror's puff of smoke! He prepared the pony's hooves by paring them with his knife before fitting the shoes. He would draw nails from the deep pocket of his apron, place two or three between his teeth before nailing the shoe into place.

" Job's right! Ned! " He said with a click of his tongue when he finished.

Ned went out to cut the meadow at the back of Tom Byrne's farmhouse. The air was hot and dry that morning and alive with the hum of insects as he fetched the scythe from the barn. Slowly, deliberately, neatly, he rolled up the sleeves of his striped shirt sans collar, lifted his soft hat briefly to wipe his brow with his kerchief. He held the angled stock of the scythe firmly upright against his body, the great blade arcing away from him like the crescent of the moon. With slow methodical strokes he caressed the razor edge with the stone, pausing now and then to moisten it with a spit. He took the skewish handgrips, described a few practice swings before wading into the sea of lush green grass that undulated back and forth to the music of the unseen breeze. He swung the scythe then with deliberation. Like a pendulum it swung, back and forth, back and forth in mini-hemispheres, the blades of grass collapsing silently from the cut to lay gently in neat lines, criss-crossing the field. Slowly he swathed with nothing but the sound of the bite of the blade guillotining the grass, and the startled twitter of a bird to disturb his composure. All around the border of the field the ash trees trembled. Now and then a frantic insect interloped: buzzing like a bee, crackling like a cricket or silent like the butterfly, fluttering on the wing. Ned would pause with regularity to wipe his brow again, and to cast a backward glance to survey the extent and progress of his handiwork. As the grass fell the perfume began to rise and dissipate. The scent was barely perceptible to the nostrils at first, but soon it drowned the very air with its overpowering narcosis. The sun was high in the sky before Ned finished his cutting. Hoarsely he called across the levelled field for a cup of cooling water as the releasing of the grass seed seemed to have shocked the oxygen from the very air.

On the following day Ned returned to turn the grass. For this task he used the twin pronged fork. He would lift the grass and toss it and tease it and twist it to help it to dry. In the merciless heat the grass slowly cooked to a crispy brown colour. After a few days incineration it was time to build the *ricks*. Bit by bit, fork by fork the *ricks* took their traditional shape bound together by the brittle hay.

So the haycocks would sit and fructify warmed by the sun, flavoured by the scent of the spent grass,

blending together safe from the rotting rain. It was the proverbial pastoral scene: Tom Byrne's field dotted with drumlins of hay.

Ned was really great to be with because he trusted us to work alongside him, helping him in any way we were capable. He knew that we had respect enough to follow his instructions, and the savvy to be careful with cutting tools though he always supervised our efforts. It was easy to chop the smaller branches of wood with the slasher. This made up the tinderwood for to restart the fire in the morning. The larger trunks were laid out astride the wood-saddle. The cross-cut saw was then drawn across the wood back and forth, using the straight handles. Ned would be on one end and Jimmy and me on the other. " Now, follow the rhythm!" Ned would admonish us.

'*Crish-crash! Crish-crash!*' That's what it sounded like sawing with the long jagged toothed blade. It seemed now that everything in Life had acquired a rhythm, a musical angle with which a body got into tune. I could sense it: The swish as Ned swung the axe to crack the wood. The hollow sound as he drove the wedge into the bigger logs to shear the wood's resistance. The crackle as the wood burned on the fire. The wet acrid smoke from damp turf, swirling with the backdraft from the chimney. Carroll coughing in protest, her countenance dark like smoky bacon. Sad scatterings of sawdust stuck into the mud and shavings of wood curled like fallen Autumn leaves.

" Let's run through this field," Jimmy suggested on our second day: " It'll be fun, playin' hide n' seek in the barley!"

It seemed like a good idea so we climbed over the wall at The Pike and raced through the stalks of barley which seemed to stretch for miles. The harder we ran the sharper the whip-lash from the stems of the barley. And when we finally pulled up, panting we barely could see over the myriad of arrowheads of barley swaying in the wind.

" Hoi! Wha'd ye tink yaar doin' daar!" A voice roared out in anger.

Immediately I ducked and lay doggo. Jimmy stood his ground as two other boys came shuffling towards us through the barley.

" Wha'd ya tink yaar playin' ah!" The shrill voice of the taller boy demanded again impatiently.

" What's it to you!" Jimmy laughed imperiously, watching the stranger warily as he approached.

I peeped out from beneath the blades of barley on my hunkers. The taller stranger was a dark haired wiry boy, almost as tall as Jimmy if a little thinner, and he had a sunburnt face. He may have been more ruddy because he was evidently angry at us or because he had been working as he was wearing muddy boots. His eyebrows quivered. He was obviously spoiling for a confrontation.

" Who in blazes gave yaas permission to trespass in *my* field?" He bellowed, and he went on to answer himself: " I did not anyways!"

" Haugh! " Jimmy scoffed, trying to bait him: " Do I have to have permission....Not from you surely?"

" This happens to be *my* field an' yaar trespassin'!"

" I've as much right to be here as you have!" Jimmy went on stubbornly.

" No ya haven't, because I live here, so I do!"

" And so do I " Jimmy scoffed again: " I live over there with Carroll, so there!"

" Ya're livin' wi'h *The Goose*!" The stranger laughed: " Ha!"

" Don't you dare call Carroll a goose!"

" I ken call her wha' I will for that's her name; *The Goose*!"

" Take that back!" Jimmy cried out, making a lunge for the boy. They grappled, stumbled and fell, rolling around through the barley in an ever increasing circle, flattening it as they wrestled.

" Hoi! You! L'ave my brother alone!"

The smaller boy now intervened. But he paused momentarily as if pondering something, and then he took off his glasses and stuffed them into his pocket before attacking. He danced and shuffled about the other two with his fists held up like a prizefighter. Now and again he would aim an odd kick at the other pair grappling on the ground. I decided I may as well joining in the fray so I launched an assault, whooping like Crazy Horse! A general melee ensued until gasping from the effort we mutually fell apart exhausted with honours just about even.

" This is getting us nowhere," Jimmy sighed and held out his hand to his adversary: " *Pax*, okay?"

" Okay, a truce anyways!"

" I'm Jimmy, and this is....."

" An I'm Jimmy, an' this is m' brother, Liam!"

We all roared with laughter at the co-incidence of names.

" Partners then!"

We spit on our palms and shook hands all round: "Friends forever!"

" Eh, there's only one problem," I ventured: " Just how are we going to tell the two Jimmies apart when we call out?"

We scratched our chins, pondering this dilemma.

" I know !" Liam cried: " We'll call m' brother Jamesy !"

" Jamesy !" We all repeated the new name, gauging the sound, its weight of authority.

" Well wha' else would ya call him ?" Liam asked superciliously. He was the more erudite one,

especially when he looked down his nose at you through his wire-rimmed spectacles

" Jamesy it is so !" We all agreed and shook on it a second time.

" Come on so lads!" Jamesy called out: " Last one home's a dunkey !"

Dinny Murray, the father of our new found friends, farmed about eighty acres at that time in Broadstone. A pillared entrance led to their farmhouse just at the dip in the road before the stone bridge over the Leer stream on the road to Graney. Their avenue was gravelled and lined with neat hedgerows. A sharp right at the top of the avenue took you to their substantial two-storey farmhouse, and on into the farmyard. In the hollow of the yard, which was quite extensive, lay the dungheap.

The dungheap which was to become a favourite haunt for us was situated close to the byres and pens, more easy for the cleaning out. A sort of duckpond formed by muddy brown water lay adjacent and here geese would wallow when not engaged in grazing the tufts of grass that fought for existence in the cracks around the yard. The front door of Murray's farmhouse was only used on rare ceremonial occasions; we boys always used the back porch which led into the kitchen. The kitchen was arranged with labour saving devices and a massive cooking range. It seemed to us when we visited that there was always something simmering on the stove. Mrs Murray baked appletarts like Carroll and boiled potatoes for animal feed. Off the kitchen there was a little larder cum dairy and here Mrs Murray made fresh creamery butter. She had all the necessary utensils from the wooden churning barrel which was turned laboriously by hand, to the various spatulas and strainers and muslin cloth and mashers.

The Murrays had two other young children then: John who was a toddler and Nora who was still a baby. Mrs Murray definitely had her hands full raising four offspring not to mention numerous animals and helping to run the farm. But she was an indomitable woman equally at home driving a car or a tractor. She had strong greyish hair and a ready wit, and like Liam, she too wore glasses. She had met her future husband in of all places *Dun Laoghaire* when she lived in Dublin and he was up for one of the Farming Shows. Early every morning she and Dinny and Bowbee, the ancient farmhand would milk the herd by hand. The cattle were mostly Friesian. Twice a day at first light and in the evening the herd would automatically trudge, triggered by an instinctive signal, to the gate at the end of the lane that led from the farmyard to the bog. Here they would gather patiently, chewing the cud, awaiting access. Slowly, ponderously, trampling and heaving and pausing, they picked their way along the well trodden lane, mooing occasionally or nibbling at some grass that clung perilously to the side of the ditch. The stocks in the byre could hold about ten cattle for milking.

The milkers sat on three-legged stools, manipulating the teats on the udders before working them. '*Squish, squish* !' The jets of milk would squirt into the silver buckets, sitting beneath the cows. The milkers would rub the flanks of the animals with their cheeks, changing cheek from time to time, to prevent a rash forming. As each bucket was filled it was strained off into the milk churn. The milk churns had codes painted onto them in red so that the farm and owner was identifiable to the creamery. The cows seemed utterly content during the milking as they chewed the hay in the manger. Strong wooden stocks locked into position either side of the cows' necks: this prevented sudden movement though a novice milker would be wary if an animal lifted a hind leg in case it should inadvertently kick out.

It would take about two hours to milk the entire herd. They would then be shunted back down the lane to the bog for the day's grazing. Usually they were more reluctant to leave the sweet taste of the hay so now and again an encouraging prod with the cattle stick was required to shift some of the more stubborn beasts. The milkers would rise up wearily in relief, massaging their backs and stretching to regain their mobility, no doubt looking forward to the whole process being repeated that evening. The amount of gallons milked would be recorded for the creamery and the churns carted down the road to be collected by Snell in his Thames flatbed lorry. A hearty breakfast would then follow for the milkers; but this repast would often be disdained by Bowbee: " I have to go and fix that harrow!" He would insist huffily. The next morning it might be a mangle. I think he fancied himself as a mechanic for he always wore a boiler-suit when working, and his wellies were always turned down at the tops just like Ned's. I think he may have been related to the Murrays: he looked vaguely like Mrs Murray except for the four o' clock shadow. He wore tight fitting wire glasses and favoured the peaked cap like Tom Byrne. Bowbee was the drover par excellence. Driving and coaxing the herd with his favourite prod which always sat by the kitchen door, he would wave it and toss it like a bandleader, singing rebel songs under his breath, encouraging his charges for Bowbee spoke that secret language know only to the likes of Dr Doolittle. The herd knew him for this and followed him: an age old understanding gleaned from the land, a lowing back to older times when man and beast were one in a primordial existence.

The weather forecast, the farming news from Michael Dillon, market prices for cattle, hoggets and ewes and politics, roughly in that order, ruled the airwaves in Murray's kitchen. For a farmer like Dinny this was like vital intelligence. Dinny too smoked a pipe like Sherlock Holmes and he would peruse *The Irish Independent* for up to date information on how the country was doing. He was a smallish man with a deep, growling voice. Like Ned he walked slightly bent, a condition no doubt acquired from the constant bending and stooping that was par for the course in everyday farming like thinning beet. But Dinny had a jutting jaw that always meant business:

" Have ye lads done yore chores yet....No excuses now....Yeas have an extra pair o' hands, I see....Out with yeas now....Clean out the byres....An' don't forget the sow....An' when yeas have done tha'....I thinks year mother needs some spuds lifted in the garden....Are yeas listenin'....Or do yeas need tha' in writ-ing m' be....Be tel-e-gram m'be....!"

In those days Dinny followed the fortunes of the greyhounds. He became so hooked on the science that he bought a few pups to raise and to breed for racing, to supplement the farm income ostensibly. But it was more important for him as a pure hobby. He used to bring us off to the racing track at Naas to watch his dogs racing. Dogs like his favourite ' *Blue Lightning Boy* ' fly through its paces like a cheetah, golloping up the ground and we on the rail cheering him on madly. He wasn't a bad dog really whether first to the bend or last coming down the finishing straight. A galloping greyhound was pure streamlined motion and we had ' *Blue Lightning Boy* ' well trained dragging drogues up and down the back field behind the tractor, to entice him. Dinny's dogs won a few races in their day, nothing spectacular though like The Puppy Derby as far as I know. But it was great to see Dinny's sheer enthusiasm and his love of the animal and the sport. His dedication and his pride as he paraded his dog along the floodlit track before the handlers took over to install it in the starting gate. The racing world seemed like an out of world experience to me. There was the misty atmosphere around the track captured by the lights, the secret signs of the bookmakers, the six dogs straining at the leash in their individual coloured jackets, the whirr of the mechanical hare, the thrust of the chase, all seemed pure theatre to me. And to top it all off the roar of the crowd encouraging, driving their chosen favourites on to the winning line. And almost as soon as it had begun it was all over, in elation or anti-climax!

Afterwards there was the drive home in the back of The Hearse- that was the Murray's

Ford Prefect with the straight-backed rear end, the walnut panelling and the leather seats, the dogs in the trailer, fuzzy headlights lost in fog, following the dark road, the dark trees looming either side like tentacled monsters. Everybody chattering in the flush of victory, or making excuses in the post-mortem of defeat. Discussing strategy and training schedules before the next outing. Happy banter in the kitchen over a cup of cocoa and a raspberry and custard biscuit in Murray's kitchen, and then the run home to bed through the fields under the star spangled sky. Then crazy dreams of crazy races with giraffes and elephants and snails and frogs, and every sort of living thing except greyhounds!

" Aye! She'll do!" Dinny always said when he came up with another brilliant idea that might require his wife's mental or physical input. Her imprimatur.

" Yea!" Mrs Murray would drawl: " But not in here she ain't!"

Dinny would shake the catalogue, and give it a clatter with his hand:

" Sufferin' saints! Tis a grand tractor!"

" An' what's wrong with the one we have, I ask yea?"

" Tis only fit for the museum!"

" An she still goin' strong!"

" She wouldn't pull a combine!"

" Now tell me year not dreamin' ag'in!"

" She'll bring us a good trade-in, mind."

" Are yea tryin' to convince, yea are!"

" Well she wouldn't pull the new trailer....Aither!"

" Now year definitely gettin' stronger!"

" Tis called the *'Dexta'* so it tis!"

" Well ain't that the fancy name for a tractor!"

" D'yea think so then...So will we bring her out for a test run?"

" I wouldn't mind....Year the man who'll be payin' for the privilege!"

The Massey Fergusons, the Fordsons, the David Brown tractors proliferated around the farms in those days. The teams of workhorses had all but died out. Only aficionados like the ploughing competitor or poor crofters would consider keeping such anachronisms as a horse and plough. But once upon a time the draught horse towered over the land like Samson and Goliath, cutting the sod and sculpting it, forcing it to yield its bounty. A well trained pair of Shires or Clydesdales could turn a green field brown on their own encouraged by the ploughman's directions:

" *Come around now....Eazey....Whooo....Whooaa
....Hup,hup,hup....!* "

There was method to it from the arms to the voice, and
through the collar and the reins slung over the shoulder: from the
man to the horse through the plough to the earth. The collar grew
to fit the horse, the imprint of its straining forever moulded into its
form. The bit to savour before the effort of erupting and moving
the earth, then turning it. The intrinsic plodding along invisible
lines, the noble horse responding to the *flic* and thug of the leather,
the urging, the praise of the ploughman's voice. The shudder of the
head. The snort and whistle of triumph, coming around the line
once more, the land laid bare by the trenches, and the dive-
bombing of the birds, extracting struggling worms from the soil.
The horse team had culture, had vitality, had romance. Hadn't
Robbie Burns written about it and performed it with eloquence,
scratching verses over his land in Ayrshire; and our very own
Paddy Kavanagh over his stony grey soil of Monaghan! How much
richer we had become to see that last ploughman in action: gouging
a furrow over the hill on the farthest horizon, heading into the
twilight of history, a silhouette in the sunset, the heavy smell of the
loam permeating the evening air.

Jamesy and Liam, Jimmy and me, we were *pardners*. We
were the Haggard Gang. Because we derived most of our fun and
games in the environs of the hayshed. Unlike haycocks, the
hayshed was supplied with a ladder for the less agile of us to
climb- those who were unable to sally up a roof support. While the
hay tended to be prickly it was a smart place to hang loose even on
a wet day. None of us as yet had succumbed to the temptation of
smoking cigarettes. We had dudeens from Tom Byrne which we
filled with hay once and lit up for a puff, but it was like smoking
Jimmy's smelly socks after a wade through the dungheap and it put
us off for life. We were not impressed; and neither was Jamesy as
it turned out. He got a good tanning from his mother for pinching
the matches, and she ranted at us fiercely about the stupidity of

lighting matches around hay. Jamesy took it on the chin, but blamed Liam for peaching on him, calling him a *'So-in-so!'*

" Stick an' stones....!" Liam jeered as Jamesy chased him around the haggard; but his tormentor escaped to the safety of his mother's apron strings within the house.

The hayshed was great for sky-diving. The mountain of hay acted like a trampoline. We twirled through the air, pirouetted and spun like tops, doing stunts worthy of the circus. The hay was great for burrowing and hiding in or courting in for that matter if you were lucky to become acquainted with one of the local girls. We knew a few of the local girls but they weren't really part of our gang as they were possessed of different priorities, being under their mother's wing or being not quite as wild as us. There was one girl that I did rather fancy. Esther Kelly lived in a Council Cottage back up the Baltinglass Road from Carrolls. I often made excuses to call upon her. We would chat to each other on the stoop or perhaps go for a stroll, and sometimes we would play at Mammys and Daddys , using her old shed for a house. We would pretend to go to bed and wrap ourselves in the old musty carpet. I even ventured to kiss her goodnight, curled cosily beneath our makeshift duvet, dozing off then. I think Esther was one of the first girls I ever kissed and contrary to all reports it proved fine and free and natural and perfectly intimate. Esther was a lovely girl to know anyway: slim and fair with a friendly smile, the sort of girl who wouldn't put you down for your deficiencies. But then we were friends. It proved a magical time beneath that dusty carpet like a scene from the Arabian Nights. Me the Sheikh and Esther with her long golden tresses , wearing a chequered dress with ragged ribbons in her hair. She was like my *Sherherazade*!

There was only one problem playing in the hayshed : before long you might begin to itch. The   ticks were the biggest turn off because they would burrow under your skin in the most embarrassing of places. The ticks used to drive us wild: the constant scratching served to turn our skins blotchy, and they were a bugger to shift and extract even if you had long dainty nails like Liam to eradicate them.

" What ails yea now!" His mother would complain: " Can't yea see I'm busy...Wait for year bath!"

There was a certain amount of relief in water alright. The Leer stream ran through the bog on Murray's farm It was a fresh and bubbly cataract with a smooth rocky bed. At intervals along its course there were old rusty sluice gates that were inoperable, and it was beside one of these that we constructed our swimming pool. We picked the sluice beside the grassiest bank , the better to act as a diving platform. The pebbly foreshore acted as a sort of beach. We would lift sods and pack them into the gate of the sluice to form a dam. The water rose about three feet behind the dam which was deep enough for our purposes as we were no champion swimmers.

Here on sunny days we would strip naked and plunge into the cold water regardless, bumping on our bottoms on the bottom, throwing in coins and crab apples and trying to retrieve them like at a Hallowe'en party, and splashing like seals! We would dry ourselves by running around in the pelt like young stallions, scattering ferns and reeds and getting snared in the yellow gorse so painfully.

We might wrestle then like Classical Greek Heroes. We would playact: slapping each other and tickling each other, and feeling each other. Charging around I felt the first stirrings of manhood rise within me through the flow of adrenalin and hormones, the thrill in the groin, leading to kissing and biting and us mounting each other like adults:

" This is the way that grown-ups do it!"
" No! It has to be face to face!"
" No! Backwards!"
" That's a load of bull!"

The prized bull arrived in a Department of Agriculture trailer: a mean and muscular minotaur with a metal ring through its nose. The bull's handler drew him out into the yard to perform his duty. Three heifers might be segregated in the byre and all exits from the yard were blocked off. We boys were confined to the kitchen porch along with Sixpence, the Murray's pure bred collie who would bark incessantly at the goings on. I thought Sixpence a strange name for a dog but he was a good companion although

Jamesy would often torment him by masturbating him just for devilment.

It was like love on a hot afternoon, the imminent coupling of bull and cow. Bowbee was in control of the heifers. He tapped them on the back with his stick urging them to get acquainted with their suitor, their rude Casanova! Neither lover seemed interested at first, the heifer lowing and shifting, the bull groaning and sniffing. Steam rose up from their mouths and nostrils

Bowbee would egg them on further, circling the pair at a safe distance while the Department Official supervised the event. Then it would seem to happen in an instant. The heifer would stall, standing her ground at the ready, waiting for the bull to get connected. He responded by rearing up and mounting her hindquarters with a bellow. The act of mating hardly seemed to last a minute, just enough time for to allow Bowbee to close in on the couple and confirm that penetration indeed had taken place to guarantee conception, all things being equal.

" Hup ya boyee!" Bowbee would roar to register his approval at the successful outcome. He would then lead the cow away like a bridegroom, talking affectionately into her wagging ears, before lining up the next candidate for the bull's service.

In later years Dinny favoured the A.I. man's approach. If unexciting it was more clinical. When the cow came into season it would be placed in the stall, awaiting the arrival of the A.I. man with his bag of instruments. He would be dressed like one of those guys in *Country Life* and smell of antis- septic. On went his rubber glove, up poked his forearm, and if everything was in order, the long syringe with the selected sperm was guided in and injected, and hey presto! The cow was in calf! A quick wash-up and a cup of tea and it was on to the next farm.

" Whaaaat a job!" We all gasped after witnessing it.

" Yea know lads," Jamesy commented in a deadpan sort of way: " They wank them bulls in Carlow!"

" No way! Ye're pullin' our leg now, so ye are!"

Baltinglass like any other country town had a certain hierarchy among its citizenry. At the top of the pile would have stood the Parish Priest, followed by the Doctor, and then The Headmasters of the local Primary and Secondary schools. Then perhaps it would have been the local politico like Godfrey Timmons in his day. The local lawyers might then get a look-in followed by the higher echelons of the Merchant Class and Civil Service like the Postmistress and the Telephone Operator. After that might come the humble shopkeepers, publicans cum hoteliers like Germaine, the tradesmen and labourers, the pensioners and the children and finally the drifters and tramps who might wander in and out of local society.

The town held a certain importance because of its hospital. This gave the town an almost regional status which belied its own size and its hinterland. Baltinglass then was basically a crossroads near the bridge over the river Slaney with a main street and further development to the east. The town had boasted a train station, but this was now closed and the tracks lifted, and the beautiful terra-cotta station buildings were held in private ownership, doubling up as a private dwelling. Close by to it was the essential Mart used for the buying and selling of livestock which abounded. A small Church of Ireland church St. Mary's stood beside the old ruined Abbey near the river. This church was almost colonial in style with partitioned pews and scant ornamentation. St Joseph's the Roman Catholic Church which stood further up the town to the east was a much more formidable structure, serving as it did the greater population and need.

The highlights of St Joseph's were the glorious stained glass windows with the glazed admonitions to: *'Pray for the Donor'*. It also had a huge polished altar gilded with metal which stood to high heaven. Around the walls stood sympathetic statues of saints like St Anthony, and there was a doleful crucifixion scene, made sadder and more immediate by the waxy smell of candles burning on drizzly days. Two substantial confession boxes stood out from the walls on the main aisle and this is where we went to whisper our venial sins to the priestly voice which spoke in the darkness and sent us on our way purified and white and clean to finish the Saturday shopping, saying 'Three Hail Mary's for Penance'.

On Sundays at Communion the paten was held under your chin to save the Sacramental Host in case it slipped out of the priest's hand or out of your mouth if you didn't suck it in with your tongue. That would have been every kid's nightmare, and a moment of shame: to be seen to spit out The Lord! The linen cloth along the altar rail acted as a back-up; but even if the Host should roll and fall onto the dirty wet floor, you had to stand back immediately while Fr. Brophy delicately retrieved it. The soiled Host would then have to be interred reverently on sacred ground like under the *aucuba* shrub out in the churchyard. This I imagined to be the scenario for these disasters, but for as long as I wished and waited for it, the Host was never dropped accidentally.

The bicycles were parked on the channelled concrete slabs along the sides of the driveway that led to the portals of the church, two long rows of splendid machinery. If you wanted one of these customised parking slabs though you had to come early and beat the rush. Cycling was the preferred mode of transport to church, to anywhere for that matter, and there would be no need to lock your bicycle when you got there as thievery was practically unheard of then, on hallowed ground anyway.

The menfolk went bareheaded into the church to attend Mass while the womenfolk went head covered as appropriate. The mantilla was the simplest, the most fashionable, most respectful and most favoured head covering for the women, and it was always worn in black. Dark apparel in fact was the order of Sundays. Bright gay coloured clothing might have drawn comment and unwanted attention or worse still, a diatribe on the sin of Pride from the pulpit, in which case the congregation would have no difficulty in picking out Dives: the rich man or the rich woman for that matter. Better to blend in and conform while the priest mumbled on in Latin. Ostentation was alright at the Barn Dance where people were free to laugh, but at church it smacked of vulgarity. This outlook, however, solely applied to the adults, the children could be dressed to the nines, and get away with it. Well dressed children conferred a certain status on the family, as well as boosting the ego of the children themselves. As for us, being on holidays, we were dressed neatly in shirts and short pants, socks pulled up to the knees, shiny shoes from the dew, and shiny teeth from eating all the crab apples, slicked hair and scrubbed faces with just a little crescent of froth above the upper lips from draining the green bottles of porter off Kehoe's bar, to where Ned and the rest of the menfolk would retire after Mass. That was our main Sunday morning occupation after Mass, rinsing out the porter bottles for in those days they were worth money on deposit! The women were busy too, doing the rounds and gossiping, picking up the papers or visiting their late lamented in the steep graveyard up the hill at the back of the town.

Wood is what I remember most about Sunday mornings: the smell of varnished wood in the church, of smoky wood in the bar, the spicy wood of the beer barrels, the smell of the damp wood on the banks of the Slaney, pine scent, and honeysuckle.

The Slaney was a powerful river. A noble river, fast flowing and scenic as a classic river should be. It was also a good fishing river. There was a weir on the river upstream before the bridge and sometimes we would head there with our makeshift rod to fish. Though we cast our baler twine more in hope than expectation of catching a fish on the bent staple baited with some unfortunate worm, now and again we did manage to land the odd boot or other bric-a-brac from the bed of the river. If nothing else boys are born optimists as far as fishing is concerned. As far as ' *An Bradan Feasa* ' was concerned it was only the professionals who managed to land them. We could only brag about the size of 'our boot'.

We used to love playing in the grounds of the ruined Baltinglass Abbey. It was the nearest thing that we had to a castle with its tall rookery tower, its thick crumbling walls and the massive pyramid that marked the Stratford Family tomb. Drawing the battles lines it usually ended up with the Two Jimmies against me and Liam. Broken branches doubled as swords and lances with a bit of a cardboard box for a shield. So we jousted, charging the length of the cloisters, trying to knock each down off our charges. Somehow we never managed to gouge our eyes out or hurt ourselves perhaps due to the grace of God or being as we were on hallowed ground.

Baltinglass Abbey stood close by the Slaney to the north of the town. It was originally a Cistercian Order house founded in 1148, the first sister house of the primary monastery foundation of the order at Mellifont which was founded in 1142. Baltinglass Abbey was given the name *'Vallis Salutis' or 'Vale of Salvation'*.

The Abbey prospered so much so that four daughter houses were subsequently founded after it:- Abbeymahon, County Cork in

1172; Jerpoint, County Kilkenny in 1180; Abbeyleix in 1184; and Monasterevan in 1189. That infamous King of Leinster, Dermot Mc Murrough, 'Diarmaid na nGall' granted the monks large tracts of land in the surrounding countryside. Outfarms were developed away from the main Abbey and were called granges like:- Grangecon, Grange Beg and Grangeford. These farms were worked by lay brothers. The Abbey was first populated with Irish , but with the coming of the Normans, it eventually came more under English influence. Because it became identified with the interests of the invader, the Abbey became what might be described as a 'legitimate target' for raiding parties of the O'Tooles and O'Byrnes of Wicklow.

The Abbot at this time was a Mitred Abbot, and sat as one of the 24 Spiritual Peers in the Irish Parliament. In 1379 the Parliament actually sat at Baltinglass Abbey for three days. With the Reformation under Henry VIII the monastery was dissolved in 1536/37, one of the first Cistercian victims, and the property was granted to Thomas FitzEustace later Viscount Baltinglass.

Though none of the usual Abbey buildings like a refectory survives, the ruins of the monastic church built between 1148/80 are impressively interesting. There is an imposing nave arcade and an assortment of sculptural details. The square ended chancel and the relatively low arches leading into the transepts reflect the influence of early Cistercian churches in Burgundy. Neat carvings at the eastern end of the church are the work of local Romanesque craftsmen. The nave arches are supported on alternating square and round piers, the capitals of which are decorated with a variety of designs by the so called 'Baltinglass Master' , whose work is also to be seen at Jerpoint. There are the bases of two Romanesque doorways in the nave aisles and a well preserved sedilia in the chancel. In the 15th Century a substantial tower was erected in the old crossing, the base walls of which remain. It collapsed sometime around 1800 and was replaced by the present slender Neo-Gothic tower in 1815. The gate surround at the west end also dates from this time. After the Reformation the Abbey Church became the Parish Church and a wall was built across the nave. It thus consisted of the chancel, the crossing, one bay of the nave and possibly the transepts.

When the modern St Mary's Church was built the old Abbey Church was left to deteriorate. A large task of excavation and preservation was carried out in 1955. The granite Egyptian-style Mausoleum of the Stratford Family was built by Lord Aldborough in 1832, partly on the site of a side-altar in the south transept.

About a mile down the road eastwards from Carrigeen Cottage stood the handball alley. Naturally this was a big attraction for athletes like us boys who fancied we had the stamina of Hercules. We often trekked down to the alley to play ball, sometimes singles, and sometimes family doubles, and mixed doubles or young lads against old. 21 was always the winning score to reach. Handball was a handy game for small parties: to have a good game of football you needed a crowd and such was never readily available to us so scattered were the younger generation in those parts. Jamesy and Liam took a hand at Gaelic Football and Hurling: they both wielded the *caman* and *sliothar* with an easy skill which us city kids mostly bred on soccer could not hope to match though we gamely tried to acquire the knack of scooping the *sliothar* with the hurley, and soloing with, and striking the ball from the hand and the ground.

Beside the handball alley stood the Community Hall. It was a spacious building largely neglected during the summer months, but readily used during the other seasons for family, school and charitable events and the odd Saturday Night Hop.

Opposite the handball alley stood the Big Stone school. It took its name literally from a big stone that lay at the nearby road junction. The school was a typical rural alma mater with just two rooms where all the grades of children were taught by their teachers. The school was a source of vague memory to us: we were aware of its existence, we were aware of its function, we were aware that we would be re-inducted into its regime come Autumn, but for the present it meant a place for bantering and witless displays of bravado about how little we cared about school and how much we knew without it. Peering in through its dusty windows at the forlorn lines of empty desks devoid of their fidgety, restless captives, its use and purpose seemed oddly obsolescent.

"Look lads! There's my desk, second row back, third to the left," Jamesy asserted: " It's got my name on it carved into the wood!"

" And there's mine! " Liam added: " Tis the one wit' the copy book on it....ready for next term! "

We all groaned after that remark, hastily counting down the days of free enjoyment left to us. A last glance through the window: the frayed linen atlas of the world hanging on the wall with most of the countries of the world painted red from the British Empire. On the blackboard a faint tracing of the last problem presented on the last day of school could be vaguely deciphered by the keener eyes among us. The schoolyard itself seemed like a moonscape bereft of the shouting and jostling of its internees. But we drank greedily nonetheless from the water tap on the wall before restarting our game of handball, schooldays forgotten already.

In those days our range was quite extensive. Eastwards beyond the Big Stone, northwards to Baltinglass, southwards to Graney, and westwards to the hilly country of the Chulchie Macs. We foraged off the land, plucking leaves of cabbages, and pulling carrots, and depodding peas as a means of sustenance. We searched the wetlands for frogs: fat brown toadlike varieties and slimline green varieties. These we would race, endeavouring to keep them in a straight line using hands and feet. Invariably we allowed them escape as we got bored.

There were many rabbit burrows about the countryside. Some of the obviously more used were set with wire snares. We often inspected these traps to see if any unfortunate rabbit had been snared and maybe throttled to death. It was not a pleasant way for a rabbit to die; but fare worse was the strain of *myxomatosis* that had been introduced into the population to control it. Indeed wild rabbits were a rarity in those days because of this disease. The wilder variety of rabbits were much leaner and had or seemed to have much longer ears than the docile domesticated varieties that the Murrays kept. The long ears of the wild rabbits always pointed skywards as they sat on their hind-legs, sniffing the air for intruders like those prairie dogs. Ours was a quest for the mutant, the unnatural and different. Despite the legend of St. Patrick having banished the snakes from Ireland, we forever searched the watery ditches and the boggy canals of the drainage land for elusive serpents; and on dark nights we would listen out and strain our vision for the bats as they whizzed imperceptibly through the air, homing in on unseen moth, making for the safety of the lamplight over the door to Murray's kitchen.

Before retiring for the night, as we sat by the fire, Tom Byrne snug in the ingle-nook might tell us a story. Long, long ago there lived a King of Leinster called *Bran Dubh Mac Echach* or Black Bran for short. Although only twelfth in line to the kinship of the *Ui Cheinnsealaig*, and a member of the *Ui Felmeda* branch of the clan, Black Bran through bravery, fearlessness and determination wrested the Lordship of the Province from his rivals, *Ui Mail* of West Wicklow and *Ui Dun Lainge*, and became Overking of the Leinstermen. At this time the *Ui Neills* were the High Kings at Tara and demanded and levied a tribute from the Leinstermen called *An Boruma Laigen*- The Cattle Tribute of the Leinstermen. This was an exorbitant tribute of cows, swine, wethers, mantles, silver chains and copper cauldrons which was exacted from pre-history down to the time of Black Bran. Now Black Bran determined to stop payment of this unfair tribute, and he fought many battles with the *Ui Neills* to this end, his most notable victory occurring at *Mag Ochtair* in 590 A.D. So the great Blood Feud began between Black Bran and the Northern *Ui Neill*. *Aed Mac Ainmerech* of the *Ui Neill* came to the High Kingship in 595. Two years later his impetuous son *Cummasach* invaded Leinster on a stripling's circuit of Ireland, claiming his *Droit de Signeur - The Right of the Lord* to sleep with the wives of his father's subjects en route. *Cummasach* demanded fealty and obedience of Black Bran who pretended to comply, but withdrew from his house at *Bealach na Dubthaire* near Baltinglass. Black Bran's wife escaped to *Dun Buchat* at Kilranelagh. While *Cummasach* with 300 other King's sons feasted at *Bealach na Dubthaire*, Black Bran, with the aid of the *Ui Failge* Kings, *Airnelach* and *Oengus,* Sons of *Airmedach,* set fire to the Great Hall of his own house to flush out the invader. Many were slain in the confusion. *Cummasach* escaped the slaughter only to be caught and killed by *Loichin Lonn* on the green at Kilranelagh. On hearing of the death of his son, *Aed Mac Ainmerech*, enraged and seeking revenge, crossed the King's River and invaded Leinster. He drew south to *Dun Bolg* near Baltinglass to replenish his supplies. Unbeknownst to him, the Leinstermen hid in the hampers and food baskets, that were supposed to contain the provisions for his army, and in a twist to the tale of the Trojan Horse, when night began to fall, Black Bran emerged with his Leinstermen and massacred their foes as they settled down for the night. Ally *Ron Cerr*, son of Dubhanach, King of the *Ui Mail,* slew the Northern Kings of *Airgialla* and *Tulach Og* and after chopping off *Aed Mac Ainmerech's* head, he presented it to Black Bran. Thus the Kings disguised as servants defeated the power of the Northern *Ui Neill.* The site of this battle in 598 is reputedly the ringed hill-fort of Brusselstown near Baltinglass

[Baltinglass Hill has much prehistoric remains such as Neolithic Passage Graves. Even on the older ground surface beneath the cairns of the tombs there is evidence of habitation floors. Recent finds have included stone axeheads, flint scrapers and a quantity of wheat grains and a saddle quern in 1980 which would suggest proof of cereal cultivation near the hilltop. Megalithic Art on the stonework like geometrical motifs of circles, spirals and triangles are to be found, giving certain meanings to certain symbols. Earthen banks and stone facings often go with passage graves, dating from the Late Bronze Age].

Black Bran didn't last too long to enjoy the fruits of his victory. The struggle continued, and after being defeated by the *Ui Neill* under *Aed Uaredach* at the Battle of *Slaebhre* in 605, Black Bran was assassinated through treachery by his own people. Other accounts suggest he was slain by *Saran Saebderg*, High Warden of *Senboth Sine*, east of Mount Leinster; while a later tradition says he was killed at the Battle of *Dam Chluain*. Perhaps his people were tired of warring or had reached an accommodation with the High King to end the conflict, the price being Black Bran's head. The Cattle Tribute of the Leinstermen was brought to an end some years later. It is said that St. Moling who died in 697 tricked the *Ui Neill* into remitting the tribute forever, according to the *Boruma Laigen* which was inscribed by St. Mullins of the Barrow Valley. Much of Black Bran's exploits were recorded in the Annals of Ulster.

Another great folk-hero of Tom Byrne's stories was Michael O' Dwyer of 1798 rebellion fame. The tales of his exploits and hair-raising escapades were legendary. The United Irishmen were numerically strong in Wicklow: about 13,000 were enrolled. Despite acquiring arms from earlier raids on Baltinglass when the rebellion broke on May 24th, the insurgents failed miserably to invest and take the garrison towns of Baltinglass and Dunlavin, and were slowly dispersed. The insurgents had been left largely leaderless by the arrest of many of their leaders, and the self-appointed and self-styled 'Colonel' Holt was an ineffectual and indecisive commander. It was left to local clerics like the famed Fr. Murphy of Old Kilcormac, and Fr. Philip Roche who defeated the Yeomanry at Clough in Tuberneering, to organise and lead the resistance, mainly in Wexford. All attempts to unite the various rebel contingents faltered, and with the defeat at Vinegar Hill, the cause of a United Ireland and the United Irishmen was effectively quashed.

Those insurgents who had escaped the slaughter had to go 'on the run' and melted into the mountain fastnesses around *Lugna-coille*. Among these was Michael O' Dwyer. He soon developed the skills required to live off the land while carrying out a guerrilla type of warfare to keep the Yeomanry at bay. So disruptive were his activities that the Crown had to initiate the building of the Military Road to bring in additional troops, and to safeguard supplies and communications. O' Dwyer had many hide-outs and safe-houses where he could lie low in between harrying the Local Administration, and upsetting the governance of the county. He had two well known cottages where he stayed in at Glenmalure and in the Glen of Imaal. He was almost captured at one of the cottages when it was raided on an informer's tip-off early one misty morning. He was delivered by the quick thinking of throwing damp straw on the smouldering fire which caused a smoke screen throughout the house and out onto the lawn. He disappeared through the resultant smog in his nightshirt, and gained the safety of nearby woods. O' Dwyer was a prototype of what you might call a cross-dresser or impersonator. He would dress up as a woman to enter the garrison towns to reconnoitre troop disposals, and fetch supplies and garner the latest news on the street corners. In fact he aided a compatriot to escape from captivity in jail by donning the uniform of the Yeomanry. O' Dwyer also laid up in mountain caves which like rabbit burrows, allowed various bolt-holes for easy escape.

For five long years O' Dwyer held out against all the efforts of the Crown to apprehend him. He was still active in the revolutionary sense, and helped Robert Emmet to plan his ill-fated rebellion in 1803, promising to support Emmet with reinforcements. This, however, proved to be a futile hope, and fearing the worst, O' Dwyer travelled hurriedly to Dublin to plead with Emmet to abandon the enterprise as ill-conceived. O' Dwyer was too late and was helpless to prevent the so called rebellion from developing into no more than a street-brawl.

O' Dwyer by this stage must have been tired and disillusioned, and with the offer of an amnesty as an incentive, he surrendered. So ended one of the most single-minded and heroic resistances of an Irish rebel. Michael O' Dwyer was to eventually end up in Australia where he had a most successful life like many Irishmen and Irishwomen who had been transported before him and since.

In such a healthy climate as that which prevailed at Carrigeen Cottage, Jimmy and me rarely fell ill. Granted we got the occasional cough or cold or cut ourselves at horseplay or had a tummy upset. No matter it seemed that whatever the ailment, Granny Nowlan had the cure. She possessed the ancient knowledge of the folk remedy for various illnesses, and concocted different potions and treatments to combat these. For gashes for instance she would make up a poultice of chickweed. For colds she would use elderflowers and peppermint leaves, boil them and strain off the juice, and serve with honey or sugar to taste. For coughs proprietary eucalyptus oil and wheat-germ oil would be mixed and rubbed into our chests. For inflamed eyes, boiling up bags of tea, letting them cool and then applying them over the eyes helped to soothe them. Nowlan kept a herb garden just for such purposes or else she picked the ingredients straight from the wild source. The common nettle made an infusion to combat allergies, and could be taken to ease the stinging that the plant itself caused. If we got stung with nettles away from the cottage we could always fall back on rubbing the inflammation with dock leaves. Nowlan made Turnip Syrup whenever she got a touch of bronchitis; and she took a thimble full of Cider Vinegar to ease her arthritis. Her fennel tea was really tasty like aniseed and she used to use it when we got indigestion or became bloated from eating too many biscuits from the package of sweet goodies that Mammy used to send us by post every week.

Nowlan knew the ancient cure for tapeworms: boiling pumpkin seeds, removing the skin, and then mashing up the green pulp to a paste with a little milk. After 12 hours of fasting, this mixture was taken followed by Castor Oil two hours later, and within 3 hours the tapeworm would have been usually passed safely. That was one reason why Nowlan was fanatical about hygiene, and the washing of hands after the toilet. She always prepared her concoctions and decoctions scrupulously. One thing she warned us about was eating mushrooms. Some toadstools like the yellowish green Death Cap, the red cap of the Fly Agaric and the pure white Destroying Angel were deadly and to be avoided. The leaves and seeds of trees like the Laburnum and Yew were also to be avoided.

If it was the case that Nowlan or Doctor Lord, the family physician, couldn't provide the cure, a body could always turn to one of the Holy Wells that abounded in the parishes around Baltinglass. There was one *tobar* or well near the town itself that was said to have been blessed by St. Patrick himself, hence the dedication. The exact location of this well has been lost in time, but patterns were held there regularly up to the time of the Great War. There was one well at Tobersool (*Tobar na Sul*) at Knocknareagh in Ballynure Parish west of Baltinglass that specialised in eye treatment. The Faithful bathed their eyes in the waters of the well three times to effect a cure. Another well reputedly blessed by St. Patrick (or according to other accounts blessed by St. Palladius) lay at Tobermacargy, Kelshamore in the Parish of Donaghmore, north-east of Baltinglass, At this well water taken against the stream would cure one ailment while water taken with the stream would cure another. Donaghmore Parish was particularly blessed with Holy Wells. There was a well at Moorstown dedicated to St. Brigid which provided a good flow of water, and the stone at the well was known as St. Brigid's Elbow. Holy Well at Talbotstown Lower in the Parish of Kilranelagh, east of Baltinglass, boasted many cures to do with the washing of clothes; while another St. Brigid's Well at Colvinstown Upper also in the Parish of Kilranelagh, provided cures for headaches, vomiting and retching. There was a well devoted to St. John, *Tobar Eoin* at St. John's in the Parish of Kiltegan, east of Baltinglass that has many cures attributed to it. A Station was held here regularly on St. John's Eve up to the 1960's. On June 23rd 1798, John Moore, a comrade of Michael O' Dwyer was hanged from a tree near the well. The branch from which he was hanged subsequently withered. Attempts at piping water from this well proved unsuccessful though many cures have been reported here and many offerings have been left. St. Bernard's Well at Rampere in the Parish of Rathbran, north of Baltinglass held a pattern every August 20th up till the late Eighteenth Century. It was discontinued after a man was killed there engaged in a faction fight. Such patterns and pilgrimages to the Holy Wells were often regarded as more like a Fair Day rather than as a solemn occasion for reflective contemplation, humble intercession and penitential weeping and gnashing of teeth! All manner of Humanity besides the Believers would be attracted whether to peddle their own wares or cures, to perform their own 'miracles' of trickery, and to flog their bodies for profit rather than salvation.

Of course like all children we were no angels. Particularly when it came to the Fordson Dexta tractor. Driving the tractor came as naturally to Jamesy as swearing, and he would often 'borrow' it for a spin around the back field when his father's back was turned. We would all hop up on the back of the tractor, sitting on the huge mudguards over the huge rear wheels or standing on the towbar, hanging on for dear life as Jamesy roared around the field like a demented Stirling Moss. In those days anti-roll safety frames or enclosed cabs were not standard or enforceable by law, and I often marvelled how we were never killed or injured, practising numerous 'stunts'. I was lucky though on one occasion. I was sitting up on the rear mudguard, facing inwards when Jamesy decided he might as well lift the hoist. Whatever way I was sitting the knuckle of the towbar jammed my knee against the metal guard, slowly crushing it. I screamed blue murder until Jamesy realised my predicament, and released the pressure. I hobbled down off the tractor, walking wounded, and sprawled out by the ditch, sore and physically sick. I recuperated fairly quickly and was soon back to my old tricks. In all the times we travelled on tractors and trailers and hay wagons and combines it was the nearest any one of us came to having a nasty accident.

The super-efficient Combine Harvester was making its first appearance over the fields of Ireland at around this time. These latest examples from the *Claas* firm were self-drive models. The farmer hired them or leased them to harvest the corn. Entering the field, the great jaws with their incisor edge teeth and flailing paddles gobbled up the corn, threshed it, bagged it, and baled the straw, shoving it off the back all in one movement. Sometimes a tractor and high sided trailer would shadow it alongside while the Combine spat out the grain from its chute like a gigantic peashooter to load it. The bales of straw were simply loaded up and carted off to the haybarn for storage. Earlier Combines were pulled by a tractor and its machinery run through the universal drive shaft at the rear of the tractor. These machines were a far cry from the simple grass mower with the long toothed cutting blade that was used at right angles to the tractor or pulling horse. For a time the Binder was the state of the art for cutting corn; this machine simply cut the corn, bound it with twine and deposited the resultant stooks on the stubblefield. The stooks were stacked like tepees to dry out, before being threshed and gleaned. In the even older days of course the great Steam Traction Engines undertook the processing of corn; but this practise would have been utilised only by the richer landowners with the greater acreage of corn to be cut. After the corn was harvested the stubble would be burnt off, giving off thick acrid smoke, highly toxic, then the field would be harrowed and finally ploughed for the next rotation crop.

The best part of the harvesting was eating doorstep sandwiches and drinking tea from Billy Cans as we stretched out by the ditch, basking in the sun in our vests.

" What are you doin'? " I asked Bowbee one day. He was mixing up a large barrel of chemicals in the yard.

" I'm makin' Bluestone," He explained: " Copper Sulphate and water fer to spray the *pratais.*"

" And why is that, why is that? " I kept asking ignorantly. He shook his head, stirring all the more:

" To combat the Potato Blight, that's what! This here country was hard hit by The Blight when the potato crop failed three years running: h-in 1845,46 an' Black '47."

Bowbee paused from his labours and swept his arms across the land, musing, as if talking to himself as he resurrected some folk memory of harsher times.

" All the land as far as your eye can see was blackened by The Blight. 'Twas heartbreakin' to watch. All o' them beautiful crisp and green potato plants, shrivel up, blacken and rot away, the tubers dug up like balls o' mush. Thousands starving: bloated and black...."

Bowbee shuddered as if overcome by a deathly chill even in the humid heat of the day:

" An' thousands more fleeing, runnin', stagg' rin', crawlin'......"

He spoke with increasing anger now and palpable resentment:

" Anys where for sustenance. The towns, the cities, the workhouses, the slums of Liverpool, New York, even as far as Bot'ny Bay in h-Australia, any wheres to h-escape the scourge of the rotten potato, they travelled in their coffin ships: them who was lucky t' escape!"

Bowbee's voice calmed then:

" Yis, m'boy we was hard hit be The Great Famine, an' many's the ancestor o' mine what's buried out there in an unmarked grave.....An' many more in unknown lands...."

Just then I fancied I saw tears well up in the old man's wrinkled and glassy eyes. And I too felt sorry for his Lost People.

The Murray's parlour was out of bounds to dogs and children ,except when they were entertaining. Then we kids would be allowed entry to partake in the festivities provided we discarded our muddy boots and shoes; less to be heard in our stocking feet. The parlour was a bright airy room with polished furniture and crystal glass and sumptuous drapes and rugs. It was most convivial, a place for friends to gather to make general conversation about the events of the day: local, national or worldly, and with the launch of Russia's Sputniks, universal. After High Tea, the whiskey and sherry would flow, and with the relaxing of inhibitions, Dinny might break into song. He was a fine baritone, and with his eyes gently closed, he would give a powerful rendition of ' *The moon behind the hill*' or one of the favourites of the company: ' *Boolavogue*'. Visitors were encouraged to participate if they came prepared with a fiddle or harmonica or accordion or tin whistle all the better to improvise a session. So it would go on long into the night; long after we were sound asleep in bed with the milch cows looking forward to a lie in too, on the following morning.

The older generation like Eileen could go out dancing, and once they had dancing shoes they were prepared to travel as far as Carlow or Naas or Tullow or Athy, anywhere for a hop be it ballroom, old-time, Latin, Ceili or the latest Rock n' Roll. Eileen used to love dressing up and going out. She would spend hours getting ready. She was like Cinderella every time except she had no time restriction. Lifts were arranged, or a bus provided for transport to the chosen venue, and before she left she always gave us a twirl in her *'bop skirt'*.

" How do I look , lads? " She would ask gaily: " D'think I'll get a dance t'night? "

There'd be no doubt that she would get a dance, any night. Eileen had her fair share of boyfriends, I would have no doubt, but that still didn't stop us lads from trying to play Matchmaker. We always pestered Sheammy Buchaill with the idea of walking out with Eileen. We would arrange to accidentally bump into him as he ambled home from work. He would always be chewing a length of straw and may be crooning to himself, sauntering along oblivious to his surroundings.

" Do you like Eileen? " We would demand of him in turn: " Would you ask her out?.....She likes you, you know.....She's great fun....Do you not think you'd make a great pair? "

In the end I think Sheammy agreed to our scheme to get us off his back. He agreed to call on Eileen on a certain night. She laughed when she heard the news; but she agreed to co-operate, to appease us, I think. Sheammy turned up freshly shaven and dressed like a stuffed turkey, straightening his tie at the door as he knocked, proffering Eileen a bunch of wildflowers when she answered the door. We were all hiding around the gable end, pinching each other and tittering.

" Would ye like t' come for a walk wi' me? " He asked her nervously after lingering somewhat.

" I thought ye'd never ask! " She replied with a sigh: " 'Tis a lovely evening for a stroll!"

" That it tis, that it tis! " Sheammy kept repeating.

" An' where would ye be takin' me for a walk? " Eileen asked, fluttering her eyelids, and squinting around at us.

" Well, Eileen I thought we might take a walk as far as The Pike, have a chat like, watch the sun go down like...."

" Well isn't that the dandy idea," Eileen swooned : " But why bother strainin' ourselves when we can watch the sun settin' from here, just as well.....Better shtill why not come in and have a cup o' tea with the Daddy....Ye'll have so much in common to talk about, being in the same line o' business! "

" But I thought...." Sheammy faltered: " I thought...."

" Thought what? *A leanna!* " Eileen said, trying to keep a straight face: " Don't ye know ye shouldn't believe ever'thin' ye think.....I'm away now....I has a bus t' catch! "

She departed for the dance, leaving Sheammy standing at the door dumbfounded. I went up to him brazenly and said:

" I'll take those flowers if you don't mind...I'm sure Carroll will be delighted with the thought! "

Mammy and Daddy came to visit us on the odd Sunday, bringing more supplies. We always went out for a drive after lunch packed into the old Bedford. We would go off to Castledermot may be which was fabulous because it had a real castle. Sometimes to Rathvilly which was one of the tidiest towns in Ireland. It had a shop that served ice cream cornets. On the last weekend of our holidays, our parents came to stay over and slept in John's old room in the back of the kitchen. We would often go to see a film in Bradley's Picture House in Baltinglass on these occasions. Gary Cooper as Marco Polo was one movie I recalled; but we were more into Cowboys and Indians. We could always hear the flicking of the projector over the sound , and the silhouettes of the backs of the heads of the audience, sitting on their benches, caught in the smoky pallid white beam of its light.

Parting was always hard on all of us. Reluctantly we prepared ourselves on the Sunday evening, making sure everything was packed, especially any favours we had collected during our stay. We did the round of our last goodbyes. This would include a visit to the Kellys usually; and perhaps we would drop into Ger Miley's cottage above the crossroads. We had befriended him when he moved into the cottage; helped him set up house and did a few odd chores like gathering kindling wood. He was convalescing after an illness. Murrays was a must to say thanks and farewell to Dinny and his Mrs and Bowbee and Sixpence. Jamesy and Liam would come to the cottage to see us off; and we would exchange a Roman handshake like true Gladiators. We kept the biggest hugs for Tom Byrne and Ned and Carroll and dear Eileen, not to mention The Howlers! We clung on as long as we could, reluctant to go. The tears would be welling up in our eyes; but we endeavoured to bite our lips, resisting the ignominy to be branded as Sissies.

" See you all, come summer, Please God! " This was always our last hurrah.

It was only when we had waved our last goodbyes from the back windows of the Bedford that we were free to release our emotions. So our holiday that had begun in tears now ended ironically in the same way. The long drive home always proved a quiet anti-climax, even the twinkling lights of the night time city seen from The Embankment failed to move us, and the house when we arrived back inside seemed somehow changed and strange.

We boys spent a number of idyllic summers with the Carrolls until we got too big to manage. Our sisters Anne, Mary and Paula took our places instead. Theirs' would have been a different experience for like life itself, we move on. By that time John and Nora Murray had grown, and these five formed a new relationship. Anne always told me that she got her first kiss from John in the hayshed. Mary, who was always a lover of animals, used to crawl into the rabbit hutches and pet them. Paula like us before was carried around on the back carrier of Eileen's bicycle; and fell into ditches and got stung with nettles. She would have had to rely though on dock leaves to relieve the stinging for by this time old Granny Nowlan had passed on to her eternal reward. As the old saying might suggest: as much as everything changes, everything remains the same. But perhaps the greatest change of all was the advent of the electric light, and Carroll's new bottled gas cooker.

Towards the last summer of our stays with the Carrolls, Eileen had a young baby girl called Mary. She often called into our house during her visits to the hospital clinic. Carroll herself had had only one child, Eileen because she had had a difficult time during her pregnancy. It was the same with Eileen, but her first confinement went well. Mother and daughter were doing fine when we visited. Our Mammy then arranged to sort out a few things for the new mother and child with baby clothes. Our old cot and pram was pressed back into service and Daddy hauled them to Carrigeen Cottage. Mary was a beautiful baby soft and dark like her mother. I always remember her sleeping peacefully in her cradle; and she rarely cried the way a baby might do. There was consternation one morning though when Mary wouldn't wake for her bottle. Doctor Lord was sent for, but it was no use. A cot-death was the verdict it seemed. We boys were sent down to the Murrays during the funeral, but I still remember that sad little white coffin being carried out the door. Mary was buried with her Great Grandmother as far as I am aware.

Mammy always said that Eileen changed after that: she wasn't nearly as gay, not nearly as focused. In time though she grew strong again, and some time later she met Lar who came a courting. Lar was a widower himself with grown-up sons over in England; but nevertheless they made a match. Lar would take Eileen out in his Morris Minor and park outside the garden gate for a kiss and a cuddle with her before she came in. We used to watch for their return and when they arrived we'd sneak out to the car and start tapping on the steamy windows to annoy them. We tried it once too often though. On this particular night when we sneaked out Lar was waiting behind the bushes to ambush us and he chased us off down the Big Stone Road, crying 'Spoilsports!' Lar was great fun though. He had a ready smile and a freckly face and red wavy hair. A hard worker too in Morrins' Mill and he was to make a good husband for Eileen.

Lar and Eileen got married in St Joseph's in Baltinglass, and the reception was held in Lawlors of Naas. Eileen had come to town to see Mammy to arrange her trousseau. It seemed that Carroll herself wasn't much use for that sort of thing. Eileen picked a blue Georgette style dress for the wedding; and Mammy also arranged the cake. Eileen was to have two more girls: another Mary and Cathleen, named after Carroll.

Life can be cruel and unpredictable, perhaps inevitably so. One single event was to alter utterly the fortunes of this lovely family. While having her second child Eileen was kept in hospital for observation. Lar and Ned and Carroll would drive to Dublin to visit her, and it was on one of these return trips that their car was hit by a drunken driver. Ned was thrown against the windscreen with the force of the impact and suffered head injuries and both Lar and Carroll broke a leg.

All were taken to the hospital in Naas, and Lar in fact was still a patient when Mammy and Daddy and Eileen called in to show him his new daughter on their way home to Baltinglass. Lar was to recover eventually, but Carroll's leg never properly mended and she had to employ a stick for the first time in her life to help her get around. Such an incapacity must have hurt her pride if not her composure. Ned never got over the experience and he visibly faded until he succumbed to heart failure, years before his time. Lar and Eileen lived in Baltinglass after they were married and one day while pregnant on Lar's third child, poor Eileen died of a heart attack while hanging out her clothes on the line. (There was obviously a coronary weakness in the family). She died within the Month's Mind Mass for Ned. Lar was devastated. He mourned her, and buried her, and then packed his bags and took his daughters over to England. For Carroll this must have been the last straw. Alone now in Carrigeen Cottage with just her memories, she too soon pined away and departed on her sad final journey, back to the bosom of her lost family.

It's left to the likes of me to have known such caring simple people, and record their simple story. These are people who do not walk the world's stage or who leave no lasting imprint on the fleeting affairs of humankind. These people like their neighbours were tolerant people; and they loved their own. How welcome and doted upon the ill-fated first Mary had been. There was to be no orphanage for her, no *Magdalen Laundry* for her mother either. Just a loving home environment as should be any mother and child's due. The people of Baltinglass were largely the same. They had demonstrated it graphically during the so called *Battle of Baltinglass* when the first Coalition Government had replaced the postmistress with another of their own choice whom they felt was more qualified for the position.

The position of postmaster/postmistress at Baltinglass had been held in the Cooke family since 1870 when Michael Cooke had been granted the position by the grandfather of Major General Meade Edward Dennis. In 1936 a granddaughter of Michael's, Bridget Cooke was the postmistress, but she became unwell, so much so that her niece, Helen Cooke was asked to relinquish her post office position in Rathdrum, and come to live with and assist her ailing aunt. The aunt died some weeks later, and her sister Katie Cooke, then aged 68, was appointed to the position, after some wrangling it must be said that Helen had to undertake to secure her aunt's tenure because of her age with the Postmaster at Naas who controlled the district. Katie was nominally the Postmistress, but Helen ran the business. In April 1950 Katie suffered a second stroke which incapacitated her further so she decided to retire, secure in the knowledge that her niece would succeed her.

It was in the gift of the then Minister for Posts and Telegraph, Mr James Everett to select the nominee for the post. Both Helen Cooke and Michael Farrell, whose family had a drapery store in the town, had applied for the position. The appointment dragged on with Helen Cooke still running the Post Office until in November 1950, Michael Farrell was surprisingly appointed.

This controversial selection aroused the anger of some influential inhabitants, leading some to claim that there was a hint of corruption behind it. After all Helen Cooke had been performing an admirable job, and besides her family had held the position for 80 odd years. Bernard Sheridan resolved to do something about it and Ben Hooper, Principal of the Technical School was approached to form a support committee under the auspices of the School Board. This, however was not practical because Michael Farrell's father was a member of the school's governing body. So an alternative arrangement was made under the auspices of the local Catholic Boy Scout Troop's Association! A public meeting was organised for the green painted Town Hall to ascertain the attitudes and opinions of the general populace about the issue. The question of who would chair this meeting was the main problem. The priest of the parish Fr.Doyle and his curate, Fr.Moran were not inclined to become involved directly though they both supported the Helen Cooke cause. It was then the agitators struck on the idea of asking Major General Meade Edward Dennis to chair the meeting. The General was reluctant to oblige until it was subtly pointed out to him that his Grandfather had made the original appointment. With the Family Honour involved, the General agreed. The meeting attracted a full attendance; but when the pro-Farrell faction challenged the General's right to chair the proceedings, he turned to the audience and asked: " Do I have the right to represent you? " Yes ! " came the resounding reply. Thus, the Nationalist Card was nullified.

A strategy to preserve Helen Cooke in her position was planned and devised. Petitions were organised and local representatives like Deputy Cogan, Independent, and Councillors Kehoe and Timmons, as well as Government Ministers like Sean McEoin of the Department of Justice, were approached for support. It was the opinion of the Minister of Justice that the appointment was a *fait accompli* and would be difficult to overturn.

James Everett insisted that his hands were tied in the matter. In an instruction to his Department in 1948 on taking up office, only the immediate family of outgoing incumbents could inherit posts   which excluded Helen Cooke. The engineering gang under McNulty was dispatched from Waterford to lay the new cables into Farrell's shop on December 1st. They began to dig up the road outside the drapery, and attracted a least one cynic to observe their progress:

" There's a terrible smell around here! " Tom Morrissey asserted.

" What'd ya mean!" One of the gang retorted angrily.

" I mean, I think you've just hit the sewer with your pick! "

The Helen Cooke Action Committee knew it would be only a matter of time before her lines outside the Post Office would be disconnected so a picket was organised round the clock to patrol and cover the concrete slab that gave access to the telephone services outside the Post Office. This picket of ordinary townspeople was so strong that McNulty couldn't carry out the work.

By this time the newspapers were alerted to the events and Martin Fallon was the first reporter on the scene to record the shenanigans. The matter had been raised in Dail Eireann by Deputy Cogan, and as the Opposition saw the potential of embarrassing the Government, stormy debates ensued on the morality of the appointment long into the night. Threats were hurled across the benches of the House as well as insults and calls for impeachment! Deputy Cogan went so far as to write to the Taoiseach, Mr John A. Costelloe, to withdraw future support for the Government in the Division Lobbies.

The Action Committee planned to picket the Dail to further escalate their campaign, but were wisely advised against it because it would be against the law, and might damage public sympathy which was slowly growing in their favour. Helen Cooke had become a *cause celebre*, at home and even now abroad, and hundreds of messages of support were daily arriving at the Post Office.

For fear of antagonising the more liberal support the Action Committee decided to scale down the strength of their picket, but not wholly eliminate it. Bernard Sheridan arranged for an early warning system so that protesters could occupy the Post Office should the engineering gang come to close it. From Pat Dunne's garage he obtained a motor siren which he mounted in his home to warn the Mill Street area around the Post Office. He arranged that Morrin's Mill should ring their old brass bell to warn all those around Main Street.

The word got out that Monday, December 11th was going to be *P.O.Day*. At 7.30 in the morning McNulty would be arriving with his gang to disconnect Helen Cooke, supported by a force of at least 70 Gardai. The alarms were sounded as the enemy army approached and the citizens gathered around the Post Office. The Gardai moved in to try and move the crowd, but without forcing them. It was not a successful manoeuvre. Stalemate ensued briefly until someone came up with the brilliant idea of using a lorry to slowly push the demonstrators away from the concrete slab of the services manhole. This was achieved successfully. The Gardai therefore could establish a cordon upon moving the truck so that the gang could get to work.

It seemed then that the Action Committee was defeated, but this is when the passive resistance began. A picket on the G.P.O. was to be arranged, and members of the Committee would attend the Public Gallery of the Dail to aggravate proceedings in the Chamber. An Auster light aircraft piloted by Norman Ashe was hired to broadcast over Dublin City to alert the inhabitants during these initiatives! Bernard Sheridan would speak through a microphone that had been rigged up by the pilot. The telephone subscribers in the town held a meeting in which a boycott of the telephone exchange would be instigated, but following strong opposition Mr Redmond of R.N. Gillespie's Ironmongery suggested that all telephones should be left off the hook every Thursday, and that on every other day of the week the exchange would be pestered by nonsense calls to make it virtually inoperable. This was adjudged to be an eloquent compromise and the subscribers went home happy.

O'Neills shop in the town was licensed to sell stamps so this was used by Helen Cooke's supporters as a mail centre. Finally a plebiscite was arranged in the town to determine the true level of support for the cause of Helen Cooke as there were still many who supported Michael Farrell's position. He himself had after all merely applied for the post and had done nothing wrong, but despite pleadings on behalf of the Cooke's who would be left destitute if Helen Cooke was to loose her position, Michael Farrell would no step down.

On December 21st the final results of the referendum became known: 87% of the population had voted to support Helen Cooke. Some time later the shock news was brought that Michael Farrell had resigned as Postmaster, and the *Battle of Baltinglass* had been won in the face of Government in-

transigence and the Red Tape of State against the wishes of the majority of the people of the town.

Life would return to normal as it always does, but the battle served to demonstrate the true strength of democracy or People Power when properly and peacefully organised. It served to demonstrate the triumph of justice over cynicism and opportunism. " What can the people of Baltinglass do? " A proponent of the Government stance was heard to remark arrogantly, during the height of the month long battle. The people of Baltinglass had a ready made answer that they had employed as one of their slogans: ' *Baltinglass Demands Clean Administration*! '

With the Carrolls of Carrigeen Cottage and such People, this world was a better place, and a less hurtful place, a more tolerant place, and a more loving place when it was graced by their brief , unassuming presence. Much more so than other glib commentators would have us believe.

END

Martha's Hat by Jean Harlow

It had long been my theory that you could tell a lot by the way Martha's hat behaved. It was made of straw, with faded blue flowers and green leaves on the brim and a shallow, tatty crown.

Some said that Martha, the Vicar's wife, had bought the hat at a car boot sale; some said that, like the majority of her wardrobe, it had come from a charity shop; others asserted that she had inherited it from a maiden aunt. In any event, none dare ask where the hat came from. She wore it throughout the cricket season, and my Gerald swore that she slept in it! In spite of all these theories, I felt it should be watched carefully. We always seemed to win if it sat confidently on her head, but if it looked forlorn and disconsolate we invariably lost.

"It's absolutely unthinkable that we should lose this game," Gerald announced as he pushed a white cricket pullover into his bag. "I can't bear to think that lot from Lower Croft might lift the Cup."

Now what I know about cricket could be written under the proverbial postage stamp – 'silly mid on' and 'square legs' are foreign to me – and the same about making sausage rolls could be said for Gerald, so we make the perfect couple. He bats at number three for the Highill village team, and I provide two dozen sausage rolls to be consumed at their tea interval every summer Saturday.

Well, it's usually two dozen sausage rolls, but yesterday I had a breathless telephone call from Martha, who is in charge of catering. Her nervousness made me think that she must be hatless.

"Make it four dozen, can you, Beth dear? That rough team from Lower Croft will be here, and you know how greedy they are. Common lot!"

Sentiments not befitting a Vicar's wife, I felt. However, I did as asked and turned up early on the Saturday afternoon. I saw Gerald practising at the nets behind the pavilion and felt a surge of pride. He looked so handsome in his immaculate whites, although I noticed with dismay that his knuckles matched.

Wives and girlfriends were busy filling the urn and spreading tablecloths on the two trestle tables. They worked in silence and the smell of tension was suffocating. I grabbed four large plates and arranged my sausage rolls.

"Well done, Beth! Could you fetch the sugar bowls, dear?" Martha was still nervous as I could see by the inevitable straw hat perching uncomfortably on her yellow perm.

On my way to the kitchen I saw, and heard, the Lower Croft team arrive. A cloud of dust, a screech of tyres and loud singing heralded the arrival of their coach. They spilled out, led by their captain, Big Mick. He ignored the polite outstretched hand of the Vicar, instead slapping him on the back and sending him reeling against the pavilion. It was obvious that they had visited the Black Bull on the way.

"Heads!" shouted Big Mick, winning the toss and deciding that Lower Croft would field first. I watched with apprehension as I glimpsed Martha's hat looking limp and sad. The motley crew took up their positions, most of them in 'off whites'. Their burly Captain, however, was dressed head to toe in pale pink, obviously the result of a red sock in the washer.

He thundered towards our opening bat, delivering a menacing ball that uprooted and scattered all three wickets. In no time at all it was Gerald's turn and, my tea duties over, I gave him a reassuring wave from the pavilion balcony as he walked into battle. He tried to look confident but I knew different.

I glanced at Martha's hat but found no reassurance there. It now looked in danger of plummeting to the depths of the tea urn.

Gerald 'took guard carefully as if he intended to bat all afternoon but Big Mick had other ideas. He lobbed a ball that may or may not have clipped Gerald's leg and in one swift leap he went nose-to-nose with the umpire, yelling "Owzat?" A chorus of similar loud queries rose from the entire Lower Croft team and the umpire felt it in his best interests to lift a finger and seal Gerald's fate.

Our Highill team put up a noble fight but at tea-time they were all out. Before the ladies could take up their positions behind the trestle tables all the egg sandwiches and most of my sausage rolls had disappeared. It was just as well that our team had no appetite because the visitors swooped on the food, cleared the tables, and left nothing but a few crumbs.

Martha sat near the wall, hat now ominously poised over closed eyes. "Ssh," warned the Vicar, "she's praying for rain."

Either she didn't pray fervently enough or she'd forgotten to give the correct location. Under a bright blue sky our team downheartedly took up their fielding positions to the rather weak encouragement of the Vicar's, "Come on, men, do your best."

Big Mick, bat held aloft, strode to the crease, giving loud, concise orders to his second batsman – "Give 'em hell, Steve!"

And so they did.

Big Mick never moved from the crease. He slammed every ball to the boundary. Our poor wicket keeper became redundant but the scorer could barely keep pace.

Martha abandoned prayer and dragged a deck-chair near to the boundary – a hazardous position, I felt.. However, I took heart from seeing her hat, though at a grotesque angle, sitting firmly on those yellow curls.

My confidence was short-lived. Big Mick faced an untypical slow ball and he was ready. With an almighty swipe the ball ricocheted off what I think they call the 'sight screen', snatched Martha's hat, flew over the pavilion and scattered the ducks off the village pond as it plunged to the depths.

If I'd had any say, Lower Croft would have been given the Cup there and then. I knew it was all over when the search party gave up hope of finding Martha's hat. Without it, I felt we hadn't a cat in hell's chance. I was so sorry for Gerald and the rest of our team.

The new ball inspired our bowlers, however, and soon Lower Croft fell like ninepins.

Highill set about their second innings with a will, and, in the three hours of remaining daylight, began to run up a healthy score.

It was my turn to help with the washing-up and when I finished I walked out on to the pavilion balcony, drying my hands on my apron. The hatless Martha and the Vicar were standing near the boundary in a state of high excitement.

"One more run and they're done for," she shouted. Flushed and jumping up and down, the Vicar called out to me.

"Did you hear, Beth? I think we've made it!"

"Go on, then, rub it in!" moaned Big Mick who was sitting on the grass, head in hands, looking forlorn in his dirty "pinks". He looked much in need of sustenance that only the Black Bull could supply.

As I turned to look at him I saw something on the pavilion roof. Silhouetted against the early evening sky it looked like a dead pigeon fluttering in the gentle breeze. But, no, it was Martha's hat! The breeze brought it sailing down to Martha's feet and, without removing her gaze from the match, she plonked it firmly on her head. It looked triumphant and everything, I knew, would be OK now.

The match ended with a 'four' struck by my Gerald and I can tell you that there was much back-slapping and free pints from the landlord of the Black Bull as Highill celebrated that evening. It was late when we arrived home.

Handing Gerald his cocoa I snuggled into his shoulder and announced, "I knew we'd win."

"How?" he asked in amazement. "You always say you don't understand cricket."

"Maybe not, but I only need to understand Martha's hat!"

IN HIS IMAGE By Noel Bailey

To describe George Taylor as unimpressive would be to state the obvious. Seriously height-challenged, even built-up heels would have left Tom Cruise towering over him. As a scrawny youth, he didn't exactly have sand kicked in his face whenever he ventured to the beach – instead, the local kids built sand-castles on his *chest*!

Charismatically speaking, George was quite obviously AWOL when that little number was being handed out and in his later teenage years, discovered that any attempts to ingratiate himself with members of the opposite sex were more or less doomed to abject failure.

"It's not that I don't *like* you George," one girl had heartlessly relayed to him during recess, "I'm just not that desperate…sorry!" Even as she re-joined her chosen clique, the joint laughter then emanating from the group was something less than a self-confidence boost it must be said.

Sadly, his physical shortcomings were not even compensated-for by an above average intellect. George in fact was academically adrift from the pack. Majoring in the lower percentile bands mathematically, the youngster had trouble with anything much over his six-times table. *Pi* might well be 22/7 but as far as Master Taylor was concerned, *Pi* was at best – "Shepherd's" and at worst – "rhubarb and apple." History had him completely flummoxed with regards to anything in the wake of "Genesis," while his ability to memorise the element-chart for Chemistry, took on legendary proportions the day he answered his teacher's (in hindsight) critically unwise question, *"What does the symbol Au indicate George?"* with, *"August Sir!"*

Sport? Now that was another embarrassing little chapter to be endured. With the outright coordination skills of Porky Pig himself, football, cricket and basketball were never going to present themselves as viable options to one struggling to find his niche in school life. Fact is, he could neither kick, catch or throw. For the best part of ten years, the simple rigours of philately were to be the extent of his physical exertion.

And where were his parents all this time you may well ask? Spending quality moments with their other two children is the sad but truthful answer to that insightful ponderance. They found in the presence of their youngest boy, an inexplicable *awkwardness* if the truth be known.

"George must find his own water-level in life" his father would comment sporadically, never once feeling disposed to offer his son it seems, the least word of encouragement.

The fact is though, not only had George already *discovered* his own water level, he had, in his relatively brief tenure upon the planet, unlocked (albeit accidentally) the very key to personal contentment and oneness of being.

Not for him, the transient pride of material ownership. *His* pleasures were selfless. Feeding the squirrels and birds on the heath, lending the occasional arm to the blind or infirmed, in their quest to navigate a street-crossing safely. Simply talking to the elderly and companionless in his home-town of *Kettering Fields,* afforded George that which the educational curriculum itself had failed to deliver. Lonely they may have been, but the knowledge and experiences of the old he discovered, outstripped any worthwhile gains to be had by associating with those his own age. That included his two siblings naturally.

Where others may have commented "It's getting dark," George would gaze upwards at the shimmering sunset and see there, the beauty of the cloud formations as they extended their multi-hued fingers of tangerine and red ochre, back-lit still by the dying orb. During the winter months, while others would rug-up against the frigid elements, futilely complaining of the bitter cold, George would sit alone in the small summer-house, admiring the purity and cleansing nature of the silent snowfalls. Occasionally he would extend a gloved hand to catch a few eddying flakes that he would observe with fascination, until they passed from existence in his upturned palm.

The scent of flowers, the gently directed symphonies of falling autumn leaves, the majesty of fork-lightning, an animal's trust.....*these* were the important things he knew.

Twenty now, he had been employed as an assistant at the local library since leaving school. Scholastically out of touch perhaps, nevertheless the solitude yet orderliness of his chosen environment, appealed strongly to him. Bereft of scientific and historical knowledge himself, his incapacity to understand the words *within*, in no way detracted from his ability to chronologically sort, categorise and recollect titles!

Fully unable to have ever understood the morbidity that led Roderick Usher to entomb the Lady Madeline, the personal descent into Hell of Dorian Gray, the technical innovations of Verne, the grotesque nature of Mr Hyde, George was still fully able to direct without hesitation, readers to the exact location of any book sought. Whilst co-workers had nothing but praise for the lad's efficiency, female companionship remained for him, a seemingly insurmountable stumbling block.

Naturally, the discovery of 2006JY12 some three weeks before Christmas that year, put this minor contingency into perspective.

In astronomical terms, one might say the 'discovery' as such, was a tad *overdue*. Becoming aware of an object the size of Lower Manhattan, just three months ahead of it's impact with what Scientists unequivocally agreed would be central India, was not cause for universal gratitude.

With an estimated impact speed of some eighteen miles per second, there was no need for a second opinion. This was your standard, garden variety L.E.E. – Life Extinction Event!

Pity the media – trying to publish headlines in fifty-point print on the average tabloid just wasn't working! After the inevitable *"How could so much technology have failed us?"* it was recognised and understood by those still lucid in their thought processes, that "what difference anyway?" the outcome was as inevitable as it was unaddressable.

George quite enjoyed it.

Just *three* months to build underground bunkers capable of withstanding the incomprehensible fury of an inter-stellar collision – always assuming Earth wasn't fatally fractured at the point of impact. Vaporised cities, a heat-blast beyond comprehension and three-hundred mile-an-hour winds, with the potential for a super-heated atmosphere scattering red-hot debris for months. One that indubitably could not sustain life for decades. Matters were not helped when it was pointed out that the slightest miscalculation might involve an oceanic splash-down that would result in mile-high tsunamis that would likely place the strategically placed bunkers at the bottom of a new ocean. Options were thin on the ground. Less bunkers – but with fully self-contained survival chambers for the chosen few, was the universal decision.

Now that was a problem. *Who was to be chosen?* The final countdown was based on the frenetic building activity involved in the construction of just three bunkers. One in Colorado, one in Central Europe and the third near Alice Springs in Central Australia, *this* being given the most likely chance of preservation, having regard to its geographic remoteness from the impact zone.

The Internationally-approved edict that no-one over forty be eligible for selection was not popular let's say! Professional forgers of birth certificates, licences and other forms of id had never had it so good, wasted as their efforts ultimately were, given the individual Governments' electronic public records.

The bunkers were scheduled to hold just eight-thousand people each, which meant that aside from the eight-hundred pre-selected technical and medical staff needed to oversee operational function-ality of each bunker, only seven thousand two hundred people could randomly be selected by computerised lottery…and the greater percentage of that algorithm was to be slanted towards children.

For two weeks in the lead-up to Christmas, TV programming on all channels was no more than twenty-four hour live-cross updates on the building schedule, panels of 'experts' airing their opinions of the coming Armageddon and incredibly, Banks offering fixed short-term deposit options at 75% interest.

At the library it was business as usual for George. Every book even skirting such subjects as 'meteorology,' 'astronomical facts,' 'survival of the fittest,' 'religions of the world,' even 'self-help programs,' were out on loan.

"Live" feeds from the Hubble telescope of the inbound 2006JY12, showed at this stage no appreciable change in either aspect or size of the approaching asteroid. Scientists the world over were however united in their view that this would change rapidly come late January and in the weeks leading up to the actual collision on March 7th.

While panic began to set-in shortly after Christmas as people the world over sensed more keenly than ever, their hopelessly vulnerable mortality, George noticed how the older citizens faced their Waterloo with so much more dignity. He still fed the birds and the squirrels on the heath and felt no bitterness towards his maker as the count-down neared the seriously worrying stage.

The authorities left the *really* bad news until early the third week of January. Resources it was admitted, could only guarantee the completion now of just one bunker and *that* in Australia was the logical choice. As the previously selected twenty-three thousand, four-hundred lottery winners had now to be short-listed to just seven thousand two-hundred names, teams of local and imported workers worked frantically round the clock, that these people might carry with them any and every chance to perpetuate humanity in their brave, if not fully inhospitable new world.

George watched almost unemotionally as the telescope showed now, with just twelve days to go, the incoming nightmare, twice the size it had appeared to be a week earlier. He would have walked up to the heath but the birds and squirrels had long since forsaken the place. He hoped they would not suffer when the time came. Standing now outside his own front gate, he could see his father with the familiar upraised bottle in the kitchen – quite obviously seeking-out his own water-level. George would like to have walked inside and comfort him but knew he was not wanted. He sensed correctly that his very acceptance of what was to be, irritated his parents no end and that nothing he could say would endear him further. His sisters were no longer living at home, having been entrusted to relatives in northern Scotland, under the misguided belief that safety might be found there.

Come March 1st, the first tidal waves had already been recorded in Japan with enormous loss of life. Electrical storms were already cutting a swathe through the residential populous and triggered by a combination of wildly fluctuating weather patterns and unprecedented solar activity, the world's terrified population bore witness to the sun's total discolouration as dense cloud formations formed an unearthly yet atmospheric guard of honour for the incoming destroyer.

George glanced around his bedroom one last time. A gentle person's conclave. On his desk, two slender stalks partially extruded from between the pages of an old encyclopaedia that he had used to press a pair of primrose flowers he had picked from nearby parkland the day he started High school. A certificate of merit for an essay he had written hung on the far wall, over the desk-lamp – the only award he had ever won. The old radio that had once belonged to his Grandmother but which still worked admirably, sat on his bedside table. How many hours had he spent lying there, listening to music and wondering what was to become of his life? Outside, the wind howled.

Straightening the corner of the pillow-case he left the room, closing the door softly behind him. He knew where he had to go.

The residents of *Kettering Fields* who had ventured outside, preferring to face their fears, gathered in a group outside the King's Arms near the small roundabout. They idly watched as a young man made his solitary way along Pinewoods Road towards his intended destination.

Above the shrieking wind another sound could clearly be heard now, one that none could identify. Fearful glances were exchanged. Descending abruptly through the opaque cloud-cover, the enormous craft hovered, its fusion reactors issuing a thudding vibration. Concurrently, every computer screen in the free world blanked out, being replaced with the enigmatic but ultimately simple message:

"GEORGE TAYLOR born Oct 12th 1986: Left March 7th 2007"

Atop the heath, a lone figure walked towards his destiny.

WHEN WHAT TO MY WONDERING EYES SHOULD APPEAR By Noel Bailey

You think Christmas is only for children? That's what old Jim Hadfield thought too and as he was to discover, it is simply a matter of never losing sight of what Christmas intrinsically *means* and what magic exists still, in those remote places holed-up between fantasy and reality, hope and disillusionment.

Jim dreamed – just like everyone else. He dreamed of bygone days when he would leap from his bed Christmas mornings, a flushed and excited eight-year old, taking the stairs two at a time on his descent to the lounge-room. Pushing wide the door respectfully, a trait often exhibited by only-children, you could have lit-up a thousand cities from the glow on the youngster's face as he gazed in awe at the presents piled up around the tree.

Jim's parents had never been what you might call well-heeled, yet they had ensured that at whatever cost, their little boy would remember the happiest of childhoods, most especially during the Yuletide season. Their efforts had paid-off handsomely.

Marrying in his mid-twenties "for better or for worse," it had proven most definitely the less desirable of those two options. Cathy, fundamentally was a bitch. He remembered back, not long before his mother's death in fact and how she had more or less laid that particular fact out for him. His father had died years earlier and had been spared the worry of his son's great unhappiness. All Jim had ever done was to love his wife unconditionally and in doing so, managing somehow to overlook her complete selfishness, emotional detachment and cruel insensitivity. For thirty-four years Cathy drove, while he sat out life in the back-seat!

Bereft of meaning, the marriage had produced two daughters equally bereft of paternal interest and consideration. Perhaps genetically influenced, both girls from their teenage years onwards found a plethora of reasons not to be home, staying either with girlfriends or maternal relatives. Of little concern to Cathy, it simply afforded her more time to spend in front of the television. The few times Jim tried to talk to either girl about their school-work, their futures, even the most mundane of topics…it was obvious, they had little need for his input into their lives….*that* having ended one might conclude, with Cathy's abrupt announcement of her subsequent pregnancies. After a while he left them to their own intractable devices. Both girls left home soon after completing school and their finding local employment. He saw them perhaps once a fortnight, usually when they came to visit their mother.

Jim would console himself some nights recalling the Christmases when they were yet children and the pleasure he had gotten in recreating for them what still stood-out so vividly from his own past. How had everything gone so wrong? he mused. All he had ever wanted was to love…and *be* loved!

Many years passed. Cathy had died of kidney disease, his daughters had married and moved away to the north of England. A postcard from Marion in the late eighties had put him on notice that he was now officially a grandfather. He had seen the lad but half a dozen times since, the last being when his daughter called in at the local hospital briefly following his triple-bypass .

He was in his sixty-fourth year now and living alone in a shabby semi in Portsmouth, the area's solitude matching his own bleak and wind-swept life. Still, he took pleasure in wrapping-up during the wintry months and spending hours on the seafront, looking out at the gray Atlantic, perhaps sensing in the uncompromising and harsh environment, a kinship somehow with his own unstinting tidal existence.

The one thing that adverse circumstance had failed miserably in trying to dull or nullify in Jim's life however, was December the 25th. Each year he would decorate the little tree using the same tinsel and colored balls he had so religiously protected and stored away following his parental loss. Within the limitations of his meagre savings, he would even buy himself a few presents to be religiously wrapped and placed beneath the tree on Christmas Eve.

To the outside world that year, it was an elderly and rather melancholy-looking gentleman that took his time wandering around the stores, picking up and studying the latest toys, deriving tactile pleasure from simply *holding* the many items that represented those seasonal childhood yearnings. Occasionally he would smile as he held aloft a doll or a farm animal. Mothers would glance at him warily and shepherd their youngsters into the adjoining aisle. They could not know that inside that tattered old coat and scarf, an eight-year old child looked out at his beloved world of remembrances.

In *Brackensfield's*, one of the largest Department stores on the east-side, the newly installed Santa was entertaining a long line of expectant children as their mothers jostled for the dubious privilege of parting with six pounds 75p in exchange for an instant photo of their loved one/s posed on the man in red's knee. No-one noticed the lonely old figure standing alongside the racks of games nearby, watching the awe-struck children as they progressed excitedly along the queue. The moment they had to relinquish their mom's hand and take that last step up to that lofty perch. The encouragement to smile for the camera and then finally those few words with Santa himself. Unseen also, the occasional yet involuntary tear trickling down the man's cheeks.

He stayed until the last child had scampered back to his mother and the helpers were hanging up the sign which read "Santa has gone to feed his reindeer and will be back at 6 p.m."

For a moment he was lost in his own thoughts.

"It means a lot to you doesn't it?"

The words jolted him upright. Kindly eyes considerably older than his own even even, looked down at him.

"I was just remembering," he half-stammered and feeling not a little embarrassed.

The eyes smiled. "Ah, the memory of happier times perhaps?" Then after the briefest of pauses, "And what then would *you* wish for yourself on this cold Christmas Eve?" came the question from deep beneath the bushy beard.

"That's easy, " Jim responded. "I'd wish that for just a few hours even, I could spend time with a young lady who might love me for simply myself. Someone I wished I could have met when I was young and had a future."

The hand caressed the white moustache. "*All* of us have a future my friend. It's just a matter of recognising when it actually started! We must enjoy the opportunities that come along and for some of us," he looked at Jim almost sympathetically, "such times may be of regrettably brief duration."

Smiling now, he took Jim's hand. "Well, a very merry Christmas to you Sir. I must be going now. Those reindeer of mine are eating me out of house and home."

Jim watched as the tall figure disappeared around the sporting aisle and decided to head home. Although not snowing, it was icy cold outside and he was looking forward to the familiarity of the snug confines of his little home. Perhaps he would indulge himself with a small bottle of brandy, after all, Christmas *was* but once a year.

Entering the small latched gate that opened upon the narrow crazy-paving pathway that led to his front door, he felt upon his forehead first one, then another touch of crystalised cold. He looked up. The weather bureau had been right for once. For only the eleventh time since the turn of the previous century, a genuine white Christmas had been predicted for the south of England. He watched for a few moments, the sporadic flakes as they eddied silently downwards, not yet in sufficient a flurry to lay the groundwork for their heavier relatives.

The front door closed behind him, sealing off once more his own little eco-system from the withering elements. Everything was as he had left it. The tree over by the small French doors, those ancient but so well-loved glass balls reflecting the small lights as they winked on and off – tiny beacons of cheer in a room of such gentility and misplaced affection.

Beneath the lower branches upon the threadbare carpet, four neatly-wrapped presents lay clustered there. So sad their message of loneliness, yet so *inspiring* a tradition of hope and goodwill. Jim knelt down and re-arranged them as he liked to do occasionally. He had long since put out of his mind what they contained and was rather looking forward to the morning's discoveries. He allowed his fingers contact with some of the long strands of tinsel. It took no effort on his part to recall his mother kneeling there beside him, showing an eager son how to hang them properly. Closing his eyes, it was *her* fingertips he now felt, *her* breath that perceptibly disturbed the symmetry of those lower branches.

The plummeting outside temperature was more than enough reason to light the fire in the open hearth that he had earlier prepared. He knelt there watching as the embryonic flames consumed the kindling, giving them sustenance to take-on the challenges of the thicker wood above. Within ten minutes the hearth was ablaze with pyrotechnic good cheer and Jim began to set strategically in place layers of coal that would keep the entire house warm during the night. There is something intrinsically magnetic about an open fire. A lifetime's thoughts and recollections can pass in an instant watching those glowing embers, the small pockets of gas igniting within the lumps of coal and the curious behavior of those tiny flame-creatures as they scurry along the base of the conflagrated logs.

Jim walked over to the small but serviceable kitchenette and cooked himself a couple of pork sausages with potatoes and mixed vegetables and with the small room at its optimum temperature now, he watched on television, as he had done every successive Christmas for as far back as he could remember – *Miracle on 34th Street*. Some years it was *A Christmas Carol*, but always one or the other. The brandy saw admirably well, to his transition from well-fed comfort to yawning tiredness. The last thing he did was to lay out a final layer of coal before drawing the fireguard across in front of the hearth.

He was aware of the old clock in the lounge-room striking, having listened to its comforting message of hourly regularity since he was a small child. Subconsciously he realised it was midnight. It was the *other* sound however that had him struggling between wakefulness and confused unreality.

It's repetition brought him fully awake. Someone at the front door?...*his* front door? It was only the lightest of knocks.

It would have been hard to tell what shocked him more. The inbound blast of freezing air with not a few flurries of heavy snow or the young girl standing on his doorstep shivering there, in just a thin dress.

"Could I come in for a few moments please, I'm lost." was all she was able to mutter.

The girl was in the last stages of hypothermia to judge by her color and aggravated shaking. Flakes of snow covered her shoulders and long brown hair. He did not fail to notice how pretty she was either and the likelihood that she was surely no more than seventeen or eighteen. He pulled her gently inside and closed the door.

"Good heavens child," he said, propelling her gently towards the fireplace. "What on earth are you doing walking around the streets at this time of night...*and* with no warm clothes."

"I...I don't remember," she said, crouching down near the hearth spreading her small hands before the resuscitating heat. "Something happened and I had to leave....that's all I recall. I don't even know this place!"

Jim selected a few small logs from the pile nearby and tossed them on the fire ahead of some more coal to bring up the level of flame.

"Are you hungry missy?" he asked. The girl looked-up at him and nodded shyly.

"Well you just stay there love – get yourself nice and warm and I'll fetch you something to eat," he said to her.

As he pottered about in his little kitchen alcove tossing some bacon and eggs into a frying pan, and a couple of pieces of bread into the toaster, he looked back at the girl. Obviously benefiting greatly from the warmth of the fire, she looked back at him once or twice, smiling and quite obviously at ease in his presence. Looking at her delicately formed body hunched up there on the floor, he realised he wasn't yet too old to recognise the physical attraction of one so young, despite the obvious futility of such recognition.

"What about a mug of hot chocolate to be going on with love" he enquired, turning the eggs as he did so.

"Oh, yes please," she answered gratefully, hugging herself around the knees as she sat there, seemingly entranced by the flames. Little wispy clouds of steam were rising from the sleeves of her dress and he realised that besides being half-frozen to death she must have been soaked through from the melting snow-flakes. She sipped her hot chocolate delicately.

By the time he took out the tray of hot food to her, the color was back in her cheeks and she was altogether a healthier-looking proposition to the freezing and bedraggled young thing that he had first ushered across his minimally populated threshold.

He had wanted to ask her all sorts of questions but thought better of it, preferring to watch as she relished the simple but satisfying meal he had brought her.

"What's your name miss?" he found the courage to ask her.

"Cassandra," she replied, but most people call me "Cass, or Cassie." she added, looking up at him between mouthfuls.

"Well, I like Cassandra," he told her, "If you don't mind I'll call you that – it's a lovely name....for a lovely young lady, if you don't mind me saying so." he blushed at his own words and she caught the color rising in his cheeks.

"You're a little shy with girls aren't you?" she asked. "Oh, and you haven't told me *your* name either, have you?"

"Ohh, sorry...no I forgot," he said to her. "I'm Jim...just *old* Jim!"

"You're not *that* old," she observed with a commendable degree of tact.

"Ah, but I *am* Cassandra," he smiled at her wistfully. "Way *too* old I'm afraid."

"You're a very *kind* person, I know that much," she smiled up at him. "A girl knows instinctively who she's safe with and who she can trust."

He was watching her now, noticing just how young she was, the beautiful unlined face, blemish-free skin, girlish figure that promised more than he dared remember. He wondered how he must look to her? Never realistically having been even "handsome" in his youth, his skin was old and sagging in places now – all the *wrong* places at that! Beneath his eyes, his jowls, around his considerably expanded and flabby waistline, even the tops of his gnarled old hands were wrinkly, the veins standing out like speed-humps gone feral. Liver-spots were starting to make their presence known and to describe his hairline as receding, would not begin to recount the cranial carnage wreaked over the past twenty years. Reduced to a few white hairs, those currently on-site presented themselves as little more than a ruffled patchwork at the best of times. As if subconsciously aware of his hirsute shortcomings, he ran his hand across his head suddenly, flattening a few rogue strands.

"Well to *me* you're not old Jim....just a really nice man," she smiled up at him sweetly as she finished her food, offering him up the tray.

Her words touched him and quite without any logical reason, he wanted to put his arms around her and hold her tight....the daughter he had never had... the wife he had never known....the lover he had so futilely longed for. Instead however, he simply took the tray and trudged back to the kitchen, aware for the first time since he had let her in, how additionally grotty he must appear to her in those tatty old pyjamas and dressing-gown he was wearing.

Seemingly reading his mind, she called out to him,

"Jim, come and sit beside me in front of the fire for a while."

Not even questioning why she would ask such a thing of him, he shuffled back to the fireplace and eased himself down beside her. For a while they both stared into the dwindling flames. He noticed now the little silver chain around her neck and the tiny locket that she seemed to be holding for comfort as she sat there.

"That's a very pretty little treasure," he said to her.

Looking at it for just a few moments she smiled back at him. "Yes, it was given to me by a very dear person. It means everything to me."

Now her immediacy was affecting his judgment and he took her hand in his. "May I please?" he asked, looking at her delicately shaped hand resident now in his own palm, "Only for a moment Cassandra.....I just want to remember what it feels like..it's been such a long time."

Whatever response he had been expecting, he was not prepared for that which he received, as she leaned across and kissed him softly on the lips. It was not a long kiss but in the three or four seconds contact he was treated to a kaleidoscope of emotions. Shock, pleasure, embarrassment, disorientation and not the least – arousal!

Pulling back, but still holding the girl's hand, which for some reason was recalling impossible memories, he was momentarily lost for words.

"You....you shouldn't be doing that," he stuttered.

"Why not?" she said, looking as cute as a button, "I *wanted* to! Didn't you like it?" she teased, then looking serious for a moment. "You have been very kind to me...I just wanted you to know I really appreciate it.

As she was speaking, he found himself studying her closely once more. The little wisps of brown hair curling around her ear-lobes, the almost unkempt locks that fell across her forehead and which jiggled as she emphasised her point. Her pretty and expressive little face without a trace of make-up, not that any could possibly improve on what nature had already set in place. Despite her youth, something about her was bordering on the old-fashioned. Perhaps it was the dress. Although well fitting – *especially* so he noted, in areas he hardly dared contemplate – the hemline was longer than girls her age tended to wear and certainly was without any mainstream appeal so far as he could judge. On *her* though it looked perfect and he found himself wishing he could hold and caress something other than her hand.

A log suddenly crackled and the girl started in surprise. He took the opportunity to put his arm around her shoulders hoping against hope she would not react unfavorably. How he wished it was a young arm and not that of an old man that carried now the fully unrealistic hopes of its owner.

Far from rejecting the gesture though, Cassandra snuggled in to him.

"You make me feel safe and protected," she whispered, turning her head slightly. The movement caused her dress to gape slightly at the front and for a moment he saw the onset of the downward curve of her cleavage. She had fairly small breasts he had determined and again inexplicably, something of a hazy remembrance came to him. She was saying something to him. It surely *couldn't* be what his mind was hearing?

"Kiss me again Jim.....please,"

In that instant he fell apart emotionally. With what would appear to any onlooker to be the sad, if not pathetic spectacle of an old man trying to resurrect his forgotten romantic habits, he pulled her back until she lay in his arms and lowered his mouth to hers. Soft, gentle and confidently pliant lips met their coarse, trembling and long-since used partner's. As both the beauty and hideous reality of the interaction washed over him, he was unable to prevent the tears building up.

"I'm so sorry Cassandra," he cried...."I don't know what's come over me. I'm just a really lonely old man and.....and well, you're just so pretty...." He was wracked in an agony of despair.

She smiled at him.

"You're not an *old man* Jim....you never were.....Look, see!" So saying, she held his hands up before him.

Unable to accept what his eyes would have him believe, he stared at the strong and well-shaped hands. No hint of a wrinkle. Wide wrists heralded the onset of muscular arms that disappeared up beneath the sleeves of his old pyjamas. He had no need of a mirror, he knew his face was that of a young man. He could feel the weight of thick and luxuriant hair which even now curled almost to the nape of his neck.

He sought not to question this miracle, merely to address its purpose.

Carrying her to his bedroom later, where neither the crumpled bed linen, nor the faded and decrepit wallpaper held sway any longer, he laid Cassandra on the top sheet. Turning away from him she sat up and raised her arms. Gently he unzipped the dress and watched as she pulled it over her head. She wore nothing beneath.

Her needs mirrored his own and he found himself kneeling beside her on the bed, caressing her hair, her shoulders. She raised her arms above her head needing his full complicity in what ultimately was to follow.

He found disrobing in front of her, an act easily effected without the slightest inhibition. He remembered then, how it was something neither he nor Cathy had ever been comfortable with. He couldn't recall ever actually *seeing* her fully naked – nor having the desire to!

After their frenetic early needs subsided, Jim lay down behind her, pulled her close to him and tugged the bedclothes up over them. Cassandra with her back to him, pulled his arms tightly around her and lay still, listening to their respiratory rates even out. She didn't want to think about having to leave, or about what she knew had shortly to be.

All Jim was able to think about was by whatever miracle, an angel had been delivered to his door this night. He would worry about an explanation in the morning. God willing he should never lose her again, yet somewhere deep in the recesses of his mind he knew he had experienced these thoughts some time in the past.

An old man awoke Christmas morning. His cries of anguish at his loss would have melted the heart of the least compassionate of men.

"How could a dream be so real?" "How could any God be so cruel?" were just two of the questions he suspected he was never likely to be receiving an answer to. Determined however that nothing would ever undermine his love of the festive season, he decided he would first make himself a pot of tea and entering the tiny kitchen he had to grasp a hold of the door-frame to steady his nerves…if not his sanity. Sitting there on the bench was the tray, containing one dirty plate with traces still of bacon rind and a small yellowish stain.

Struggling to make sense of the non-sensical, the only rational explanation in his view was that whilst in a semi-delusional state, quite obviously brought on by the brandy, he had actually *cooked* that meal last night….and presumably eaten it. He made his pot of tea and whilst waiting for it to draw, went to the front door and opened it. Snow must have been falling all night. The front path, grass and flowerbeds were now but a uniform white blanket, the trees - icy sculptured sentinels. All around, picturesque serenity, a silent white matte-work.

Returning to the living room, he went across to the little tree – and stared! *Five* presents now sat in a cluster-pattern beneath those lower branches, one far smaller than the rest, slightly away to the right. The wrapping looked faded but again, somehow familiar. As he picked it up he felt a decided chill.

His hands trembled as the little heart-shaped box was exposed. It looked quite old. Removing the lid, he saw what was inside and his world spun away. With shaking fingers, he opened the tiny silver locket, then with tears of passion raking both cheeks, he read what he already knew was so minutely inscribed there.

"To Cassandra from your loving husband Jim. Christmas 1832"

Funk By Noel Bailey

An inevitable confrontation in the mind of the average cynic - a journalist down on his creativity and a well-stocked bar somewhere this side of desperation.

Personally I would have called it a slow-news week, but at the insistence of my editor, who running the numbers under psyche-evaluation mode, famously decreed that I could use a week off, had subsequently checked myself into a hotel, one of those atmospheric and gothic edifices fronting the main highway through Sydney's Blue Mountains. Peace and tranquility had been the order of the day. What I pulled down was nearer *The Twilight Zone* - a movie-length episode at that!

Just twelve hours earlier, I had been sitting alone in the corner of Kelly's Bar on Devlin Street, a quiet and little known area of Blackheath, an historical and somewhat picturesque little township, similar - rather in atmosphere than architecture - to it's counterpart in South East London and after which it was named in the 1800's. A haven for the seriously romantic, the dreamers, mid-life crisis sufferers and aspiring writers – all of which in retrospect, I laid claim to holding temporary membership. Some half a mile or so from my hotel, I probably would never have stumbled across it had it not been for my nose for a decent scotch - and *Kelly's* had plenty on tap.

Besides, the place suited me, hardly anyone except the locals knew it was there. Even Kelly himself would drift off into his own reverie between serving customers. The room, for there was only the one lounge, was quaint rather than spacious. An attempt most likely by the owner, to resurrect the image of a typically English pub here in the Colonials, one might say with but moderate success. At intervals, from the prolific cedarwood panelling, brass ornaments hung in appealing disorder. The chairs clustered into a flanking pattern around the occasional table, housed to a man, characters, each of which had experienced something more than that which comes from a lifetime's devotion solely to the nine-to-five grind.

I was romancing my third scotch - the tide was definitely receding, when the front door imploded, ushering in not only the dishevelled newcomer, but a blast of sub-arctic air and a few flakes of snow, the first of the season. The bringer of this instant confusion was a young woman somewhere in her late twenties. To describe her condition as hysterical would be kind though inaccurate, screaming as she was and pleading for help of some kind. Beyond this she was incoherent. Kelly, who it would appear had a way with women, seized the initiative and swiftly handled the somewhat delicate situation by seizing the girl by the shoulders and delivering a well-directed slap across her right cheek. A fierce intake of breath could be heard around the bar, but to be sure, the screaming stopped.

"Here Miss, have a sip of brandy," said Kelly, handing her a small glass of the calming liquor. The girl took it with shaking hands, downed a mouthful before spluttering uncontrollably as the spirit temporarily took her breath away. "Now then, what *is* it girl?...what's happened?" he asked. Reduced now to intermittent sobs and violent fits of trembling, the young woman was able to tell how her young son aged eight had not returned from the corner store some three hours earlier. Further questioning revealed that she had spent the intervening time roaming the "Heath," looking for the lad. It should be made clear to the reader that the township does not have there a permanent Police presence. Crime rates lower than stale bread in these mountain outposts and the constabulary are better served in larger populated areas at lower altitudes of the Blue Mountains.

Thus it was decided then and there that the entire patronage of Kelly's Bar, a force of nine (including Kelly), would immediately instigate a search of the area. Kelly first escorted the young lady home, little more than a street away, promising that the young lad would be found and returned, or his name wasn't Kelly! Between us of course, we gave ourselves a couple of hours which if still unsuccessful would mean calling in the appropriate authorities. With that, we set off with high expectations of finding the lad.

The locals, having an unsurpassed knowledge of the area, split the densely wooded sections to the immediate west of the corner-shop between us. The boy it seemed had made it that far, and according to the proprietor, had left for home well over two and a half hours earlier. Myself and two others were accorded the south-western perimeters which bordered upon the sheer cliff faces of Govett's Leap - a near three- hundred metre, ninety degree descent to the valley floor. By day a touristy venue for the amateur photographer - by night, best avoided unless an experienced hang-glider. It was considered highly unlikely that Mike, for such was the lad's name, could have strayed that far, but a search is a search, and must be treated accordingly.

Of concern, the weather was closing in, the snow intensifying and visibility down to yards now given the pockets of thick mist drifting across from the higher reaches of Mount Victoria. With barely an hour before dusk additionally, the element of time was coming prominently into play.

Firstly checking with a few local residents, none had seen the boy although one elderly lady thought she might have seen a youngster resembling his description, crossing the road further up towards "The Castle," a fancifully named rock formation standing silently if not introspectively, beside the eastbound track to Govett's Leap.

Leaving the others to patrol the wooded region to the north of the track, I took to the southside where the trees were few and far between, the buildings mere isolated cabins and the general outlook - bleak, in a word. Calling out intermittently, "Mike ......can you hear me?" and similar equally useless phrases that spring to mind when one instinctively realises the inadequacy of the situation. I knew he was not around here and yet, I was impelled to keep going. Perhaps it was fuelled by the image of his distraught mother, maybe I had to placate my own sense of self-importance but as darkness finally descended, my ears were strained for some response......anything!

At length the trees gave way to bushes and the road was left way behind. Ahead I could make out a low fence through the heavy mist. With little or no light to guide me, the moon having but the occasional victory in its quest to penetrate the thick cloud-cover, I stepped over the fence and crunched on to light gravel, the noise quite incongruous in the enveloping silence. Directly ahead, the mist and blackness combined to present anything but a welcoming presence. Suddenly stubbing my toe on an outsize rock, seemingly placed there for that very purpose, I tripped and fell forwards. Lying there momentarily, I realised that my head appeared to be without support. Normally I reasoned, when one falls, the head is either cushioned, bruised or otherwise ill-treated by the ground itself. This not being the case tonight was a definite worry! No support meant no ground, which threw up but one inevitability .....I was right on the cliff edge! This was indeed the case, and it took every ounce of courage I didn't have, to get to my feet.

Shaking worse than a first time lottery-winner, my eyes gradually accustomed to the gloom and I could see just how close to death I had come. The reality brought on shock and I wept there, crouched on my knees, vulnerable and emotionally violated.

My self-pity was interrupted by a sound - faint, but clearly audible. I stood up, listening intently....it came again, far to my left. Surely a cry for help? Following the low fence, barely three metres from the cliff face, I called out desperately,

" I hear you, can you hear me?"

Within seconds the call came again...clearer this time.

"Help me please - I'm down here." Undoubtedly the voice of a young boy.

The ground began to slope upwards and the fence came to an abrupt end causing me further insecurity. Making progress somewhat gingerly now, and ever aware of the imminent presence of that drop-zone, there came another plea,

"*Here*, I'm right here!"

The words were almost directly beneath me, and lying full length, I could now make out the edge. Staring down into the darkness, I called out,

"Mike, is that you?"

"Yes," came the reply. "Please get me up, I want to go home."

I could hear sobbing and forgetting my own immediate danger, I craned my head downwards and called to the lad.

"How far down are you Mike?...are you hurt?"

The lad was able to describe how he had slipped on the edge trying to peer over and had fallen, perhaps three metres, on to a small rock-ledge below. I was just able to make-out his situation beneath me as he spoke. He didn't appear to have suffered any serious injury, but was obviously now freezing cold and with no way up was understandably close to hysteria. How he had survived these past few hours without 'losing it' was remarkable.

Obviously too far down to reach, I pulled off my belt and leaning downwards, hung the belt as far as I was able. Even standing on tip-toe, the boy was barely able to reach it, let alone grab hold of it. I judged the distance to be a fraction more than three metres. His only chance was obviously with me down there to help him up the rock face. No chance to leave him there and go for help - the boy was exhausted and terrified. Thus, using the belt as a guide, and with Mike's help, I was able to pinpoint near enough, the centre of the ledge. This done, I lowered myself, facing the cliff-wall, until I was hanging precariously from the safety of the overhead ledge. Mike was barely able to reach my knee. Something less than a man in the peak of fitness and with less experience of rock-climbing than most ten-year olds, I was not overly confident of my ability to drop cleanly, so to avoid any further negative deliberation on the matter - I let go!

It wasn't pretty! Lying there crumpled up and temporarily unable to move by virtue of muscular paralysis, my heart was thudding unmercifully and a full-on coronary surely but seconds away! Mike took my hand...the poor kid was freezing. Overcoming my physical adversities, I managed to get to my knees as the lad clung to me - for warmth as much as security I imagine. Discarding my outer coat, I pulled off my thick woollen cardigan and zipped it back up around his shivering little body. Perhaps a no-go in the fashion stakes, but in the thermal-preservation department, an instant winner! The coat, I replaced around my own shoulders.

The boy's teeth were still chattering and he kept muttering, "I want my mum, I want my mum!". I wanted her *myself* at that moment!

I calmed him down as best I could and explained that he was going to have to stand on my shoulders and haul himself up from there. It seemed good in theory, there being no other immediate solution evident. Before hoisting him up, I thought it prudent to determine the exact size of the ledge on which we stood. I could pretty much see it in the gloom, but knowledge is preferable to guesswork any day! Thus crawling very tentatively on hands and knees I took stock of our rocky life-support. Probably less than three metres in width and half that in depth, it didn't leave much room for line-dancing. Beneath it was an unknown quantity, the blackness, for the moment at least, blotting out our dire predicament. Fighting back tears, Mike climbed on to my shoulders as I crouched down. I told him to keep in contact with the cliff-face at all times and he was dutifully heeding my instructions as I began to stand up. With absolutely no warning, the ledge beneath us cracked and split-across just left of centre, the right-hand section giving way as I instantly changed footing to the residual left fragment. The rock slithered and crashed out of view, slamming into the cliff face with a monstrous reverberation during its epic fall to the valley-floor. The shifting of my own centre of gravity dislodged the boy from my shoulders. As he flew past me, primal screams tearing at the night air, I grasped at his flailing limbs. Somehow I caught his left arm in passing and throwing myself backwards, was able to arrest his fall. I heard simultaneously, the impact of the fractured ledge as it struck bottom. My grip on the boy was loosening, the strain telling on my shoulder-joints, as he slid now up to the wrist, hanging clear in mid-air with only death beneath him. I called down to him to reach up for my other arm, there being no way I could support him for many more seconds like this. Somehow, amidst his desperation, the human spirit which so covets life at its most crtitical hour, took over, and swinging in an arc he grabbed my right hand. In an instant he lay beside me, a spent force, just whimpering quietly.

We remained there unmoving for maybe two or three minutes. Time wasn't of real importance given the prevailing circumstances you will understand. Gradually I pulled him to me and sought to comfort him in some small way. Was there *ever*, I wondered, a more defining example of the blind leading the blind? Realising that I had to get the boy to safety now, I moved to stand. The remaining half-ledge shifted, creaking as it tilted downwards at an angle of some fifteen degrees. Obviously critically weakened by the events of the last few minutes, the slab was threatening to precipitate us now on a one-way descent to oblivion.

"Hell, and no-one will ever know," I thought to myself ruefully.

With obviously nothing but danger inherent in any upright movement, I pulled Mike close-up to me mid-slab, right alongside the cliff-face, so as to limit the downward pressure of our combined weights. Whilst a definite shifting was still detectable in the ledge itself, the tilting was partially rectified. For an hour or so, I called out, not with any realistic expectation of being heard, but rather to give the boy some hope in what was, to surely the most optimistic person, a near hopeless situation. No-one at Kelly's Bar knew me intimately and would have presumed I had simply gone home....wherever *that* may have been!

Hunched up there, hour after hour, additionally with the onset of hypothermia, knowing that at any second whatever was still supporting the slab may well tire of the effort, plunging us to our deaths, was no cause for real positive thinking and by the time the first rays of light appeared, the true aspect of our situation became apparent.

A cursory examination of our immediate environment was negative in all aspects. The cliff top appeared now higher than had seemed its reality during the night. This however was the least of our worries. The cliffs themselves were absolutely sheer, no other rocky outcrops to speak of and the view in all directions, one of sublimal terror. For souls such as I, afflicted with vertigo at the top of a step-ladder, this was really bad news!

Of prime concern, the slab we were hunched-up on was, by the light of day, so small, it defied logic how we had not slipped off it already. Barely a metre and a half square, it was so tiny the only thing more fearful was wondering what exactly was holding *it* up? I told Mike that whatever he did, not to look down.....advice I should most certainly have followed myself.

Salvation now could only come through our being heard by someone hopefully out for their early morning constitutional, well off the beaten track! Conserving myenergy and voice-box, I began calling out at six-thirty am. Limiting my message to "Help" or "Anyone there?" I continued unabated for almost an hour. Except for one terrifying jolt, when I tried standing at one stage, our situation remained unchanged. By seven-forty-five I had grown inwardly despondent. The boy was suffering from exposure and no evidence had been seen or heard that any local authorities were searching for us, not that they had any reason to be scouring the lookout and its immediate area. Still I called aloud! Just before eight thirty came an unexpected answer,

"You there...where are you?"

Immediately, I knew how the lifeboat occupants must have felt when the *Carpathia* steamed into view!

Without thinking, I leapt up calling out, "*Here,* down here!"

Too late I remembered our insecure platform. To my horror the rock tilted further - no stopping it this time. As if in slow-motion, I saw the view beneath us expanding as our tenuous support lessened. Clutching Mike's hand, I saw his eyes widen in terror. The tilt increased and I prayed that we would be dead before impact. Something struck the rock-face behind me It was a rope-ladder. Holding Mike by his right hand, I grasped the life-giving rungs, swinging the boy up to my waist, where he took desperate hold.

"For God's sake, don't look back," I cried, as the entire slab broke loose and fell into the yawning abyss...just as we were drawn up to safety. I had erred in my logic. The search squad *had* realised my disappearance and had called in Police Rescue at first light. They had been searching for almost two hours.

Mike was reunited with his mother and *I* with a glass or three of Kelly's very best scotch. It was on the house!

Funny thing, anyone mentions Govett's Leap these days and I leave the room, even now, a quarter of a century later!

A WOLF BY THE EARS
A One Act Play)
By Mattie Lennon.

Characters;

SERGEANT MARTY McAteer; A man in his late thirties.

When the play opens McAteer looks slightly dishevelled with shirt open and tie loosened. He seems confident when talking to his friend on the phone but for the reminder of the time he appears to be unsure of himself.

GARDA BILL KILGANNON; A man in his mid forties.

He looks clumsy, moves slowly and has an "agricultural" appearance about him. He wears the heavy Garda overcoat and cap at all times and mostly keeps his hands in his pockets. He tends to lean against something whenever possible.

GARDA PADDY BLACK; A man in his late thirties.

He is dressed fairly tidy and is wearing well-worn shoes and a very old watch. He shows signs of parsimony when parting with coins and on more than one occasion he rummages in his pockets, finds a very short cigarette butt, which he lights from the fire with a paper spill.

GARDA LIAM SMITH: A man in his early thirties.

He is impeccably turned out; his uniform trousers pressed like razor blades and his shoes shining. He wears a signet ring, tie-pin, cuff-links and a fashionable watch.

He has a habit of filing his nails, replacing the nail file in his tunic pocket only to retrieve it a few seconds later. At every opportunity he looks in the mirror, combs his hair or straightens his tie. He also admires his reflection in the window.

HUGHIE DOHERTY; A man in his mid twenties.

He is dressed in farmers working clothes with turned down Wellingtons. His boots, trousers and jacket show traces of "bovine excrement" and judging by the expressions on the faces of the Gardai his clothes are offensive to the olfactory sense. He is unshaven.

MAIREAD FRIEL; A scantily-clad, well-spoken, voluptuous blonde in her mid to late twenties.

****

SCENE;

(ALL DIRECTIONS ARE GIVEN FROM THE AUDIENCES VIEWPOINT)

The action takes place in the dayroom of a small Garda Station in a village in south Donegal. The time is the late sixties.

There is a fireplace in the back wall, left of centre. To the right of centre is a door leading to the living quarters. On this door is a badly handwritten notice, "PRIVATE".

In the right hand wall there is a window and a door leading to the street.

Near the front in the L/H wall is a door leading to a cell.

A baton and Garda raincoat hang on a Peg-board on the L/H wall and beside it an old advertising mirror.

Notices on the wall include an advertisement for a Garda Benefit Concert, a sign about the licensing of firearms and another giving a list of penalties under the Noxious Weeds Act 1910.

There is a desk in front of the fire and a metal filing cabinet stands in the back R/H corner. There's a Garda cap on top of the filing cabinet.

When the play opens a clock on the mantelpiece is showing five minutes to five and a desk calendar proclaims it to be Friday, November 07th.

(*Sergeant is sitting at desk*)

SERGEANT; (*Leaving down Sporting Press and making phone call*) Hoya Mick.....Marty here.....I see you have Scotstown Squire running in the fourth race at Lifford tonight.......is he in with a chance or is he........?

No. I'm on my own here.......right so......Smith, The Male Mannequin from Cavan, is due in any minute.....of course all he wants is the station to himself so that he can ring the quare one in France. What?......Oh I think he wields his baton a bit nearer home as well.

I sent the other two gobshites out to bring in the Poet Doherty........Oh he done nothing.....He was in the wrong place at the wrong time....or the right place at the right time for us. Remember when Dinny Gallagher's rick o' hay was burned six weeks ago?......Oh it was an accident; John Bryan was in it with the Cassidy one and one of them dropped a cigarette butt.....it wasn't all they dropped says you..... But I can't let that out. The Bryans look after me....Oh I might be from the stony grey hills of Monaghan but I know which side it's buttered on alright.

An' you know what Dinny Gallagher is like ....but he's "good to us", so I have to do something... I can't be seen to ignore the destruction of two hundred pounds worth of hay...Oh he is..Oh Dinny has the connections all right...through his missus.... Oh it's better to have him on your side sure enough.

Anyhow I discovered that the Poet was out the night it was burned... Oh I didn't make the boys any the wiser....I told them he done it...

Oh, we'll get something out of him anyway.....that's right...it'll give him something to write about......it's about time someone took that lad down a peg, him an' his songwriting an' his rhyming...... Right, I'll see you in Lifford tonight....the dog is......

Enter Garda Liam Smith

SMITH: ' evening Skipp..er.. Sergeant.

SERGEANT; (*looking at the clock*) Hello Liam. Anything new?

SMITH; No. The Nailer Dunne was telling me that our friend "The Boxer" is driving around without any insurance. We'll keep an eye on him. Where's everybody?

SERGEANT: I sent them out to get Hughie Doherty. you know the poet fella... he burned Dinny Gallagher's rick.

SMITH: Dinny Gallagher's rick?. That's an unusual pastime for a literary person. Eliot wrote of the "burnt out ends of smokey days" but he didn't say anything about setting fire to hay. And Dinny Gallagher of all people.

SERGEANT: Aye, well you know what to do when he comes in.

SMITH: Yes Sergeant, but that Hughie Doherty is a dangerous bastard. He's a bit too handy with the pen for my liking. He'd write to the papers or report us to the Minister or anything.

SERGEANT: If he hasn't an alibi for the night of Saturday 27th September he can write to who he likes.

SMITH: OK, when he comes in we'll use the usual tricks...

(*Enter Gardai Bill Kilgannon and Paddy Black pushing Hughie Doherty a man in his mid twenties ahead of them*)

SMITH; Well?

BlACK;(*Hanging his cap on a nail, in R/H wall, between the window and door*) He didn't tell us anything yet.

SMITH: He will (*to Doherty*) Well, Hughie, what have you to say for yourself?

DOHERTY: I believe I'm supposed to have burned a rick of hay.

SMITH: There's no supposing about it, we know you were out that night.

DOHERTY: I was out. I got a lift home with the Doctor McHugh. Another man and myself.

KILGANNON: We know to the differ.

SMITH: Who was the other man that was...

SERGEANT: It doesn't matter who he was.. We know this lad burned the hay.

SMITH; Would it surprise you if I told you that you were seen lighting it?

DOHERTY; nothing you tell me would surprise me. I know your pedigree and if you were a greyhound pup I wouldn't buy you. A man can't be seen where he's not. I didn't burn any hay.

KILGANNON; We know to the differ.

DOHERTY; *(RAISING HIS VOICE)* I didn't commit any crime and you know it.

SERGEANT; Keep your voice down. I have enough evidence here to charge you.

SMITH: Will I put this man in the cell, Sergeant?

BLACK; You'll get out when you decide to tell the truth.

(The Sergeant nods his head and Smith-careful not to soil his uniform with "farm waste"- ushers Doherty into the cell, As Doherty is being pushed into the cell he sings (to the air of The "Ould alarm Clock";)

"It happened up in Largabeg,

In November sixty nine,

I was makin' rhymes an' feeding pigs,

The day was far from fine.

The Gardai got contrary

And they..... "

Doherty's voice fades off as Smith bolts the cell door with a flourish.

SERGEANT; Right lads, you know the drill. I have to collate the census returns from Barnafadda. I'll do it in the kitchen an' have a cup of tea. (*He takes folder from filing cabinet and exits rear*).

SMITH: (*To Kilgannon, grinning and nudging Black*) Will you see what you can get out of the Poet, Bill? (*Kilgannon exits left into cell*).

SMITH: If the Poet starts about John Keates to Bill Kilgannon he'll think he's talking about a cattle-jobber from Ballymote.

BLACK: He mightn't be a match for the Poet sure enough.

SMITH; He wouldn't be a match for anything. It's a struggle for him to read the Sligo Champion. But he's been out to get the Poet for quite a while. He said that the Poet was lazy, in the wrong company, and Doherty heard it back and had something to say about it. Yeats described Irish Landlords as being: " lazy, trifling, inattentive, negligent, slobbering and profligate". I suppose Kilgannon would have attributed these qualities to Doherty if he could get his tongue around them. To hear an "alternatively motivated" individual like Bill calling anybody lazy is a joke.

BLACK: I know. I was in the squad-car with him one night, months ago, and we met the Poet behind at Rory's Brook, and him walking home.
Bill stopped and accused him of making faces at us and anything else he could think of. He tried every trick he knew to provoke the Poet into saying or doing something that would land him in trouble.

SMITH: Seemingly the townland that Kilgannon comes from has nothing to recommend it only a legend about a graveyard that's supposed to have re-located itself one night. It's a sort of a hamlet where everybody is related if you understand what I mean. It's a, "if she's not good enough for her brothers she's not good enough for me", sort of country. It just shows you the sort of place it is when even the dead don't want to stay in it. But I suppose anywhere that would produce the likes of Bill....Anyway, the Poet juxtaposed those two pieces of information into some sort of doggerel or a ditty and our colleague was less than enamoured of it. So he'll do his best to pin him now. You could say it was Doherty's own fault: Patrick Kavanagh, your fellow county-man, said:" anybody who writes poetry that a policeman can understand deserves anything they get".

BLACK: Bill must have understood whatever he wrote anyway.

SMITH; *(fake innocent as he notices a speck on his uniform and reaches for a clothes-brush)* Do you think he did it?

BLACK: I don't know. He's a know-all and could do with a bit of a come-uppance but I'm here since 1955 and the Poet hasn't done anything like this before.

SMITH: There's always a first time and according to the Skipper this is it for Hughie Doherty.

BLACK: Maybe he didn't do it.

SMITH: *(Thoughtfully)* Maybe not, but in the words of one of our most famous playwrights: "Some men were born to take raps or to be made into scapegoats."

BLACK: Who said that?

SMITH: It was John B. Keane but a more appropriate quote of his comes to mind right now. In "The Farmer's Boy" he said;" There are instances when your farmer's boy was not above setting fire to a haystack rather than take his grievances into court".

BLACK: We don't know of any grievances that the Poet has against Dinny Gallagher.

SMITH: No, but he would look on Dinny as being as thick as bottled pig-shite and as John Lydgate said;" Comparisons do oft get grievance".

BLACK: Talking about farmer's boys, what keeps Hughie Doherty there on a few acres of bad mountainy land? Old Master McCauley in Largabeg school told me that Doherty was one of the brightest lads he ever taught. He didn't do much with it.

SMITH: Ah, he's an only child. His father is old and his mother is an invalid and I suppose he doesn't like to leave them.

BLACK; Having him hauled in here won't do his poor old mother much good.

SMITH: It certainly won't but your fellow Monaghan-man didn't think that when he sent you and "Constable Addledepete" out to lift him.

BLACK; Marty Mcateer is only here twelve months. He has built up his own little network of snitches all right but he still doesn't know the score.

SMITH: He might know it by the time he's finished with the Poet. Doherty knows people and he's very pally with O'Donnell the Labour Councillor.

BLACK; I know. Did you see the write-up about him on last week's Donegal Democrat?

SMITH: No. The only things I read in local papers are the GAA results. And, lately, you don't have many exhilarating ones in the Donegal Democrat. What did they say about Doherty?,

BLACK:I left it in the squad car. (*exits, stage right*)

(*Smith rushes to phone and starts to dial but drops the phone when Kilgannon enters, stage left, out of cell*)

SMITH; Well? Was he on about Robbie Burns?

KILGANNON: No. He didn't say anything about Bobby Byrne, he said him and Liam O 'Shea got a lift home with Doctor McHugh the night the hay was burned. Maybe Black'd get something out of him.

SMITH: He might. Black is not too fond of the Poet.

KILGANNON: No. The poet made a bit of a song about him one time. Remember when Paddy had the house rented off Dick Egan. A dacent man Dick. A Protestant but a dacent man. When Black was leaving the house, after he'd built his own house, it was wrecked. The childer had it wrecked. So he went in to give back the key to Dick at twelve O'Clock at night. But Dick was cute enough; he wouldn't take the key until he examined the house in the daylight. He was after getting legal advice don't you know.

SMITH: Yes, and then Paddy wanted us to do Dick's son for everything from an uncut ragworth to an unlicensed dog.

KILGANNON: It's true for you.

SMITH: And then the morning the Post Office here was robbed and Black got a blow of an iron bar on the head the Poet recorded it for posterity. (*sings*)

Oh Garda Black

He got a smack,

At twenty past eleven.

It missed his eye

By half an inch

And his brain by two-foot seven.

KILGANNON: Where is Black?

SMITH: He's gone to get an article about Doherty that was in the paper.

KILGANNON: Oh Paddy'll have plenty of information as long as it doesn't cost him nothing.

SMITH: He treats us very much on a need to know basis. He only tells us what suits him. He grew up only five miles from the Skipper. They're the same age so he couldn't be in the dark about him. Did you know Marty was a mental nurse before he joined the Guards? Paddy didn't tell us that.

KILGANNON: A "keeper" like?

SMITH: Yes. He worked for four years in the Mental Hospital in Monaghan Town.

KILGANNON: They say some of them keeper lads does be as bad as what they do be minding.

SMITH: If you lie down with the dogs you'll get up with the fleas. It's not a great grounding for a career in the police sure enough. For, as John Clare said"...in a madhouse there exists no law".(*mischievously*) Wouldn't the Poet have a field-day with that information?

KILGANNON; Oh them Monaghan boys won't tell you nothin' unless it suits them.

SMITH; Did you know that Paddy claims to be a descendent of the Earls of Belmore?

KILGANNON: There was a Jimmy Earls lived in Dun.........I think he was a Monaghan man.....

BLACK: (Entering opening the Donegal Democrat and reading)

" When Hughie Doherty is not working on his small farm he puts the stories of contemporary "doin's an' sayin's" to verse in the time-honoured manner of the Bards of old.

In ancient times the Bard was respected and feared in the community;

but with the passing of the old, Gaelic way of life the status diminished

and in the nineteenth century the term was just used colloquially to denote any local character who put the happenings of the locality to verse.

Many such local troubadours were people of genuine ability who could catch the mood of the community ethos, which they mirrored in their 'versifications.'

I would place Hughie Doherty in that category and I feel he would rightfully

be awarded the title of 'Bard' in his local community had he lived in earlier times.

His works range from the whimsical to the sombre and from the irreverent

to the sublime. However, life, in the Ireland of yesteryear mirrored all of those aspects and what Hughie does is in direct

line of descent from the wordsmiths of yore."

KILGANNON: Did ye ever hear such a load of rubbish about a fellow that....

(*Sergeant appears in rear door, excited*).

SERGEANT: A guard shot dead in Falcarragh......one o'clock today...Jim Mahony..I served with him in Letterkenny...A Bank Raid ......five armed men..Jim was always a plucky lad..it said on the news headlines that it's thought they're the same gang that robbed the Raphoe bank on the eight of October.

BLACK: That was a tidy one. They walked in dressed as FCA men, robbed the place and were gone in a few minutes.

SERGEANT: According to the wireless they escaped today, with two thousand pounds, in a red Zepher.

BLACK; Two thousand pounds?

KILANNON: Will we set up a checkpoint?

SERGEANT;(Impatiently) They'd be in Dublin by now. Unless they're walking... Poor Jim Mahony God rest him. (*exits rear*)

KILGANNON: Nothing ever happens here.(*under his breath*) Thanks be to God)

(Sound of heavy vehicle stopping briefly and taking off again)

SMITH: There's the Dublin bus . He'll have the Provincial papers (*walking towards door*) I'll go in next door and get The Celt.

BLACK: Get me twenty Sweet Aftons (*gives him coins*)

SMITH: (counting money) Twenty cigarettes are one and tenpence. You're fourpence short.

BLACK: Amby always gives me a cut. Tell him they're for me.

(*Phone rings. Kilgannon answers it*)

KILGANNON: It's for you Liam.

SMITH: Hello...ah Tom..No, you didn't flummox me. I'd know a Glangevlin accent anywhere. No I didn't.....I had " a bit of business" to attend to in Bundoran ...I would have put a few bob on Knockroe Hero if I was there...no I suppose there isn't...and there's not many heroes in Glangevlin either. .yeah...Why am I not surprised?...I'm not surprised at that either...Well, if he knows there's no point in telling him. As Willliam Blackstone said "It is better that ten guilty persons escape than one innocent suffer" . But of course Blackstone didn't spend four years working in an asylum. You may be sure of it....thanks Tom..I'll see you. (*hangs up*) That was Tom O'Reilly. He was stationed with me in Manorcunningham. He was talking to John Mc Bride at the races on Saturday. And guess what John told him? That he burned Dinny Gallagher's hay accidentally, he was in it with Julia Cassidy, and that the Skipper knows all about it.

BLACK and KILGANNON: What'll we do with the Poet?

SMITH: The words of Thomas Jefferson were hardly ever more apt: " We have the wolf by the ears and we can neither hold him, nor safely let him go. Justice is in one scale, and self-preservation in the other". (*exits, stage right.*)

KILGANNON: That fellow is as bad as Doherty, with his spakes. He hardly got that class of learnin' at Gurtnacloca National School.

BLACK: Ah, he's getting a bit of "private tuition", I think. There's a certain schoolmistress above at Barnesmore Gap and he puts the cuffs on her now and again.

KILGANNON: Do you notice how Smith seems to be more or less on the Poets side?

BLACK; Poetic courtesy?

KILGANNON; No.I think Doherty knows something about Liam. Remember he said something about pedigree to him when he came in.

BLACK: The Dohertys are great men for "the Pedigree." Hughie's father always says," Ye should always look at the Stud-book."

KILGANNON: An'do you remember the night young O'Donnell was knocked out here on the street with the belt of a baton? Well the Poet seen it..he knows that it was Smith's pal McMahon, that was transferred to Tubbercurry that done it.

(*Smith enters*)
SMITH: There seems to be something going on I see..................

BLACK; Where's me fags?

SMITH (*Ignoring the question*) There's something going on. They were talking in the shop about something that happened this morning. The Special Branch was mentioned but they all clammed up the minute I went in.

KILGANNON: (*looking out through window*) There's that Friel one heading this way and she looks to be in a class of a hurry.

BLACK; (*looking out*) She's not dressed for the Donegal winter anyway.

SMITH; (*Pushing them out of the way to get to the window*) She's a good journalist, Maraid, and a fine looking bird too.

KILGANNON; (*to Black*) Liam's mind is dropping below his belt again.

SMITH; (*laughing*) Maybe she wants to do a special on Doherty in custody.

(*Mairead Friel enters from stage right. She makes straight for smith and flirts with him*)

MAIREAD: Liam, I'm after getting a scoop in Corock. Would you ever be a darling and let me phone in my copy to the Independent?

SMITH; Sure. Go ahead.

(*Mairead sits up on desk, exposing a lot of limb and dials a number*)

MAiRAID: Hello. Irish Independent? This is Mairead Friel, South Donegal correspondent, could you put me through to the news desk please?....Hello...Mairead here....I have a story....Ready? (*Reading from an A4 typed sheet*) "...Chief superintendent Seamus Fennell, this morning, led a mixed force of heavily armed Special Branch Detectives to a galvanised-roofed two roomed cottage at Corock in a remote area of South-Donegal, used from time to time as a hide-out by five wanted men."..

SMITH; That's just across the field from the Poet's house...

MAIREAD: (*Reading on*) "The men, who rented the cottage from Joseph Browne, are all wanted for questioning about the robbery of the Raphoe Bank on Wednesday 08th October. It was suspected at the time that the raiders were holed up in the mountains of South Donegal and the local Gardai carried out house-to-house enquiries.."

SMITH;...I like that..we didn't do any house to house enquiries anyway..

MAIREAD;(*Reading*) "The raiding party was wryly amused by what they found lying on the floor..................Some of the residents had been studying detective methods. Their reading matter included at least one copy of the American magazine 'The Detective'. Also found in the cottage were items of clothing and other things indicating that it possibly had been used as a cache by an illegal organisation. The clothing found included five FCA uniforms ....got that?...great. (*She hangs up the phone jumps off the table, without taking the typed sheet, bumps into Smith, says a hurried "Thank you" and runs out the door*)

(*Black and Kilgannon stand open-mouthed*)

SMITH: I must say it's going to look great. Two Banks robbed, a Guard dead and the perpetrators living on our doorstep. And here are we looking after the important business of the day; interrogating a peasant/poet about a heap of dog-rushes that was burned accidentally; and all to appease a half arsed farmer-cum-huckster, like Dinny Gallagher, who might tip us off occasionally about some young lad riding around on an untaxed Honda Fifty.

BLACK: What's going to happen now?

SMITH: What's going to happen? What do you think is going to happen? Every last man of us will be transferred. (*Lightning up*) Ah, well. It'll be nice to get out of this kip. They'll probably send you back to Howth, where you started. (*recites*);

The boy stood on the burning deck

With arse against the mast,

And faced the opposition

'Til the hill-o'- Howth was passed.

And when the hill O'_Howth was passed

They threw.......

BLACK: It's all right for you to titter an' grin. You have nothing only a pair of football boots and what you have in your trousers. I have a family and I'm after building a house.

SMITH: Ah; yes, but the house owns you. You see I listened to John Donne.

KILGANNON: John Dunne? Would he be one of the Dunnes abroad in Clougher........

SMITH: (*reciting dramatically*)

And seeing the snail, which everywhere doth roam

Carrying his own house still, still is at home.

Follow (for he is easy paced) this snail

Be thine own palace, or the world's thy jail.

BLACK; That's all very well but..but...

SMITH: I suppose I'd better bring the "Psychiatric Nurse" up to date on happening in Corock (*He partly opens rear door and shouts "Sergeant have a look at this"*)

(*The Sergeant enters*).

SMITH: Mairead Friel is after phoning this in to the Irish Independent. (*Sergeant takes papers and becomes increasingly agitated as he reads*)

SMITH: (*Taking obvious pleasure from the Sergeants discomfort*) What do you think of the reference to us "making house to house enquiries"?

SERGEANT: (*Annoyed*) I don't have the manpower for house to house. I'm asking for months for extra men to police this place properly.

BLACK: We'd want to be able to show that we put some effort into looking for the Bank Robbers.

SERGEANT; I'll...I'll ... Shiela Mc Gonigle in Largabeg Post Office is one of our's. I'll get Mary, the wife, to type a letter, marked "confidential" like, asking for information. We'll back-date it and address it to Largabeg Post Office) They don't postmark anything with the harp on it).Shiela won't let us down. But Mary is with her sister in Pettigo and won't be back 'til Friday. I suppose I'll have to try and type it myself. You couldn't trust anyone else with a job like that.

You get out there to Corock and put up some kind of a show. The place is going to be crawling with Branch men. But what can we do. They're laughing at us anyway.

(*Black and Kilgannon exit*)

SERGEANT; Let that lad out before you go.

SMITH; (*Opening cell door*) Come on. Get out. We're letting you go for now but we'll be taking you in again. (*Smith exits*).

DOHERTY; Sergeant, thank you very much for using your discretion and exercising your prerogative in issuing the instruction to have me released from custody.

SERGEANT; If you don't shut up you'll be back in that cell.

DOHERTY; And a very interesting cell it is too. Though it's a pity that the Office Of Public Works, or it's imperial predecessor didn't invest more thought in the soundproofing of the aforementioned place of incarceration. A person of my acute auricular perception could, AND DID, pick up some very interesting information through that door.

SERGEANT; (*Moving forward to put Doherty back in the cell*) I'm not going to listen.....

DOHERTY; Ah, hold on now Sergeant. I have just one further, small, observation to make about the design and construction of your detention quarters. It lacks toilet facilities and it has been said that "improvisation is too good to leave to chance". Your next prisoner may very well lodge a formal complaint about a slightly damp mattress....

SERGEANT: (*Rushing into cell*) You didn't........

DOHERTY; (*Bolting cell door*)

With apologies to the late Oscar;

I know not whether laws be right

Or whether laws be wrong.

But if the mattress isn't changed tonight

There'll be a right ould pong.

SERGEANT; (*Banging on door*) You won't get away with this...I'll .I'll...you'll be locked up.

DOHERTY: Relax Sergeant, Relax. You are the one that's locked up. You'll have a nice long rest. You said your wife is not back until Friday? And the boys won't be in any hurry back from Corock. Didn't you tell them to put up a good show. But you have nothing to worry about. I'll lock the outside door when I'm going.

(*Phone rings, Doherty answers it*)

DOHERTY (Mimicking the Sergeant) Hello. Carrigbeg Gardai....Sergeant Marty MacAteer speaking.... Who's this?....Telefis Eireann is it?....Yes there was a bit of action out in Corock this morning....No...I can't do a live phone interview, during the next news bulletin because I'm walking out the door this very minute.. I'd be gone only you rang...I have a dog running in Lifford...Oh I can...I can no bother. I'll give you the whole lowdown on the situation now. (*Banging on cell door and shouts of "Let me out"*) Sorry about that. We have a prisoner here and he thinks he should get out. He's a local farmer who claimed his rick of hay was burned maliciously but we know that there was an insurance connection. He hasn't admitted it yet. But he will. I have that lad's measure. You see..and you can broadcast this.. I worked in the Mental Health Service before I joined the Guards. Anyway, about the job above in Corock this morning. Oh we knew the boys were there all right. Right from the time they robbed the Raphoe Bank. We had them under cover you see. We knew they'd strike again, But we didn't think it would be so quick. We were up to our eyes here anyway. Crime here has gone out of all proportion. Just to give you an instance. Last Friday night week Mickey Browne the grocer in Bunmore, in the course of his deliveries, left a bag of messages at Johnny Maguire's gate. When ohnnie went out to bring in his groceries wasn't there a half pound of cooked ham missing. We interrogated the usual suspects but none of them would squeal. Oh we aven't closed the file on it yet. What....oh the lads in Corock..oh we'll apprehend hem boyos yet, don't you worry. I can tell you as an experienced and accomplished fficer (I'd go so far as to say that I'm genetically disposed to law enforcement; wasn't ny father a member of an auxiliary police force below in Monaghan in 1920). We'll et them yet.   But as I was saying to you, crime here is gone mad. The place is urning into another Derry. Only last Monday morning, first thing, Ted Crampsey eft his bike at Morris McLoughlin's Corner, across from the Barrack here, while he vas going into Millar's for a bale of binding twine. When he came out ten minutes ater his pump was stolen. Of course nobody saw anything.

(Banging at cell door and shouting)

I'm sorry I'll have to sign off. Our prisoner is getting a bit obstreperous.

(He hangs up phone and immediately takes it off the hook)

SERGEANT; If you let me out now I'll see to it that you are treated leniently.

DOHERTY; *(Moving towards cell door)* Sergeant, my good man, it takes wo to make a bargain and you are not exactly negotiating from a position of strength.

How about this? On your release-whenever that is- if you say nothing about his I wont tell the Commissioner that you authorised my wrongful arrest and illegal detention for a crime that you knew wasn't committed. You see, Sergeant, given the present climate and today's happening a complaint from me could mean that you would, once again, revert to being "an Asylum Seeker" in Monaghan; if you follow my meaning.

SERGEANT: If you open the door we'll talk about it.

DOHERTY; You know Sergeant, I was just pondering on the important part that burned hay played in world history. Think of the number of times, here on our own island, that a blazing load of hay was used to ignite an RIC Barracks. And then there was the encounter of Liutenant Clemens (Mark Twain to you) at Garrett's barn.

(sarcastically) You are of course aware of the story behing the painting "Burning of the Hay At Coram" by Thomas R.Bayles.A considerable amount of hay had been collected by the British Army and stored at Coram on Long Island. It's burning was planned and carried out by Major Benjamen Talmadge and General George Washington considered the burning of the hay more important than the capture of the fort at Mastic. Who knows! Maybe yours and mine will yet be household names, linked in the minds of future generations with the burning of a rick.

Doherty moves to front of stage and sings, to the air of "The Old Alarm Clock).

It happened up near Largabeg

In November sixty nine,

I was feedin' pigs and makin' rhymes

The day being far from fine.

When the Gardai got contrary

And they gave to me the knock

But somehow or other chanced to miss

The gunmen in Corock.

They took me into Carrigbeg

Which made me swear and curse.

My internment was authorised

By "the Psychiatric Nurse".

They said "We're going to charge you"

As Smith the door did lock.

But from the cell I could hear quite well

Of the happenings in Corock.

(Doherty takes Garda cap from top of filing cabinet, puts it on at clumsy angle, looks in mirror and recites;)

"Caps tilted, fag drooping, every one

Looks like a jailbird on the run."

(He sits down, puts feet up on desk and is about to start reading the Sporting Press when he appears to have a brainwave. He enthusiastically reaches for the phone directory and rapidly traces lines with his finger).

DOHERTY: Irish Pneumatic tools......Irish Potatoe Growers Association.......Irish Pre........(*He suddenly reaches for the phone and dials*)

DOHERTY: Hello. Irish Press? Could you put me through to the News Desk please. ...Hello...This is Garda William Kilgannon, Carrigbeg Station..I'm acting Sergeant...Sergeant McAteer is gone to the dogs..Ah, no...no...I mean he's gone Greyhound Racing... I have a news tip for you...it should be worth a few pound..You had a piece in this evenings paper about the Branch raiding a cottage in Corock..Well we have one of the robbers in custody here..he headed back to Corock after the Bank raid in Falcarragh...A local farmer,Hughie Doherty caught him trying to rob Seamus O'Neills's van. Fair play to Hughie he made a citizens arrest and brought your man in here at the point of a four prong fork before..*(shouts from cell; "We can talk.Let me out and I'll make some arrangement with you"*) Shut up you robber you..no..no.not you, sorry about that do you hear your man in the cell an' he lookin' for mercy? As I was saying about Hughie Doherty..we could have done with

Hughie here last week. Wait 'til I tell you. Didn't Guard Black leave the keys in the squad car and it parked abroad on the street. There's a boyo here in the village he's known as "the Jackal" and nothing would do him only to rob the squad car.. He kept it for two days so he did..Oh we got it back..an' Black an' Smith bet the shite out of him..(*Banging at cell door*)..I'll have to let you go this buck is not too happy with his lodgings...Thanks.

(*He leaves phone off the hook, takes* "PRIVATE" *notice from rear door and puts it on cell door and then goes to front of stage and sings;*)

Back to a dark October day

As autumn mists hung down,

A daring raid was carried out

In Raphoe's little town.

To all Tyrconnel's homesteads

The Guards were told to flock.

But they let the boys return in peace

To the hideout in Corock.

To keep the law I have been reared

An' that's how I mean to stay,

Though I'm slightly disillusioned

By the goings-on today.

But if I were a robber

And the law I chose to mock

I could live without disturbance

In a hideout in Corock.

(He exits, stage right, closing outside door)

CURTAIN

Pass the Parcel by Maria D'Silva

It was the perfect summer romance. The sun, the sea, the sand. Mia knew he was 'the one' the moment she saw him and she'd never felt so happy. But it all ended that beautiful, moonlit night, in tragedy.

It was a spur of the moment thing, and before they knew it, they had booked themselves a last minute holiday. The girls chatted excitedly as they collected their luggage and made their way to the apartment in Kos. Two weeks of freedom. It was a gorgeous summer day, the sun was shining and there was not a single cloud in the sky. The girls treated themselves to some ice cream and found that they were edging closer and closer to the sea. There was a pebble beach, with clusters of dark brown rugged looking rocks scattered all around. Mia took off her flip-flops and carefully made her way through the rocks until she reached the water. She looked out towards the horizon; the sea was a mixture of blue, green and turquoise and glistened in the sunlight. The waves came in sequence, making clunking noises as they hit the pebbles. The sound was so calming, it reminded Mia of when she was a little girl and her dad would take her to the seaside. She would just sit and stare at the sea and clap her hands in sheer happiness. She was experiencing that exact same feeling, the sea was hypnotic, her eyes felt heavy and she closed her eyes. It was then that she heard his voice.

'It's amazing isn't it, the way the sea is so inviting, you just want to close your eyes and shut yourself off from everything'.

Mia opened her eyes; it was almost as if he had read her mind. At first, she thought she was dreaming, it was, after all, a very hot day and she felt totally relaxed. She could hardly believe her eyes, he was beautiful. He had the perfect physique, she could feel his muscular shoulders resting against hers, his dark brown hair and tanned olive skin seemed to shimmer in the sunlight, but it was his eyes that drew her to him. They were a mixture of browns and sparkled as he spoke and she felt as if he was looking right into her soul. His name was Luca and from that moment they were barely apart from each other.

He was a native of the island and as Mia loved her food she was more than happy to experiment with all the Greek dishes. Kleftiko was her favourite and so Luca would take her to places off the beaten track where she could enjoy the finest home-made cooking. They were quiet, local tavernas, away from the hustle and noise of the tourist hotspots in the main town and Mia loved being amongst the locals. They would spend their days lazing by the beach with her friends, but the nights were their own personal time alone together. Often they just walked and talked and walked and talked some more and watched sunrise together on the beach. Other times they just sat in silence, and Mia couldn't help but laugh out loud at times and then they would both be consumed by laughter. They were soul mates and she almost felt guilty for being so happy.

It was not any surprise to Mia's friends when she decided to stay on in Kos. Mia had adapted easily to her new way of life and when she wasn't out snorkelling she would help out as much as possible on Luca's boat. His father was a fisherman by trade and left the business to Luca to manage as he wanted to retire. He would go out early in the morning and come back triumphant with an array of fish, octopus and squid. Seafood was in high demand and so Luca was always busy as he supplied all the local restaurants. Fishing was in his blood. Mia and Luca would often go out fishing to an isolated part of the island and stay there all day. Mia would sit beside Luca occasionally dipping her feet in the sea, only to be told off by Luca for disturbing the fish. It was complete relaxation and there was no other place on earth Mia would rather be than by Luca's side and by the sea.

Soon it was her birthday and Luca arranged a special evening for her. He gave her his gift. It was a necklace made out of pearls and the finest shells she had ever seen; Mia treasured it and promised him she would never take it off for as long as she lived. Luca expressed his love for her and she would never forget his words,

'My darling Mia, my mother told me that you can't search for love, it just catches you by surprise and once you find that person you just know – It's like a game of pass the parcel, you cross your fingers and unwrap each parcel, but only one of them is the prize.'

That night, under the moonlit sky Mia thought to herself this will be a night i'll remember for the rest of my life.

Having fallen asleep on the beach, they awoke to a mighty crashing sound. They immediately jumped to their feet only to see huge boulders falling around them from the cliff top. The sea was lashing against the rocks and the previously clear, moonlit sky was now full of raging storm clouds. Part of the cliff had been totally destroyed by the storm. It all happened so quickly. 'Watch out!' he yelled as he pushed Mia so hard she went flying backwards and the boulders came down on him from the cliff edge. Despite, the thundering noise of all that was going on, in Mia's world everything had stopped. She stood there in stunned silence as she saw Luca disappear before her eyes. There was nothing she could do but run to safety.

After that fateful night, Mia couldn't live in Kos without her beloved Luca and so she went back home to England. Six years on, Mia has never returned to Kos, as far as she is concerned her world fell apart there. But she has never forgotten Luca and she has kept her promise and his necklace remains firmly around her neck and will continue to do so until she joins him wherever he may be.

Friend or Foe by Maria D'Silva

It was snowing heavily. Winter was definitely here with a vengeance and everything was covered in a blanket of white snow. Karl shivered and wiped the snowflakes from his eyes. He had been running for over an hour now, through the forest and narrow streets and he couldn't seem to shake them. The men following him were liked wild animals hunting their prey and they weren't about to give up. Karl crouched on the ground and looked at the map; he had to be near his final destination. It was then that he spotted a row of old workshops in the distance. He had finally made it. Karl sighed with relief. Nicole was waiting for him, waiting for him to hand over the mystery key he had in his possession. He had risked his life to get hold of it and he was determined not to let her down, not when he was this close. The key was the final piece of the jigsaw; it would unlock valuable information that was being held in the national database. He pulled down his hat over his forehead, adjusted his coat and then ran, as fast he could, through the thick layer of freshly fallen snow. When he reached the brown door he knocked three times just as he had been instructed. There was no answer. Karl looked around hesitantly, and not knowing what to do slid the key under the door. He could hear footsteps closing in behind him; he tried to run, but slipped. Lying on the ground, he looked back only to see a blunt object coming down towards him. Then it all went blank.

'Where is it?' barked a rather fierce and agitated voice. Karl opened his eyes and feeling a little dazed, he looked his captor straight in the eyes. 'I don't know what you're talking about', Karl replied confidently. Blood was trickling down the side of his face, he had taken a strong blow to the head and it was starting to ache. It was dark, a damp smell lingered in the air and he could hear some water dripping off a pipe behind him. His hands were tied tightly to a chair and so he shuffled uncomfortably, trying to loosen the ropes. 'There was nothing on him boss, maybe we were chasing the wrong guy?' remarked a tall, rather odd-looking man standing in the corner of the tiny room. He started to pace up and down, waving his hands frantically at the other man and they both started yelling at each other. It was then that the taller man's mobile phone started ringing; there was an eerie silence for a couple of seconds before he answered the call.

'Aaarghh- we'll have to let him go- another wasted day!' grunted the man, the frustration resonating in his voice. Karl couldn't believe what he was hearing, the men were obviously amateurs and he couldn't believe his luck. They grabbed him and took him outside with them then jumped into a car that had just pulled up and drove away.

Karl's wrists were sore from the ropes and now he had a grazed chin from being thrown out, face first, onto the snow paved road. Dusting himself off, his thoughts turned to Nicole and the key he had pushed under the brown door. He hoped it was the right door, if not he'd have to go back and retrieve it and that would be dangerous. After walking for about a mile he was able to place exactly where he was on the map. He made his way to the nearest town and found a phone booth. He rang Nicole's number and, after a few rings, she answered. 'Hey Karl, it's all been taken care of – our guy in the government has the key and he will pass it on safely, away from corrupt hands, if you catch my drift. A job well done.' Karl took a deep breath. He had completed his mission.

There was a mole in the government office and it was difficult knowing whom he could trust, he had become good friends with Nicole over the past year and he was glad she had got the key. He and Nicole had worked together on a number of missions in recent months and they made the perfect partnership. They certainly were a formidable team. Nicole had actually saved his life on their last mission. A bullet had somehow penetrated through his bulletproof vest and Nicole was on hand to give him first aid and rush him to hospital. Karl had never been so scared in his life, the blood was pouring out of his side and he remembered the feeling of his life ebbing away from him. He was completely helpless and would have died if Nicole hadn't come back to carry him to safety. He owed her his life and he'd be forever grateful to her. It was inevitable then that they would have a relationship outside work. Karl couldn't help thinking that he had it all, the perfect job and the perfect woman.

It had been a successful day, despite the little 'interrogation' he had earlier, but to Karl it was all in a day's work. It was the danger and uncertainty of the job that he loved the most, being a spy was exhilarating. He had tried the 9-5-desk job, but hated being tied down to the office environment and so handed in his notice after only a week. He had never looked back since.

On returning home Karl thought he'd make a celebratory dinner. But first he had to check in with head office and so he logged onto his email account. He could see that an email had come in from head office and so he ran the decoder. It had only just started to unscramble the code when the phone rang. Karl ran over to pick up the receiver. It was head office. He began to enter into some friendly conversation, only to be stopped abruptly. 'Karl' said the voice 'I'm sorry to have to tell you', there was a distinct pause, 'Nicole is the mole' and the phone went dead.

Once Upon A Childhood By Noel Bailey

Completely true in every detail, I remember after all these years, how she sat, the little silver bracelet she wore on her left wrist – even the charm that hung off it – a small fish. I can describe her dress, her shoes…slip-ons actually, smell her hair, hear her soft voice – tell you what the weather was like. I don't have to imagine the tears which come to my eyes as I write this either. She was so ethereally beautiful and I would give anything to be able to go back to her and that time so long ago. I never *ever* wanted to grow up. It was the cruellest thing ever happened to me.

Of course, having five children now, more than compensates for my lost childhood and I love *them* more than life itself, but Ruth was my first real experience and with all the limited knowledge of worldly things I possessed at thirteen, I loved her with every emotion that crowded in upon me. The incident is mentioned briefly in a companion autobiography I have recently published, *"Cool Among the Flames"* – compiled mainly to shut my second eldest daughter up, as she kept demanding to know what I had been doing for the last forty-five years. It does not however plumb the emotional and physical depths that I am about to relate to you. It is I admit, a very slow-to-develop recollection, nothing wondrous and impassioned should ever be *rushed* should it?

Living then in the county of Kent, just a couple of miles outside the Greater London border, I grew up cocooned in a world of Harry Potter type kids all with their middle-class Brit accents. Ruth herself was so very like Emma Watson who plays Hermione in the HP films, right down to her hair, facial features and totally

adroit Englishness. She was fourteen, just a few months older than
Emma

Most years our family, of which I was an only child, would
head-off to my Great Aunt's farm, set in the wilds of the Yorkshire
Dales. Only twenty minutes or so from the tiny village of Hawarth
where Emily Bronte and her sisters lived and where Heathcliff
wanders still his beloved *Wuthering Heights*. The nineteenth
century farmhouse where we stayed had neither sewerage or
electricity but no-one in 2006 even working with the most
technologically advanced kitchen equipment available, could cook
anything to compare taste-wise with what was served-up in that
tiny farmhouse beneath a flickering gas-light. I lived for the next
steam-train trip that would take me north to my closeted and
remote little spiritual home.

Immediately adjacent to the farmhouse was a good-size
barn in which my Uncle would feed and milk the cattle, daily
occupations as far removed from my own experiential domesticity
as Hans Solo and the Millennium Falcon might be adjudged so far
as the Wright Brothers are concerned. Nevertheless, I slipped into
"farm life" without the least parental urging.

The summer holidays then, some five months subsequent to
my thirteenth birthday, saw us enjoying another farm visitation up
there on the picturesque moors. It was a Friday. I recall this clearly
because mom had promised to take me to the local movie-house, a
decrepit but intimate old relic in a nearby township, some twenty-
five minutes walk from the farm, alongside those old stone walls
which separated field from field, property from property...and on
those cold misty nights – legend from legend. That's what one did
in those days – walk! Films were only run there Saturday nights
and I recall it was the following day!

Some time around mid-afternoon that Friday, while chasing
cows, sheep, chickens and poor old Dobbin - so ancient a sway-
back, it was definitely a dead horse walking - around their own
fields, I heard my dad call me from far-off. Scooting back up to the

farmhouse, Mom, Dad and my Uncle were chatting to another family.

"Say, this is my son Noel," said dad. I shook hands with the man and nodded to his wife. Evidently they were staying for the week in the farm-house right across the way. The "way" being a road no more than twelve feet wide between the properties. I could have tossed a stone from my bedroom clear through their kitchen window......could probably have flicked it come to that.

"And *this* is their daughter Ruth," Dad was continuing. I looked up at her and lost my power of speech. Nothing was working.....neither my arms, voicebox...or brain!

"Well say *hello* to Ruth, Noel," said my mom, "She's just fourteen – a bit older than you. Maybe you'd like to play with her? Show her over the farm maybe?"

I managed some strangled sound like "Y-oh"....a resulting cross between "Yes (mom)" and "Hello." Ruth looked less than impressed but allowed me to direct her back the way I had just come.

"You two be back for tea in an hour or so!" called out dad. If I had been seventeen, I wouldn't even have been *back!*

Now, I was hardly what you'd call a 'smooth operator' at thirteen. I had known from the first time my eyes fully focused shortly after birth that I liked girls! My best friend at junior high, she who I had sat beside since day-one in primary school was most *definitely* a girl and I'd had a thing for my younger cousin since she was eight. Sexually however, aside from a couple of show and tell sessions behind the lounge with my cousin when age-wise, we were yet to hit double figures, and hot little Carmen who had charged me threepence to "have a feel" in fourth grade one afternoon, I had no reason to doubt the stork theory!

And yet, as I helped Ruth over that first stile (a wooden 'step' arrangement, built to enable one to cross those old stone walls, between fields) and the briefest flash of underclothing as she climbed over...I knew instinctively that some up-till-now unutilised software was kicking-in.

One thing I *did* have going for me – I could hold a conversation and with Ruth this was a ground-level entry requirement. Well read, intelligent, but equally (so I discovered) impulsive and adventurous, she was no wimpy arm decoration.

"This is such fun," she called out to me, crossing her fourth stile. She wasn't far off the mark either.

The extreme southern ends of the property were marked by the onset of the banks of the beautiful river Nidd. A timeless old waterway whose shallow but crystal-clear waters were stocked with enough trout to satisfy generations of retired Yorkshiremen. Linking my Great Aunt's farm with the neighboring property across the river was a sturdy but none too steady 'swing bridge.' Only able to carry one abreast, it was aptly named, as Ruth found out.

"Oh Gosh!" she uttered, as almost mid-center, the bridge's lateral motion caused her to slip backwards. She fell against me as I caught her. Just for a moment I held her there and she turned as if to say something, her face but inches from mine. Even in that instant, I knew she was everything to me…completely nonsensical as that sounds and especially with the benefit of but thirty minutes relational co-existence.

Whatever awareness came to her at that second, she held-on to it, but from that moment on, existed an unspoken bond between us. Having wandered across a few neighboring fields, we returned to the farm property and I took the opportunity to demonstrate my prowess skimming stones downriver.

"Let *me* try that," she said and promptly buried my best throw with a perfect flat trajectory that pulled in ten "bounces" before heading into some distant mud-flats. My highest had been eight! That was Ruth!

As feminine as they come, she knew all the tricks. The cutesy smile, hair tossed over her shoulders at strategic moments, eyes wide for effect, "helpless little girl" routine" (as if!) Fact is, the gulf, both physically and emotionally, between a thirteen-year old boy and a fourteen-year old girl is laughably distant.

Not that I was feeling out-matured or even out out of my depth as such. I was enjoying every moment of her company. We sat there on that lush green river bank and talked about just about everything. School to home-life, pasts and futures, likes and dislikes. At one stage I was just so enraptured, I must have been staring at her. She stopped and asked,

"What are you looking at?" I remember just saying simply, "You!"

She actually blushed and that made *me* feel self-conscious. Right about then I heard my father calling-out and I knew we were way past our allotted hour or so. Playfully, and I suppose in some ways with a child's enthusiasm, I grabbed her hand and pulled her to her feet as we took off across the fields. She didn't let go of me until we reached the front gate.

After tea we played multiple games of "Concentration." Just sitting on the floor with her, listening to her laugh when I forgot where the other 'eight' was…her hand brushing against mine as she leaned across to turn over the matching 'King,' her sharp little intake of breath and the way she would hold her hand to her chest when she made a pair. I see it all now as clearly as I did then. The absolute last thing I wanted to hear was mom saying,

"Noel, it's nine o'clock, Ruth has to go back over the road now." Dad walked her across, but not before I collected my shoes and went with them.

"Are you doing anything in the morning?" she asked sweetly.

If I had been due to collect the Nobel Peace prize, I would have cancelled it. I told her I wasn't and dad, looking at me knowingly, smiled and said.

"Not really Ruth, would you like to come over and spend some time with Noel?….assuming its OK with your parents?"

I really think I caught the faintest blush – I was having such trouble standing up I couldn't really be sure.

I went to sleep that night just staring out my window across the roadway.

You will notice that aside from drawing a comparison with Emma Watson, I haven't made any real attempt to described Ruth in detail. I will paint for your benefit right now the picture of a young girl that dad ushered into our tiny kitchen the following morning, just as I was finishing my breakfast cereal. Remember though this is a recalled image from a child's memory not an adult's.

Poise…that's the word for it. I didn't know it then, but she had such poise. Her shoulder length light brown hair – it must surely have just been washed, had a natural wave through it and framed her beautiful little face to perfection. She had it pulled back at either side with small mica clasps and her mother had either donated or bought her a simple but pretty pair of earrings that glinted when she turned her head. Ruth had that "just scrubbed" look and she smelled of fresh flowers and youthful promise.

As it was quite a warm morning, she was wearing the simplest of little short-sleeved cream colored tops with just a couple of buttons at the neck. I remember now, the pretty white lace-edging around the sleeves. Obviously planning on some serious cross-field hiking she had on a pair of dark blue girl's pants and matching-color running shoes.

She must have had the most beautiful youthful figure but I had as much knowledge, interest and experience in sexual matters then as I did in current affairs. What I *did* have an interest in, was getting out of that farmhouse with her at the first available second!

"No more than a couple of hours," said mom, as we hightailed it out through the main gate. "*Three* is close enough," I was thinking!

Both Middlesmoor and Nidderdale are sight-seeing valleys within commutable distance of the farm and both offer magnificent wind-swept views of the moors. We lit out for Middlesmoor, being slightly nearer. Some of the more elevated stiles I spent double the time necessary helping Ruth over – I'm sure she noticed! I think she even *took* her time climbing them.

It was the most balmy of English summer mornings, non-penetrative heat and the occasional light breeze being the order of the day. Successfully negotiating our two hundredth field so it seemed, the heights of Middlesmoor stretched before us. Acres of wind-swept heather leading the way and lending to the casual traveller a gentle if not rather exhilarating scent. Ruth and I hadn't shared much in the way of conversation mainly on account of the fact this was all so new to her and she was completely taken up with the experience. I of course had walked this way so many times with mom.

"It's just so beautiful up here isn't it?" she said to me, sitting on a huge rock that had been there long before Moses came down off Mount Ararat. The wind at that moment was blowing her hair across her face and she looked like an angel...one that Michaelangelo would have liked to sculpt. I sat beside her and without any thought for the consequences, turned my head to her and just kissed her.

It was only the briefest of contact – and I was so shocked at my own forward behavior I had no idea what to say as a follow-up. I think I stood up and muttered "sorry" or something equally inane. Half expecting a slap across the face, I was primed for *anything* except what happened. She just whispered "Come here," and pulling me back down beside her, returning the most wonderful kiss flush on my sadly inexperienced lips.

In hindsight, over the years I have experienced several electrical discharges. Light sockets, frayed wires – even taken a full charge direct off the spark plug of a V8 Falcon. *That* one put me on by back for the count. But the sensation that arced through me that second as she kissed me, ran out first place let me tell you!

It was, as far as lip to lip duration goes, brief - not much longer than mine but if I had gotten up from that rock I would have been unable to balance properly.

"You are *sooo* sweet," she said, hands folded neatly in her lap now.

"You don't have to apologise for kissing me," she added giggling.

"Can I do it again then?" I asked hopefully.

"Later maybe," she replied, teasing me unmercifully.

"C'mon," she said, "lets walk the rest of the way." She took my hand....I felt such a child!

As we walked, I was aware of a nagging irritation. It bothered me to such an extent I half whispered to her as we negotiated another stone wall,

"Ruth, have you kissed any other boys?" I desperately wanted to hear her denial.

She stopped, turned and still holding my hand said,

"Oh, that is such a funny question," but seeing as I wasn't laughing, she added, "Well actually....no I haven't – never met a boy I ever *wanted* to kiss me. You're the first – honestly!" I knew it was the truth.

"So you *wanted* me to kiss you?" I teased.

"I didn't say that," she retorted, slipping effortlessly into a demure, "I'm much more grown-up than you" mode....which she was!

"You did *kinda*...." I replied, trying to get full mileage out of my deductive brilliance. She just flashed me a pretty smile and the subject I knew, was at an end.

No sooner did we make the summit of Middlesmoor than it was time to head back and even then the three-hour time allotment was looking iffy. We saw so much....the old Roman ruins atop

Scanlon's Ridge, the tiny bus-stop in Summerbridge called "New York," the caverns where a family of black panthers were said to have made a home for themselves.

None of them though came close to watching Ruth. Crouching down smelling the heather, brushing her beautiful hair out of eyes after the wind had taken liberties with it, hugging herself as she sat down occasionally to take in the view.

As the old farm came into distant focus, I felt the magic unravelling - my most acute pleasure up for imminent termination. I held her hand ever tighter, I never wanted to let her go.

Riding out the inevitable "Didn't I tell you just two hours Noel?" cross- examination, after we had winged-it across the last couple of fields to the gate, mom relented and in just one sentence, restored my faith in miracles. Turning to Ruth she said,

"Would you like to come to the cinema tonight with us?"

Ruth looked as happy as my heartbeat was suddenly irregular.

"I spoke to your mom and dad," she was continuing, "They said its fine with *them* if you'd like to come."

As it happened, they were screening Disney's *Peter Pan* that night. It may as well have been "A Political Discourse On the Causes of the Indo-China war," for all the attention I was paying the screen. I took every opportunity to glance at her sweet little profile, hoping she wouldn't see. Occasionally she turned and caught me looking at her but just smiled at me. She let me hold her hand right through the session and more than once I saw Dad glance downwards. If it were possible to see a replay of it all now, I think you would sense his unspoken encouragement.

"Hold-on tight son, angels like her don't drop-by all that often."

Last thing that evening she permitted me a further goodnight kiss. I was still slumped against the window-sill when I woke up the next morning.

I think by now, Ruth's parents were resigned to the fact they wouldn't be seeing too much of their daughter until they got home. Had it been *my* choice, they'd have to have been content with the odd postcard!

It was the next day that my up-till-then sublimely uncomplicated life was to be hijacked, re-formatted and dragged screaming into pleasurably near adulthood.

The weather had done a complete one-eighty, as the Brit climate is well known to do....especially during the summer vacation. Caught mid-field by a drenching little shower, Ruth and I scurried like drowned rats to the safety of the barn. Mom, dad and Ruth's parents had gone to Harrogate City together for the day – some twenty miles or so distant. Since I couldn't interest her in a handful of oats, we shinned up the ladder to the hay loft.

As luck would have it, Ruth had slipped on a new summer dress that morning, a simple yellowish cotton affair with a neat little black belt – I remember *that* well for reasons that will become obvious. The whole dress was pretty wet and she was sitting on a hay bale holding it out before her and lamenting its rapid absorption rate. Her hair even was quite damp and curling up around the edges. I was in no drier a state. We decided to wait it out and to dry off a bit. Following the last few days quite hot weather, it was very warm up in that loft and we figured our clothes would soon dry.

What *is* it with hay? Maybe it just looks inviting to toss people in ...especially girls! Whatever, we were ragging about, acting like a couple of dumbo schoolkids and while I was teasing her and holding her wrists, she slipped out of my grip and fell on her back in the hay. I saw my chance to overpower her and kneeling there, pinioned her arms above her head. She may have been more mature and definitely way prettier, but I was stronger!

At what stage exactly something tapped me on the shoulder and said "Time to grow up kid," I couldn't say, but something in her expression pressed buttons somewhere and as I moved my face close to hers I saw the 'welcome sign' flash on. *This* kiss was way less juvenile....longer too. That isn't to say I had the least idea what I was either doing or starting. What I *do* remember, she didn't pull away, she simply jerked her hands free and placed them round my neck. For the first time I think I became aware of her femininity and the effect her closeness was having on me.

Lying there as she was, her dress had risen well up her legs and way past her knees and obviously something blueprinted in the male psyche kicked in. More in an exploratory sense than with any sexual intent – God, I didn't even know what "sexual" meant - I remember just tentatively putting my hand on her thigh and being entranced by its smoothness and heat. Ruth still had her arms around my neck as we we continued kissing like laughably outright amateurs I imagine. Oh, but how wonderful was it?

I think I muttered something excruciatingly retarded like "You are so pretty Ruth" but in all honesty I had no idea what was expected of me. Maybe for a change of stimulus or perhaps she really *did* want to kill me, but as I sat there performing like a mechanical sex-toy, she took my other hand and pulled it to her breast.

Funny how most young boys always gravitate towards that area. To be honest I can't even recall *looking* at her breasts up until that point. I remember my hands on her bra-straps and wondering how she got it on....it was only a flimsy little affair and her breasts were pretty small too. But dear God, what a fantastic new sensation. Having a hand down her top. I prayed for more rain!

Again the fear of following in another's footsteps (or handprints) made me ask her if she had ever done anything like this before. Her shocked reaction, quite close to tears actually, convinced me of this improbability. I held her to me then and with my childlike inexperience I told her I loved her. She asked me if I would like to undress her.

I just didn't know what to say and must have looked such a tongue-tied dickwad. In the absence of any positive action on my part, she undid that little belt and all the buttons of her dress from hem to bra. I simply watched entranced as she let the dress slide off her.

It seemed to me she rather liked being naked in my presence.....nothing she said or did you understand - just a feeling I had. Girls are so much less inhibited than boys. Anyhow, inevitably she asked me if I would like to undress. I think I almost screamed out "Mommy!"

"C'mon," she said, "Don't be shy, *I'm* naked...take *your* clothes off too. Besides, they'll dry quicker." Actually, she had a point there – almost had me convinced! I was just sitting there unmoving.

"OK," she said, making as if to put her clothes back on. What brilliant psychology is inherent in the female make-up!

"Oh, Alright then," I muttered and standing there, undid my shirt buttons as slow as I knew how. It went OK until my underpants. *No-one* had seen inside them, let alone a naked fourteen year old girl just four feet away.

"I can't," I said abruptly.

"Why not?" she asked, "You don't mind looking at *me* do you?"

"You'll laugh at me," I said evincing my inner fears. "Have you ever seen a boy naked?" I asked, hoping against hope that she hadn't.

"No," she said, "But you're sooo cute...I'd really like to."

So refreshingly honest were her words, I felt suddenly at ease with her, and just slipped my pants off. I knelt there as naked as the day I was born and trembling in her presence.

True to her word, she *didn't* laugh. She just looked at me rather entreatingly.

After that, we lay side by side for what seemed like a couple of hours. Just snuggled up in the hay together discovering what no Biology textbook seems to exhaustively cover.

The sound of a car pulling into the driveway saw action of a different sort. So mortified was I, I started putting her dress on. We were buttoned-up though and down that ladder before they had the motor off.

We had three more wonderful days together and didn't miss a solitary opportunity. It was during that time also that I learned the wonders of a self-help program and how to handle my own affairs if you get my drift! I figure Ruth already knew.

The day that Ruth had to leave and her family lived some two hundred miles from Kent, remains the most emotionally desolate moment of my life. Even with the promise that she would come and stay a week with us at our home at the end of term, was small consolation.

Barely able to hold myself in check as they sped off down the roadway that afternoon, I watched gutted, as my beautiful Ruth waved to me from that small back window. Once out of sight and completely blinded by tears, I climbed that ladder back up to the hay loft and sat there in wretched misery replaying all that we had done together, all that she had taught me and wishing hopelessly that she would come back to me.

Now however I realise she never really left me. I see her in my own daughters' eyes occasionally, especially when they are being cheeky and manipulative. She is for ever fourteen as I am eternally just a few months younger than her.

But I know if I ever go back to that desolate and romantic moor, she will be sitting on that rock waiting for me - even now. The wind will be blowing her lovely hair across her face and she will look up and smile as I approach. She will let me hold her hand and then take me where I want to go.

I am still such a child.

CUBITUS DROPPED BY By Noel Bailey

Not everyone was sleeping in Tamarind. As the first rays of dawn swept the canyoned streets, shepherding the darkness westwards towards its inevitable twelve hours or so of enforced exile, a creature was stirring and it wasn't a mouse!

Kevin was awake! Home, was an '84 Lite Ace with bile-green trim, puke stains and a welcome mat. He didn't get out much these days, being legless, the result of an attempted field-goal with a live hand grenade, during a stint in 'Nam as a cook! He was of the happy-go-lucky nomadic mould..never concerned about the weather, politics, the Dow-Jones Index, or even the cross-eyed german shepherd which shared the van with him. Just as long as those street kids didn't bother him, wanting to clean the windshield, he was at peace with humanity. On this day however, Kevin was to save the world. Although as he struggled upright in the front seat, ran his nicotine-tinged fingers through his receding hairline and observed in the rear view mirror, a rat's tail disappearing down through the hole where once sat a pair of 250 watt woofers, this eventuality had not presented itself as a real likelihood.

He turned his head as the sixty-storey office block across the street imploded, causing small eddies of dust to float across his windshield but not much else. "Shame about the window-cleaners," he thought aloud, as a couple of buckets rolled into the gutter nearby.

The delicatessen, chinese restaurant, Citibank office and theater complex were the next to be vaporised - not twenty metres from where he sat. Again, it was intriguingly accomplished. Hardly any mess, just a neat pile of fused rubble, ready to be loaded on a truck. The image of Oddjob in *"Goldfinger,"* driving away with the compressed Lincoln in the back of his cab, came to mind.

It took the destruction of the football stadium on the next block to get his full attention. Opening the van door, he lowered the wooden ramp to the sidewalk enabling him to slide down out of the vehicle. As he steadied himself, a colossal craft, substantially wider than the street, settled almost noislessly ahead of him.

"So *that's* what this is all about" he thought to himself, "They've got nowhere to park!"

His first impressions as he stared at the alien ship, motionless except for a couple of street lamps swinging unevenly where they had been caught-up in the landing gear, was of a mutated cockroach. It seemed even to have an outside 'skin' or carapace. As he watched nonchalantly, there being really no other way to look at it, as far as he was concerned, a portal appeared at the nearside edge and through it stepped or rather flowed, a being, short of stature and positively wispy in constitution. It appeared to be struggling to propel itself under Earth's gravity. He watched as an appendage - how else would you describe a gelatinous `arm?' fiddled with what looked like a miniature "notepad" attached to the upper part of its body. At a distance of some five metres, the thing's outline shimmered and was swiftly replaced by an instantly recognizable form, right down to the sideburns, tight pants and guitar.

"Greetings Y'all, I come in peace. The Lord is my Shepherd, Don't be Cruel....and puh'lease, don't step on ma blue-suede boots," uttered the newcomer in a failed mastery of a southern accent.

"You mean *'shoes'* don't you?" said Kevin, not entirely convinced he was fronting the genuine article.

"Shoes, boots, what difference?" added the figure, strumming a few notes as if to engender a feeling of bonhommie, "I'm back, that's all that matters."

"So you're Elvis?" mused Kevin, "What was your biggest hit?"

"It's now or Never" replied the other. "Satisfied?"

"What was on the flip-side of *"His Latest Flame?"* Kevin probed further.

"Lordy, how can I remember?" retorted the newcomer running his fingers through his hair. Kevin noticed that his scalp didn't look right and rippled oddly around his forehead.

"Little Sister" he added, "that's it, `Little Sister'.....anything else?"

Kevin thought hard for a moment,

"What was your twin brother's name then?"

"Twin brother?" said the other. "Hell I never had no twin rother...."

"Yeah? so who and *what* are you then?" demanded Kevin unched almost imperiously over some fallen masonry.

The other stared back at him quizzically,

"You mean he *did* have a twin brother?" the figure looked restfallen, "Our databank does not record that information!"

Kevin noticed that the fake accent had been replaced by a flat asal Aussie twang now.

"So why are you decked out like that?" he enquired.

"We like to set the local inhabitants at ease," replied the being, taking on the appearance of a well-known planetary identity sually works," he added.

"Would you rather *this?*" Again he pressed various quadrants n the touch-screen of his "form adaptor" returning instantly to the ransluscent shape Kevin saw emerge from the craft earlier.

"Mmsgghth Ynllan shrrk imdo hrtunnsum yygh" emanated rom the being's "head."

"Could you re-phrase that?" said Kevin drily.

The figure tapped in a few commands, reconstituting himself s a Parking Police Officer.

"Sorry, that's the problem with our moleculiser. If we do not dopt human form, we cannot communicate in your language. You're wondering why we came?"

"It had occurred to me," said Kevin."You just destroyed several buildings, a high-rise and a sports complex. You probably illed more than two hundred early-morning workers!"

"But there are millions on this planet," said the Officer, "does t really matter?"

Kevin thought for a moment. He was probably right, certainly none of them were his friends - what did it matter when you came to think of it?

He noticed that the other was beginning to scribble on what looked like a small pad.

"What are you doing there?" he asked.

"Writing out a ticket," said the other, "Your vehicle i unregistered and parked on a public street - I'm just doing my job y'know!"

Kevin was outraged. "Yeah? and what about your heap o intergalactic junk illegally parked across the entire street? Yo going to book that too?

"No need to be *aggressive* human," said the visitor. "I think i you knew the fire-power of that craft, you'd show a little more respect, choose your words a little more carefully.....maybe ever apologise for your inappropriate attitude here?" He handed Kevir the ticket, "Now, where were we?"

"You were about to tell me why you came," said Kevir undaunted.

"It was an unplanned stopover actually," said the visitor, "We were en-route to the Xanthes System - you probably have never heard of it - it is only accessible by harnessing the connective anti-matter pulse waves of former binary black holes, within a fifty light-year radius naturally - when our ship was dislodged off-course by a star turning supernova less than twenty million kilometres off our port side. Our shields deflected most of the shock-waves, but to maintain them we had to exhaust our supplies of hydraxine compound. Earth has it in abundance, it being sourceable from your own atmosphere. You don't even know it!"

"Big deal" thought Kevin to himself, "They don't even know that Elvis had a twin brother !"

"So why destroy all these buildings? asked Kevin accusingly." Why not land in a desert somewhere...a jungle? Why, the middle of a city?"

"*That* craft" said the visitor, deccelerates from twice the speed of light to under two thousand kilometres an hour in less than fifty nanoseconds. Not a great deal of time to make a precision landing you'd agree. We did what we *could,* OK?" Kevin remained unmoved by this explanation.

"This Hydraxine you mentioned, how much do you need then?"

"Well, according to our calculations," replied the other, "Earth's prevailing atmosphere globally, will just about be sufficient, we need only the oxygen and free nitrogen present," he added matter-of-factly.

"Leaving us what exactly?" put in Kevin, "a few gasps of freon, carbon dioxide, neon and carbon monoxide, if we're lucky? Sorry, we need our atmosphere - that's how we breathe and stay alive!"

"We *know* that!" retorted the other, "but unfortunately, our need is greater than the perpetuance of your species, or to put it more succinctly, our intellect vastly outstrips the best this planet has to offer. Look at it this way, there'll be no more wars, famine, disease, episodes of "Survivor" to put up with. You won't feel a thing, just uninterrupted sleep!

Now, I must leave and supervise the extraction process. This conversation can serve no further purpose, please return to your vehicle and by the way, is that your creature?"

Kevin turned around.. Raz, as the shepherd was called, was sitting with his paws out of the back window.

"Yeah! that's my *creature* - we call it a 'dog.' Why?"

"It doesn't look like *it's* registered either," said the other, "you'd better do something about it!"

Kevin's brows tightened, he called out to the retreating figure,

"OK, you win, but do me just one favour. I've always wanted to see the inside of a UFO as we call them, would you allow me aboard....just for a few minutes. If I'm going to die with the rest of the planet, at least humor my inquisitiveness?"

The extra-terrestrial looked amused,

"If you can get yourself over here, I'll grant your request."

Kevin swung himself expertly on his stumps and covered the distance to the ship in less than a minute. Close to, the craft seemed even more insect like. The 'carapace' appeared to be of some organic matter which was unpleasantly yielding to his touch.   As he approached the portal, he could see no physical means by which access might be gained, since the opening was at least three metres above ground level. He paused, and the visitor looked down at him.

"To effect entry, you must link telepathically with the control and guidance system. Since it cannot recognise your primitive humanoid voice-wave imprint, I will do it for you.

To do this, I must assume my natural form however.....please stand by."

Again, depressing the touch-screen at his chest, his shape dissolved into its primary form, the colors at such close range, intriguing yet disturbing in their alien non-conformity. A few seconds passed before Kevin found himself rising above the sidewalk and within moments, abreast of the entrance itself, which he could now see towering above him.

"Hell of a tractor beam," he thought aloud, as he eased himself into the ship by way of an unnaturally cold metallic floorway. Looking about, he noticed the inside of the craft to be roughly ovoid in shape and about the size of a baseball pitch - including the outfield!

He could not detect anything which looked remotely like a control unit or instrument panel. Indeed, the inner 'wall' appeared to be composed of the same ridged organic matter as the exterior. It appeared though to be `pulsing' at various points, giving the disturbing impression of a breathing leviathan. The visitor he noted, was some twenty metres distant, communicating with another like being. As he watched, a huge 'screen' appeared in the wall behind them, upon which rows of constantly changing numbers and symbols flashed laterally. It gave Kevin the impression of an outsize 'test-pattern' you might see at an IMAX theater.

"Is this what you were expecting?" enquired his host, having taken on the appearance of a construction worker, complete with hard-hat. Kevin momentarily had fears that he was about to witness an impromptu performance of *"In the Navy,"* but answered,

"Can't say that it is, no," then feeling obliged somehow to expand upon this statement added, "As a matter of fact, I was expecting more flashing lights, gangways, control panels and banks of computer hardware!"

"Gangways?" retorted the other.."This is no interstellar warship, it has no 'bridge,' no Captain Kirk to save you, and not a solitary pointed ear in sight. You have been conditioned my friend, shaped and programmed by your environment as surely as the sun will shortly be setting for the last time on humanity."

Kevin propelled himself towards the huge display panel. The other being stood his ground or rather, re-flowed over his spot.

"Is this the guidance system you spoke of earlier?" Kevin enquired of his host casually.

"It is the Cubitus, yes," came the reply, "It has infinite knowledge of star systems, full navigational control and is the ultimate power source."

"But still it seems, without this Hydraxine, it's stuffed," interjected Kevin.

"Speak irreverently of the Cubitus at extreme risk to yourself," remarked the other.

"I thought your system could not recognise human speech-patterns" said Kevin enquiringly.

"The Cubitus is more than a guidance system - it has all knowledge and in here, your every thought is able to be interpreted, processed and if neccessary - altered!"

"How many of you are there in this ship?" enquired Kevin, changing the subject.

"More than fifty," replied the other, "But you cannot see them, they are in molecular dissociation and remain stored in the cyclorex tissue - the inner-wall medium you see around you. Only two of us are required to remain in synthesised state until we reach our ultimate destination, in this case Xanthes!" Retreating a couple of paces, he turned to Kevin,

"Now we must commence the extraction program. It will take close to forty-eight hours of Earth time. You must leave now - your last request has been granted. Goodbye human!"

As he spoke, his form returned to normal and Kevin heard the faintest echo of condescending laughter as he receded across the chamber.

Concentrating now, eyes closed, Kevin focussed his thoughts on Cubitus. He started with a series of primary numbers and was immediately aware of a response. Cubitus emanated its own string of binary code which to most others would be meaningless, but Kevin's advanced programming skills absorbed the data-flow and enabled him to repond. The effort required was enormous, and sweat ran in rivulets down his unshaven cheeks.

Cubitus was fascinated, no single entity had ever provided such stimulating thought-control patterns. Questions were answered and information flowed both ways.

Immediately, Kevin was aware of the extra-terrestrial's presence beside him - now the image of Leslie Nielsen in Forbidden Planet.

"What are you doing human? - you were told to leave this ship...you dare to try and interface with Cubitus?" Kevin sensed he was distinctly rattled!

"Extraction countdown has now commenced," intoned the other, "All oxygen and nitrogen molecules within a two-hundred kilometre radius of this ship, will be absorbed within thirty seconds, expanding then outwards at twenty quadrants an hour. Your time is up human!"

"You could be in error there Zhasti my friend," muttered Kevin, turning now and heading for the rear portal, "Or to put it another way.....*Huynworg myf iqadrst f jxxpuqqi*."

Both life-forms stared at each other, if you could accurately classify it as 'staring, ' one having no identifiable "eye."

"You know my name, you speak my language. How is this so?" called Zhasti across the cavernous chamber to Kevin, now positioning himself at the portal for descent to the sidewalk below.

"I'm a quick learner," he replied, "and by the way, don't bother Cubitus for a century or two - he's going to be tied up for a while. He has worked out some new co-ordinates for you though, deep within the Andromeda Cluster.There's several planetary systems there that can provide your Hydraxine compound without destruction of life-forms. You should make it with hours to spare"

"Cubitus *tied up?*...impossible!" sneered Zhasti, his form wavering around the edges. "He is multi, if not infinitely-functional human, there is nothing he does not know. You lie!

"There *is* just one thing, my intergalactic predator," smiled Kevin, "He does not know the full value of 'Pi'....however, by the time you reach Andromeda, Cubitus will have more information on that subject than anything or anyone before him. Until then, his knowledge remains incomplete and he is not the omnipotent creation he has been led, or has led himself to believe!" A reverberation filled the craft.

"Time now for you to leave Zhasti," he called out, "Have a nice trip and don't forget....keep your pseudopods inside the craft at all times!"

As Kevin descended to the sidewalk, his last view was of Zhasti flowing towards him. He hadn't covered half the distance when the portal sealed over and faded from sight.

Turning his back on the craft, he made his way swiftly towards the van, where Raz barked loudly and commenced licking his face furiously.

"I gotta get rid of this mutt" he thought to himself, as the craft rose silently behind him in a vertical trajectory, before whisking instantly out of sight, heading towards the northern skies.

Printed in the United States
71226LV00002B/331

9 781904 988113